BOOK 3 OF THE ORIGINS TRILOGY

ESCAPING THE CATACLYSM

A Novel about the Origin of Geologic Formations

KEITH A. ROBINSON

DEFENDER

CRANE, MISSOURI

Official Disclosure
A division of Defender Publishing House,
Crane 65633
Copyright 2011 by Keith A. Robinson
All rights reserved. Published 2011

Printed in the United States of America
11 1
ISBN-10: 0984630023 (paperback)
ISBN-13: 9780984630028 (paperback)

Cover design by Shim Franklin

A CIP catalog record for this book is available from the Library
of Congress.

DEDICATION

To all of my adventurous friends, both past and present.
You have helped to shape my creativity and provided
source material for the characters that inhabit my stories!
I am indebted to all of you.

OTHER BOOKS BY KEITH A. ROBINSON

The Origins Trilogy:
Logic's End
Pyramid of the Ancients

ACKNOWLEDGMENTS

I am grateful to so many people for their assistance in making my first trilogy a success. However, first I would like to give thanks to the ultimate Source of my inspiration. Thank you, Father, for the many blessings You have bestowed upon me. Thank you for the privilege of serving You.

To Mom, Kevin, Tim Chaffey, and Terry Cave—Thanks for all of the time and effort you put in helping me refine the manuscript. A special thanks to my fellow "time traveler" Tim for helping to keep my theology sound in the midst of a complex plot.

To Aimee and Nicole—Thanks for helping me put together the study guides for the trilogy. I pray your efforts will help readers get the most out of my books.

To Donna Howell—You have blessed me in so many ways. You are a fantastic editor and author. Thank you for your dedication to my work, and for helping me get the book finished in time.

To Pamela McGrew—Thanks for having patience with all of the changes Donna and I kept making along the way. (Wait a minute, didn't I say the same thing about *Pyramid of the Ancients*? At least *some* things never change!)

To Shim Franklin—Thank you for working so closely with me on the cover. I appreciate your cooperation and patience.

Finally, I would like to say a big "thank you" to everyone who has read *Logic's End* and *Pyramid of the Ancients*. Your support has encouraged me to continue in this grand adventure called "writing." I hope you find the end of the story satisfying.

CONTENTS

NOAH'S ARK

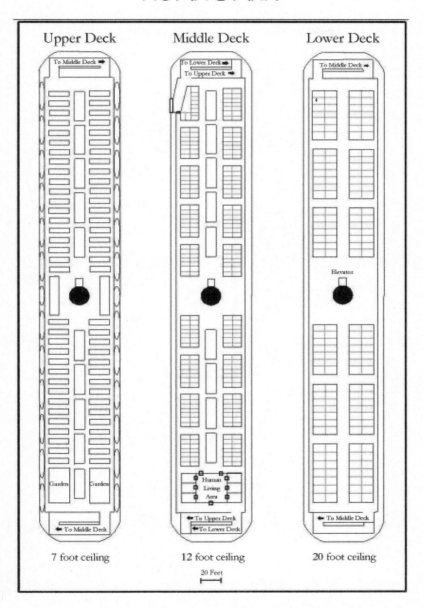

Upper Deck

To Middle Deck ➡

Garden   Garden

◀ To Middle Deck

7 foot ceiling

Middle Deck

To Lower Deck ➡
To Upper Deck ➡

Human
Living
Area

◀ To Upper Deck
◀ To Lower Deck

12 foot ceiling

20 Feet

Lower Deck

To Middle Deck ➡

Elevator

◀ To Middle Deck

20 foot ceiling

* Dimensions are from floor to ceiling. The remaining 11 feet of height (50 feet total) are used for storage below the lower deck and crawlspace between decks.

ODIN'S DOMAIN

FOREWORD

WHO WERE THE "sons of God" in Genesis 6? Who or what were the *Nephilim*? What kind of technology did the pre-Flood people have? What was the world like before the Flood?

These are questions that scholars have debated for many years, yet no clear consensus has been reached. This is due to the fact that, frankly, the Bible gives us very few details about the world that perished.

However, due to the very nature of writing a novel, one *must* choose a theory and go with it. The ideas and interpretations that I included in this book were chosen for the following reasons:

1. They **fit** the original biblical text and are based on mainstream interpretations.
2. They **make sense** of ancient cultures, ancient artifacts, and legends.
3. They follow **logically** from clues found in the Bible.
4. They make for an **interesting** story.

While I am sure that there will be many who disagree with the direction I took, I want the reader to know up front that I do *not* take a hard and firm stance on the issue of the pre-Flood world. I also *do not want the reader to confuse my fiction with the facts* that we know about Noah's Ark, the effects of the Flood, and how it explains the geological structures we see around the world. For this reason, I have reference notes starting on page 333 so that the reader will know what is based on real research and what is purely made up.

God didn't reveal much to us about the pre-Flood world, because it was not necessary to the narrative. What *is* included in Genesis is enough for us to know that the accounts are not legends or fairy tales. They contain all of the elements of a true, historical record and should be treated as such.

Keith A. Robinson

Prologue

VISIONS OF THE PAST

"WELL, THEY'RE AT IT AGAIN."

Jeffrey looked over at his new friend as he sat down at the table, an ice cold mug of Miller Genuine Draft in his right hand. Sitting on Jeffrey's left side, two of their other classmates, Kevin and Rich, were nursing drinks of their own. As the twenty-one year old African-American man rested his six-foot, two-inch, lanky form onto one of the barstools around the circular table, Jeffrey turned toward Kevin and Rich.

"Hey, guys. You remember Jerome, right? He's in Dr. Eisenberg's Ancient Civilization and Archeology class."

The three quickly exchanged greetings and handshakes before Jeffrey responded to Jerome's prior statement; his voice forced into a shout in order to combat the dissonant strains of heavy metal music that suddenly burst from the establishment's speaker system. "So, who's at it again?"

By way of reply, Jerome pointed toward the image currently being displayed on the fifty-two-inch flat screen TV hanging on the wall, just over the bar. "Those crazy creationists. They're back over in Turkey trying to find Noah's Ark again."

As one, the three other men turned to regard the picture on the screen. They watched the news coverage for just over a minute until the story finished. Turning back around, Kevin shook his head. "What a bunch of whackos!

1

You'd think they'd just give up after all these years, especially considering that the only thing they've found so far was a lightning storm," he said. Leaning back in his chair, he rubbed his right hand over his bald head and laughed. "Didn't one of them get hit and almost die?"

"Actually, I think all three of them got struck by lightning, if I remember correctly," Jeffrey smirked. "And they got guns waved in their faces by the local crazies. I don't know about you, but that'd be enough to deter me."

"What're you talking about?" Rich chimed in. "I'm deterred just by the fact that no one in their right mind believes that there even was a real Noah's Ark. Why waste your time risking life and limb looking for something that doesn't exist?"

The three other men grunted in agreement. Then, after a moment of relative silence, Jerome commented, "Ya know, I just don't get it. I mean, I was raised in the church, and I can tell you that most of the people I knew believed that Noah's Ark was just a story. It was a myth. What kind of brainwashing have these ark-seekers been put through to make them believe that there is a real boat stuck up there?"

Rich reached up and scratched the dark stubble that had already begun to form on his chin. "Personally, I think they should lock up every one of these 'creation scientists.' Anybody who thinks that two of every different kind of animal could fit on one boat is truly loony."

"Yeah, not to mention that supposedly only eight humans took care of all of those animals for over a year!" Kevin added. "There are so many species of animals, the boat would have been bursting at the seams. And can you imagine the smell? The sheer amount of waste must have been enormous!"

Jerome just shook his head. "And ya know what else puzzles me? How do they even attempt to explain where all of the water came from to cover the tops of the mountains? There's not even close to enough water on the earth to reach that high. Besides, there's not enough water in the atmosphere to cause it to rain constantly for forty days and nights. It's just ludicrous!"

Jeffrey chuckled derisively. "The water issue is just one of many inconsistencies. These Christians always talk about how God is so loving. But if that's *true, then how could He justify killing all those people in a massive flood? What about all of the innocent children? How could a 'God of love' punish them along with everyone else?"*

The more he spoke, the more his sarcasm and cynicism rose. *"Think about the carnivores on the Ark. What did they feed them? Did they bring along a year's supply of dead carcasses? Wait, I can see it all now…"* Standing up, he put his hand on his hip as his face took on an air of irritation. Speaking in a high voice, he said, *"Noah, honey, those doggone lions are at it again. They just won't leave the poor lambs alone. They ate the unicorns last week, and if you don't get over here quick, sheep are gonna be extinct next!"*

Kevin and Jerome guffawed loudly, while Rich choked on his beer, nearly spraying it all over the table. While his friends wiped tears of laughter from their eyes, Jeffrey dramatically ran a hand through his shoulder-length, dark brown hair, then resumed his seat.

Having finally recovered his voice, Jerome slapped his hand on the table. *"Man, that's funny. What a bunch of idiots! Only a fool would believe the story of Noah's Ark could be real…"*

Only a fool…

The words echoed loudly in Jeffrey's head as his mind snapped back to the present. His feet were rooted to the grass-covered hill as he stared at the boxy shape resting on the horizon in front of him; his mind stubbornly refused to believe what his heart knew to be true.

He was staring at the *real* Ark of Noah.

No! It can't be! There has to be some other explanation. Still, no matter how long he stared at it, he simply couldn't come up with anything plausible. *This has to be some kind of dream. Becky's crazy theories have caused me to start imagining things. That has to be it.*

Jeffrey felt a momentary flash of anger at the thought. *If Dr. Eisenberg had minded his own business and not encouraged Becky to come to the dig, then things would have been a whole lot easier. Sure, it wouldn't have changed the fact that we were attacked by two cyborgs…or animal-like giants…or whatever they were. And it wouldn't have changed the fact that we would have had to launch the pyramid prematurely, but at least I wouldn't have had to deal with her being around. And now that she knows about my relationship with Lisa, things can only get worse.*

For a moment, Jeffrey let his anger drown out that small, soft voice that nagged at his conscience. It was easier to focus on his bitterness than to admit the truth. Yet, like the slow brightening of a room at sunrise, Jeffrey could feel the uncomfortable thoughts returning.

Although he wouldn't—*couldn't*—allow himself to admit it openly, he knew that Rebecca's theory made the most sense of their current situation. Mack's idea that they had travelled into alternate realities explained how they could have met living Mayans and dinosaurs. It also neatly explained how the ancient Greeks they had met could have had maps of the entire globe. It even explained the intelligent Neanderthals that lived during an ice age and the high technological level of the people that were building the so-called Tower of Babel.

However, Mack's theory could never have predicted what they witnessed at the tower itself, or what they had observed just before arriving at their current location. In his mind's eye, Jeffrey could once again see the giant warrior, Nimrod, staring down at Dr. Eisenberg with sword in hand. He could hear Rebecca's cry as the cold metal pierced the doctor's body. Then, suddenly…chaos erupted all around them.

Jeffrey couldn't remember a time that he had felt such pure, unadulterated fear. Some force was at work around him…some power that made him want to crawl into a hole and flee from its wrath. He knew that he would never forget the look on the faces of those at the tower who ran here and there frantically searching for someone who could understand them. What kind of power could instantly create scores of languages and make a man lose his ability to communicate? What other things could the wielder of such power do at a mere whim? Unbidden, a stab of fear coursed through Jeffrey's body, leaving him feeling weak and causing his hands to tremble.

Even more than that, it seemed that they had witnessed the destruction of the whole world, albeit in reverse. The memory of the entire globe covered with water burst to the forefront of his mind. He could once again see the swirling clouds, the massive continent-sized hurricanes—and the water. Wherever the clouds were absent, nothing showed through but bluish-brown water. Jerome's question, spoken so long ago, now became his own: *Where did all of the water come from?*

I can't believe I'm even thinking this! Jeffrey chided himself. *Pull yourself together, Jeff. You* know *that evolution is true. Don't let a few strange experiences cause you to start doubting what you* know *to be factual. Some other logical explanation will present itself. The Bible is just a book of stories and myths. Noah's Ark is* NOT REAL!

Even as the words passed through his mind, he felt the uncertainty that came with them. No matter what he told himself, the pieces of the puzzle just seemed to fit together too perfectly, and the picture they created pointed directly to one fact: the Bible's history is true. Although, before that conclusion could even be contemplated with his rational mind, it was sent hurling to the deepest recesses of his subconscious, for the ramifications of that conclusion were simply not acceptable. If the Bible's history is true, then that means that there must be a God, and if there is a God, then He will hold all men accountable: accountable for the things they did in their past…

"Look, Jamie, can we talk about this another time? I'm heading out of DeKalb now and it's getting late. And to make matters worse, it's beginning to snow again." There was silence for several seconds as Jeffrey listened to the voice coming from the other end of his wireless, in-ear phone piece. *"C'mon, don't start that. I'm not 'blowing you off'! I'll just be in Chicago for the weekend. I—"*

Jeffrey listened once again, his hands tightening their grip on the steering wheel as his anger built within him. Barely slowing as he approached the stop sign, he turned right onto the two-lane road heading toward the bridge over the interstate highway. *"What's with you lately? Every time I turn around you're harping at me!"*

Jamie's voice dissolved into tears, causing Jeffrey to roll his eyes and curse silently to himself in frustration. "What's wrong now?" he asked, his voice taking on an unmistakable air of impatience. "Jamie… Jamie I'm really getting tired of all of the drama. I— "

Jeffrey's car climbed the bridge as his expression suddenly changed; his mind processed the words that were coming through the phone. His previous annoyance evaporated instantly, replaced first by shock, then anger. "WHAT?! Oh great. That's just great!" he yelled, his voice oozing with sarcasm. "So, what are— "

As he spoke, he yanked the steering wheel in anger; turning the car quickly to the left and toward the entrance ramp of the expressway. Suddenly, a blaring horn caught his attention. His head snapped immediately to the right to see two large headlights shining through the passenger window of his car…

Shaking his head, Jeffrey fought against the memory that stubbornly refused to return to its banished state of forgetfulness. In an effort to focus his mind, he closed his eyes to block out the sight of the Ark on the horizon. Reaching up with both hands, he began massaging his temples slowly.

Then, with a suddenness and clarity that shocked him, several thoughts came rushing at him simultaneously. *Don't dwell on the past. What's done is done. Besides, it has absolutely no bearing on the current situation. No matter what that box-like thing in the distance turns out to be, it won't change anything. Science has revealed what is true. There is no God—no "cosmic scorekeeper." And when you die, you'll simply cease to exist, just like everyone else.*

Jeffrey furrowed his brow in confusion. The voice in his head was his own, and he had certainly had thoughts like this before. Yet, something seemed different somehow. It definitely didn't feel right. Shaking his head to ward off the unsettling feelings, he opened his eyes and took a deep breath. *Get a grip, Jeff. You're letting yourself get spooked.* In control once more, he turned away from the view of the ship.

Action. That's what he needed. That's how he always handled these kinds of uncomfortable feelings. If he just *did* something, it would keep his mind occupied on the present.

Once again, he had succeeded in burying the past. But deep in the secret places of his heart, he knew it wouldn't remain buried forever...

1

URGENT DECISIONS

THE MULTI-COLORED and beautifully-shaped leaves on the myriad of different trees of the forest began to rustle, blown by a gentle breeze. Curious mammals, both small and large, flitted in and around the majestic trunks, scrounging for food. All around the forest, strange yet wonderful birdcalls and animal sounds were carried on the wind, like finely-crafted canoes floating lazily on a slow moving river. Next to the forest, gentle hills rolled, their earthen surfaces covered by wave upon wave of soft, vibrant, green grass.

Yet, despite the sheer beauty that surrounded her, only one sight held Rebecca's gaze: Noah's Ark. The rectangular barge, though far off in the distance, was unmistakable. Under just about any other circumstances, Rebecca would have been elated and overjoyed, for the discovery of the Ark should once and for all cause the others to see the truth of her theory. It was proof that they had not only gone back in time, but that the Bible's accounts were indeed true. The theory of evolution and its accompanying history were wrong.

However, Rebecca could not afford the luxury of her philosophical victory. For she knew, based on what they had viewed from space before landing the pyramid, that the worldwide flood of Noah could begin at any moment.

And the pyramid wasn't functioning.

Rebecca stared around at the others standing near her on the hilltop, just outside the main entrance to the pyramid. Based on the expressions of shock, fear, and confusion, she could tell that their minds were struggling to come to grips with this new development. She knew exactly how they felt. At least for her, the discovery of the Ark was confirmation of what she already believed to be true. For Jeffrey and the others, it turned their whole worldview upside down. She could almost see on their faces the battle being waged between their beliefs and their senses.

Well, if we're going to survive this, then they're going to have to come to grips with this reality real quick. We don't have time for them to process everything, Rebecca thought snidely.

"Are you just going to stand around here all day?" she called out, her pent up emotions from Jeffrey's recently discovered affair with her best friend Lisa mixed with her own prideful feelings of vindication to add extra bite to her words. "Whether you believe it or not, that's the *real* Noah's Ark. And in case you're too stubborn to realize it, what we saw from orbit was a *real,* global flood that could begin at any moment! We've gotta fix the pyramid and get out of here NOW!"

Her outburst had the desired effect. Turning toward her in unison, they regarded Rebecca with looks of confusion; as if they had each just awakened from sleepwalking. For once, even the normally fearless giant Goliath showed signs of uncertainty and apprehension.

Mack was the first to recover his voice. "Aw no," he said in defeat. "Becky, please say it ain't so. Your theories were fine as long as they were just part of some hypothetical discussion. But this… Wait, maybe this *isn't* Noah's Ark. Maybe there's another explanation."

Rebecca stared at her friend with impatience. "Can you think of any other boats that someone might build high up on a hill far from any body of water? Not to mention we *saw* the entire world covered with water just moments before we landed. Let's not waste time trying to come up with theories to explain the obvious."

Looking dejected, Mack absentmindedly took out his inhaler and prepared to activate it, only to realize that for once, he didn't need it. Puzzled by the fact that his chest was not constricting because of his current heightened anxiety, he frowned, then placed the medicine back in his pocket unused.

Jeffrey, completely oblivious to Mack's confusion, closed his eyes, and shook his head quickly, as if to ward off some unpleasant thought or memory. "She's right. Regardless of whatever else we believe, I think we're all agreed that we need to get the pyramid repaired as fast as possible, if for no other reason than the fact that we don't want to be stuck here if we are attacked. Let's get moving."

One by one, the others numbly nodded their agreement and began heading inside. As she turned, Rebecca saw Lisa draw closer to Jeffrey; her face awash with fear. "Is it true?" she asked him in a barely audible whisper. "Do you really think it's...*the* Ark? If it is, then...then that means..."

Rebecca felt her pulse quicken again from anger and pain as she moved out of earshot. Part of her was thankful that Jeffrey didn't argue the point about the Ark, but another part of her was disappointed. She *wanted* a fight. She wanted to unleash her frustration and bitterness at him and his...his... She stopped her thoughts short, shocked at the foul descriptive words for Lisa that were flashing through her mind. *No. I won't stoop to that level. God, help me keep my mind clear. I can't afford to let pity and resentment cloud my mind. Not now.*

Within a matter of moments, Akwen, Jerome, Mack, Goliath, Rebecca, Jeffrey, and Lisa had all gathered in the control room of the pyramid. Letting out a sigh of uncertainty, Jeffrey began speaking.

"Okay. The first order of business is to get the ship fixed. Akwen, how do we do that?"

Still somewhat disoriented by their current predicament, Akwen shook her head, her face becoming a mask of concentration. "I don't know if we *can* fix it. According to Elmer, da virus has shut down da entire system."

"What if we install the core we took from the Tower of Babel?" Jerome suggested, his dark skin wet with perspiration.

"We do need to change da cores, but dat won't get us around da virus," Akwen stated. "As long as it has da computer locked down, we aren't goin' anywhere."

"But isn't there some kind of backup system?" Mack offered. "Can't we somehow bypass the main computer and control the ship from the secondary bridge?"

"'Secondary bridge?' C'mon, Mack!" Jerome said in frustration. "We need *realistic* solutions! So unless you have any ideas that aren't based on some cheesy TV show, why don't you just *shut up!*"

The anger in Jerome's tone caused each of them to start in surprise. Before they could react, however, Mack's own pent up fear and anxiety rushed to the surface. "Back off, man! I'm just trying to brainstorm some solutions, which is more than you're doing!"

Before the situation could dissolve further, Jeffrey stepped in between them. "Stop it, both of you. Look, I know we're all under a lot of pressure, but there's no reason to take it out on each other. We need to pull together to get out of this. If anyone has *any* suggestions, no matter how far-fetched they seem, we need to hear them."

Disturbed by his own sudden loss of control, Jerome stepped backward and turned away from the group.

"Okay, so is there any way we can override this virus?" Jeffrey said, returning the conversation to the topic at hand.

"We can try. Elmer may be able to crack it, but I wouldn't get my hopes up," Akwen said.

Silence fell upon the group as they each considered their limited options. "So, what are we waiting for?" Goliath said finally. "Let's get the new core installed so that we can be back to full power if Akwen succeeds in working around the virus."

"So that's it?" Mack asked as he threw up his hands in defeat. "We just exchange the cores and wait around for the wall of water to hit us while Akwen tries to attack an alien computer virus? Man, we are *sooo* dead."

"Well, what else can we do?" Jeffrey countered.

"We can try to find help," Rebecca stated simply; her expression blank as she considered the possibilities. The others turned and looked at her questioningly.

"Help?" Jeffrey repeated. "From who?"

"Yeah, it's not like we can just call up a tow truck," Mack snickered.

Focusing her attention on them once more, she nodded as her ideas began to take on a more definite shape in her mind. "Remember that the Sacred Scrolls we took from the Patriarch had detailed information about the Tower of Babel, which just happened to have a core exactly like ours and many structural similarities to the pyramid. The people who were building the tower obviously used the same technology as those who built the pyramid."

"What are you getting at?" Jeffrey asked.

"I think it stands to reason that the builders of the tower didn't just recently develop that technology," she continued. "They must have… inherited it from previous generations."

Mack threw Rebecca a curious look. "So, you think that Nimrod and his cronies got their technology from people who lived before the… the Flood? If so, then where'd *they* get it from? Did they find some lost alien technology?"

The expression on Rebecca's face revealed her obvious disagreement with Mack's suggestion. "For now, let's not even try to speculate on the source of their technology. But, I think we can all agree that it isn't unreasonable to believe that these people might know something about how to fix the pyramid."

Everyone was silent for several seconds as they considered Rebecca's words. Finally, Jeffrey cleared his throat and spoke. "As much as I don't want us to split up again, I think Becky's right. Even if we can't find someone to fix the ship, at least maybe we can find someone who can help Doc."

"But we don't know anything about the local customs or culture," Mack pointed out. "I mean, we might as well be on an alien planet. How will we even get into the city? What kind of clothes do they wear? What currency do they use? At least with all of our previous stops, we were dealing with known human history. But this...this is... Look, what if we accidently break some weird law and end up in prison or something? That very thing happened to Picard and his team when they landed on—"

"Mack, not now," Jeffrey warned.

"Excuse me, but I wasn't finished!" Mack retorted. "I'm serious. Just because my ideas come from old TV shows and movies doesn't mean they don't have relevance to our situation. I'm gettin' real tired of you guys lookin' down on me about my taste of entertainment."

The lines in Jeffrey's face deepened in response to Mack's sudden outburst. Rebecca could read his body language well enough to know that his patience was wearing thin. If the group didn't decide something soon, they would likely be at each other's throats before long.

"We don't have to go into the city," Rebecca said, hoping to diffuse the tension. "We will go to Noah for help."

"Noah?" Lisa said in surprise. "But why would he help us after we just stole his scrolls?"

Before Rebecca could reply, Mack answered for her, his previous agitation having been somewhat deflated by this new prospect. "But that's the beauty of time travel. Although this'll be the *second* time that *we've* met Noah, it will actually be the *first* time he meets *us*. Unless, of course, we go back further in time and meet him again, making *that* time the first time." Suddenly, Mack's face brightened, his current train of thought completely dispelling the remainder of his anger. "Whoa, wait a second! Oh man, that is sooooo cool!"

"Now what are you raving about?" Akwen asked.

"Don't you remember?" Mack said as he brushed a lock of his curly black hair behind his right ear. "Oh, wait, you weren't there. Anyway, when Becky and I were meeting with the Patriarch—I mean, Noah— he said that we looked familiar and he wanted to know if we'd met before!"

Jerome, who had been leaning against the edge of the table in the corner of the control room, stood up as realization dawned on him. "Yeah… I get it. We looked familiar to him because we *had* met before! We met him—will meet him—here! Man, that messes with your head."

Although Rebecca's mind was also reeling from Mack's revelation, she forced herself to push it aside and focus on the immediate issue. "So are we agreed? Will we go to Noah for help? We need to decide quickly. In fact, it may already be too late. If I'm right and we are less than a week before the flood begins, Noah will have the ark completely loaded and he may not be willing to leave, even momentarily."

"Then let's cut out the rest of this useless discussion and get moving," Goliath commented.

Taking in a deep breath, as if preparing himself for what lay ahead, Jeffrey glanced around the room at each of them. "Right. So now the only question is: Who's going this time?"

"Mack and I must go, at least," Rebecca said firmly. "Noah…trusted me before, and I believe he'll trust me again. And I need Mack to translate."

"What else is new," Mack mumbled.

"Someone needs to stay behind and look after Doc," Lisa chimed in. "I…I guess I should be the one to do that," she said, although it was clear she wasn't happy about being left behind.

Torn between his desire to keep Lisa close and yet out of harm's way, Jeffrey merely nodded. "That would probably be best. And when Doc is resting, you can help Akwen with the ship."

"Speaking of da ship," Akwen interjected, "we need to install da new core before you leave. Lisa and I cannot do it alone."

"Good point," Jeffrey agreed. "Jerome, what about you? Are you going with us?"

"Yeah, I'm in," Jerome stated with more confidence than he felt.

Turning to Goliath, Jeffrey looked up at the nearly eight-foot-tall, wolf-like giant. "I don't think I need to even ask what your decision is. But, what do you plan to do about your appearance?"

"Although one of the dinosaurs that attacked us in the tower damaged the main controls that activate the shape changing ability of my armor, I was able to reroute the circuitry during our trip here," he replied. "I won't be able to use all of the armor's features, but I can at least appear as a normal human being again."

"Good. Then it's decided," Jeffrey said.

"But what're we going to do about our clothes?" Jerome asked. "Do you think we should wear the outfits you bought when you visited Corinth?"

Jeffrey considered the questions for a moment before responding. "I don't know. Mack, what do you think?"

Mack shrugged. "I think that anything we wear will be out of place. Greek togas would probably look just as out of place to these people as the jeans and t-shirt I'm wearing. Although the togas probably wouldn't *itch* as much. We really need to get some new clothes. I've been wearing the same pair of jeans and the same two shirts now since we started this wacky trip over…how long has it been, anyway? I never realized how hard it would be to tell time without the sun," Mack finished as he activated the holographic computer screen that was projected from the back of his right wrist.

Looking down at her own stained and ripped clothing, Rebecca had to agree with Mack. None of them could have expected that they would get stuck back in time. However, here they were, with only the clothes they had with them when they left. At least most of the others had an extra shirt or jumpsuit laying around the pyramid since this was where they had been working regularly. Rebecca, on the other hand, was more-or-less a stowaway, and as such, she only had her navy blue t-shirt, jeans, and black leather jacket. And after all that they had been through—crawling in the dirt, wading through a river, fighting dinosaurs, and getting caught in a downpour—her clothes had definitely seen better days.

"Can we get back to the point?" Jerome interjected.

"Wow! It's only been just over two days!" Mack said, ignoring Jerome's comment. "It seems like we've been gone at least a year!"

Growing impatient, Jeffrey put an end to Mack's ramblings. "We'll just go with the clothes we have. We're only going to talk to Noah anyway, and our strange clothes didn't seem to bother him before. So let's not waste any more time. Grab what you need, and let's get this core installed so we can get going."

2

LISA

"**JEFFREY, CAN I** talk to you for a second?" Lisa asked as she, Jeffrey, and Jerome reached the bottom of the stairs leading from the control room.

Sensing the emotional conflict in her voice, Jerome politely excused himself. "I'll go grab the levitation devices and meet you two by the core."

"Thanks. We'll be right there," Jeffrey said as Jerome headed around the corner toward the shared bedroom. Once Jerome was out of earshot, Jeffrey gently placed his hands on Lisa's upper arms, his six-foot height forcing him to look down at her. "What is it, honey? You're trembling. What's wrong?"

"What's wrong?" she replied in a forced whisper. "What *isn't* wrong?"

Jeffrey frowned. "You know what I mean. Besides the obvious, what in *particular* is bothering you?"

Lisa looked away from Jeffrey, her gaze wandering around the hallway as if the answers to her concerns were lurking in some corner. "I don't...I don't even know where to begin." Returning her attention to him, she stared intently, her face lined with worry. "Everything has gone wrong. When...when it was just us, things were so much simpler. Even when the girls came to live near the dig, I felt... I felt like there was so much possibility. We clicked—all of us—just seem to get along so well. It has been one of the most wonderful years of my life."

Jeffrey studied her expression. Guessing the source of her concern, he attempted to cut it off before it could escalate further. "I know that Becky's presence here makes you uncomfortable. It bothers me too. I wish things had turned out differently. But there's nothing we can do about it right now. Let's just get through this, and when we get home, it'll be the beginning of a new life for us."

As her frustration began to build, Lisa's eyes flashed. "Don't try to just blow this off," she said, the volume of her voice rising slightly. "You know I hate it when you do that. I'm not some immature girl who doesn't know how to deal with random mood swings."

Jeffrey's features hardened at the rebuke. But before he could respond, Lisa continued. "If it were just Becky, I could handle it. But it's this…this time machine, this mess we are in and…and that blasted boat out there!" she whispered harshly, her hand pointing behind him toward the entrance of the pyramid.

"What does any of that have to do with me and you?" Jeffrey countered. Then, his expression abruptly changed in understanding. "Oh, I get it. You're upset because you have to stay here with Doc while I'm leaving with Becky, right?"

Lisa just stared back at him, incredulous. "Ya know, Jeffrey, sometimes you can be a real idiot! This has nothing to do with that."

"Then tell me what it *is* about!" Jeffrey practically yelled back, forgetting to lower his voice.

For a moment, Lisa simply glared at him. Then, she shook her head as her lips curled in disgust. "Forget it. I've known you long enough to know when you get into your 'problem-solving' mode. At this point, I'd probably get more out of a conversation with Elmer." Stepping past him, she strode off down the hallway that led around the central core of the pyramid. Behind her, she could hear Jeffrey swear quietly in aggravation.

Reaching the hidden door on the east wall of the chamber, she paused. Leaning her head on the cold stone that appeared to be nothing more than a wall, she let out a heavy sigh. *How can someone so smart be so clueless? How can I make him understand?* she thought. *Doesn't he realize that this journey has changed everything? There's no going back. If that really is Noah's Ark out there, then that means that…that Becky's right. And if she's right, then… I don't even know what I believe anymore. And what if Jeffrey changes his beliefs? What will become of our relationship then?*

Taking a deep breath to calm her frazzled nerves, she reached down and pressed the specific section of the wall that would open to reveal the secret entrance. Once it had slid out of her way, she stepped into the room and began working on disconnecting the core that had been damaged when the pyramid slid down the ice-covered slope during the Ice Age. Within moments, Akwen arrived and began assisting her. Another minute later, Jeffrey and Jerome stood in the opening with the new core carried between them, its bulk being held aloft by the blue-glowing levitation devices they had acquired from the Tower of Babel. Although the work served to keep her mind occupied, it failed to dispel the raw emotions that clouded her mood, and the fact that the main person responsible for her current emotional state was standing next to her in a small, enclosed room didn't help matters.

Before long, the job was complete. With barely a look in her direction, Jeffrey left the room along with Jerome to begin preparations for their trip. As Lisa watched them go, she heard Akwen say something beside her. Focusing her attention on the tall, Cameroonian woman, she said, "I'm sorry, what did you say?"

Looking at her with impatience, Akwen repeated her previous statement. "I said, 'I need your help upstairs. Go check on Doc, den meet me dere.'" As the dark-skinned woman headed out of the central chamber, she paused and glanced over her shoulder at Lisa. "And by da way, get your head on straight first. I don't know what dat little spat between you and Jeffrey was about, but now is not da time to be distracted." Turning back around, Akwen disappeared into the hallway.

As much as she didn't like the woman's attitude of superiority, she had to admit to herself that Akwen was right. Lisa's training in the Marines had taught her to concentrate under extreme pressure. Yet somehow, this was different. This was too personal to just brush aside. Her thoughts still dwelling on Akwen's words, Lisa exited the chamber, shut the hidden door, and went to visit Dr. Eisenberg.

Opening the door to the bedroom that the women had been using, Lisa stepped inside and closed it softly behind her. Because this room was the closest to the main entrance, and was one of the only areas in the pyramid with a bed, it became the default emergency ward. Furthermore, with a second bed nearby, it allowed Lisa a chance to rest, yet, be close enough that she could respond quickly should her patient need anything.

As with every other time she had checked on the doctor's condition, she felt her pulse quicken anxiously, wondering if he would still be alive. Unconsciously, she held her breath as she stepped closer to the still form and searched for any signs of life.

She let out her breath in relief as she noticed the gentle rise and fall of the older man's chest. Reaching out toward the controls on the wall, Lisa turned up the lights in the room well enough for her to see, yet not so much as to disturb her sleeping patient. "I'm glad to see you're still with us, Doc," she whispered. As she went about the task of reading his vital signs, Lisa continued to speak to her unresponsive friend. "We need you to stay with us. Don't you go checking out early. You're strong. Just hold on until Jeffrey and Jerome get back. They're going to get some help from…"

Lisa paused, as once more the reality of her predicament hit her full force. "Doc, we need you. We need your wisdom and advice. What do we do? What do *I* do? I…I've really messed things up. How can I even begin to—"

The door to the room suddenly opened, causing her to stop midsentence. Looking over toward the entrance, she felt the bitter rock of her own guilt drop down, landing hard in the pit of her stomach at the sight of the woman who had once been her best friend; the woman who had been with her in the Marines; the woman who had travelled with her to 2021PK.

The woman she had betrayed.

"How is he?" Rebecca asked, her voice cold and clipped.

For a second, Lisa struggled to find her voice. Swallowing hard, she averted her gaze and looked down at Dr. Eisenberg as she responded. "He's...he's still alive. Actually, his vitals are somewhat surprising. For someone who has lost as much blood as he has, he's doing very well. He appears to be stabilizing. If we can just get him to a doctor, I...I think he'll pull through."

Despite the awkwardness her proximity produced, Rebecca stepped closer to Lisa and studied the face of the wounded man. Several moments passed in silence as the two women, bound by their love for their friend, stood side by side next to his bed. Finally, Rebecca leaned down and kissed his forehead. "We'll be back soon, Doc."

Without even acknowledging Lisa's presence, Rebecca straightened and headed toward the door. Lisa stood staring at the wall, her body as rigid as a block of granite. She wanted to say something, *anything*, but as soon as the words and sentences formed in her mind, she quickly discarded them. Then, just as Rebecca opened the door and was preparing to leave, she managed to get a phrase past the blockade in her throat. "I...I'll take good care of him, Becky."

Rebecca froze, the door obscuring her face from Lisa. "You had better. And by the way, my name is *Rebecca*. Only my *friends* call me Becky."

Hot tears dropped from Lisa's eyes to land noiselessly onto the bed next to the sleeping doctor as her one time friend closed the door with a thud.

3

RODINIA

ONCE THE INSTALLATION of the new core was completed, Jeffrey, Jerome, Rebecca, Mack, and Goliath assembled at the entrance to the pyramid, the few meager possessions they felt would be useful on this trip tucked away in their backpacks.

"Okay, Akwen," Jeffrey said into his commlink, "we're ready to leave. Open the front door." Before he had even finished his sentence, the two thick slabs of stone that covered the entrance began sliding along their tracks and moved up into the space between the inner and outer walls of the structure.

"Dere you go. Be careful. And hurry back," came Akwen's reply through the comm.

Despite the calm demeanor with which she spoke, Jeffrey had been working with the Cameroonian long enough to tell by the subtle tension in her voice that she was as worried as the rest of the group. Just the fact that the normally stoic woman was expressing her concern for them at all reminded Jeffrey of just how serious their predicament had become. "We'll check in every twenty minutes and swap updates. Good luck with fixing the ship. And hey, when you do get it fixed, don't accidently set it off, okay? I think I can safely speak for the rest of the group when I say we don't want to be stuck here."

Jeffrey's attempt at humor elicited only a short "hmph" from the other end of the line. Setting his commlink to standby, Jeffrey looked over at Mack. "Do you have the technical journals containing all of the pyramid specs?"

"Yeah. They're right here," the language specialist confirmed as he patted his backpack.

"Good, then let's get moving," Goliath said, his voice muffled by the helmet. Activating the cloaking device, the suit shimmered briefly before its silver metallic sheen changed into the likeness of a dark-skinned man dressed in leather garb, similar to that of a Roman centurion. Once the armor had completed its transformation, Goliath strode out of the entrance and into the sunlight.

As the giant passed, Jerome eyed the four-foot-long sword strapped to Goliath's back in a makeshift scabbard. Grabbing Jeffrey's arm, Jerome indicated for him to wait as Rebecca and Mack exited the pyramid to follow the giant.

"What is it?" Jeffrey asked once the others were out of earshot.

"I still don't like the idea of Goliath carrying around Nimrod's sword," Jerome whispered. "With its ability to shoot energy off the blade, it's every bit as powerful as the laser pistol Rebecca's carrying."

"Which is why we *need* him to have it," Jeffrey countered. "In case you hadn't noticed, we're a little short on weapons. If we happen to encounter any resistance, I think you'll change your opinion. Whether we like it or not, we're all in this together. Now c'mon."

Swallowing his concern, Jerome frowned as he followed Jeffrey down the steps and out onto the open plain. Within a matter of moments, the two of them caught up with the others. As Jeffrey pulled up alongside the giant, he scanned the landscape that stretched out before them. "So what do you think is our quickest route?" he asked.

Goliath continued to stare straight ahead as he replied. "We should stay on these rolling hills for as long as possible. However, in order to avoid the city, we're going to have to turn northeast and cut through the forest before long. After that, we climb those hills on the other side, circle around, and approach from the east."

Jeffrey's brows furrowed as he considered the giant's suggested route. "Why the east side?"

"For two reasons: First, I don't see an entrance on this side of the Ark, so I assume it's on the other side, and second, it'll keep us from being seen by anyone in the city," Goliath said.

"Hey!" Mack suddenly called from behind them, his voice taking on an unmistakable New York accent. "Where's da fire? I'm havin' ta jog back 'ere to keep up. Slow down a little, will ya?"

The giant turned his head slightly and regarded Mack out of the corner of his eye. "Unless you feel like traveling through a dense forest filled with who-knows-what lurking in the shadows and climbing a steep, unfamiliar hill in the dark, we have to keep up the pace. The sun is already passed its zenith, and we don't have much sunlight left. We'll be fortunate if we can make it before dark. So I hope you're ready for some exercise."

A blank look crossed Mack's face as understanding dawned on him. "Uh…you's-a point is well seen," he replied in a high pitched, odd-sounding voice that sounded to Rebecca like something from a slapstick cartoon character. The wolf-like giant shook his head in obvious disgust at the linguist's silly accent and returned his attention back to scanning the countryside.

Jogging next to Mack, Rebecca looked at him with concern. "How're you doing?"

Mack cast her a sidelong glance. His expression was somewhat hard to read, due to the artificial sunglasses created by the holographic projectors imbedded under his skin. "Well, other than the sheer terror brought on by the prospect of being drowned in a gigantic tsunami, or the panic that's causing every nerve in my body to fire simultaneously, I think I'm doing okay," he responded nonchalantly.

Rebecca's face reflected her own anxiety. "I know what you mean.

Let me tell you a little secret I learned a long time ago. Keep your mind busy. Analyze things and focus on the moment. Don't dwell on what *might* happen. With that in mind, let me ask you another question. How's your asthma? Just about every other time you've been forced to run, you've needed your inhaler almost immediately."

A look of profound surprise lit up Mack's features. "You're right! I should be wheezing worse than Darth Vader without his helmet! And with all of the recent stress, I should be getting walloped by one of my massive migraines from my technology implants right about now! What…why do you think…?"

"I don't know," Rebecca replied in astonishment. "The only thing I can think of is that there's something in the atmosphere that's making a difference. Even the wound that I got on my leg from that dinosaur back in the Tower of Babel isn't bothering me as much as I thought it would. I was afraid I wouldn't be able to keep up, but I seem to be doing alright."

"Well, I for one hope it continues! I feel strong enough to pull the ears off a Gundark!" Mack commented as he quickened his pace slightly.

"Yeah, me too," Rebecca said, mostly to herself. Lost in pondering other possible implications of this new discovery, Mack's movie reference went completely unheard and unappreciated.

"So, do you still think this is Earth?" Mack asked after a brief lull in the conversation. "From what we saw in orbit, this planet only has a single massive continent. How does that fit with your theory?"

"Quite nicely, actually," Rebecca replied. "If there really was a global flood, it would mean *huge* changes in the crust of the earth and massive tectonic movement. The Bible talks about the 'fountains of the great deep' bursting open, which could very well account for the mid-Atlantic ridge."

"But, I thought movement of the plates took long periods of time," Mack stated. "Didn't the Flood last only forty days and forty nights?"

Rebecca shook her head. "That's a common error. The Bible says that the initial downpour lasted for forty days and nights. But if you read the account carefully, it clearly indicates that Noah and his family were in the Ark for over a year, I believe."

"A year?" Mack repeated incredulously. "But, how could eight people possibly take care of that many animals for that long? And I always thought that *forty* days would have been pushing it."

"We'll probably find out first hand soon enough," she replied. "As for your other question, the plates could move quickly under catastrophic conditions.[1] Evolutionary scientists often make this common mistake. They look at the way things happen in the present, and *assume* that things have *always* happened that way."

"Wait...don't tell me," Mack said. "I've heard you guys mention this before. It's called...uni...uniform...itism, right?"

Rebecca smiled. "You're close. Uniformitarianism. It means, 'the present is the key to the past.' But, what scientists fail to take into account is that catastrophes can produce similar results to the slow, gradual processes, but in *much* less time."

"But, then how would you ever be able to tell if something was formed in a catastrophe or by slow processes?" Mack wondered.

"Well, first you need a good reason to believe that a catastrophe occurred."

"Would an ancient document stating that there was a worldwide flood count as a good reason?" Mack asked sarcastically.

"Yeah, I think it would," she replied. "Also, there are other geological indicators."

"Like what?"

Rebecca's expression dropped slightly. "Unfortunately, I don't know off the top of my head. Even when I first believed in Creation, I didn't believe that Noah's Flood was universal. Everything I'm telling you now was stuff that I read years ago, but dismissed as not being true. I've only just switched my understanding of things since we've been on this trip. I really wish I'd have paid more attention to it. We'll have to do some more research using Elmer's memory when we get time."

Mack was silent for nearly a minute as he processed this information.

"You know, I've never really gotten into science that much—except science fiction. But, this little adventure through time has really taught me a lot. So, does the Bible give a name to this pre-flood supercontinent?"

Rebecca searched through her memory in an effort to find the answer to Mack's question. Finally, after several moments, her face brightened. "The Bible doesn't give it a name, but I believe that one of the articles I read gave it a name. It's on the tip of my tongue. It was some Russian word that started with an 'r.' I think it meant 'home,' or something like that."

"Was it 'Rodinia'?" Mack offered.

"Yes! That's it," Rebecca confirmed. "What does it mean?"

"It means 'homeland.'"

"Rodinia," Rebecca repeated as she looked at the beauty that surrounded them. "Yes. This *is* our homeland."

Rebecca, Mack, and the others continued jogging for more than an hour, stopping only on occasion for brief rests, even though they were surprised and amazed at how little rest they actually needed. Due to the rate at which the group travelled, they soon found themselves at the point where Goliath had indicated the need to turn into the woods. As they drew nearer to the massive trees, they slowed their pace in wonder. For although the trees themselves were similar to the kind that the travelers were familiar with, the immense size of the majestic trunks and long, flowing branches filled the onlookers with awe.

"Look at the size of these trees!" Jeffrey exclaimed. "I've seen the redwoods, but these are even bigger. You could make an entire house out of one of these trunks!"

"Man, I feel like I just stepped into the woods of Lothlorian!" Mack said, his neck craned back to look up at the branches far above them.

"Incredible," Jerome muttered to himself. "What do you—"

"Quiet!" Goliath hissed, causing Jerome and the others to freeze instantly.

The only warning they had was a low growl that emanated from a pile of brush near a fallen tree. Suddenly, a large animal the size of a lion charged straight toward Rebecca. While it looked somewhat like a feline, it was unlike any cat that she had ever seen. Its short fur was a dark brown color peppered in various places with shades of gray. The head and shoulders of the animal were devoid of any kinds of markings, but the midsection had black spots that turned into stripes near its hindquarters and legs. Its front paws were much wider and thicker than any large cat she had ever seen, and its head was more angular. Instead of fangs, the animal had strangely-shaped teeth that resembled blades or knives, and its eyes, which were locked directly upon her, promised death.

As soon as she saw the creature, Rebecca took off running in the opposite direction, knowing in her heart that it wouldn't do any good. Remembering her laser pistol, she reached into her jacket and tried to pull it out as she ran; all the while, she could hear the beast closing in on her.

Then, with the giant cat now less than five feet away, a loud crack echoed through the woods, accompanied by a brilliant flash. A moment later, the smell of charred flesh wafted through the air, carried by a gentle breeze as the forest once more returned to its previous tranquil state.

Her heart still pounding loudly in her ears, Rebecca looked over toward the source of the light and sound to see Goliath standing with his sword pointed at the animal. "Th...thank you," she managed, after swallowing several times in an attempt to regain her voice.

"Whoa! That thing is HUGE!" Mack said incredulously. "You could probably put a saddle on it and take it for a ride! I bet it would even give a warg a run for its money! Wow, I didn't even know they ever *came* that big!"

By now, Jeffrey, Jerome, and Goliath had moved toward the creature to examine it more closely. "They *don't* come this big. At least not anymore. And actually, I don't think it's even a cat at all. If I'm not mistaken, it's a marsupial."

"What, you mean like a kangaroo?" Rebecca asked.

"Yeah," Jeffrey confirmed as he crouched down to study it closer. "I think this is a *thylacoleo carnifex*—more commonly known as a 'marsupial lion.' They're an extinct species from Australia."

"But I don't get it," Jerome commented. "This one seems larger than most of the reported fossils of *thylacoleo*. I've read articles about giant animal fossils, but those fossils were dated to be at least…"

"Let me guess," Rebecca interjected, "millions of year old?"

Jeffrey glanced at her, but didn't reply. His face, however, reflected his confusion.

"Keep your weapon ready, in case we encounter anything else," Goliath said.

"Yeah," Rebecca said in agreement, "I think I'll do that."

"Especially since these things were supposed to have hunted in small groups," Jeffrey added as he stood and scanned the surrounding area warily.

Leaving the carcass behind, the group headed out once again, their senses more alert. As they moved deeper into the forest, it became more difficult to maintain their vigilance as their attention became drawn to dozens of beautiful, yet strangely-shaped plants and moss that lay cloistered among the roots of the trees like little children huddling around their mother's skirts. Patches of round mushrooms that were the size of baseballs lay scattered about the area. Thick mosses of vibrant purple and blue grew up the sides of the trees. Red-tinged vines as thick as a man's arm hung to the ground. Flowers of bright orange, yellow, white, and blue dotted the floor of the forest, as if a master painter had deliberately placed them in strategic locations to liven up the dark browns and gentle greens of the trees and leaves.

"Is that what I think it is?" Jerome asked, pointing toward a circular red object about the size of a small pumpkin hanging from one of the lowest branches of a tree. Running up to the base of the trunk, he began looking around on the ground. As expected, several more of the objects littered the area. Picking one up, he examined it closely. "Jeffrey, it looks like some kind of apple—an enormous, red apple!"

"Surely you jest!" Mack said, coming up to stand beside him. "That thing looks like it's been pumping steroids!"

Rebecca stepped over to join Mack and Jerome. After examining another one of the gigantic apples, she wiped it off with her shirt, then took a bite of the fruit. The exquisite flavors that burst in her mouth caused a groan of pleasure to escape from her lips. The thick, sticky juice flowed down her chin as she bit into the succulent flesh of the apple once again. "I've never tasted anything like this!" she exclaimed. "It's like…like eating apple-flavored candy, only richer. Not rich in a 'make-you-sick' kind of way, but rich in a pure, natural way."

Grabbing one for himself, Mack sank his teeth deep into it. "Man, that's good! Ya know, Becky, if this *is* Earth, like you say it is, then why do you think everything is so big? And why don't we have fruit this good anymore? Do you think it's got something to do with this environment?"

Rebecca thought for a moment before responding. "Yes, I do. If you remember correctly, when we told Noah that humans during our time only live about one hundred years, he responded by saying he believed it was due to the change in climate after the Flood." Rebecca paused to take another small bite of the fruit.

"When I first started my research into Creationism, I came across several articles about a 'vapor canopy' model," she continued. "Although many creation scientists said that it had scientific problems, the model did explain quite a bit."

"Like what?" Mack asked.

"Like why people lived so much longer," she replied, "why there are fossils of giant animals and plants in the fossil record, and why dinosaurs didn't grow as large after the Flood."

"Hey, that's right," Mack said. "Jerome and Jeffrey, didn't you guys say that those Monoclonius dinosaurs we encountered with the Mayans were smaller than the ones in the fossil record?"

Jeffrey didn't reply, but Jerome nodded once, unenthusiastically. "Yeah."

Mack grinned at the confirmation as he turned his attention back to Rebecca. "So, you think there's some kind of extra layer of atmosphere up there causing everything to grow bigger?"

Rebecca shrugged. "It's possible, but as I said, it didn't work as a scientific model. All I know is that there seems to be *something* in the air affecting these things."

"Yeah, I can vouch for that," he commented as he chewed. "We'll have to grab some of these apples on the way back to the ship. They sure beat that other stuff we've been eating."

"Jeffrey, over here," Goliath said, interrupting their conversation.

Turning to look at the giant, he saw him kneeling down and examining something on the ground. "What is it?" he said as he strode over to see what had caught the interest of his companion.

"Animal tracks, and lots of them," Goliath said as he stood. "I've been trained in tracking, yet some of these are unfamiliar to me. Look at this one," he said, moving to his right and pointing to a small cluster of four indentations. "This larger section looks similar to a horse's hoof, but I don't know what to make of the other three smaller indentations. And this other one to the left looks like nothing I have ever seen before."

Jeffrey shook his head as the truth hit him. "I *have* seen tracks like this before. Fossilized tracks. These are small, but unmistakable, *tyrannosaur* tracks."

Mack, Rebecca, and Jerome, who had overheard most of the conversation, came over to join the other two. "Wait…wait…wait!" Mack blurted out. "There must've been something in that fruit that messed with my head. I could have *sworn* that you just said *tyrannosaur* tracks. But I *know* that can't be right!"

Jerome crouched down to examine the tracks, then swore softly. "That's it, alright. It must be a juvenile, judging by the size and stride."

"I don't care if it's a lil' ol' *granny* t-rex! I *still* don't want to meet it," Mack exclaimed, all the while scanning the surrounding area as if expecting one of the creatures to lumber out from behind a tree at any moment. "Those things are *mean*! They can crush a whole jeep just by stepping on it. And they're real protective of their young. Didn't you ever see any of the *Jurassic Park* movies? I say we get moving before it, or its parents, find us!"

Not the least fazed by Mack's concern, Goliath continued to study the tracks. "I don't think we have to worry about running into any of the animals who made these," he said casually. "At least not yet."

"What do you mean? Why not?" Jeffrey asked.

"Because, they're several days old and they all lead in the same direction. Uphill."

"Were they running away from something?" Mack asked.

"They weren't running," Jerome said as he continued to study the tracks. "They're too close together."

"They were moving *toward* something!" Rebecca said in sudden understanding. "The Ark! These animals were heading toward the Ark!"

"Don't jump to conclusions, Becky," Jeffrey warned. "There could be lots of reasons—"

"Oh shut up," Rebecca said in frustration. "I'll believe my theories, you believe yours." Without waiting for a reply, she turned to look at the others. "At least now we have a clear path to follow. We've gotta hurry. If the animals are already on board, then there isn't much time left. And by the way," she said, staring directly back at her husband, "my name is *Rebecca*." Not even turning to see if the others were coming with her, she headed off down the trail.

For a moment, Jerome and Mack just looked at Jeffrey as if trying to decide what to do. As Goliath started walking after Rebecca, Jeffrey shifted the weight of his pack on his shoulders. "What are you two staring at?" he snapped. "We might as well use the trail. At least it's taking us in the right direction."

Jerome and Mack merely exchanged glances, and then followed behind him.

Although the group was forced to step around the occasional animal dropping, the trail proved to accelerate their travel greatly. After about an hour of fast-paced walking, the incline of the path increased noticeably.

Fortunately, the animals who blazed the trail seemed to have found the shortest and least strenuous route possible. The more Rebecca and the others climbed, the more they realized how difficult the climb would have been had they not found the trail.

Finally, as the sun dipped low on the horizon, they reached the edge of the forest. Directly in front of them ran a well-worn dirt road over forty feet wide. From their vantage point, it appeared that the road wove its way down the hill and headed back to the city, which now lay somewhere off to the northwest. To their right, a smaller road branched off from the main one and led north to a cluster of large buildings hidden back in a copse of trees. The main road, however, continued on another one hundred feet until it came to an abrupt end at a huge clearing at the top of the hill.

A large portion of the clearing, which spread out for several miles, was surrounded by a twenty-foot granite wall. Rising silently from behind the wall like an enormous mythical beast sat the Ark.

4

VANDALS

FOR SEVERAL MINUTES, all Rebecca and the others could do was stare at the massive vessel. From bow to stern, the ship, which ran perpendicular to their vantage point, stretched five hundred feet, covering a large portion of the hilltop. From what they could see through the bars of the heavy metal gate, the giant craft rested on a bed of planks and supports, adding several more feet to its already impressive fifty-foot height. Bathed in the rays of the setting sun, the wooden sides of the vessel seemed to glow a deep, warm amber.

The overall shape and design of the vessel reminded Rebecca of pictures she had seen of ancient galleys. Near the bow, a twenty-five-foot-long fin-like structure rose up from the roof, increasing the height of the front of the ship significantly. Projecting out an additional twenty-five feet from the stern was another fin-like structure. This one, however, pointed down and appeared to be some sort of fixed rudder. Unlike the other ships that Rebecca had seen, the Ark, by necessity, had a roof. Running down the center of the roof, there was a row of raised windows about a foot high and four feet wide, each with a covering that appeared able to swing upward to let in light and air during dry weather.

The only entrance Rebecca could see was located near the front of the ship about two-thirds of the way up the side. A huge mound of packed earth and rocks obscured nearly half of the Ark as it formed a natural ramp leading up to the ten-foot square door, which currently stood open.

The clearing surrounding the mighty vessel reminded Rebecca of a battlefield. Numerous objects that appeared to have once been neatly stacked were now strewn about the area, broken and crushed. Piles of wood lay splintered and disorganized, shards of pottery appeared to have been trampled, and wooden wheelbarrows were tipped over and smashed. In addition, large stumps the diameter of a small house remained standing as a testament to the number of trees required to build the massive structure. Scattered among all of the debris and stumps were animal droppings, and lots of them.

"Look at the *size* of that thing!" Mack stated.

"I…I never imagined it would be so…so *big*," Jerome said at last, the amazement in his voice palpable. "It's gotta be over one and half times the size of a football field! For some reason I've always had this image in my head of a small boat with giraffes and elephants sticking their heads out through open windows."

"That's because, too often, well-meaning people draw it that way when they tell the story to their children," Rebecca commented. "Or, when they teach it in Sunday school."

Jerome turned to look at her, his expression revealing his growing respect. "You're right. That's where I saw it. I remember thinking it was an insult to my intelligence that they'd expect me to believe it was *real* history. But, they never described it to me like *this*."

A sense of superiority and vindication suddenly came over Rebecca. "Maybe you should've read your Bible more. It has the dimensions of the Ark listed right there in Genesis 6. Of course, the Bible gives the dimensions in cubits, which is the distance between a man's elbow and the tip of his finger—roughly eighteen inches. However, the cubit in the ancient world varied from place to place. By the looks of it, Noah must have used the larger cubit, which would make the Ark over five hundred feet in length."

Jerome's countenance darkened at Rebecca's know-it-all attitude, causing him to keep any further comments to himself.

Recalling a previous conversation regarding Jerome's loss of faith due to his experience with hypocrites in the church, Rebecca pressed her philosophical advantage. "And that's one of the problems with our churches: we teach the *history* in Genesis as if it were just *stories*."

Highly uncomfortable with the current topic of conversation, Jeffrey drew the other's attention back to their immediate situation. "I never expected there to be a wall. How are we going to get past it?"

"Maybe we could figure out some way to use the levitation devices to get us over it," Jerome suggested.

"It's too high," the tall, dark-skinned man that was Goliath replied. "It looks like there might be some kind of…Quick! Everyone back behind the trees!"

Although none of the others saw any signs of immediate danger, they nevertheless reacted instantly to Goliath's command. Once they were all safely crouched behind one of the trees, they searched the area for the source of the giant's concern. It didn't take them very long to find it.

In one of the windows of the buildings that were off the main road, a soft, orange light began to glow. As they watched, it began to grow steadily brighter until they could make out the telltale signs of a fire. A moment later, the same scenario repeated itself as each of the other four buildings was set ablaze.

As they watched, Rebecca and her companions saw shadowy figures emerging from the flaming structures. From the way they moved, and based on the fact that they all held some kind of torch-like object in their hands, Rebecca knew instantly that the figures were not the local residents.

They were vandals. And they were heading straight toward the road.

"Hold!" Goliath called out as they watched the approach of the shadowy group. "They probably don't know we're even here. With dusk upon us, the lighting is poor. We'll most likely escape their notice."

As the thirteen tall figures approached the road, the torches in their hands seemed to wink out one by one even as the conflagration behind them consumed everything in its path, sending dark plumes of smoke into the air. Sure enough, when the vandals reached the road, they turned toward the metal gate protecting the Ark, completely ignoring the travelers.

"They don't look any older than teenagers," Rebecca said as the young men reached their destination.

"Probably some kind of street gang," Goliath stated. "Notice how each has a black band wound around his head. I saw some kind of symbol drawn there."

"And they're all wearing the same type of sleeveless shirts and dark colored pantaloons," Jeffrey added.

Rebecca's eyes narrowed as she continued watching the men. "What are they...oh, no," she said, realization suddenly striking her. "They're going to burn the Ark!"

"What?" Jeffrey said, his head turning quickly in her direction. "What makes you—"

Before he could finish his sentence, the gate suddenly swung inward. Immediately, the men poured through the opening and sprinted toward the wooden vessel. As they ran, tongues of fire sprang into existence in the hands of several of them.

"We have to do something!" Rebecca nearly shouted in panic.

"Isn't this supposed to be God's Ark?" Jeffrey asked spitefully. "I want to see *Him* protect it."

Leaping to her feet, Rebecca shoved Jeffrey hard, sending him sprawling into the dirt. "You're such a jerk! I for one am not going to just sit by and do nothing." Without another word, Rebecca darted forward onto the street, her laser pistol held ready in her right hand.

Seeing that their element of surprise was about to be lost, Goliath quickly turned to the others and spoke rapidly. "They'll likely be armed. As soon as I take one out, grab his weapon. Until then, activate the levitation devices and use them as a shield." Rising gracefully to his feet, the giant sprinted after Rebecca, his lengthy stride rapidly closing the gap between them.

"Oh man, I…I don't know if I can do this," Mack muttered worriedly. "I'm not a fighter."

Jerome, his own face radiating fear, looked at Mack and swallowed. "We'll just have to do what we can. C'mon." Searching the ground around him, Jerome grabbed a broken branch to use as club. Taking a deep breath as if preparing to dive into water, he ran out into the street, followed by Mack who was brandishing his own makeshift weapon.

Cursing loudly in frustration, Jeffrey reluctantly followed.

Rebecca had just passed through the open gate when Goliath caught up to her. Grabbing her by the arm, he pushed her to the ground behind a large stump just as two of the men turned in their direction, their attention drawn by the sound of the running figures. Holding a finger to his lips to indicate silence, the giant peered around the curve of the stump.

The two men immediately spotted Mack, Jerome, and Jeffrey who were nearing the open gate. Crying out in alarm, the two men grabbed their nearby comrades, and the five of them turned and began heading back toward the newcomers.

Goliath held up his hand, indicating for Rebecca to wait. In his other hand, he held Nimrod's sword ready. Because the attention of the group of men was focused solely on Jeffrey and the others, they walked right past Goliath and Rebecca without noticing them. Silently, the pair held up their weapons and took aim as the five men drew out their two-foot-long, thin short swords from sheaths on their hips.

Jerome, Mack, and Jeffrey halted their charge at the sight of the men. Suddenly, to their great surprise, beams of energy lanced out from the swords in the vandals' hands, narrowly missing the newcomer's heads. Instantly reacting to the attack, Jeffrey dove to his right while Mack and Jerome dove to their left, each of them using the granite fence as a shield.

"Great!" Jerome called out sarcastically. "It looks like their swords can do the same trick as Nimrod's!"

"Now whatta we do?" Mack asked.

"Jerome, toss me the other end of the levitation device," Jeffrey said.

"There's no time! Here they come!"

The five men, now seeing their attackers taking up positions on each side of the open gate, slowed their advance, unknowingly positioning themselves as easy targets for Goliath and Rebecca.

"NOW!" Goliath called.

As one, he and Rebecca let loose with a coordinated attack. Two of the men fell immediately, while the remaining three spun around in an effort to locate the source of this new attack. Just as their gaze fixed upon Rebecca and Goliath, a second volley of shots dropped two more of them.

The remaining man sprinted toward the opening to escape from the ranged attacks only to be felled by a well-placed blow from Jerome's club as soon as he came around the edge of the wall. At once, Jeffrey, Mack, and Jerome threw down their primitive clubs and grabbed the swords out of the hands of the downed men.

"Look!" Mack called out as the three of them ran to join Rebecca and Goliath. While their companions had been fighting the newcomers, the rest of the vandals had been busy piling up any debris they could find that would burn near the stern of the Ark.

"How did they get so much piled up so quickly?" Rebecca wondered aloud.

"Rebecca, Mack, and Jerome—take out the four on the left, we'll handle the three on the right," Goliath commanded. "Keep low to the ground and use the stumps for cover."

The instant the travelers began to fan out and make their way forward, they heard a cry of warning from one of the vandals. Five of the men immediately dropped what they were doing and turned to face the attack, leaving just two gang members to finish the job of stacking up the combustible material.

Combatants on both sides of the battle sought cover among the debris and stumps. A moment later, bolts of white energy and small cracks like thunder split the evening air. The flashes of light joined with the deep orange of the burning buildings and the purplish-red of the setting sun to create a kaleidoscope of color, all under a covering of thick black smoke that was beginning to blot out the sky.

For several seconds, neither side gave ground, causing Rebecca to fear that they would not be able to stop the vandals in time. Her fear was increased a moment later when she saw the two men closest to the Ark set fire to the brush pile they had created.

"Cover me!" Rebecca yelled to Mack and Jerome as she leapt out from behind her cover and began running left toward the mound that led to the entrance of the Ark, hoping to be able to flank her attackers. Blazing white energy bolts flashed all around her, narrowly missing. Reaching the mound, she dove behind a crate to catch her breath. Peering around the corner of the wooden box, she was encouraged to see that Goliath had mimicked her maneuver and had worked his way to the right, thus trapping the gang of vandals between their own rapidly increasing bonfire and the attackers.

As Rebecca added her laser to the deadly light show, she heard a cry of pain come from Jerome. Watching in horror, she saw his body jerk backward and fall out of sight behind one of the large tree stumps.

"JEROME! Oh God, help us!" she prayed fervently. "Lord, we need you. Please—"

From behind another crate near her own, a figure rose up and knocked Rebecca onto her back, sending her pistol flying from her grasp. Reacting on instinct, she reached up just in time to keep the blade in her attacker's hand from piercing her heart. As she fought to turn the blade aside, Rebecca got her first glimpse of her assailant.

The face that stared down at her nearly caused her to lose the battle for control of the dagger. Under normal lighting conditions, the features would have been frightening enough. Yet, the reflection of the fire and the strobe-light effect from the energy blasts made the young man's face seem demonic.

Although he appeared to be no more than thirteen years old, his body was already over seven feet tall and very muscular. The tips of his ears were pointed, and his nose was flattened against his face. As he sneered, she could see razor sharp teeth and two large fangs hiding behind his cracked lips. The jet-black hair that crowned his head was pulled back into a tight ponytail and encircled by a matching headband bearing the symbol of fangs dripping blood. Even in the approaching darkness of night, she could tell that his skin was thin and appeared almost transparent. However, more disturbing than anything were his eyes. For in them, she saw a lust and desire for evil that rivaled anything she could ever have imagined in her worst nightmare. If this being had once had a soul, it had been lost long ago.

Leering down at her, the aberration grinned wickedly, fully revealing his fangs. Summoning all of her strength, she brought her leg up and rolled her body with the kick. Her leg connected with her attacker's body, knocking him off balance. Nimble as a cat, the vampire-like man quickly regained his feet and lunged at her once more.

Looking around desperately for her gun, she noticed a discarded hammer half buried under a wooden plank. Diving toward it, she grabbed the handle in her right hand and yanked it out just as the man drove his dagger into the plank, barely missing her arm.

Crying out in fear and rage, Rebecca twisted her body and swung the hammer at the man, but he moved quicker than she would have imagined. Ducking under her swing, he threw his body into hers, knocking the wind out of her. She collapsed to the ground, gasping for air and knowing that she would feel the bite of the vandal's blade—or teeth—at any second.

Suddenly, from somewhere behind her came the unmistakable twang of a bowstring. The man that had been attacking her let out a garbled cry as an arrow pierced his chest. Before the body had even hit the ground, several more twangs sounded and the air around her was alive with more of the deadly shafts.

As the breath came back into her body, she looked up to see that all of the remaining gang members lay dead or dying. Rising slowly to her feet, Rebecca turned around and froze at the sight of her rescuers. Standing just outside the open doorway of the Ark, bows in hand, stood Noah and his three sons.

5

THE INVITATION

BEFORE THE LAST of the gang members had slumped to the ground, Noah and two of his sons dropped their bows and ran toward the growing bonfire, while the fourth man held an arrow to his string and kept it pointed in the direction of Rebecca's companions. Approaching the bodies of the vandals closest to the fire, Noah and his sons reached down and grabbed some kind of objects from their hands. Darting over to stand next to the Ark, they pointed the newly acquired devices toward the blaze. Then, to Rebecca's surprise, a circular disc about three feet in diameter sprang into existence in front of each of the men and began moving away from them, pushing the burning materials past the stern of the ship and into the clearing. Although she had seen gravity-control technology used in the Tower of Babel to lift objects, she found it odd that these creatures would have access to that technology and that it could be used to *push* objects laterally.

With the bulk of the bonfire moved away from the Ark, the three men turned their attention to removing any smaller pieces of burning debris that still clung to the sides of the ship and inspected it for damage. Satisfied that no damage had been done to the hull, Noah and his sons heaved sighs of relief as they turned to survey the rest of the area.

Several soft gasps could be heard coming from the entrance to the ship, causing Rebecca and the fourth man still holding his bow to spin around. Standing in the doorway were four women, their gaze riveted to the sight of the burning buildings on the other side of the massive stone fence.

The archer spoke brusquely to the women, then immediately went back to guarding the strange newcomers. The three younger women were attempting to comfort the older, dark-haired woman, whom Rebecca now recognized as Noah's wife. After a few moments, the younger women led her back into the interior of the Ark.

The immediate threat having been removed, Rebecca suddenly remembered Jerome. Despite her desire to rush over to him, she forced herself to stand slowly, so as not to startle the bowman guarding her. Holding her hands in the air, she looked directly at him and hoped that the expression on her face would be sufficient to convey her intentions. It appeared to be enough, for as she walked toward Jerome's position, the archer merely tracked her movements with his eyes, but did not aim directly at her. Finally deciding that the unknown visitors were not the perpetrators of the vandalism, the man with the bow relaxed and lowered his weapon, allowing Rebecca to focus on finding and helping her friends.

As she neared the stump that Jerome had been using for cover, she saw Jeffrey, Mack, and Goliath rise slowly from their own concealed positions, their weapons held loosely at their sides. Rounding the edge of the stump, she nearly collapsed with relief.

"Hey, Becky," he said with a painful grin from where he lay on his back, "what happened? Did we win?"

"Yes, we did," she said. Kneeling down beside him, she removed his left hand from his right shoulder and began examining the wound. "You were lucky, tough guy. It hit your collarbone. A couple inches more to your left and you'd have a new hole in your neck."

As he returned her stare, the lines on his forehead creased. Rebecca felt a lump rise in her throat at the raw emotion she saw in his features. "It looks like maybe Someone was looking out for me," he said, his voice cracking as he spoke. In the fading light of the sun, she saw moisture begin to fill his eyes. Fighting back her own tears, she simply nodded in reply.

Sensing the approach of someone behind her, she turned to see one of Noah's three sons striding over to her. The six-and-a-half-foot-tall man appeared to be in his late twenties, yet his eyes seemed to hold the wisdom of a man much older. His wavy brown hair and short, trimmed beard and mustache accented his handsome features. The finely wrought, gray robe with gold trim that hung from his shoulders was cinched at his waist with a simple, yet beautifully-crafted crimson belt. Although the robe was loose-fitting, Rebecca could tell by the size of his arms and calves that his body was toned and muscular and was accustomed to hard, physical labor. As she studied him, she couldn't help but draw a connection between him and the warrior Nimrod that they had encountered on their incursion to the Tower of Babel. However, where the other's face had been hard and cruel, this man exuded trust and empathy.

Speaking a few words in his own language, he bent down and indicated that he would like to help Jerome to his feet. At the sight of the large man, uncertainty spread over Jerome's features. Laying a reassuring hand on her friend's arm, Rebecca said, "It's okay. This is one of Noah's sons."

At the sound of Rebecca's words, the man cast a strange look at her, as if he was questioning her sanity. Despite his sudden wariness, he reached down and helped Jerome to his feet.

As he walked between the man and Rebecca, Jerome whispered in her ear, "He looks a little bit like Nimrod, don't ya think?"

"Well, considering that he's either Nimrod's grandfather or granduncle, that doesn't surprise me," Rebecca replied.

"Oh, yeah. I didn't think of that," Jerome said, wincing in pain as the three of them headed over to where the others had gathered. While one of Noah's sons had been helping her and Jerome, one of the other men checked the gate, searching for signs of damage. The third son, along with Noah himself, had rounded up the remainder of Rebecca's companions and stood near the side of the Ark, waiting for the rest to join them. As she and Jerome approached the group, Rebecca looked toward the entrance of the ship for signs of the women. However, the warning from Noah's son had been enough to keep them from venturing back to the ship's door.

Although her rescuers no longer held bows in their hands, the posture of the four men left no doubt in Rebecca's mind that they were still wary of the newcomers. She also observed that they had gathered together the bows that they had discarded in order to fight the fire, all of the weapons that Jeffrey and the others had "borrowed" from the gang members, as well as her own laser pistol and placed them near the door of the Ark.

Standing before this much younger Noah, Rebecca was surprised at how tall he seemed. She also caught herself staring at the physical strength he obviously possessed. Instead of his thin frame, light skin, and gray hair that he possessed as an old man, he now had thick muscles, dark, bronzed skin, and a full head of golden hair streaked through with veins of silver. Like the older version of himself, his shoulder length hair was pulled back into a ponytail that reached down to the base of his neck. His beard, however, which also displayed slivers of silver hairs, was not as long as when Rebecca had last seen him.

Despite the fact that each of the three younger men shared the same father, Rebecca was surprised by their differences. While the one that assisted Jerome had brown, wavy hair, one of his brothers had reddish-blond, curly hair and light skin, and the tallest of the three had black, straight hair and darker skin. The men all wore robes similar to the one which their brother was wearing, each beautifully made despite their simple design.

Once Noah was convinced that all immediate concerns had been taken care of, he turned to Rebecca and the others and, in similar fashion to their previous meeting, began examining each of them in turn. An odd sense of déjà vu settled over Rebecca as he studied them. As before, he looked at each of them briefly before stopping in front of her, his expression becoming suddenly filled with surprise.

Still standing before Rebecca, he spoke, his eyes boring into her soul. Glancing over to Mack, she found him focused on their host, completely oblivious to the fact that she needed his help. Seeing her turn to look at him, he suddenly remembered, and after a brief apology, he began to translate Noah's words. "Who are you, and why are you here?"

Based on the group's past experience and their current urgent situation, Rebecca decided to try the direct approach. "Mighty Noah, favored servant of the Most High God, blessed be His Name, we come seeking your help. I am Rebecca Evans. My companions and I are travelers from far in the future, brought here unwillingly in a machine we believe was built by someone here in the past. The machine is no longer working properly and we are hoping that you may be able to fix it, or know someone who can fix it. Most of us do not speak your language because…" she paused, wondering for the first time if they might not be irrevocably altering history by their very presence here. Deciding not to reveal too much in her explanation, she continued, "…because in our time, language has changed greatly, and only my friend, Mack, now speaks the original Language of Eden."

As Mack translated, Rebecca noticed that although Noah's expression remained curious and unchanging, his sons glanced at each other, their faces a mixture of wonder, mistrust, and confusion. When her host didn't respond, she continued. "It is the greatest honor of my life to meet all of you. These are my companions: Mack, Jerome, Goliath, and Jeffrey," she said, taking a bit of twisted pleasure in introducing her husband after the giant. Judging by the look on Jeffrey's face, he didn't appreciate the slight.

After a moment of processing her reply, the Patriarch responded. "These are my three sons. This is my eldest son, Shem," he said, lifting his hand to indicate the man with the curly blond hair as Mack translated his words, "my second son, Japheth, was the one who assisted your injured friend, and this is my youngest, Ham," he finished, pointing at the tall youth with the straight black hair. "I see that you have the Spirit of God, may He be eternally glorified, residing in you, yet your friends do not. Can you vouch for their intentions?"

"Yes," Rebecca said emphatically.

"Then you are welcome," Noah stated. Although his physical stance relaxed, she could tell that his sons were not as quick to welcome these strangers. Ham leaned forward and whispered briefly to his father. Without even turning to face his son, Noah simply spoke a couple of words and his son backed off, clearly not happy with his father's decision.

"My son, Ham, worries that this gang may have others working with them," Noah continued. "We need to remove their bodies from here, and secure this area. It appears that somehow, this group obtained the key to our gate. We must change the lock before anyone else tries to destroy the Ark. If you would pardon my sons, they will attend to this matter while we discuss things further."

Before Mack had even finished translating his words, Noah's three sons began using the newly acquired gravity devices to push the bodies toward the gate, in much the same fashion that they had used the devices to move the burning materials.

Turning his attention back to his guests, Noah smiled widely. "I wish to express my gratitude to you and your companions for your timely intervention. I am forever amazed at my Protector's infinite wisdom and power. For surely He brought you across space and time to arrive at precisely the right moment to prevent this group from destroying His Ark of salvation. We thank Him, and you, for your intervention."

As Mack translated the words, his own astonishment was reflected in his voice and expression. "That's just freaky!" he exclaimed. "I mean, what are the odds? If we had showed up even just a couple of minutes later…"

"Yes, Mack," Rebecca replied, her own mind reeling from the implications. Then, turning to Jeffrey, her face became suddenly smug. "You said you wanted to see God rescue His Ark, well, now you have."

Although he didn't respond verbally, she could see the muscles in his face twitch, clearly showing that he was not amused by her attitude. The slight grin of pride on Rebecca's face died instantly as she turned back to face their host. For despite the fact that Noah could not understand their speech, the look of disapproval on his face left no doubt in her mind that he found her behavior disturbing.

Immediately, Rebecca felt her face flush as a deep sense of shame overwhelmed her. *What's wrong with me?* she thought. *How can I expect to win Jeffrey and the others over if I'm constantly rubbing it in their faces when I'm right? Lord, forgive me! Help me show them love, not pride.*

Turning back to Jeffrey, she opened her mouth to apologize, but was cut off by Goliath. "Ask him if he has any idea how long it will be before the Flood starts."

Suddenly remembering their greater danger, Mack nodded and began speaking to Noah. A moment later, the Patriarch replied, his tone grave.

"Five days ago, the Creator, just and righteous are His acts, told me that in one week, He would bring the Deluge. Alas, this entire world has but two days left before destruction."

As Mack relayed Noah's words, a heaviness settled upon the group. Jerome was the first to speak, his words giving voice to the thoughts that were running through each of their heads. "Two days? That's…that's not enough time. It's already evening and we haven't even… We're…we're not going to make it."

"Hold on, buddy," Jeffrey said, attempting to calm his best friend. "We don't even know what's wrong with the ship. It could be something simple. Don't give up hope yet."

Noah, sensing their fear, began to speak, his face filling with hope. "You are welcome to come with us. The Ark has more than enough room for everyone. The offer of salvation is available to all who humble themselves and accept it. The Lord, who is Truth and Life, is full of compassion, wishing that none would perish."

Rebecca and the others just stared at him as Mack finished translating the offer. *Would that even be possible?* she wondered. *But, if we went with them on the Ark, wouldn't that change history, and even change the Word of God itself?* Shocked by the offer, she was lost in her thoughts for several seconds and nearly missed the others' response.

"…can't be trapped here. Tarshwa needs me! She can't afford the hospital bills without the extra money I—" Jerome suddenly stopped himself mid-sentence as if just remembering something. Then, he hesitantly finished, "She just can't afford it."

Jeffrey, slightly confused by Jerome's reaction, placed a comforting hand on his friend's shoulder. Turning to look at Mack, he said, "Tell him that we appreciate the offer, but we have to get back to our own time. We have families who need us there."

For a split second, Rebecca felt a jolt of pain stab her heart at his words. Maybe *he* and *Jerome* had families to return to, but not her. Not anymore. For an instant, the possibility of accepting Noah's offer flashed through her mind, only to be immediately discarded. *What would I do then? Live out the rest of my life alone on a barren landscape with no husband and no children—always being the outcast. No. It'd be better to drown in the Flood.* With bitterness in her heart, she focused once more on accomplishing what they came to do.

Crestfallen, the patriarch let out a sigh. "Then, for your sakes, I pray that I can help you. However, won't you at least come see the Ark first? Perhaps you may change your minds. Besides, darkness approaches, and it would not be safe for you to return tonight. With the gate secured, and with the Master of All watching over us, we will be protected here."

Rebecca felt her heart leap into her throat as her face lit up with excitement. Never in her wildest of dreams could she have begun to come up with a scenario that would have allowed her to walk through *the real Noah's Ark* during her lifetime. Yet, here she was. This was the ship that would preserve every kind of plant and animal life to repopulate the world. This was the ship that, for so many years, she had believed was just a myth. She would actually get to see how Noah and his family planned on storing, feeding, and caring for thousands of animals for over a year. She would get answers to questions that people had wondered about for centuries! As she looked at the others, she could tell that despite their lingering fear and trepidation about their fate, they were fascinated by the prospect.

Except Jeffrey.

Although she could tell that at least some part of him wanted to go inside, there was another part of him that feared what he would find. His face revealed his conflict, and she wondered momentarily if he was going to be sick. For a moment, Rebecca began to pity him. She knew what it was like to have everything that you believe suddenly turned on its head. *Lord, open his eyes. Let him see Your truth,* she prayed.

"What about Doc?" Mack asked worriedly. "We need to get him help immediately. He may not last the night."

"You're right," Rebecca said, chiding herself for not thinking of her friend's needs first. "Mack, tell Noah about Doc's situation. Ask him if he has any medicine that would help."

Upon hearing Mack's explanation, Noah shook his head. "We do have medicine that can help, but you would never make it back to your vessel. There are many other dangers far worse than Blood Drinkers that roam the forest and fields at night. I am sorry, but you would be throwing your lives away."

Not happy with his response, but seeing no other option, Rebecca sighed. "We have to at least call Akwen and Lisa to let them know the situation, and to check on Doc's condition. He was doing better before we left. Perhaps he'll make it until tomorrow."

Agreeing with Rebecca's assessment, Jeffrey pulled out his commlink and called Lisa while Shem, Ham, and Japheth returned from moving the bodies and began to converse with their father. Judging by their body language, they didn't appear to be in agreement with their father's decisions. A minute later, Jeffrey shut off his commlink and reported. "Lisa says that Doc is stable and sleeping soundly. She thinks he'll pull through."

Rebecca and the others, encouraged by the news, relaxed for the first time since they had landed. For the moment, they were safe. Returning her attention to their host, Rebecca bowed slightly. "We would be honored to visit the Ark."

"Wonderful. Our wives will prepare a meal, and you will be our guests," Noah said. "It has been quite some time since we have had the pleasure of entertaining someone who has love for our glorious Creator. Once you are fed and your wounds are bandaged, we will offer you our full hospitality for the night."

Reaching down, Noah's sons retrieved the stack of weapons and handed Rebecca's pistol, Goliath's sword, and the other smaller blades back to their owners. Then, turning toward the vessel, they headed through the doorway into the Ark. Gesturing toward the entrance, Noah beckoned for Rebecca and the others to follow. Leading the way, he walked up the mound and entered the massive structure. With her heart beating wildly in her chest from excitement, Rebecca walked as if in a trance toward the ship. Barely aware that the others were right behind her, she crossed the threshold and entered Noah's Ark.

6

THE NARROW DOOR

AS REBECCA STEPPED into the Ark, she began to shake with excitement and awe. Although she always struggled to put into words the thrill she felt when she had first set foot on alien soil during her trip to Ka'esch, that feeling paled in comparison to the overwhelming sense of grandeur and majesty that settled into her soul. *Is this for real?* she wondered. Even though she had recently come to believe that the "story" of Noah's Flood was more than just a myth, her brain had yet to fully comprehend all that her belief would entail. Numerous questions that she had heard scoffers pose regarding the Ark wormed their way to the forefront of her mind: How could Noah get all of those animals on the Ark? How could eight people care for that many animals? How would they manage the feeding, watering and waste removal? The sheer logistics involved boggled the mind.

Yet here she was! She was going to find answers to questions that had caused countless numbers of people throughout the years to doubt the historicity of the Flood, and by extension, the Bible itself. Next to the resurrection of Christ and the Fall of Mankind into sin, no other event in the entire history of the world has had such a sweeping impact as the Cataclysm, and, few other events had such far-reaching implications.

These thoughts and more assailed Rebecca as she took her first steps into the massive structure. Beyond the fifteen-foot-wide door was a short hallway of the same width that curved to their left, heading toward the bow of the vessel. A normal-sized, wooden door was built into the wall on their right several feet from the main entrance.

Once they were all inside, Noah turned toward them as Shem, Ham, and Japheth headed off down the hallway to their left. As Noah spoke, Mack immediately fell into the role of translator. "Please excuse the departure of my sons. They have gone to assist the women in preparation for your stay. Before we proceed, I need to secure the outer door."

Rebecca and the others stepped away from the entrance as Noah reached up and released a lever attached to the wall. Immediately, the massive door began to rise, its bulk being lifted by two thick ropes attached to each of the top corners. Once the door was in place, Noah moved another lever, causing a massive rectangular slab of wood more than half a foot in width and height to slide slowly down from above. As the beam divided the door vertically into two equal sections, Noah guided it through three loops of thick cable that were attached to the door itself.

With the first beam locked securely in position, Noah walked over to the left side of the door and moved yet another lever, which caused a nearly identical beam to slide across the door horizontally. Rebecca gasped quietly as the second beam came to rest in the bracket mounted against the opposite side of the entrance.

Walking as if in a trance, Rebecca moved over to the door and began to caress the wood like one would stroke a beloved child. The moment her fingers brushed the lightly colored beams, she felt a tingling sensation course through her. The feeling grew until it felt as if her whole body were aflame with purest joy. Unadulterated tears of pleasure streaked down her cheeks as she closed her eyes and sank to her knees, both of her hands sliding down the wall and remaining over her head in a posture of worship. For what seemed like an eternity, Rebecca remained in that position of reverence as her soul bathed in the presence of her Master. Oblivious to her surroundings, Rebecca wept as an unfathomable peace washed over her. A single thought replayed over and over in her mind: *He is HERE!*

However, along with the joy came the mirror of truth. In its reflection, she could no longer rationalize her recent petty behavior, her impatience, or her lack of forgiveness toward her husband. *Lord, I'm so sorry,* she prayed silently. *I know there's no excuse for my actions. I don't know what's come over me since we arrived here. Please help me to do better.*

The gentle pressure of a hand on her shoulder roused her from her prayer. Looking up from where she sat on the floor, she saw Noah standing over her, his kind eyes staring deeply into her own. After speaking a few words, the patriarch removed his hand from her shoulder and nodded at her as if in understanding. Smiling broadly, he raised his hands above his head, closed his eyes, and appeared to offer thanks. A moment later, he opened his eyes once again and reached out a hand toward Rebecca to help her stand.

Realizing that everyone was staring at her and waiting for her, she brushed the tears from her eyes, accepted Noah's offered hand, and stood. Once she was back on her feet, she turned to Mack and the others. Gesturing toward the door with her right hand, she reached out with her left and gripped Mack's arm. "Don't you see it? Don't any of you see it? The two beams form...a cross." As she spoke, her face radiated so much love and assurance that the others were stunned into silence.

"Jesus once taught that we should 'Make every effort to enter through the narrow door' because many won't be able to. He then said that once the owner of the house closes the door, many will stand outside knocking and pleading, and saying, 'Sir, open the door for us.' "[1] Although she half expected her friends to cut her off or dismiss her point as foolish religious nonsense, she found that she couldn't stop herself. And, to her great surprise, the looks on their faces showed that they were actually listening to her intently. Emboldened, she continued. "I've never thought of it this way before, but just as the door to the Ark is the 'narrow door' that leads to salvation from the flood for all who enter, so, too, is Jesus the narrow door that leads to salvation of the soul for all those who come in through Him. And the Bible says that God Himself shut Noah and his family in the Ark, just as 'the owner of the house' closed the door."

Somewhat taken aback by the whole scene, Mack regarded Rebecca with a newfound respect. "Becky, I, uh…I don't know what's going on, but I…I felt something when we walked through the door," Mack said, causing her to turn her attention back to him once more. "It was almost as if…as if some pressure had lifted off of me. I feel…lighter. It's kind of…freaky, but in a nice way."

Rebecca smiled at her friend. "God is real, Mack. Just because we can't see Him and don't always feel His presence doesn't mean He isn't there."

"Yeah…" Mack said as he glanced at their surroundings somewhat nervously. "But what creeps me out even more is what Noah said to you a minute ago. He…uh…he said that the…presence of the Almighty is very strong here and that we should be at peace, for no…" Mack swallowed hard as if the words he had been about to utter became stuck in his throat, "…no…evil forces…can harm us here."

Turning to regard the others, she saw a look of reverent respect on Jerome's face, while Goliath looked uncomfortable and Jeffrey appeared downright ill.

Gazing intently at Mack, Rebecca spoke the words that burned in her spirit. "No matter what happens to us on this trip, we need to remember that God is in control. We need to trust Him." Taking her own advice, she offered up a silent prayer for her friends and husband and turned her attention back to their host, who was waiting patiently, his son Japheth having returned to stand by his side.

"My friend," Noah said, addressing Jerome, "if you will follow my son, he will see to your wounded shoulder, and then bring you back to join your friends."

Offering his thanks, Jerome crossed over to where Japheth stood. "You guys will have to fill me in on what I miss," Jerome commented as Japheth led him deeper into the ship.

Turning his attention to the rest of his guests, Noah began walking down the hallway, beckoning for them to follow. With the initial burst of excitement beginning to ebb, Rebecca and the others began to take in their surroundings. Oil lamps hung on both sides of the hallway and were spaced at regular intervals, lighting the interior of the Ark with a warm, amber glow, despite the blackness of the outer wall, which was covered with pitch. A symphony of muted animal noises came from the end of the hallway and bounced off the walls, floor, and ceiling around them, and, as they headed down the short hallway, their nostrils were assailed by a plethora of smells that, due to the visitors' mostly sterile lifestyles, were quite repugnant.

As the first wafts of unpleasant odors invaded Mack's delicate senses, he raised his hand to cover his nose while he began to gag and choke. "Holy Stench, Batman! I betcha a roomful of flatulent Hutts wouldn't smell *this* bad! Yikes!"

"What did you expect?" Rebecca said, laughing at her friend's discomfort. "You obviously haven't spent much time on farms or visiting zoos."

"You got it," he replied, his voice sounding nasally and muffled. "I don't go anywhere *near* those places for exactly this reason."

Before Rebecca could reply, Noah brought the group to a halt at the end of the hallway, causing her to forget all about their conversation. In front of them, a twenty-foot-long platform extended out from the main floor and had two ten-foot ramps connected to it: one descending and the other ascending. The descending ramp, which was closest to where the group stood, angled down to another identical platform that extended out from the deck below them on the opposite side of the ship, and yet another ramp led down to the lowest deck. The ascending ramp mirrored the design and ended at the deck above them.

To their right, the floor ran along the edge of the ramps nearly the full eighty-foot width of the ship. Along the opposite wall, a narrow four-foot-wide passage opened up and appeared to head toward the back of the vessel. Closer to where they stood, however, was another, much larger passage that ran down the center of the ship. It was from this passage that the majority of the animal sounds, and stench, emanated.

Turning to face his guests, Noah began to speak. With his hand still pinching his nose, Mack translated for their guide. "We are now near the very front of the ship. The ramps you see here lead to each of the other decks, and there is a duplicate set of ramps in the aft. There are three decks, and two other four-foot-high crawlways about ten feet wide that run above the lower and middle levels used for storage and maintenance. Each of the floors has a main central aisle large enough for the animals, and two small aisles intended just for my family to use: one on each side of the ship. All three aisles run the entire length of the ship."

Still in awe of his surroundings, Mack asked nervously, "So...so the door we saw to the right of the main entrance...did that lead to one of the aisles?"

Nodding in affirmation, Noah continued. "In addition to the storage walkways, there are many rooms along the outer walls of the ship that hold food, bedding, and other items, as well as animals that prefer the darkness."

Finally recovering his ability to speak, Jeffrey picked up on the older man's implied point. "Which means that all of the rest of the animals are housed in the central part of the ship."

"Correct," Noah confirmed. "This design aids in ventilation, temperature control, and lighting. It also makes waste elimination easier, but we'll get to that later." The Patriarch continued speaking as he stepped out onto the platform and began walking up the ramp leading to the upper deck. "If you would please follow me, I have found that you get a better view of the ship by looking from the top down."

As they ascended the ramp, Rebecca was once again struck by the sheer immensity of the vessel. Walking to the edge of the ramp, she looked over the railing and stared straight down between the ramps toward the bottom deck, several stories below. Lost in the grandeur of the sight, it took her a moment to realize that Mack had just called her name. Turning, she saw him looking down at her from the platform attached to the storage crawlway.

"Are you coming?" he repeated.

"Yeah. Sorry," she said. As she jogged up the ramp toward the others, she studied their faces once again, hoping to gain some insight into what each of her companions was thinking or feeling. *I wonder what Jeffrey and Goliath think. Seeing as how neither one has said much since we've entered, I can only assume that they're trying to process everything. After all, I believed in the Ark, and I'm having trouble processing it.*

Reaching the platform, Rebecca glanced briefly at the storage area to see row upon row of barrels, piles of hay and straw, wood, jars, and containers of every imaginable shape and size. Due to the dim light illuminating the paths leading down the length of the ship, it appeared as if the deck continued on forever. Rejoining the others, Rebecca crossed the platform to the final ramp and climbed toward the uppermost deck.

As they reached the halfway point of the ramp, they caught their first sight of the central corridor of the top deck of the ship. The twenty-foot-wide corridor was split into two five-foot-wide walkways, one on each side, and a middle area that opened to the decks below. Each of the outer sides of the walkways was packed from the floor to within two feet of the ceiling with wooden bars and doors that led to different animal enclosures. Some appeared to be no more than inches high, while others were several feet tall. On top of the cage-like structures, colorful birds perched, strutted, or huddled in their nests, many of which were separated by carefully designed netting. Although the ceiling of the deck was no more than seven feet high, what looked to be an observation platform rose up an additional seven feet above the central opening in the floor.

Their curiosity escalating rapidly, the visitors quickened their pace. Within moments, they had reached the end of the ramp and stepped foot onto the top deck. Facing outward toward the ramp were several more of the enclosures, each containing tufts of fur partially buried by piles of straw, moss, and other bedding materials, making it nearly impossible to determine the type of animal contained in them. Above each of the individual animal enclosures were small storage boxes.

As Noah led the group toward the central aisle, he resumed his instruction. "When the Almighty Creator, hallowed is His Name, charged me with the construction of His Ark of Salvation, I knew that one of my first tasks would be to make a list of all of the various kinds of animals that my family and I would need to take on board. So, for many years I traveled, studying and writing down everything I could about each of the many animals that inhabit this wonderful world, even as I preached the message of salvation to the people." At this last statement, Noah's features drooped in sorrow. A moment later, however, he continued speaking, his face reverting to its previous joyful countenance as he pushed aside his disturbing thoughts. "The more I learned about the animals, the more I realized how much I had yet to learn. I was familiar with the needs of many of the animals. After all, I was already nearly five hundred years old when the Lord of Hosts spoke to me. But, I also realized that there were many more that I needed to study in depth. Then, to my wonder, pairs of animals began appearing on my doorstep. The Mighty One sent animals to me so that I could learn more about how to care for them. Eventually, I built a menagerie to house them all."[2]

"What's a menagerie?" Rebecca asked.

"It's basically a zoo," Mack explained quietly, "but it specializes in exotic animals. It was the only word I could think of to fit what he was describing in his language." Once Mack had finished his explanation to Rebecca, Noah began speaking again.

"Over time, and with the help of my fathers, Lamech and Methusalah, as well as my sons, I learned about the eating habits and survival needs of every animal on earth," Noah said. "In addition, the menagerie allowed me to train many of them to be accustomed to me and my family."

"Amazing," Rebecca said softly. "I never thought about what Noah might have done to prepare for the Flood. So then, those large buildings that the vandals burned were the remains of the menagerie, right?"

Noah nodded affirmative. "That and the lumber mill."

"But doesn't the Bible say something about God calling the animals to go to Noah *after* the Ark was completed?" Mack asked.

Rebecca shook her head. "No, I don't think so. It *does* say that God brought two of each kind of animal to him, but it doesn't say *how* or *when* He brought them."

Mack was still digesting this new information as Noah continued his explanation. As he spoke, he guided the group toward the central aisle.

"Once my family and I knew the size and exact number of animals, we were able to create stalls and nesting areas, each of them within the overall dimensions of the Ark, as revealed to me by the Lord, the Righteous Judge." Reaching the central aisle, Noah stepped to the side, affording his visitors a view that took their breath away.

7

THE ARK: UPPER DECK

REBECCA FELT AS if every sense in her body was being overwhelmed simultaneously. A cacophony of animal sounds invaded her ears—chirps, squawks, caws, whistles, hoots, hisses, and numerous other unidentifiable noises. The smells of hundreds of animals increased exponentially as Noah led them into the walkway on the right. Her eyes were dazzled by feathers and animal pelts containing hues from every portion of the spectrum. Numerous plants and beautiful flowers growing out of pots, urns, and baskets hung from the ceiling at various locations, adding even more color to the already awe-inspiring display. Even the air seemed alive with an energy and excitement that Rebecca could feel permeate through her skin.

But even more than the attack on her senses, she stared in awe at the sheer length of the Ark. For although the ship had been immense on the outside, it never really registered just how much volume a vessel over five-hundred feet long and eighty feet wide could hold. The size was magnified by the central opening that ran nearly the entire length of the ship, enhancing its grandeur. A railing ran around the edge of the ten-foot expanse, and several five-foot "bridges" spanned the gap at regular intervals. Leaning over the railing where the two walkways diverged, Rebecca stared down in amazement. The opening ran through each of the decks, allowing Rebecca to see all the way to the bottom of the vessel.

Although the lengthy shaft offered a tantalizing view of the decks below, Rebecca forced herself to return her attention to her immediate surroundings. The outer edges of the two walkways straddling the central opening contained row upon row of animal enclosures, all running perpendicular to the length of the ship. Each row was between four and six feet deep, five feet tall, and an impressive twenty feet long. Five-foot-wide paths ran between each row, allowing Noah and his family access to the animals on the each side of the rectangular group of enclosures.

With the light of numerous oil lamps mounted along the sides of the animal pens, Rebecca began counting the rows. However, due to the sheer length of the ship, she was forced to give up the endeavor after her count reached a dozen.

Although the opening and the two central aisles had a combined width of twenty feet, the presence of so many creatures in such close proximity, combined with the low, seven-foot ceiling, served to intensify the feeling that the walls were closing in. At only five-foot-four, Rebecca found a sense of claustrophobia creeping up on her. She could only imagine how it must feel for Noah and Jeffrey, who were six-feet tall or greater, much less the nearly eight-foot giant who was forced to stoop to prevent his head from banging on the ceiling.

"Well, I'll be a monkey's uncle," Mack exclaimed quietly next to her, his jaw falling open. "It…it just goes on and on! I never imagined it would be so big!"

A disgusted grunt came from behind Mack, causing him and Rebecca to turn around and look at Goliath, who spoke for the first time since entering the Ark. "If this thing's so blasted tall, then why didn't he make the roof a bit higher?"

Noah, observing the giant's discomfort, guessed the content of his question and responded. "To conserve as much space as possible, and based upon the various sizes of the animals we needed to take on board, we decided to divide them into three basic categories: small, medium and large. We then built the heights of the three decks to match the sizes of the animals. The lowest deck is the largest, the middle deck, as you saw, is quite average, and," lifting his arm, he placed it against the ceiling less than a foot above his head, "since the animals housed on the top deck are the smallest, it was unnecessary to make the roof any higher than was comfortable for us to move around. Furthermore, the midday gives us a little extra head room."

" 'Midday'?" Rebecca repeated, wondering if she had understood Mack's translation correctly.

"Yeah, I think that's what he said. I believe he's referring to those," Mack said, pointing above the central opening to where the observation deck began.

The Patriarch guided his visitors down the aisle on the right so they could get a better view of the "midday." Rebecca could see now that this was the row of "windows" that they had seen from the outside that ran along the top of the Ark. Except now that she viewed it from the inside, she could see that it was so much more than she had originally thought.

The wooden frames extended up above the ceiling an additional seven feet. Although the "midday" spanned the entire ten-foot width of the central opening, only the middle six feet opened to the deck below, for identical two-foot-wide walkways were built along the sides, allowing anyone within the ark a clear view of the surrounding countryside. Thin, three-foot-wide "bridges" connected the two sides every twenty-five feet, and ladders reached down to the deck at regular intervals.

As Rebecca studied the layout, she was surprised to see the dark evening sky peering down at them. "That must be why he called it the 'midday' instead of 'windows,'" she commented to Mack, who stood beside her. "Look! The windows are on the side, but the entire roof of the observation area is split down the middle and hinged, allowing each side to open like a hatch![1] Do you see?"

"Right," Mack said in sudden understanding. "That would allow the 'midday' sun to come shining in."

Noting the topic of their discussion, Noah offered further details.

"By leaving the middle of the ship open and adding the midday, the warm, stale air from the lowest deck can rise and escape through the ceiling. It also gives us the ability to close them once…once the water begins to fall from the sky."

A sudden heaviness rested upon the group as their host's words reminded them of the seriousness of their predicament. Brushing aside the unsettling feeling, Noah smiled and began walking further down the aisle. As the group followed behind him, Rebecca whistled in amazement. "There must be thousands of animals on just this one deck alone! Mack, ask him how many animals are caged in each row."

After a brief exchange of words, Mack answered. "He says it all depends on the animal. There are some sections that contain hundreds of tiny animals, and others that just hold a few dozen. He also said that most of the animal enclosures have food in drawers and cabinets above the animals, which are attached to self-feeders."[2]

Moving over toward a row of animal cages, Rebecca began studying the design curiously. Each cage rested over a short piece of wood that was set at a forty-five-degree angle. At the bottom of the wooden board was a five-inch-wide gutter that sloped downward gently as it ran the length of the row. The gutter ended over a hole built into the floor.

Noticing her perusal of his handiwork, Noah explained. "The droppings and urine from the animals in the cages passes through the grate in the bottom of the cage and rolls down the slope into the gutter. From there, it is easily washed away to be disposed."[3]

Smiling at the ingenuity, Rebecca stepped back from the cages and followed after Noah, who had already begun leading the group further into the interior of the Ark.

They walked on in silence for several minutes, their senses drinking every sight and sound. Once they had passed about a dozen rows, Noah headed toward an enclosure facing outward toward the central opening. Perched on top of the five-foot-tall structure was a beautifully-colored bird about the size of a pigeon, but with a long, curved neck and wide, plumed tail. Its green and yellow feathers shimmered as the bird walked toward the Patriarch on its two thin but muscular legs. Reaching toward the animal, Noah held his hand steady as the bird hopped up onto his arm. "Ah, how are we today, my little friend?" Noah said soothingly as he stroked the bird. The beautiful bird stared up at its master without the slightest hint of fear.

Giving the animal one last loving stroke on its head, Noah put it back onto the top of the enclosure. Enamored by the beauty of the bird, the guests watched for several seconds as it strutted over to a board that contained several small holes and stuck its beak into one of them.

"What's with the holes?" Goliath asked.

Rephrasing the question to their host in a more appropriate manner, Mack listened to the brief response, and then translated it. "Water. They put the water in these boxes to keep it from spilling once the Ark is launched.[4]"

As the bird drank, a sudden question entered Rebecca's mind. Scanning several of the nesting areas in the row of enclosures, she noticed that each one had similar water containers with a tube attached at the top. "How do they keep them all filled? It seems like it would take one person all day just to refill the water."

A moment later, Noah gave his reply while Mack translated. "Each of the water containers is connected to a small reservoir built into each row of nests. That way, all we have to do is fill the tank, and it keeps all of the containers filled."

"But where do you get the water from to fill the reservoirs?"

Instead of replying, Noah gestured for them to follow him. They all complied, with the exception of Goliath, who had become completely bored with the slow pace of the tour. Moving over to stand on one of the nearby walkways that spanned the central opening, he extended his height up into the observation area and stretched, glad to no longer be hunched over.

Reaching the end of the row of animal enclosures, Noah led Rebecca, Mack, and Jeffrey into the five-foot-wide aisle that ran along the outer hull. From their vantage point about a third of the way through the ship,

Rebecca could see that doors were built into the wall every twenty-five feet for the entire length of the ship. It was to one of these doors that Noah led them.

After removing the latch, the Patriarch grabbed the circular pull ring and opened the door to reveal a small, five-foot square room. At first, Rebecca was confused and wondered at the room's purpose, for it appeared empty. While the back of the closet revealed the same solid black as the rest of the ship's pitch-covered, outer hull, the right and left "walls" curved away from the center slightly and were made of an odd, plastic-like material. Extending out from the bottom of both of the curved plastic containers was what looked to be a kind of pipe about three inches in diameter and made of curved wood that resembled bamboo.[5] Reaching up, Rebecca pressed her right hand against the smooth object.

"It's a huge water tank," she stated in awe.

"And judging by the placement of the doors along this wall, each one must be about twenty-five feet long," Mack added.

"These large tanks of water line the walls of the entire ship on this deck, supplying us with enough water for quite some time," Noah said via Mack's translation. "Bamboo pipes are attached to the bottoms of the tanks and are spread throughout the entire ship, connecting to each of the rows of enclosures. From there, a network of smaller pipes distributes the water to each of the individual animal enclosures. This not only provides the animals with drinking water, but we can also use the water to clean the nests, flush down waste, and wash the floors."

"Unbelievable," Mack muttered. "They've got their own built-in water towers. And here I thought pipes were modern inventions. Shows you what *I* know."

"I was aware that the Chinese used bamboo pipes for thousands of years,[6] but I wouldn't have thought people this far back in time would have learned how to do that," Jeffrey commented.

Rebecca considered pointing out how his evolutionary beliefs had blinded him to considering other theories, but decided against it.

Instead, she turned her attention back to her guide. "But even with that much water, aren't you worried about running out?"

The older man nodded. "We are not sure how long the waters will cover the earth, so that *is* a concern. To solve the problem, we decided to use many smaller tanks instead of a few larger ones. That way, once one tank is empty, we begin using another nearby one until the first is refilled."

"Refilled?" Rebecca repeated. "But where will you get the new water?"

"We designed a system that channels the water that falls from the sky into the empty tanks, thus providing a nearly unlimited supply of water,"[7] Noah replied.

Mack shook his head in amazement as he finished translating. "You gotta admit, they've thought of everything."

"They'd have to," Rebecca countered. "With something like this, you can't leave anything to chance."

"What do they do with the animal waste and dirty water?" Jeffrey asked, his tone flat and cold.

Once Mack had translated the question, Noah motioned for them to step back over to the end of the row of animal enclosures. Lifting his foot, he stepped down upon a small lever built into the bottom of the wooden structure. Immediately, a two-foot, square trap door opened in the floor next to him, revealing a dark shaft below.

"Each of the rows of animal enclosures has one of these," Noah explained. "Most of the waste from the small animals and birds will simply be left to accumulate. The smell is minimal once it dries.[8] I will show you how we dispose of the waste from the larger animals when we get to the other decks. As for the dirty water, the chutes lead to holding tanks beneath the floor of the lowest deck, or are drained overboard through the grated outfalls.[9]"

Without further discussion, Noah led the group back to the central aisle where Goliath had been waiting. They walked past several more rows of animals as they drew nearer to the middle of the vessel. Ahead, they could see that the two thin, center walkways converged and the deck became solid across the entire width of the ship—with one exception. In what the visitors guessed to be the very center of the ship was a large hole twenty feet in diameter that was surrounded by a rail on all sides. Running the full, forty-foot length of this open area sat a pair of ten-foot wide groups of animal enclosures, one on each side of the hole. They were each placed five feet from the outer hull, leaving a spacious amount of room between the enclosures and the hole in the middle of the ship. On the edge of the circular opening, near to where Rebecca and the others currently stood, was another hole.

This one, however, was square, and was a mere eight feet wide. Next to the square opening, a series of thick ropes came up from under the deck and were wound around several pulleys attached to a pair of massive crossbeams. One of the beams was positioned directly over the deck near the edge of the hole, while the other was mounted over the square opening.

Noah pulled on one of the ropes, sending the pulley system into action. A moment later, an eight-foot square platform, complete with wooden railings, rose through the hole as it was drawn by the ropes.

"They've got an elevator too?" Mack commented, shaking his head in amazement.

Once the platform drew level with the floor of the upper deck, Noah swung open a section of the railing, stepped onto the platform, and invited Rebecca and the others to join him. Stepping onto the platform, Rebecca's gaze drifted toward the back of the ship as she waited for the others to climb aboard.

"Patriarch, what is that near the back of the ship where the animal enclosures end?" she asked.

"That is our garden and library," he replied. "In addition to the animals, we had to bring seed from many of the plants. Some seed will survive the floodwaters outside the Ark,[10] but we also brought a large variety of seed with us to plant after the flood. We designed a large indoor garden and placed it as close to the midday as possible to receive the maximum amount of sunlight. In addition to providing us with some fresh food, it also serves as a place of calm and tranquility. It is the perfect location for reading, praying, and meditating."

"What kind of writings are in the library?" Rebecca asked, although she already guessed at the answer.

"Since we will be the only ones left alive after the Deluge, we wanted to preserve as much of the knowledge as we could about the world around us," he explained. "There are scrolls about how to farm, how to mine for ore, how to build with wood or stone, and many other topics, as well as the writings of many of my forefathers."

Rebecca's thoughts flashed back to the library they had seen in the Tower of Babel. Briefly, she wondered if these scrolls were some of the same ones that they had seen there. With everyone safely on board the platform, Noah closed the gate in the railing and pulled another one of the ropes. With a slight jolt, the lift began its descent, taking its passengers down to the level below.

THE ARK: MIDDLE DECK

AS THE GROUP descended on the lift, Rebecca gazed once again in wonder at the size and scope of the Ark. "Great Patriarch, how long did it take you to build all of this?"

"It has been over one hundred years since the Creator of all life first spoke to me about the coming destruction," Noah replied. "But it took much less time than that to actually build the Ark. Once we started construction, the project was completed in just over sixty-five years."

Rebecca stared at her host in surprise. "How could you and your family complete such a massive undertaking in such a short amount of time?"

Noah smiled. "We did not do it all by ourselves. The Mighty God, powerful is He, had blessed me abundantly. I had become quite wealthy, and for many years I hired workers from the city. I also had the help and wisdom of my fathers, Lamech and Methusalah, as well as the aid of a very intelligent and good friend who helped me with the design and oversight. In fact, it was his idea to add the high stem on the bow and the protruding fin on the stern. However, over the years, the problems with theft and poor workmanship became so bad that my family and I were forced to complete the project on our own. Even my friend eventually turned away," he added sadly.

The lift came to a halt as it became level with the middle deck. It quickly became apparent that although the deck itself was identical to the upper one, the ceiling was nearly double the height, the enclosures were much larger and they were laid out in a completely different arrangement. While the rows of animal pens on the top deck were perpendicular to the length of the ship, the ones on this level ran parallel to it. Each combined row of enclosures was nearly twenty feet wide and thirty feet long. In some places, two or three of the smaller animal stalls were stacked upon each other separated by their food storage containers, while other stalls reached up to within two feet of the ceiling. Instead of the sloped board and waste collection trough they had seen on the top level, many of these enclosures had large, sliding drawers beneath them that collected the waste. Where the cages were stacked, movable ladders were stored nearby. Lining the bottom of the upper deck was a network of the bamboo-like pipes that transported water and waste to various parts of the ship.

As the group stepped off the platform and onto the deck, they saw Japheth and Jerome walking toward them on one of the two central walkways that led to the aft section of the ship, two large wolves trailing behind them.

"Hey, guys," Jerome said as he and his escort entered the area near the lift.

Mack drew back at the sight of the wolves. "Uh…are those things tame?"

"Yeah. They're actually quite friendly, believe it or not," he said as he reached over and scratched one of the animals behind the ear. The other wolf examined the group, sniffing each of the strangers. It spent several moments taking in Goliath's scent, as if confused by what it was sensing. "So, what'd I miss?" Jerome asked as the animal eventually lost interest in the giant and returned to stand by his master.

"We'll fill you in later," Jeffrey replied. His countenance and manner were clear indications that he was not in the mood to discuss what he had seen. "How's your shoulder?"

"Much better, thanks to Japheth's wife. I don't know what was in that stuff she rubbed on the wound, but between that and the medicine she gave me, I feel great," Jerome announced. "Now, show me around. I want to see more of this place. Did you know that they have all sorts of dinos back there in cages?!" he said, pointing back the way he came.

After a brief word with his father, Japheth excused himself from the group, the two wolves following obediently. Looking at his guests, Noah asked, "Shall we continue?"

Choosing the walkway on the right, Noah led the group back toward the front of the ship. As their guide had indicated earlier, the animals that were housed on this deck were of average size. To her surprise, she noticed that Noah had put each individual animal in its own enclosure, separating the males and females from each other. Of the animals housed along the center aisles, Rebecca identified sheep, monkeys, rodents, weasels, and pigs. However, she also saw several other kinds that, while they looked similar to animals that she recognized, she couldn't exactly say what they were.

Seeing that Rebecca had taken a particular interest in one, Noah stopped the group. "What kind of animal is this?" she asked, pointing to a long-tailed, furry creature with pointed ears.

Mack translated Rebecca's question, received a reply from Noah, then turned back to her and shrugged his shoulders. "I don't know how to translate it."

Opening the enclosure, Noah began to pet the animal, which lay completely still and unmoving. Gently grabbing the animal's legs, Noah stretched them out so his guests could seem them better.

"It almost looks like some kind of small, weird kangaroo!" Jerome exclaimed.

Leaning closer, Mack studied the animal, a confused look on his face. "I think you're right. It looks like it has a pouch on its stomach. But...but, how could a kangaroo get all the way here from Australia?"

Rebecca smiled as she placed a hand on her friend's shoulder. "Think about what you just said, Mack. The continents before the flood were totally different. There *is* no Australia here."

"Oh yeah, I forgot," he said, looking somewhat embarrassed. "But that brings up another point: how did the kangaroos get to Australia *after* the flood?"

Rebecca was silent for a moment as she considered the question. "They probably crossed over on dry ground! Since we now know that the Ice Age was a result of the Flood, it makes sense that the sea level would have been lower *after* the Flood because of all the ice on the land. That would've created all sorts of land bridges connecting the continents.[1]"

"Then why don't we find any fossils of kangaroos between the Middle East and Australia?" Jeffrey asked in challenge.

Rebecca was not daunted. "Because, as you well know, animals have to be buried rapidly to become fossils. If a kangaroo died as it was migrating, it would've been eaten or it would've decomposed. It wouldn't have turned into a fossil. Isn't it true that hardly any fossils of bison have been found in North America? Yet, we know that there were *millions* of them roaming the prairies!"[2]

Although neither Jeffrey nor Jerome responded, Rebecca knew that she had hit a nerve. Judging by the frowns on their faces, she feared that she may have pushed them too far. Letting the topic drop, she focused her attention back on their host, who had just let go of the animal and closed the door of its cage. As he did so, Rebecca commented on the drawer below the cage. "What do you do with the waste once it gets full?"

Noah reached down and pulled open the drawer, which was filled with wood shavings and a few of the animal's droppings. "We discovered early on that if we used several wooden bars laid together for the floor, but left space between them, the animal droppings fall through[3]. This keeps the animal enclosures from being fouled by the waste. We then placed drawers filled with wood shavings underneath to collect it. Depending on the size of the animal, these drawers can go months at a time without needing to be emptied. When they *do* need to be changed, we scoop out the waste and send it down the chutes to the holding tank below and replace the shavings."

"You mentioned holding tanks before," Rebecca said. "Won't those fill up quickly with all of the animal waste?"

Noah shook his head. "While taking care of the animals in the menagerie, we discovered that certain earthworms can decompose animal waste.[4] So, we placed large numbers of them in the holding tanks."

As Mack finished translating, his face screwed into a grimace. "Ah, man, that's just foul! Earthworms that eat manure? Now I've got even more reason to hate those nasty things."

"Aren't these cages a little small?" the giant asked, surprising the others with his sudden question. "How do you expect these poor animals to survive in such cramped conditions?"

Once Mack had finished translating the question, Noah replied. "Actually, the smaller enclosures provide an advantage. First, the animals find the enclosed space comforting. I believe it reminds them of their natural dens. Second, it will keep them from getting injured when we encounter rough weather. Third, the confined space forces the animals to step on their waste, pushing it through the slats into the waste bin. Finally, this arrangement is only for short term survival, not for long term captivity.[5] For the larger ones, we do let them out and exercise them on the central openings and walkways. We have even trained the wolves to help us herd the animals, allowing us to continue with other tasks."

"But wouldn't it have been better to at least put the males and females together?" Rebecca asked. "Why put them in separate cages?"

Noah smiled. "The main reason is that we don't want them to procreate; at least not yet. We have enough food and water for the animals currently aboard. We don't want extra mouths to feed and waste to clean up."

Jerome suddenly called out in excitement, drawing everyone's attention. "Jeffrey, check it out!"

Staring in the direction Jerome indicated, Jeffrey's jaw dropped in shock. Housed in the next row of enclosures were several dinosaurs.

"Look at the crest on its head! It's gotta be an Oviraptor!" Jerome exclaimed. "And this one looks like some kind of cross between a Stegosaurus and a Kentrosaurus! Next to that is some kind of…"

Jerome's voice trailed off and his face became pale. Staring at him from the other side of the bars was a Deinonychus dinosaur. Although this specimen was smaller and younger than the ones encountered in the Tower of Babel, the reptiles still appeared powerful. Stepping slowly back from the stall, Jerome leaned against the railing near the central opening of the ship.

Noah approached the enclosure with a profound look of confusion on his face. He spoke, but Mack was unable to translate his words due to the intense horror that overtook him; for as Noah spoke, he opened the door of the cage.

Goliath immediately pulled his sword from its sheath and prepared to strike as Mack let out a strangled cry and dove away from the opening. Rebecca reached for her pistol but froze with her hand on the grip. Noah, staring at them as if they were all mad, reached into the enclosure containing the dinosaur and began stroking its head gently. The creature cast the visitors a disinterested glance, then lay down on the floor of its stall.

"What the…" Jerome said in shock.

"For a second there, I thought we were all going to be dino chow," Mack said, finally recovering his voice. "I had some major déjà vu."

"How…how did you calm it like that?" Rebecca asked Noah in awe.

"Calm it?" he replied, his brows furrowing. "It was already calm."

"But weren't you afraid it was going to attack us?" Golia th asked.

"No, of course not," Noah said. "Animals do not attack humans unless provoked."

A sudden thought struck Rebecca. "Wait a second. The Bible mentions something about God putting the fear of mankind into the animals *after* the Flood[6]. Which means that *beforehand*…"

"…they all got along," Mack finished her sentence. "And that explains why the wolves we saw were friendly also."

"But what about that marsupial lion?" Jeffrey asked. "If animals don't attack humans, then why did that one attack us?"

"Perhaps we frightened it or were close to its den," Rebecca suggested. "Or perhaps something else spooked it." Still hesitant, but trusting Noah, she moved closer to the enclosure. "May I?" she asked.

Receiving a nod from Noah, she reached cautiously into the stall and gently stroked the head of the Deinonychus. The creature opened its eyes momentarily before drifting back off to sleep.

The aftermath of the adrenaline rush stole much of the initial excitement the group felt upon first setting eyes on the dinosaurs. Deciding it was time to move on, Noah closed the door of the creature's enclosure and began heading down the walkway once more. Goliath, still unnerved by the reptile's appearance, waited until they were well past its cage before finally sheathing his sword.

Noah led the group back to the main ramps that they had seen upon first entering the Ark, explaining as they went how he solved some of the dietary needs of the animals by compressing hay into pellets.[7]

"So what do you do for meat-eaters," Jeffrey asked, his mind still dwelling on their recent scare.

Noah frowned at the question. "Our blessed God, Ruler of all, originally gave man and beasts all of the seed-bearing plants to eat for food. Alas, after the curse, some of the animals have started feeding on one another. However, none of the animals that the Lord sent to me have begun that detestable practice."

"So, *none of them* eat meat? Even the T-rexes?" Jerome asked. "Have you been to the museums and seen their teeth? We *know* they were meat-eaters."

"You have to remember that fossils don't speak for themselves," Rebecca said. "They must be interpreted. Just because an animal has sharp teeth doesn't mean it is necessarily a meat-eater. And even though some of them probably *were* meat-eaters, it doesn't mean that that's the way God *originally* designed them. Sin has affected many aspects of creation."

Casting her a mixed look of thoughtfulness and incredulity, Jerome didn't respond, choosing instead to let the topic drop.

As they began descending the ramp toward the lower deck, Rebecca changed the subject. "Patriarch, you mentioned earlier that a friend of yours helped design the ship and that it was his idea to add the high prow and fin on the stern. What purpose do they serve?"

Noah smiled as he related the story. "My friend always did love challenges. When I first approached him with the concept, his initial reaction was to scoff. But once he realized that I was serious, he offered to help. Although I told him the dimensions the Eternal Father gave me, he insisted on constructing various models to determine which ones would work best for a vessel of this size."

The Patriarch laughed as he continued the story. "Some of his results were quite comical. One of the models was very long, but shallow. It cracked easily. Another was very deep, which made it quite strong, but it capsized. Then, to keep it from capsizing, he made it extra wide, but then it was too shallow. This would have made the journey very rough for those inside the ship."

"What about the dimensions given by God?" Rebecca asked.

"As you would expect, my friend found that a ship built with those specifications would have the perfect balance between strength, stability and comfort,"[8] Noah said in triumph. "Despite all of his experiments, he could discover no better proportions."

"And the raised prow?" Jerome asked.

Noah nodded. "It is designed to catch the wind. The tapered protrusion at the end serves to anchor the vessel while the prow catches the wind and turns the ship to face the waves 'head-on,' making for a much smoother—and safer—journey."[9]

"I have another question for you," Jeffrey said, his face expressing no emotions. "Wooden ships are prone to leak. How did you solve *that* problem?"

"We devised a system that uses wooden dowels to join together the outer shell of planks to the internal frames,"[10] Noah explained. "When the dowels get wet, they swell, causing the ship to get tighter and prevent leaking. The Ark has four layers of planking, each overlapping the others at the seams."

"It sounds like the type of mortise and tenon-jointed planks the Greeks used to use four centuries before the Common Era,"[11] Jerome added. "Wasn't the ancient catamaran galley, the *Tessarakonteres*, around four hundred and twenty feet long?"[12]

Jeffrey ignored the question, for at that moment his attention was diverted elsewhere as the group reached the bottom of the ramp and stepped onto the lower deck of the vessel.

THE ARK: LOWER DECK

THE TALL, TWENTY-FOOT ceiling, combined with the open shaft that led up to the windows and observation area above, served to enhance the overall size of the lower deck. Noah led the group in silence, allowing his guests to soak in the sights and sounds. Unlike the floors above, which had two small walkways on each side of the central opening, the middle aisle of this deck consisted of a single, ten-foot-wide walkway. Due to the larger size of the animals housed on this level, the stalls were grouped into large sections, each one stretching fifty feet in length. A ten-foot-wide passage separated each of these sections, allowing Noah and his family access to the outer storage areas along the hull of the ship, as well as access to the animals located on the opposite side of the section. Similar to the middle deck, a storage walkway ran along the hull above some of the shorter stalls near the ramps.

Hippos, giraffes, oxen, rhinoceroses, elephants, and many other beasts lounged in their small, narrow stalls. They glanced up lazily at the group of humans as they walked by, completely undisturbed by their presence.

Before Rebecca had passed more than five or six stalls, a truth about the animals on the Ark became clear to her. Shocked by the simplicity of it, and its implications, she smiled broadly.

"They're all juveniles!" she proclaimed.

It quickly became obvious that the others had come to the same conclusion, for they began to look at one another with questioning expressions on their faces.

"I can't believe I never thought of it before!" Rebecca said, her gaze still sweeping over the numerous stalls. "It makes so much sense! Why bring full-grown animals onto the Ark? The younger ones would be stronger, take up less space, eat less, drink less, and produce less waste![1] Not to mention the fact that the whole purpose of the surviving animals is to reproduce after the flood."

As she spoke, her gaze settled upon an animal stall further down the row. Jogging up to it, her eyes grew even wider. "There's a small Triceratops in here!" she exclaimed. Looking as if she were about to spontaneously combust with excitement, she turned to face Mack. "That's it! That's the last piece to the puzzle!"

"What puzzle?" Mack asked.

"The puzzle about how dinosaurs were still alive during the time of the Mayans," she said. "If dinosaurs were alive *after* the flood, then that would mean that they *had* to have been on the Ark. What I couldn't figure out, though, was how Noah could have gotten the big ones to fit. But this explains it! They were juveniles!"

"But there are still too many animals alive in our time for them *all* to have fit on the Ark," Jeffrey countered, his tone sounding desperate. "Where are all of the dogs—the coyotes, the dingoes, the stinking poodles? Where are all of the monkeys, or…or the lions and tigers? Yeah, we saw a few, but where are the rest? The answer is: they're not here! I'll admit now that the story of Noah's Ark is based on reality. But, all of these missing animals proves that it couldn't have been a *global* flood. It had to have been just local."

"Not necessarily," Jerome said quietly.

Wheeling around to look at his friend, Jeffrey noticed him staring at another of the cages. "What do you mean?"

"Look," Jerome said flatly. Behind him, Noah stood in silence, watching his visitors with intense interest.

Glancing into the cage, Jeffrey frowned. "It's a large cat, so what."

"Did you see the markings?" Jerome asked. "Have you ever seen a cat that has some stripes, some spots, and some solid colored fur? And over here," Jerome said, pulling Jeffrey toward another enclosure, "look at this large, horse-like animal. It has reddish brown hair along its back and legs, like a horse, but its stomach is white, with black stripes and its mane is short and black."

"So? What are you getting at?" Jeffrey said in frustration.

"Remember Dr. Wasmundt's genetics class, Jeffrey," Jerome stated. "The reason we haven't seen any other dogs, or monkeys, or lions and tigers, is because each of those animals are descendents of the pairs of animals on this boat."

As the truth sank in, Jeffrey began shaking his head in denial. "No. I don't believe it."

"You know I'm right," Jerome said. "Remember those pictures Dr. Wasmundt showed us of ligers—a hybrid of a male lion and female tiger? Or a zorse? This thing looks like it's a mixture of zebra and horse. Even though there are hundreds of discovered dinosaurs, you and I both know that you could probably combine a bunch of them into one family. The only reason there are so many to begin with is that everybody and their brother wants a dinosaur named after them. If you take out all the repetition, it'd probably reduce the number of dinosaurs down to about fifty."[2]

"The biblical 'kind,'" Rebecca said, causing Jerome to turn in her direction, his expression requesting further explanation. "In Genesis, the Bible talks about animals reproducing 'after their own kind.' That must be what it means. So, before the flood, there were no lions, tigers, or cheetahs, only this original cat 'kind,' which had all of the genetic information for all of the other types. Then, after the flood, they spread across the earth and diversified into the animals that we know today."[3]

"Wait a second," Mack interjected. "So you're telling me that those two wolves we met early were the great, great, great grandparents of my mom's Chihuahua, Tigre?"

Rebecca nodded with a crooked grin. "It may seem hard to believe, but it's true. However, many of the breeds we see from our time, like Chihuahuas, are not the result of natural selection, but artificial selection. So, we can blame humans for all of those tiny, yappy dogs."

Jerome's expression suddenly lifted as a new thought occurred to him. "Since Noah didn't have to take every breed of dog on the Ark, it means that the total number of animals would be greatly reduced. So instead of having to take *millions*, he only needed... Mack, ask Noah how many animals he brought on the Ark."

Turning to Noah, who was waiting patiently for his guests to finish their conversation, Mack relayed the question. Once he received the answer, he turned back to his friends, a look of astonishment on his face. "Only 15,352."[4]

Silence settled over the group as they considered the number. Even the stoic Goliath, who had previously been impatient to finish the tour, had been listening intently to the conversation and was surprised by the low number.

"But...that's impossible," Jeffrey muttered.

"No, it's not, Jeffrey," Rebecca replied. "Think about it, many of the animals in the world are small. I would venture to guess that more than 85 percent of all of the animals on this ship are smaller than a sheep.[5] Also, Noah wouldn't have to take any marine animals on the Ark. And although the Bible says that he took seven pairs of each kind of 'clean' animals with him—which are those that have a divided hoof and chew the cud[6], such as sheep, cattle, and deer—there are really only about twenty animals or so that fall into that category."[7]

No one spoke for several moments. Finally, Noah broke the stillness. "Your surprise at what you have seen on the Ark leads me to believe that the world in the future is very different. It appears that I have given you much to discuss and ponder. I have learned that deep thinking is done best when one has a full stomach. So, I recommend we move to the living quarters and partake in a meal."

The mere mention of food caused Rebecca's stomach to rumble, reminding her that she had not eaten in many hours. Thanking their host for his generosity, Rebecca, Mack, and Goliath followed him as he headed toward the elevator. Jerome put a hand on Jeffrey's shoulder as the others moved further away.

"Are you okay, man?" Jerome asked, concern etched on his face.

"Yeah," Jeffrey said dispassionately. "It's just...just so hard to believe. All of those years, I mocked the very idea of Noah's Ark. But to see all of this," he said, looking around him, "it...it makes the story so...so real."

"I know," Jerome agreed. "I certainly never learned any of this in church. They always taught the story with those cheesy flannel-graphs, and this tiny little Ark picture."

Jeffrey grinned, despite his serious demeanor. After a moment, he looked straight at Jerome, his eyes reflecting his inner conflict. "Jerome, do you...do you really think...?"

His best friend shrugged. "I don't know, man. A few days ago, before this whole trip began, I was convinced of what I believed. Now, after all we've seen...I just don't know. We've always prided ourselves on 'letting the evidence speak for itself, no matter where it takes you.' Well, I hate to say it, but Rebecca's explanations are starting to make better sense of the evidence than...than what we've always believed."

When Jeffrey didn't respond, Jerome put his arm around his friend and began leading him toward the elevator. "C'mon. Let's go get some food."

Once Jeffrey and Jerome reached the elevator, Noah flipped the lever that sent the platform rising toward the middle deck. Once there, he led the group around the central shaft and toward the rear of the ship. Unlike the bow, the center aisle did not lead directly to the ramps that led between decks, but rather ended at a wall that stretched nearly the entire width of the ship. Two doors were set into the sixty-foot wall, each opening out onto the twin walkways that straddled the central shaft that led up to the midday above.

The door on the right opened as the group approached it. Noah's wife stood in the doorway and greeted them, her expression warm and inviting. "Japheth said you were on your way back," she said, then kissed her husband on the cheek.

Taking her hand, Noah turned to face his guests. "Friends, this is my wife, Eema." Each of the visitors offered a word of greeting, then followed Noah and his family through the doorway and into the living quarters.

They entered a square room that was thirty feet on a side. A ceramic stove sat between two beautifully-crafted rosewood tables along the north wall between the two doors that led out onto the walkways. The central portion of the room had no ceiling. As Rebecca looked up through the ten-foot-wide rectangular opening, she could see that the midday was open above them, revealing the clear, night sky, resplendent with stars. Green tendrils from some of the plants in the garden above the room draped through the opening, adding life to the dark amber support beams of the roof. Three doors were spaced evenly on both the eastern and western walls, and a single, solitary door was set into the eastern edge of the south wall. Judging by the layout, Rebecca guessed that the six doors led to bedrooms or storage rooms, while the door on the south wall led to the ramps in the stern of the ship.

Once the door was closed behind them, the sounds of the animals became muted, with the exception of the chirps and squawks of the birds that filtered down through the ceiling. Flowers spanning every color of the rainbow brightened the room, and a circular rug of bright red, purple, and gold covered the center of the floor. Several delicately-embroidered cylindrical cushions were placed on the rug in a circle. Shelves with railings designed to hold their contents firmly lined the empty spaces of the walls, each filled with clay and ceramic pots of all shapes and sizes. A number of large wooden chests and storage boxes were fixed to the floor along the southern wall.

Although the visitors noticed all of these details of their surroundings, their sense of smell by far demanded most of their attention. The moment they entered the room, the heavenly aroma of freshly-baked bread infiltrated their olfactory receptors and banished the pungent stench of the animals from their minds. The wonderful smell drew their eyes to the two tables, which, they now saw, were laden with an assortment of fruit, lentils, beans, rice, bread, cheese, and nuts. Noah's three sons and their wives were busy about the room, making the final preparations for the meal.

"Ohhhh, that smells *soooo* good," Mack said, his eyes resting hungrily on the food laid out before them. After surveying the offered choices, he leaned over to Rebecca and whispered. "Not that I'm complaining, but where's the steak? I would love something I could really sink my teeth into. Do you think these guys are vegetarians?"

"You forget what Noah told us earlier about the meat-eaters," Rebecca responded. "In the beginning, God gave every kind of seed-bearing plant and every fruit with seed in it as food to both beast *and* man. It wasn't until *after* the Flood that God told Noah that it was acceptable to eat meat.[8] So I hate to break it to you, but don't expect any steak anytime soon."

"Oh well. 'Beggars can't be choosers,' they always say," he replied. "Then again, if their fruit is anywhere near as good as the ones we tasted on our way here, then bring it on!"

Eema strode up to them, a bowl of water in each hand and two towels draped over her shoulder. "Please, wash," she said, handing the bowls and towels to Rebecca and Mack. Once they had finished their preparations, Noah encouraged his guests to sit in front of the cushions on the rug as Eema and the other women placed the food in the center of their circle. When all was ready, Noah offered a prayer of thanksgiving, and the meal began.

Just as Mack took his first bite of bread, he suddenly paused, a strange expression on his face.

Leaning over toward him, Rebecca whispered, "What's wrong?"

"It just dawned on me. Noah's wife's name is Eema," Mack replied.

"So, what's so strange about that?" she asked.

"Eema, in Hebrew, means 'mother,'" he said.

10

ANCIENT DOCUMENTS

AS EEMA AND the other women cleared away the last remnants of the meal, Noah reclined against his cushion as he addressed his guests. "Now, tell me more about what brings you here. And please start from the beginning so that my wife and the other women may hear the whole tale."

After Mack had relayed Noah's request to the rest of the visitors, Rebecca cleared her throat and began relating their story. "We are travelers from your future—from a time over four thousand years from now. We uncovered a pyramid-shaped...vessel...that was buried in a chamber under a desert," Rebecca paused momentarily to allow Mack time to finish his translation. "In addition to the pyramid, we also found two books that explained how to complete construction of the vessel, as well as two dead bodies. Both were...were human shaped, but with animal-like features. And one was twelve feet tall."

At this last statement, Noah and his family exchanged curious, and disturbed, glances with each other. Noting their concern, Rebecca asked, "What is it?"

Noah shook his head in dismissal. "Continue please. We need to hear the whole tale before we begin our search for answers."

Somewhat disconcerted by the reaction of her audience, Rebecca continued. "With the help of many others, we used the information in the books to complete the pyramid. However, before we could test the completed device, we were attacked…" Rebecca trailed off as she glanced at Goliath and considered how to proceed. Deciding to leave out the involvement of the giant and his now dead partner, Hercules, she resumed her account. "…and were forced to activate the pyramid. When we did, it launched us into…the heavens. After we landed back on Earth, we discovered that it had taken us back in time."

Rebecca was actually surprised by the *lack* of surprise exhibited by Noah and his family. *If someone came to me with this kind of crazy tale, I would've had them locked up in a loony bin!* she thought. *Yet, they don't appear skeptical. Do they really believe me?* Still confused by their lack of reaction, Rebecca decided to plunge ahead. "The pyramid was somehow pre-programmed…uh…following instructions given to it by someone else. We made several journeys through time until we ended up here."

"At first light, you must return to your vessel and leave immediately," Shem said, his face revealing open disgust. "The time in which we live is cursed. For the wrath of the Almighty, may His glory shine forevermore, is about to be poured out upon all flesh."

"But that is our problem," Rebecca replied. "The pyramid is no longer working. We don't know what's wrong with it. There doesn't appear to be any damage, yet it just suddenly pulled us out of time and landed us here."

An expression of deep concentration clouded Noah's expression. Hoping for some insight, Rebecca paused. However, when none was forthcoming, she decided to press on. "And even more, one of our friends was grievously injured in our last journey and is in desperate need of medical attention. Please, can you help us?"

For the first time since they had finished dinner, Eema spoke up. "What kind of injury did your friend receive?"

Mack translated her question to Rebecca and the others, then answered the question himself.

Eema nodded slowly as a compassionate expression spread across her face. "We brought medicine with us on the Ark. We will give you something to help your friend."

Japheth's wife turned to face Eema, a questioning look in her eyes. "But mother, surely one of us should go and show them how to use the ointment."

Noah leaned forward and shook his head sadly. "We cannot violate the Lord's command. He told us to enter the Ark, and it is here we must remain. My daughters will teach you how to apply the medicine before you go. I am sorry, but we cannot leave."

Rebecca inclined her head. "We understand, and thank you for your assistance."

"Now, let us discuss this pyramid further," Noah said. "Why did you come to us for help? What makes you think that we would know anything about how to repair it?"

"Mack, show him the technical journals," Rebecca said. As the language specialist withdrew the two ancient books from his backpack, Rebecca once more addressed their host. "These are the books that we found in the chamber with the pyramid. Since it was written in the Language of Eden, we assume that someone from before…before the Flood must have written them."

Noah reached out and accepted the books from Mack. As he opened the ancient tomes, Japheth, sitting to Noah's left, leaned closer while Shem and Ham moved over and crouched behind their father. All four men studied the books intently for several minutes without comment. At last, Noah looked up at the five travelers, his expression dark.

"I must implore you, my friends. Make your peace with the Creator, blessed are the works of His mighty hands. For you will need His guidance and protection in order for you to return home."

Mack's voice began to tremble as he related Noah's cryptic words to his friends.

"What's that supposed to mean?" Jerome asked, his own words catching in his throat as fear began to well up within him.

"It's obvious he knows something," Goliath interjected. "But I wouldn't let his religious superstition bother you. We make our own destinies, not some…invisible, vindictive god. I'm getting tired of all of this. Let's find out what he knows and get out of here." Despite his dismissal of Noah's comment, Rebecca could see clear traces of uncertainty and trepidation reflected on the holographic image that represented the giant's face.

"I agree," Jeffrey said curtly.

Rebecca could only guess as to what her husband was truly feeling, but judging by the pale tinge to his skin and the sickly expression he wore, she knew that *something* was afflicting him. Just an hour ago, she would have relished watching him suffer, and in the eyes of many, she would have been justified in doing so. However, right here, sitting inside the Ark, she knew it was not the kind of response that God would approve. As she studied Jeffrey's face, she felt a gentle presence nudge her spirit, like a downy feather lightly brushing against her skin. Feeling reassured that the affliction was something sent on him to bring about a change for the *good*, she prayed quickly for him, then turned her attention back to the conversation.

"Mack, ask him to explain!" Jerome implored. "Can he help us?"

After a brief exchange with Noah, Mack began to translate his response to the others. "He wants to know how much we know about the history of…of *this* time period?"

"Not much, really," Rebecca replied, speaking directly to Noah. "We have a few ancient, sacred documents that describe your account of the Flood and the account of Adam. But many believe that they are simply myths and legends—fictional stories that are not true. And even those of us who *do* believe they are true, know very little, since the documents are very short and don't contain much information about this pre-Flood world."

Noah frowned. Rising to his feet, he handed the technical journals to Japheth, walked over to one of the chests, opened it, and withdrew two scrolls. Returning to his seat, he unrolled the larger of the two and handed it to Mack. The language specialist took one look at the document, then, looked at his friends; his face riddled with guilt.

"What is it?" Rebecca asked.

The corners of Mack's lips twitched into a week smile. "Uh…it's… it's Noah's journal."

"His…his journal?" Jerome repeated. "As in, his personal journal that we took from the cave?"

"Yep. That's the one," Mack confirmed.

Rebecca shot him a look of disapproval. "Just remember, when we get that contraption working properly, we're going to return the copy we stole, right?"

"You mean, *if* we get it working," Goliath mumbled.

"Right. Of…of course," Mack stuttered.

"So, why is he showing it to us now?" Jeffrey asked.

Glad to be changing the subject, Mack turned in Jeffrey's direction. "He wants to know if this is one of the ancient documents that Rebecca was referring to."

"What did you tell him?" Jerome asked impatiently.

"Nothing yet," Mack responded, his own irritation beginning to show.

"Well, what are you waiting for?" Jerome countered.

"I'm waiting for you to stop asking me stupid questions," Mack shot back. "Sheesh! Give a guy a break. If *you* want to take over the translation job, feel free to step in at any time. But let me warn you, the pay is terrible and the working conditions *stink!*" As he turned back to face the Patriarch, he mumbled under his breath, "Who would've ever thought that I would sympathize with Threepio? How pathetic."

Once Mack had answered Noah's question, the older man's face fell. "That is unfortunate. I had hoped that my journal would survive for many years as a written testament of the truth. I am keeping an accurate, detailed record so that my descendants will know what the world was like before the Deluge, as well as why it deserved destruction."

Taking his journal back from Mack, he rolled it up and set it next to him on the rug. "But, you have traveled many years into the past. I cannot expect that my journal would survive all that time." Picking up the other scroll, he gently unrolled it as he had done with the other. Rebecca and her friends could tell that while the first scroll had been new and undamaged, this second one was old and obviously precious to its owner. For as he handed it to Mack, he cradled it in his arms, like a loving parent holding a newborn. "What about this one. Have these words escaped the ravages of time?"

Matching the other's care and respect for the scroll, Mack drew it towards him. Looking down at it, his eyes suddenly grew wide as he stared at the intricate, flowing letters scrawled on the page. Gently, yet impatiently, Mack unwound the scroll to reveal the next section.

"What is this one?" Rebecca asked, intrigued at Mack's reaction. "Do you recognize it?"

Looking up from the text, Mack stared at Rebecca, Jeffrey, and Jerome as a look of confusion spread across his features. "It…it contains the first several chapters of the Hebrew Torah. This is the Creation account from the Bible."

"But how is that possible?" Rebecca said, her own expression mirroring Mack's. "I thought that Moses was the author of Genesis?"

Jerome glanced at Jeffrey, who averted his gaze, clearly not comfortable with the current discussion. Left to answer the question himself, Jerome sighed. "Although the rest of the Bible often refers to the first five books as the Law of Moses, many have speculated that Moses was only the *compiler*, or *editor* of Genesis. After all, Genesis is divided up into several 'accounts,' such as the 'account of Adam,' the 'account of Noah,' and the 'account of Abraham.' Furthermore, supporters of the theory cite the fact that there are several alternative names written in parenthesis, as if Moses was converting the ancient names for cities and countries into their more modern names."

"I always thought it was odd that Moses would have written the account of Creation, since he wasn't even there," Mack commented. "I mean, did God sit down with Moses and *dictate* to him how He created the world? But if Moses was the editor, then…"

"…then who wrote this original scroll?" Rebecca finished for him.

"I see that you *do* recognize this writing," Noah said. "I had expected nothing less—for these are the writings of my forefather, Adam, which were passed down to me. Although the words were written by human hands, they are inspired by the Author of Life—glory to His Name—and therefore, shall never pass away."

Rebecca smiled broadly. "There's your answer, Mack. Moses *didn't* write the account of creation: it was written by someone who spoke with God personally. That means the accounts in Genesis are *eyewitness* accounts."

"But, if Noah didn't write his own account, then who did?" Mack asked.

"He probably *did* write his own account," Rebecca added. "He just hasn't written it yet. In fact, he could have even written it after we had met him during the Ice…" Her voice suddenly trailed off as a look of shock registered on her face.

"What's wrong?" Mack asked, concerned.

"Don't you see?" Rebecca said, her eyes still unfocused, as if she were staring at something in another time and place. "When we first met Noah, he hadn't written his biblical account yet because he still had his journal."

"But since *we* took it, he was forced to write a summary—which is what we find in our Bible," Jerome said in awe.

"For some reason, maybe God didn't *want* the world to have Noah's full account," Mack suggested. Rebecca smiled as something within her leapt with excitement. *Mack actually accepted the existence of God!* she thought.

"I'm sure this is all quite fascinating," Goliath interjected sarcastically, "but do you mind if we get back to the more important topic of finding out what Noah knows, so that we can get back to our own time?"

Rebecca, Jerome, and Mack, as well as Noah's entire family, all turned to look at the giant, who stood behind them near the door, his posture communicating his impatience louder than his words.

"Your friend appears disturbed," Ham commented. "Is something wrong?" Judging by the stiffness in his body and the dark inflection of his voice, Rebecca could tell he was distrustful of the giant.

"No, everything is fine," Rebecca replied. "Please accept my apologies for my...friend's...behavior. It's just that he is eager to hear more about...about this land."

Noah cast one last, brief glance in Goliath's direction before returning his attention to the scroll still held in Mack's hands. "Since you are familiar with the account of Creation, the Fall of mankind, and the history of my forefathers, I will begin with my own story."

"Great Patriarch, although we don't know all of the details contained in your journal, we *are* familiar with your story," Rebecca said. "Our sacred documents *do* contain an account of the Flood, although I'm sure it is not nearly as detailed as your journal. We know that because of the wickedness of these people, God decided to destroy them with a Flood. He instructed you to build this Ark," she said, her eyes scanning the room for emphasis, "and care for your family and the animals. But, we know very little about this world. Is there anyone here who can help us fix our vessel? And what is it about these books that makes you so concerned for our safety?" Rebecca asked, pointing to the technical journals from the pyramid that Japheth still held.

Noah paused momentarily before answering. As he began to speak, Rebecca saw Mack sigh heavily in relief. Turning to his friends, he translated the Patriarch's words. "He says that he believes there is someone living here who knows how to fix the pyramid!" At the news, Rebecca, Jerome, and Jeffrey all duplicated Mack's response, while Goliath merely muttered, "Now we're finally getting somewhere."

Their host's face darkened as he observed their relief. "You misunderstand me. Although I know who might be able to fix your pyramid, I do not think they will be willing to do so."

11

DARK DISCUSSIONS

MACK'S CRESTFALLEN FACE told the others that something was wrong before he ever finished the translation. "What?" Jeffrey asked in frustration. "Why won't they fix the pyramid?"

Noah stood and walked over to the chest. Placing the scrolls back into it, he turned around once again. Based on the expression of concern and helplessness on his face, it quickly became apparent to Rebecca that his news was not going to be good. "I recognize this kind of technology. But very few know how to build it or fix it, for the self-proclaimed gods are very jealous of their secrets."

As Mack translated the last sentence, Rebecca and the others turned to look at him. "Are you sure that's what he said?" Jerome asked. "What do you think he means by 'self-proclaimed gods'?"

Mack shrugged. "Don't look at me. I'm just an interpreter."

"Well, ask him what he meant," Jeffrey urged.

Noah began to pace the floor slowly, his gaze becoming unfocused as Mack relayed the others' request for clarification. Placing his hands behind his back as he walked, Noah began to speak. "My father Lamech often told me how, when he was young, he would sit on the knee of *the* Patriarch, our father Adam. The firstborn of all men would tell my father how the world was once perfect and free from sin, and the garden in which he dwelt was free from thistles and thorns of any kind.

Then, with the terrible heaviness of sorrow upon his shoulders, Adam would relate the tale of how he and Eve, the mother of all mankind, disobeyed their Creator, and brought ruin upon the world." Noah paused in mid stride as he became lost in long forgotten memories. "But for the forgiveness of the Almighty Father—righteous, yet full of mercy is He—Lamech believed that Adam would have long ago perished under the crushing weight of his guilt if it had not been for the hope given him by our merciful Creator. My father said that Adam often spoke of the One who would someday come to strike the head of the serpent and redeem mankind."

Noah paused to allow Mack time to catch up with his translation. After he had finished, Jerome made a comment before the Patriarch could continue. "Wait a second. Did you say that Noah's father Lamech used to sit on Adam's knee? But that's impossible! Adam would have been long dead before Lamech was born, wouldn't he?"

"I'm not so sure," Rebecca said. "I do know that most of the patriarchs lived to be over nine hundred years old. I never thought about it before, but it would make sense."

"It's just…just so hard to believe that someone could live that long," Jerome commented.

"If Doc were here, he would probably know their exact ages," Rebecca said wistfully.

"Then again, we've got someone right here who knows firsthand how old they were," Mack added. "We could ask him."

Goliath rolled his eyes in frustration. "No thanks! He's having a hard enough time getting to the point as it is without you giving him something else to talk about. Now, if you three would kindly shut up, maybe he would get back to his explanation," the giant growled.

"Don't be hasty! It's not like we've got anywhere else to go tonight," Mack shot back. "You know, in fantasy stories, elves and other long-lived races are always commenting on how humans are always in such a hurry. Maybe Noah and his family are like them. Just be glad he's not an Ent. If so, we'd still be waiting for him to finish saying 'hello'!"

Goliath ignored the comment and leaned back against the wall of the chamber.

Although the rest of his family still seemed disconcerted by the giant's presence, Noah appeared unconcerned. Seeing that the interchange had apparently run its course and that no questions were forthcoming, he continued his explanation.

"As more and more time passed, and more and more children and grandchildren were born, Adam watched as sin worked its poison deeper and deeper into his offspring." Now that Noah had resumed his narration, he began pacing around the room once again. "In the course of time, many turned from the Creator and began following in the path of Cain. Cities grew and flourished, but so did evil. Before long, Satan intensified his attack upon Adam's seed.

"When the first parents were expelled from the Garden, the Mighty Lord of All spoke a prophecy to the serpent: 'I will put hostility between you and the woman, and between your seed and her seed.' Before long, the fallen angel, Lucifer, who had taken the form of the serpent in the Garden, began to corrupt the minds *and* bodies of mankind. He and the rest of the angels who had followed him in rebellion, began to prey upon men. Being bigger and stronger then the seed of Adam and Eve, they set themselves up as gods."

A chill wind seemed to blow through the room. Rebecca couldn't tell whether it was from the open shaft above them or from the direction in which Noah's narrative had taken. Crossing her arms in front of her, she hugged herself to try to ward off the uncomfortable feeling.

The dark tale had a chilling effect as well on the mood of the rest of the listeners. Everyone in the room remained still, including Goliath. Even Noah himself ceased his pacing and stared out the window of the door that led toward the animal enclosures.

"Great wars were fought between the self-proclaimed gods and their armies as they sought dominance and control of the humans," Noah explained further. "Eventually, boundaries were established and most of the fighting ceased. Great cities, temples, and palaces were built in honor of these false gods. Often, many of the sons of God ruled a territory together, using their combined power to influence the people. These pantheons of gods molded the humans into their own likenesses, developing their own forms of worship, philosophies, and religions."

Jerome's brow furrowed in confusion. "Did he just say, 'sons of God'? Is that another name for these…demon-gods?"

After Mack translated the question, Noah nodded his head. "We call all of the heavenly host 'sons of God' because they were created directly by the Maker Himself. Even our forefather Adam was called a 'son of God' for the same reason."

Noah paused and placed his hand upon his head, as if this particular part of the story caused him great pain to divulge. "Once they had established their power, the sons of God began to…to…*take*…our women. Our mothers, our daughters, and…and our sisters." Standing to her feet, Eema crossed over to where Noah stood and placed a comforting arm around his waist. After a moment, he allowed her to guide him back to where the others sat. When he and Eema were settled onto their cushions, Noah turned his attention back to his guests.

"Forgive my emotion. It has been a long time now, but I will never forget what they did."

"Please, noble Patriarch, we don't want to cause you further pain," Rebecca said gently, "but we don't understand. What did they do?"

His face burned with a righteous anger such as Rebecca had never before seen. "They took our women for their 'wives.' They seduced them, used them, and then discarded them. Furthermore, they impregnated our women and created abominations. They were giants—perverse, half-humans. Many of the women, including my sister, died giving birth to these monstrosities."

"The Nephilim," Jerome stated quietly.

Noah nodded in acknowledgement as he recognized the word.

"That gives me the willies!" Mack said, shivering. "It almost reminds me of some of those alien abduction stories you hear about."

When Mack did not translate his own comment, Noah continued. "Many who trusted in the True God believed that by breeding with our women, Lucifer was attempting to pollute the 'seed' of man and create his own 'seed,' thus preventing the prophecy from being fulfilled. If there were no 'seed' of mankind left, then there could be no Redeemer."

Japheth leaned forward. "If that was truly his aim, then he is close to achieving his goal. As far as we know, we may be the only eight yet alive that are of pure blood. The rest have either been polluted by normal procreation, or they have had their bodies altered before birth through the evil technology of the sons of God."

"What kind of technology?" Goliath asked.

"The sons of God, and all of the other heavenly hosts, whom the Creator made before mankind, dwelt with Him in the heavens," Noah explained. "As such, they were not bound by mortal bodies and had access to knowledge and understanding that is beyond what man has been able to obtain in the past sixteen centuries."

Shem, who had remained silent through most of the discussion, took over the thread of explanation from his father, his youthful, tenor voice a contrast to his father's more mature baritone. "They understand how to manipulate the very laws of nature. They make machines that can lift massive stones, as if by sorcery, which they use to build great temples and palaces. Their knowledge of the healing arts is unsurpassed, for they seem to know the inner workings of the human body even to the point where they can…pervert life before it is born!" Shem exclaimed, his voice trembling and his face reflecting his revulsion. At his side, tears began to fall silently from the light green eyes of his wife. Taking her hand in his, he paused a moment before continuing. "They can alter the invisible structures that our Maker, blessed be His name, placed in each living being at the Creation of the world. As if to mock our loving Creator, they twisted life, mixing the seed of one animal with the seed of another to create horrible…abominations. But worst of all, they perverted mankind, who bears the very image of God! Through their wickedness, they formed

terrible, half-human…soul-less monstrosities! And some men even will-
ingly volunteered to have these horrors visited upon them, solely for the
sake of the power and strength it brought them!"

As he spoke, Shem's voice became louder and louder as his indig-
nation and anger rose. Leaning over, Noah placed a hand on his son's
shoulder and whispered in his ear. Closing his eyes momentarily, Shem
visibly relaxed as his father's words drained the anger from his body.

"It sounds like these 'gods' know about genetic manipulation,"
Jeffrey said quietly as he looked around at the others. "I bet those vampire-like things were some of these genetically altered creatures."

Rebecca shivered involuntarily as the image of the pale, tight-skinned
faces appeared in her thoughts. Next to her, Mack sat motionless, a sickened look on his face. Glancing at Goliath, she noticed that even *he* wore
a disturbed expression.

Shem, still shaking slightly, put his arm around his wife and drew
her close. Noah leaned back and returned his attention to his visitors
once more. "My son has been given a love of nature and animals that
rivals any I have ever seen. It grieves him deeply to see what the enemy
has done. It is for this reason that my family and I were disturbed by
your description of the beings you found with the pyramid. If they were
Nephilim or altered abominations, it would mean that the false gods
continued to corrupt mankind *after* the Deluge."

Rebecca and the others remained silent, each lost in his or her own
thoughts. After a moment, Noah resumed his narration.

"Many of these abominations were set loose in the wild, often killing
off other animals," Noah said. "Some were so ruined by these experiments that they fled to live in caves, or deep in the forests in lairs, cursed
to live out the rest of their days in pitiful solitude. Other, more intelligent creatures formed packs, such as the Blood Drinkers that attacked
the Ark tonight." Shaking his head in sorrow, Noah spoke softly. "So
many were seduced into service by the lure of the power that the Fallen
Ones offered."

Goliath shifted his weight as he grew more and more restless. "This is all quite fascinating," he snarled, "but we are still no closer to getting a straight answer to our question! Who is it that can fix the pyramid, and why doesn't he think they will help us?"

As Mack translated the question, Noah gave Goliath a quizzical look, as if he guessed that there was more to this tall human than his outward appearance indicated. "I know that you are eager to find answers to your questions, but it is imperative that you understand what it is that you will face."

Mack listened intently as the Patriarch continued to speak. Suddenly, all the color drained out of Mack's face. Seeing her friend's obvious distress, Rebecca placed a hand on his forearm. "What did he say?"

Mack slowly tore his gaze away from Noah to look at her. Staring into his eyes, Rebecca was stunned by the depth of fear reflected in his greenish-blue orbs. Mack swallowed hard and he licked his lips in a vain attempt to bring moisture back to his dry mouth.

"He…he said that…um," Mack stuttered, "that the only beings who have the knowledge we need to…to fix the pyramid are…are the Fallen Ones themselves!"

A deep sense of foreboding settled on the group at Mack's statement. Jerome began to shake slightly as he began wringing his hands in his lap. Taking a shallow breath, he spoke, his voice coming out in a slow, raspy whisper. "Are you telling me that the only way we can fix the ship is if we can get some…demon 'god-wannabes' to agree to help us?"

From the expression on his face, Rebecca thought for a moment that Mack was going to be sick. Not knowing what else to say, the language specialist simply nodded weakly in affirmation.

Noah began speaking again, snapping Mack out of his feeling of nausea by forcing him to serve as translator once more. "Do you see now why I urge you to make peace with the One True God? It is only with His help that you have any hope of succeeding."

"Isn't there anyone else who can help us?" Jeffrey asked, desperation beginning to take hold of him.

After a moment of silence, Ham turned toward his father and began speaking. The two exchanged words briefly. Although a frown creased Noah's features, he seemed to agree with his son. "There may be one who could help you, but it would be very dangerous to seek his help. His name is Arngrim. He is a…a friend of mine who is very knowledgeable about technology. For many years, he was a servant of the sons of God and learned some of their secrets. He is one of the most brilliant men in the world. In fact, it was for that reason that I hired him to help us build the Ark.

"However, many years ago, he began working on a special project," Noah said. "We have not seen him since, but his business is still operating. Perhaps if you go there, they may be able to locate him. But, as I said, it will be dangerous. For his business is located near the 'World Tree,' as they call it; where the borders of the realm of the false gods, the realm of the Nephilim, and the middle enclosure all meet. You must beware. The streets are deadly, even during the day, and *especially* for strangers. Gangs roam about everywhere, and Odin's soldiers and servants are corrupt, always willing to turn and face the other way for the right price."

A look of astonishment lit up Jeffrey's face as Mack finished translating this last statement. "Wait a second. Did you just say, 'Odin's soldiers'?"

Mack nodded, confused by the shocked look on Jeffrey's face.

"Oh no," Jerome replied, his expression indicating that he had reached the same disturbing conclusion. "Please tell me that you're not thinking what I think you're thinking."

"What?" Mack asked, suddenly worried. "What are you two talking about? What are you thinking?"

Jeffrey looked at the others solemnly. "We appear to have landed next to the dwelling place of Odin, king of the gods from Norse mythology!"

"Whoa…Norse mythology? As in, Thor and Loki?" Mack exclaimed in with a mixture of excitement and apprehension.

Jeffrey nodded. "Thor and Loki were the children of Odin."

"But what makes you think this has anything to do with Norse mythology, besides the reference to Odin?" Rebecca asked.

"According to Norse cosmology, there were nine realms, each connected to the 'World Tree,'" Jeffrey explained. "The realm of the Aesir, or the war-like gods, was called Asgard; Midgard, which means 'middle enclosure,' or 'middle earth,' was the home of humans; and another realm was called Jotunheim, which means 'Giant's Home.'"

"The home of the Nephilim," Rebecca breathed softly.

"But, how could it possibly be referring to the same legends?" Jerome added. "After all, those Norse myths were so goofy, they didn't even make any sense. I mean, it talks about a giant who gives birth to a six-headed son who receives nourishment from a cosmic cow! Or that a giant serpent Nidhogg is always chewing on the root of the World Tree until it eventually collapses!"

Jeffrey shrugged. "I didn't say I believed in any of that stuff. All I'm saying is that it sounds like someone here is using the same kind of imagery."

Rebecca frowned, then turned to Mack. "Ask Noah if there are any other realms besides the three he named." Her friend did as requested, and responded a moment later. "Yep! He confirmed that there are nine total!"

"But, do those nine realms refer to the whole earth?" Rebecca asked, a sudden thought striking her. "Or do they just refer to this country?"

After Mack translated the question, Noah confirmed her suspicions. "The nine realms refer to the areas directly under the control of the sons of God in this country. They call themselves the Aesir and Vanir. As I mentioned previously, the false gods fought for many years for the territories they now hold. Their armies still fight to this day, but for the most part, they seem content to merely control those unfortunate enough to live in their domain. Each country is ruled by a different pantheon of false gods."

"What are the names of some of these other gods?" Goliath asked, intrigued.

Before Noah could reply, Ham answered for him. "Directly to our north, Zeus, Poseidon, Apollos, Aphrodite, Hera, and the rest hold court. To the west, there is Ra, Sekhmet, Anubis, and others. The gods Marduk, Tiamat and Apsu, plus several more, reign in the south. These are the closest to our home. There are many more in other distant lands."

"The only place left undefiled by their evil is the east, wherein lies the great rivers—Pishon, Gihon, Hiddekel, and Euphrates—and Eden, the birthplace of mankind," Shem added.

Silence fell over the visitors as their minds attempted to digest the implications of Ham's statements. "Greek, Egyptian, and Babylonian," Jerome said at last.

"Yeah," Mack said, a frown darkening his face. "But…I don't get it. How does it all fit with everything else we've seen?" he asked, looking at Rebecca.

Caught up in trying to solve this riddle, Rebecca was oblivious to Mack's attention. A moment later, however, the blank look on her face suddenly dissolved as the pieces fell into place in her mind. "Wait a second! Do you remember the paintings that were hanging in the library within the Tower of Babel? They were paintings of many different gods."

She paused as the others retrieved the mental images from the recesses of their memories. "Dr. Eisenberg mentioned that they were pictures of Zeus, Baal, and *Odin!*" she said with excitement. "It makes perfect sense! All of the stories and legends of ancient gods from around the world were based on the truth. They all stem from real beings that lived prior to the Flood!"

Jerome raised an eyebrow. "So, you think that all that stuff from Norse mythology about a six-headed man getting nourishment from a cosmic cow was real? That's crazy."

Rebecca shot Jerome a frustrated look. "I'm not saying that *everything* contained in the legends was true. Many of them were no doubt embellished over time. But what I *am* saying is that it makes sense that, like the dragon legends, the stories of these ancient gods have a *basis* in reality."

Sensing the intensity of the discussion, Noah and his family exchanged glances, but remained otherwise patiently silent as Rebecca continued. "Think about it; after the Flood, future generations would have asked Noah and his family what the pre-Flood world was like. They told them about these powerful beings who called themselves gods and ruled mankind. As time passed, the stories…evolved. Then, as they dispersed from the Tower of Babel, some of the different people groups based their new civilizations and religions on the pre-Flood legends."

Jeffrey still looked unconvinced. However, wanting to finish their conversation with Noah, he let the matter drop. "Whatever the case, it looks like we'll need whatever information Noah can give us about how to find…whatever-his-name-was."

"Arngrim," Mack offered. Next to him, he could see that Rebecca was frustrated by Jeffrey's blatant disregard of her theory.

"Right," Jeffrey continued. "I think it's time you stop playing translator. That way, you can get things done more quickly. See if Noah has a map of the city. Find out everything you can about what kinds of problems we could encounter. The more we know, the better our chances of success will be. Meanwhile, I suggest the rest of us turn in early. We've got a busy day ahead of us, and we need to start as early as possible."

Rebecca practically bit her lip to keep her from saying something she would regret. *Why does he continually turn away from the truth, despite all of the proof right in front of him?* she wondered. *Lord, what's it going to take to get him to accept You? He's so blasted stubborn!*

Jeffrey stood and thanked Noah and his family for the meal. Mack translated and explained to their confused hosts Jeffrey's intention to retire for the evening. Noah immediately stood and stepped closer to Jeffrey, a pleading look on his face. "Please, you must listen. Without the protection of the Lord, who can be a shield to protect you, I do not believe you will live! Only He can save you from the snare. Only He can rescue you from the pit."

For a moment, Rebecca thought her husband might reconsider. Then, he reached out and placed a hand on Noah's shoulder. "Thank you for your concern and your help. It's greatly appreciated." Turning away from the Patriarch, he began heading toward the room on the left side of the common room that Noah had indicated had been prepared for them. Jerome quickly bade them goodnight and followed after Jeffrey. Without saying a word, Goliath nodded his thanks and moved off to join the other men.

Just as Jeffrey was about to open the door to the room, Noah spoke up once more, his voice infected with foreboding. "I warn you, my friends. Do *not* let the sons of God learn of your machine. For if they do, they will surely take it from you to use for their own twisted purposes."

Throwing one last glance over his shoulder at their host, Jeffrey nodded, and then entered the sleeping quarters. Although he immediately lay down on the bed, sleep eluded him for hours as his mind wrestled with all that they had learned.

When sleep did finally overtake him, his dreams were fraught with disturbing images of giants and half-human beasts...

12

MEMORIES AND PREMONITIONS

WHILE MACK, NOAH, and Japheth discussed plans for the next day, the rest of Noah's family had gone to check on the animals and to douse many of the lanterns that lit the interior of the ship. Rebecca volunteered to go along to help with the chores, as she was glad for the opportunity to be of use. Although she couldn't speak their language, she simply mimicked Eema's actions and, before long, became quite adept at dimming the lanterns, checking the quantities of food and water, and shoveling waste into the gutters.

When Rebecca and the others returned from their chores, they found Noah and Japheth leaning over Mack, who was hunched over and crying softly. Immediately concerned, Rebecca went to her friend and put her hand around his shoulders. At her touch, he looked up at her with a smile on his face.

"Becky, you were right," Mack said softly. "I…I should have seen it long before now. I guess I just…just never gave it much thought. But now…I believe!"

Overwhelmed by emotion, Rebecca felt tears of joy moisten her cheeks as a broad smile spread across her face. "I'm so glad!" Pulling him into a tight embrace, she laughed and buried her face in his curly black hair. Leaning back to hold him at arm's length, she stared deeply into his strange, greenish-blue eyes. "What made you change your mind?"

Mack chuckled. "What *hasn't* happened to help me change my mind? Everything that we've experienced—the dinosaurs, the Tower of Babel, the Ark—has forced me to reevaluate what I believe. It just got to the point that I couldn't deny it anymore. When it came to religion, it wasn't that I rejected it, I just…never gave it much thought. Now, after all we've been through, I'd have to be dumber than a Gamorrean to not see it."

Rebecca raised an eyebrow and smirked. "Well, I don't know much about the intelligence levels of Gamorreans, but if they're as thick in the head as a couple of men I know, then they must be pretty slow indeed."

Mack grinned. "Yeah, well don't give up hope on them. They may be slow, but Jeffrey and Jerome are bound to come around. There's too much evidence."

"I sure hope you're right," Rebecca said with a sigh. "I just hope they don't wait too long. Who knows what's going to happen tomorrow."

"Actually, that's one of the things that really pushed me to make a decision tonight," Mack commented. "The more I talked to Noah about that city and what we're likely to face tomorrow, I decided that if there *is* a real God, I want Him on my side!"

Rebecca smiled at him warmly. "You made the right decision. Welcome to the family."

At her words, fresh tears filled his eyes. Dropping his gaze to stare at the floor, he spoke softly. "You don't know what that means to me." Wiping the tears away, he looked back at Rebecca. "I don't think I've ever told this to anyone, but…I've never really had a family. I never knew my father. He took off as soon as he found out my mom was pregnant with me. And she was messed up with drugs and stuff most of the time. I locked myself in my room so that I wouldn't have to be around her and her latest boyfriend."

Waves of compassion washed over Rebecca as she listened intently. In her mind, she imagined Mack as a boy, his curly hair dangling in front of his chubby little face; his eyes haunted by abandonment. After a moment, he continued, his expression vacant, as if reliving his past pain.

"I basically raised myself. I watched hour after hour of TV, particularly the Sci-Fi/Fantasy channel. I especially loved the crazy languages that the aliens, or the elves, or the other fantastic beings would speak. Eventually, I hooked up with some other outcasts at school who were into the same stuff. Nathan and Kayley were bilingual, and they taught me to speak some Spanish and German. Then, we decided to learn Elvish and Klingon, so that we could talk to each other privately when others were around. After awhile, we even made up our own language. Sure, we were geeks, but we had each other. We were our own kind of family."

A wistful look spread across Mack's face. "Eventually, we grew up and went our own ways. Although I didn't have such great grades, I seemed to have a knack for languages and ended up getting a scholarship to college. I messed up quite a bit, and did a lot of stuff I regret. But no matter what I did, there was always something missing in my life. I never would have admitted it, and I probably didn't even recognize it myself, but I think what I was looking for more than anything was a family. I wished, just for once, that my mother would tell me how proud she was."

Losing his battle to control his emotions, Mack began to weep softly. Pulling him closer, Rebecca hugged him and began to stroke his hair. Taking in a shuddering breath, Mack let it out with a sigh. With his head buried against her shoulder, Rebecca had to strain to hear his next sentence. "I even used to dream that a man would knock on my door. When I opened it, he would introduce himself and tell me that he…that he was my father." Leaning back, Mack continued speaking; his voice quivered as he struggled to contain his emotions. "Then, he would grab me in his big, strong arms and say, 'You've done good, boy. I'm so proud to know that my son is a college graduate!' Instead, all I got was a policeman standing at my door and telling me that my mother had died of alcohol poisoning. Instead of my dream of gaining a father, I got news that I was officially an orphan."

Several minutes passed in silence as Rebecca comforted her friend and prayed. Finally, he sat up and stared at the floor again, his eyes red and puffy. "Sorry. I don't know what—"

Rebecca held up a hand, stopping him mid-sentence. "You've got nothing to apologize for." Grabbing his hands in both of hers, she leaned toward him until their faces were mere inches apart. "Now, listen to me, Mack Nielson. The Bible says that when we accept Christ as our Savior, we are adopted into His family. So you are no longer an orphan. You are the son of the King of Kings. You will never be alone again."

As Rebecca's words worked their way through Mack's mind and into his spirit, she could trace their progress through the strain of emotions that crossed his features. His initial embarrassment was replaced by confusion, followed rapidly by unworthiness, gratitude, and then joy. His face lit with excitement; he smiled broadly. "Yeah…never alone. And a son of the King. I guess that makes me a prince!"

Overcome by her own emotions, Rebecca simply nodded. A moment later, movement to her right caused her to look up to see that during her conversation with Mack, Eema, her three sons, and their wives had gathered in the center of the room beneath the shaft that opened to the night air. Noah, who had moved up to stand next to Mack, laid a hand on his shoulder and began to speak.

"He wants to know if we would join his family in their evening worship," Mack translated.

"Please tell him that we would be honored," Rebecca replied as she and Mack rose from where they were seated on the floor. Taking Mack's hand in hers, they followed Noah toward the center of the room and took their place in the circle.

Lifting his hands into the air, Noah began to pray. Although Rebecca could not understand his words, the now familiar sense of peace settled over her as he spoke. As if prompted by some unseen hand, Rebecca, Mack, and the rest of Noah's family all lifted their hands toward the night sky above them.

All sense of time vanished as they worshiped. Lost in adulation, Rebecca suddenly felt a change in the presence surrounding them. Fleeting images began to appear before her, as clear as if she were looking at them with her physical eyes. The first image filled her with both joy and concern, for she saw Dr. Eisenberg leaning back against some pillows on a bed, his expression peaceful and his eyes alert. However, as she watched, fear flashed across his features. Dark figures rushed toward him as he struggled to get out of bed, pain suddenly spreading across his face.

Doc! Doc, no! Rebecca screamed in her mind. As quickly as the image appeared, it was replaced by another.

Akwen and Lisa sat huddled together in a dark corner, their backs leaning up against a wall of stone with their knees drawn up to their chest. Lisa had one arm around her companion, who simply stared blankly ahead, her expression devoid of emotion even as tears cut wide paths through the dust and grime that covered her face.

Father, what is happening? Rebecca asked. *Why are you showing me these—*

Before she could finish her thought, yet another image invaded her mind. Mack was sobbing uncontrollably on the stone floor of a room that somehow looked vaguely familiar. Several feet away, she could see the form of a man who appeared to have his arms bound above his head, his body stretched to its limit. Then, as the image focused in on the man's face, the sight caused Rebecca's heart to nearly break with anguish. Although his face was bloodied and swollen, she could still recognize the strong cheekbones and handsome features that she had once caressed with affection. Powerless to help him, Rebecca merely watched in horror as his face contorted in agony.

Jeffrey! NOOOO!

Instantly, the images vanished, leaving her broken and afraid. For what seemed like an eternity, Rebecca stood silent and still, her emotions running out of control until she could no longer feel anything. Then, as if soothing a deep cut, the powerful sense of peace returned and drained away the pain caused by the visions, renewing her spirit. Drinking in the calm assurance, her weeping eased and eventually ceased.

"Rebecca…Rebecca, are you okay?"

Coming to her senses, she saw Mack standing in front of her, a concerned expression on his face.

"Man, you really gave me a scare," Mack said as he let out a slow breath. "One minute you were standing there with your hands raised, and the next thing I know…you totally zoned out and you had this… weird look on your face."

Still shaken by the visions, Rebecca had a hard time comprehending his words. Seeing Noah and his family still standing around her, she attempted a smile of reassurance. *Should I tell them about the visions?* she wondered. Then, just as clearly as if it had been uttered by an audible voice, she knew the answer. *No. Mack is worried enough as it is and his faith is new. And I can't talk to Noah without going through Mack. Lord, you gave these visions to me. They are my burden to bear. Help us. You know what's coming. Protect us. Prepare us. And more than anything, don't let my friends die without knowing you.*

Her face dour, Rebecca turned toward her friend. "Please thank Noah and his family once again for their kindness, and ask them to pray for us."

As he studied her face, Mack became serious. "Something happened a moment ago. You didn't just zone out, did you?"

"No, I didn't," she said, choosing her words carefully. "God was… God wants us to pray. We must be ready for tomorrow, and the best way to do that is to pray."

Nodding solemnly, Mack began to translate Rebecca's request. Kneeling down on the wooden floor, Rebecca bowed her head and began to converse with her Lord. A moment later, nine other pairs of knees joined hers.

Huddled close together, Rebecca, Mack, Noah, and his family all bombarded heaven for the next hour. The burden to pray was so strong, that even when she had bid the others good night and retired to her bed, she continued to lie awake and pray. For she knew that her life, the lives of her friends, and even their eternal destinies hung in the balance.

13

FAREWELLS

AS THE FIRST few rays of the rising sun set about their task of chasing away night's darkness, a gentle hand on her shoulder roused Rebecca from sleep. Turning toward her visitor, she saw Mack crouched next to her bed, his curly hair looking even more unkempt than usual.

"Sorry to wake you, but Jeffrey and the others want to get going as soon as possible," he said softly. "Noah says it should be safe in about another twenty minutes. Eema and the other women are making breakfast."

Rebecca sat up and ran her hands through her own tangled web of hair. "Thanks for waking me," she replied, her voice sounding scratchy and dry. "I'll be out in a moment."

Nodding in acknowledgment, Mack stood and retreated out of the darkened room. Kneading the muscles in her neck with her right hand, Rebecca's thoughts returned to the visions from the night before. The memory of the images had a stimulating effect on her mind, causing all drowsiness to immediately disappear. Closing her eyes once more, Rebecca reiterated the previous evening's prayers. As before, she felt the comforting presence of God rest upon her. *Thank you, Lord. I trust you and know that you'll see us through.*

Despite the disturbing uncertainty of what might lie ahead, Rebecca was somewhat surprised to find that she had slept soundly and felt completely rested. She wondered briefly if it was due to the oxygen-rich air that filtered down through the opening hatch of the Ark, or from the overpowering peace that dwelled within the ship. Either way, she was thankful for the energy that she knew she would need.

Pouring some water into the bowl sitting on the small table near the bed, she freshened up as best she could. Thankful for the soft nightgown that Japheth's wife had loaned her, she turned toward the chair on which she had placed her ripped jeans and dirty t-shirt the night before. To her surprise, she found that while she slept, her clothes had been washed, dried, and folded. Thanking God for the thoughtfulness of Noah's family, she dressed quickly.

Crossing to the wooden door at the end of the room, she opened it and stepped out into the common area. Immediately, the pleasant aroma of freshly baked bread assailed her, causing her stomach to growl and her mouth to water in anticipation.

Upon seeing Rebecca enter the room, Eema greeted her with a smile and motioned for her to sit on the cushions. Jeffrey, Jerome, Mack, and Goliath were already seated and appeared to be discussing with Noah a map that was spread out on the floor before them while the final preparations for breakfast were made.

As Rebecca approached the circle, Noah stood and bowed his head slightly in respect. Noticing that the others did not stand or hardly even acknowledge her presence, Noah raised his eyebrows questioningly and spoke in a firm voice. Embarrassed, Mack translated as he stood. "It is our custom to show honor to our women by standing while they are seated. Although this may seem odd to you, I would respectfully request that you honor this tradition while you are my guests."

The men quickly rose to their feet at their host's admonition. Unaccustomed to such attention, Rebecca was both honored and self-conscious. Thanking Noah, she quickly sat down. When the others were seated once more, they resumed their conversation. As they spoke, Jerome turned to her and began to fill her in on what she had missed.

"Good mornin'. Nice of you to join us," he said lightheartedly. Becoming suddenly more serious, he added, "Noah just finished showing us a map of the city, the best way to get to Arngrim's shop, and what sections of the city to avoid. As Noah stated before, the shop lies near the heart of the city and reaching it in one piece is going to be tricky. Noah suggests we hire a couple of bodyguards to take us."

Rebecca frowned at the suggestion. "And how are we going to pay for that? Somehow I don't think they'll accept my Visa card."

Jerome grinned slightly despite the seriousness of their conversation. "Noah said that he had some currency hidden down in the cellar of his house. Even though the house is burned to a crisp, he said that the cellar should still be intact. He'll get us the money before we leave."

Apologizing for breaking up the conversations, Eema politely announced that breakfast was finally ready. Rolling up the map, Noah placed it on a shelf against the wall as Shem's wife pulled a string attached to a series of bells placed strategically throughout the ship. By the time the table was completely set, Noah's three sons had returned from their errands.

Once everyone had gathered around in the circle, Noah offered thanks to God as he had done the evening before, then broke the first loaf of bread and invited everyone to begin eating. Although the visitors were thoroughly enjoying the meal, a sense of urgency was constantly prevalent, causing them to eat with relative haste. Wishing that they had visited under better circumstances, Rebecca was nevertheless in agreement when Jeffrey pushed his plate aside and called for the others to prepare to leave.

"The sun is almost up," he said. "We need to finish and get moving."

As if wanting to show his willingness to depart at that very instant, Goliath swallowed his last bite and stood. A few moments later, Jeffrey, Jerome, and Mack finished their own breakfast and followed suit, thanking their guests as they stood.

Conflicting emotions warred within Rebecca. She longed to return to Dr. Eisenberg, knowing that each minute of delay could bring him closer to death, providing he even survived the night. However, the images from her vision were still fresh, reminding her that great danger lay ahead for all of her friends. If only they could freeze time and remain in this place of safety—of peace—among friends. Gently, like a feather brushing against her cheek, a simple phrase passed through her mind, almost as if it had been spoken audibly. *Fear not, for I am with you.*

Closing her eyes, Rebecca bowed her head. *Yes, Lord. I place my life, and all of our lives, into your hands. Protect us.* Despite the uncertainty of their future, she felt her confidence grow. Ready to face whatever might come, she stood up to join the others.

It appeared to Rebecca that their hosts also seemed reluctant to have their guests leave. However, knowing full well the gravity of the situation, Noah didn't wish to delay them. As the Patriarch stood, he motioned to the rest of his family, who immediately cleared the floor and began to gather up bundles of cloth and other materials. Confused by their actions, the visitors watched in silence. After a few moments, Noah's family lined up in front of Rebecca and the others, their arms laden with bundles of leather and cloth.

"My family and I wish to thank you once again for all that you have done for us," Noah said, bowing slightly.

Rebecca shook her head and frowned slightly in dismissal. "Please, there is no need to thank us. Your generosity has far surpassed anything that we did."

Eema smiled broadly once Mack had finished translating Rebecca's statement. Shifting the bundle to hold it in her left hand, she reached out with her right and placed it over Rebecca's. "My dear, you don't understand. You have done more than just help to chase off the brigands that threatened the ship. By coming here, you have given us hope."

When she saw the confusion on Rebecca's face, Eema continued. "Although we have complete trust in the Lord of all creation, blessed be His name, there are times when our faith is weak. Especially as the day draws near for the Cataclysm to begin, we have begun to wonder if we will be ready for the task at hand."

Putting his arm around his wife, Noah finished her thought. "At times, we fear that mankind will not survive…and that maybe mankind is not worth saving. But when you arrived, having traveled here from the future, you showed us that we *will* make it, and that the Almighty, who is marvelous in work and deed, will fulfill the promise He made to my forefather Adam."

A single tear slid down Rebecca's cheek as the realization struck her that, somehow, God had used this crazy journey through time to encourage His servant Noah and his family at this crucial moment, and He had used *her and her friends* to do it! Not only that, but her own peace and strength had been restored as well by Noah.

Lord, you orchestrated all of this! You're still in control, despite the coming darkness, she thought.

"Since we know you will want to attract as little attention as possible," Noah said, "we want you to take these clothes." Immediately, Japheth and Shem stepped forward and gave each of them a plain, but well-made robe and belt. With an apologetic look on his face, Noah turned to Goliath. "We hope yours fits you. We didn't have any your size, so my wife had to redo the stitching on one of ours."

Goliath nodded in acceptance of the gift, and for a brief moment, Rebecca saw a look of genuine thanks cross his features. Slipping the robes over their heads, Rebecca and the others each spoke their heartfelt thanks. Once they were finished donning their new outfits, Noah continued.

"Please do us the honor of accepting these gifts as well. This bag contains the medicine and bandages that you need for your friend." Taking the bundle from Eema's hand, Noah held it out toward Rebecca.

Gratefully accepting the brownish-colored cloth bag, Rebecca held it close, knowing that its contents could mean the difference between life and death for her friend.

"The ointment is to be placed directly onto the wound itself," Japheth's wife instructed. "And if he is able, have him drink one cup of the elixir twice a day."

"Thank you," Jeffrey said, his face reflecting his sincerity. "We are forever in your debt."

Reaching over to the shelf on which he had placed it earlier, Noah retrieved the map of the city. "Please take this. It should help you navigate the city. Remember what I said about which sections to avoid."

Nodding toward Ham's wife, Noah continued. "We pray that your journey will be successful. And if our Maker, who alone is worthy of praise, deems it necessary to prolong your journey, then we want you to have enough food." As he spoke, his daughters-in-law handed small sacks to Goliath, Jeffrey, and Jerome.

Glancing briefly at their contents, Jerome's eyes grew wide. "There's enough bread, fruit, and nuts to last us for at least a week!"

Honored and humbled by their gifts, Rebecca looked at Noah and his wife intently. "Thank you so much for the offer, but surely you have greater need of this food than we. You won't have any other source of food for over a year except what you have stored. And once you leave the Ark…"

Even before Mack had finished translating Rebecca's reply, Noah held up a hand to stop her. "Although the Lord, our Provider, had not revealed to me the exact length of time we would spend on the Ark, we have prepared enough food to last us and the animals for nearly two years. So, it appears we will have more than enough."

Realizing that she may have given away a bit of information that she shouldn't have, Rebecca remained silent. Next to her, Mack grinned. "Way to go, slick," he teased. "I'm going to have to start monitoring what you say before I translate. Otherwise, you may end up creating a rift in the space/time continuum by revealing too much information about the future."

Before Rebecca could think of a way to recover from her gaffe, Noah motioned for Ham to offer her the three folded garments which he still carried. "These are for your other friends, if they should need them."

Tears of gratitude began spilling down Rebecca's cheeks as she took the clothing from Ham. "Words are simply not enough to express our gratitude. We owe you so much. If you would permit me, I would like to pray for you and your family. In many ways, your journey will be much longer and more difficult than our own."

Although Noah and his family tried hard not to show it, Rebecca could see flickers of trepidation and anxiety about what the future would hold. For the first time, Rebecca found herself overcome with the knowledge of just how difficult this must be for Noah and his family. Just knowing that in only two short days, everyone and everything that they have ever known will cease to exist and they will be the sole survivors would be overwhelming.

Eema took her husband's hand and smiled weakly, the emotional pain reflected in her eyes. "Yes, please," she said softly.

Jeffrey, Jerome, and Goliath shifted uneasily as Rebecca began to pray. Uncomfortable with the open display of devotion, yet not wanting to offend their generous hosts, the three remained silent.

Mack glanced hesitantly at the others, uncertain how to act. He had not divulged to them the fact that he was now a believer, and was thankful that his role as translator gave him an excuse to join in the prayer.

When Rebecca had finished praying, Noah in turn began praying for his guests, causing Jeffrey and Goliath to look through the shaft above them at the ever-brightening sky impatiently. Once they had finished, Noah and Eema hugged each of them in turn and kissed them on the cheek.

Alarmed, lest Noah accidently discover that his human features were merely a holographic projection, Goliath bowed deeply, then grasped Noah's forearm before the man could move any closer. Offering a word of thanks, Goliath quickly broke his grip and turned toward the door. Although puzzled by the tall man's odd behavior, Noah brushed it off, took his place at the head of the procession, and led the group back to the entrance of the Ark.

The sun was just releasing its final hold on the eastern horizon when the group stepped out of the door of the giant ship and proceeded down the ramp onto dry land once more. Noah and his sons escorted Rebecca and the others through the gate and down the road toward the cluster of burned and collapsed buildings. Moving silently through the wreckage, the Patriarch led the group to the far side of one of the buildings. Set into the ground was the entrance to a cellar. The heavy, wooden doors that once guarded the opening were smashed into several pieces and burned. Jeffrey and Jerome immediately exchanged worried glances. If the vandals had plundered the cellar, they may have already taken the money.

Apparently unconcerned, Noah stopped the group and instructed them to remain where they were while he went below. After a few minutes of waiting, he reappeared carrying two leather pouches that reminded Rebecca of marble bags. Stepping up to her, Noah handed one to her and the other to Jeffrey. "There should be more than enough to purchase the protection of some soldiers, pay the expected bribe to the gatekeepers, pay Arngrim for his services, and anyone else along the way who may hinder you. Keep the bags hidden inside your robes. Separate the money and reveal only what you must."

Jeffrey immediately lifted the bottom of his robe and transferred portions of the money into the pockets of his pants. Seeing the wisdom in his actions, Rebecca did the same. With the money safely tucked away, Noah turned his back on the ruins of his former home and led the group back to the road.

When they neared the gate, Noah stopped and turned to face his guests. "This is where we must part. Remember, do not trust in anyone but the Lord your God—the Provider and Protector. May the Creator guide you and speed you on your way. Now go. Time is short, for tomorrow, the world ends."

With a final blessing, Noah, builder of the Ark of salvation, and his three sons—all forefathers of the human race—bid the travelers goodbye and closed the heavy wooden gate behind them.

—

As the strange travelers headed off into the woods, a shadow detached itself from one of the nearby trees. Pulling the cowl of its hood over its head with a pale-skinned hand, the dark form crept along behind them, its blood-red eyes watching their every move with intense interest...

14

RETURN TO THE PYRAMID

THE TRAVELERS MOVED cautiously through the forest, scrutinizing each shadow and hollow trunk intently, as if expecting something or someone to attack at any moment. Although none of them verbalized their feelings, they each felt an uneasiness and foreboding. The sense of peace that they had experienced with Noah was gone, replaced by a restlessness. The entire forest seemed like a cage that held some great predatory beast that awaited release.

Shortly after moving off into the forest, Jeffrey took out his commlink and contacted Lisa to update her on their situation as well as to inquire about Dr. Eisenberg's condition.

"Doc's doing amazingly well," Lisa's voice said excitedly through the communication device, "especially considering he should be dead. But, he's not out of the woods yet. I worry that he'll take a turn for the worse. Hopefully your medicine will help him, although I'm not real comfortable with giving him some unknown meds from some primitive culture. Didn't the ancient Egyptians use fly dung and stuff in their 'medicines'? How do we know this stuff is going to help him and not make him worse?"

If Lisa had been there in person, Rebecca felt she may have lost control and punched her once best friend. As it was, it took all of her strength of will to keep from grabbing Jeffrey's commlink and giving Lisa a piece of her mind. *She is totally clueless!* Rebecca vented inwardly. *This is NOT a primitive culture! In many ways, they are way more advanced than our own. Noah and his family probably know a whole lot more about medicine than any of our doctors.*

The impatient look on Rebecca's face that revealed her inward frustration went completely unnoticed by Jeffrey, who was concentrating on both their surroundings and on his conversation with Lisa. "It'll be okay. This guy who claims to be Noah certainly knows a lot about animals and how to care for them, and his 'boat-shaped zoo' is well thought out. He may be crazy, but he's definitely not stupid."

Rebecca felt her rage rise to the boiling point at his words. *'This guy who CLAIMS to be Noah'?*

Lisa's voice sounded relieved, but still worried. "I'll take your word for it. Please hurry back, and be careful."

"We will. See ya soon." Closing down his commlink, Jeffrey returned it to his belt beneath his robes.

Behind him, Rebecca seethed as memories of her husband's betrayal assaulted her. Biting her lip to keep from saying anything, she tried to turn her thoughts to other things.

Driven by the urgency of the knowledge that time was short for both Dr. Eisenberg and this world, Jeffrey set the pace as quickly as prudence allowed. Whatever effect the strange atmosphere was having upon their bodies was still present, allowing them to jog for long stretches of time without becoming winded. As such, they moved quickly through the forest with weapons raised, their thoughts returning to the nearly successful attack on Rebecca by the cat-like animal on their previous journey.

They traveled in relative silence, each lost in his or her own thoughts until they reached the edge of the forest just over two hours later. Once free of the dangers of the forest and the concealment it provided for predators, the group relaxed their vigilance and put away their weapons. Resettling their provisions and packs into more comfortable positions, they set off at a brisk run across the rolling hills and grasslands.

As they settled into a rhythm, Mack moved up alongside Rebecca. "Hey, can I ask you something?"

After glancing briefly in his direction, Rebecca returned her gaze to focusing on her running. "You just did."

Sensing that something was bothering her, Mack tried to lighten the mood. "Wow, look at you with the dry wit. Keep it up and I might consider letting you join me in my new standup routine I'm workin' on."

Casting him a lopsided grin, Rebecca relaxed, thankful for the distraction from her disturbing thoughts. "Sure. Ask away. What's on your mind?"

Glad that his humor had the desired effect, Mack turned his attention toward figuring out how to phrase his question. "Well, this might sound a bit strange, but I…do you…do you feel something odd? I mean, like odd as in…"

"…as in a heaviness?" Rebecca offered.

"Yeah!" he said excitedly. "So, you feel it too? For a while, I thought that maybe I was just going crazy. But the more we travel, the more I feel it."

Still focused on her running, Rebecca didn't look at him as she responded. "Let me guess, you started feeling it after we left Noah. Am I right?"

"Yeah, I did," he replied. "What is it? And what do you think's causing it?"

"I've been thinking about this for awhile," she said. "I didn't realize what it was though, until just a few hours ago when we left the Ark. Do you remember that when we first arrived here, we were constantly at each other's throats?"

Mack thought for a moment, trying to guess where the conversation was going. "Sure. But, I just figured it was due to all of the stress. It isn't every day that you have to face the reality that the end of the world is coming in less than forty-eight hours."

"I'm sure that had something to do with it," Rebecca agreed. "But, I think there's more to it than that. When we first walked into the Ark,

I felt a sudden sense of peace wash over me that I can only explain as coming from God. Surrounded by that peace, I suddenly saw my previous actions and attitudes in a new light. Then, as we left the Ark a few hours ago, the peace lifted and the heaviness returned. And when I heard Lisa's voice on the commlink, the old anger, frustration, and bitterness returned as if those feelings had been locked up and someone had just opened the door, releasing them."

A troubled expression settled on Mack's face as he considered her words. "Are you implying what I think you're implying?"

For the first time, Rebecca looked at Mack fully. "Yes. I believe that we are dealing with some kind of spiritual influence that feeds on our darker emotions. The reason we didn't feel them in the Ark is that God's presence was there, protecting Noah and his family. Once we left that covering, the evil forces were able to resume their attack."

Mack shivered violently as if a bucket of ice water had just been thrown on him. "Yeeeww. That gives me the willies. I used to watch a bunch of horror movies about demons and stuff, but it never really bothered me because I never thought they were real. I guess I didn't realize that believing in God also means believing in a real devil and demons, doesn't it?"

"Unfortunately, yes. They're real, and if what Noah says is true, we may even end up meeting one or two," Rebecca said. Unbidden, the images from her vision on the Ark shoved their way back into her conscious mind. "We must focus on praying. Never stop praying."

"But, there's one more thing I don't understand," Mack said. "How come I didn't notice it before?"

Rebecca regarded her friend with a warm expression. "Because, my dear friend, before, you didn't have the Spirit of the Living God dwelling in you."

Mack blushed and immediately looked sheepish. "Oh, yeah. Well, I...I guess that would do it."

"However, as much as I know there's a spiritual component to it, I also think there's something else." she stated.

"Something else?" Mack echoed in confusion. "Like what?"

"Did you see Goliath turn to look behind us just a moment ago?"

"Yeah. And I noticed that he stopped a couple of times and paused, looking around," Mack commented. "I thought he was just getting his bearings or something."

Rebecca nodded. "That's what I thought at first. But one time, I glanced over my shoulder and I could have sworn I saw something dark and shadowy about the size of a human moving among the grass far behind us. However, when I stopped to look more closely, it suddenly disappeared."

"Maybe all of this talk of demons and stuff has you a little jittery," Mack suggested. "Maybe it was just your imagination."

"I would agree with you, except I can't get it out of my head that we're being watched, not to mention the fact that judging by Goliath's actions, it appears that he feels something too. And, this grass is just long enough that it could easily hide someone if they lie flat upon the ground," Rebecca said.

"So, what do we do?" Mack asked, more disturbed than he let on. "Should we try to lose it?"

"I don't think we have the time," she answered, fighting to control her own fear. "Besides, once the outer doors on the pyramid are closed, the pyramid is pretty impenetrable. I think the best thing we can do now is be on our guard, and pray. We have a few hours left before we arrive at the pyramid. Would you please join me in prayer?"

Mack, looking uncertain, pushed a lock of curly black hair off his sweat filled brow. "Sure. But I…I'm not really sure how."

"Don't worry. It's just like talking to a friend," Rebecca replied. "I'll teach you."

The remainder of the journey was uneventful, allowing Rebecca a couple of hours of uninterrupted time to both teach her pupil some pointers about prayer, and lots of time to practice. By the time they reached the landing site, the sun had worked its way near its zenith. As they rounded the last hill, the group could see two figures standing in the doorway of the pyramid. Upon first glancing the approaching group, one of the two leapt out of the entrance and began heading toward them at a full run. The light brown skin and blond hair made the identity of the figure instantly apparent.

The moment Rebecca saw Lisa running toward them, a surge of rage welled up within her with such force that Rebecca was forced to stop running. *Here she comes, that two-faced little tramp! Running toward* MY HUSBAND *like she's some lovesick puppy. I'd like to take that pretty little face of hers and…*

Shocked by her own thoughts, Rebecca put her hands to her face and closed her eyes. *Lord, help me to forgive! I want to feed the hate, but I know that's not your will. And with everything we're facing, the last thing we need right now is to be divided. I just can't forgive them yet, Lord. But, at least help me to get through this.*

A gentle pressure on her shoulder caused her to remove her hands from her eyes to see Mack standing in front of her, concern for her clearly written on his face. "Are you okay? What's wrong?"

Not sure how to respond, Rebecca simply replied, "Just keep praying." With that, she took a deep breath and strode over to where Lisa and Jeffrey were deep in an animated conversation. As she passed them, she spoke in the most even voice she could muster, not daring to look at them. "I have the meds for Doc. I would appreciate it if you would give me a hand." Not even turning to see if Lisa was following behind her, Rebecca kept walking past Akwen and into the cool interior of the pyramid.

Going immediately to see Dr. Eisenberg, she opened the door and stepped inside the room in which he lay. To her surprise, his eyes opened as she entered and a broad smile lit up his features. "My dearest Rebecca! What a pleasure it is to see your beautiful face," he managed, his voice sounding tired, yet strong. "I was afraid I wouldn't get the chance to see you again this side of eternity."

Walking over to the massive, nine-foot long bed, she laughed as tears of joy began sliding down her cheeks. "Me too. You really gave us a scare. We thought we were going to lose you."

"I told you not to go picking out flowers for my funeral just yet," he said. "I'm a tough old bird. I've still got some fight left in me."

Taking out the medicine and bandages given to her by Eema, she laid them out on the bed. "Doc, we got you some medicine. Did Lisa tell you where it's from? Did she tell you where—I mean—'when' we are?"

"Yes. She told me everything, including the fact that we are in a bit of hot water, or at least might be soon enough," he replied.

A sour look crossed Rebecca's features at the pun. "Not funny, Doc."

"Sorry. But when you've faced death once, it tends to take the edge off," he said. "Especially when you know your final destination."

Opening the jar of medicine, Rebecca sat the doctor up with pillows and offered it to him. "Here, drink this. Noah's daughter-in-law said you were to take some twice a day."

A moment after the liquid touched his lips, the doctor scrunched his face in disgust. "Wow. What is that stuff? It's quite bitter."

Despite the unpleasant flavor, he continued to drink the elixir until he had drained the cup. As Rebecca laid him back down, the door opened and Lisa entered. The two women exchanged brief glances, then looked solely at their patient.

"We're going to change your bandages and put some ointment on the wound," Rebecca informed him as she began to unbutton his shirt to reveal his wounded side. "Then we have to go. Did you hear about what Noah said we should do to fix the pyramid?"

Wincing in pain as the two women removed the old dressing, Dr. Eisenberg shook his head slightly. While they worked, Rebecca filled the doctor and Lisa in briefly on what had happened. Although she was focused on relating the past events, Rebecca paused in astonishment as they cleaned his wound.

"Doc, this is amazing! Even with very little medical attention, your side has already begun to heal!" Rebecca stated.

"Yes, that's what Lisa tells me," he replied. "Tell me, Rebecca, do you believe it's the hand of God that is healing me?"

Taking his hand in her own, she said, "I learned years ago to always give God the glory for every good thing. So, yes, I believe it *is* the hand of God. At the same time, I believe that He often works through natural means. In this case, we've discovered that there seems to be something in the atmosphere that gives all living things extra energy or vitality. Mack doesn't have asthma anymore, we were able to run long distances without getting tired, and we observed fruit that was abnormally large. It's just a theory, but I think there's more oxygen in the atmosphere."

The doctor was silent for a moment as he considered her words. "Yes, that would make sense. There's probably more to it than that, but that would explain a lot. For one thing, it would explain why, according to the Bible, many of the pre-flood patriarchs lived to be over nine hundred years old."

Having finished cleaning the wound, Lisa and Rebecca had begun dressing it with the fresh bandages when Dr. Eisenberg suddenly spoke up, excitement in his voice. "I just remembered a study I read years ago about how scientists had found air bubbles trapped in amber. When they analyzed the gases trapped in the bubbles, they contained 35 percent oxygen!"[1]

Rebecca paused in her work, not understanding the reason for the doctor's excitement. "Really? That's almost double the normal ratio."

"This article was written from an evolutionary perspective, so I don't buy into their time-scale interpretation, but it matches what we see here," he stated. "The authors also speculated that a drop in the level of oxygen could have been one thing that led to the extinction of dinosaurs. Think about it, before the flood, they grew to be large partially because they may have lived longer, like humans, and the atmosphere was rich with oxygen. Then, after the Flood, the atmosphere changed, causing animals and humans to live shorter lives and not grow as big. Dinosaurs were then hunted down and driven to extinction."

---

1. "Air Bubbles, Amber, and Dinosaurs" U.S. Geological Survey, June 01, 2009. http://minerals.cr.usgs.gov/gips/na/amber.html (accessed December 16, 2010).

Glancing at her co-worker, Rebecca noticed that Lisa looked pale and sickly, clearly disturbed by the implications of their conversation. Fighting the urge to gloat at her former friend's apparent misery, Rebecca returned her focus to her work and their conversation. "It does make a lot of sense. But frankly, I'm just glad that this atmospheric change seems to be helping *you*."

Finished with their work, Lisa mumbled a quick goodbye and left the room. Once she had departed, Rebecca said, "Well, Doc, you're all set. Now get some rest."

"Yes, ma'am," he replied. "Be careful, and come back quickly. I really would like to make it back home, especially now that I know the truth. There is so much research I want to do, and so many people that I want to talk to, such as…my son."

"I understand, Doc," she said. "I wish you could have been with us on the Ark. It was so incredible. When this is all over, I'll tell you everything we learned. We found the answers to so many questions!"

"Please don't remind me!" he said. "I would've given anything to have been with you. I will look forward to your report on the subject."

"It was so amazing that even Jeffrey was impressed," she added. "Oh, and by the way, I have a bit of news that will help you rest a little easier. We have a new member in the family of God."

His eyes widened as joy lit up his face. "Who? Jeffrey?"

"No," she said wistfully. "Mack."

Although disappointed that it had not been Rebecca's husband, the doctor still smiled broadly at the news. "Praise God. I am so glad for him. Now maybe he will get those silly movies out of his head and start focusing on something that really matters."

Rebecca grinned. "Don't count on it." Leaning forward, she kissed him on the cheek. "We'll be back as soon as we can."

"And while you are gone, know that I'll be praying for you, and that God will open the eyes of the others as he opened Mack's eyes, and my own."

"Thanks," she said. For a brief moment, she paused, wondering if she should tell him about her vision. Deciding that it would probably only serve to worry him and prevent him from getting some much needed rest, she kept it to herself. Kissing him lovingly on his forehead, Rebecca walked toward the door. Wondering if this might be the last time she would see him, she fought to control the emotion in her voice as she said, "Goodbye, Doc. See you soon."

"I have tried everting I can tink of, and yet, I get da same result. Nuhting!" Akwen said as she slammed her hand down on the edge of the control console in frustration. "Elmer and I have been working on dis stupid ting since you left. Whatever shut it down has it locked up tight." At the mention of his name, the floating droid turned its circular head and regarded her silently with the beady pinpricks of light that served as its eyes.

"Don't worry about it," Jeffrey said, in an attempt to calm her down. "You gave it your best shot. We just have to hope that we can find this Arngrim guy and convince him to help us."

"Which isn't much of a hope at all, from what I hear," she replied, a doubtful expression on her face. "Let's face facts, Jeffrey, we're going to die."

"I'm not ready to concede defeat just yet. We'll get through this—"

"Why is it dat men are always lying about da seriousness of situations?" Akwen shouted. "I'm not some child dat needs to be comforted."

"Well, what do you want me to say?" Jeffrey yelled back. "'Yes, Akwen, we're all going to be drowned in a massive flood, so you'd better bring your snorkel'?"

For a moment, the two of them simply stared at each other, anger smoldering between them. Then, like a small crack that announces the forthcoming breaking of a dam, Akwen's lip began slowly curving into a smile until, unable to contain it any longer, she let out a full-throated laugh. With the tension released, Jeffrey joined her until they were both in tears.

Finally regaining control, Akwen said, "A snorkel? Where did dat come from?"

Shrugging his shoulders, Jeffrey said, "I don't know. I guess it's just the pressure of everything coming through."

An awkward silence descended upon them, which served to sober them immediately. "I guess I can accept da fact dat we are going to die," Akwen said at last. "It's just hard to come to grips wit da realization dat I will never see my children again."

Jeffrey paused for a moment before replying. "Seriously, we can't give up hope just yet. I know our chances seem dismal, but if we give up now, then we're *really* dead."

"Listen to you, talking about hope as if you believed in God," she stated. "Why should we believe in hope? You know just as well as I do dat dis world is random and witout purpose. Pain and suffering are just part of life," she said, as if it were a well rehearsed mantra. "Dere is no God directing our lives. And if dere is, I've got a few bones to pick wit Him when I die."

"Yeah…" Jeffrey agreed quietly, his face devoid of expression as he stared vacantly.

Before either of them could say anything further, Jerome appeared at the top of the steps. "Hey, Jeffrey, we're ready to go when you are."

Shaking himself as if to ward off whatever unpleasant thoughts were plaguing him, he stood, once more in control. "Alright. Let's get this over with. See ya later, Akwen. And don't forget to oil up the scuba gear."

Raising a sarcastic eyebrow, she said, "Sure ting, boss."

Confused by Jeffrey's last comment, Jerome shot him a questioning look as the two of them headed down the stairs. They joined Mack, Goliath, and Rebecca who all stood near the entrance waiting for them. As the group exited the pyramid and headed out across the plains toward the city in the distance, Jeffrey reflected upon Akwen's words. In his mind, he kept repeating the same things over and over, as if trying desperately to convince himself of their truth. *Death and suffering are just part of life. There is no God directing our lives. There is no God directing our lives…*

15

ENTERING THE CITY

THE GROUP REMAINED silent as they ran, each preoccupied by his or her own thoughts. Working their way across the rolling hills, they eventually came upon the road that led to the main gate of the city. Small caravans of people, animals, and carts made their way to and from the city along the wide road. Since there were few trees or other objects to hide behind, Rebecca and the others pulled the hoods of their robes low over their heads and nervously made their way toward the road, expecting at any moment to draw the attention of some of the other passersby. Although many on the road *did* see them and cast uneasy glances at Goliath, the appearance of Rebecca's group didn't herald much of a disturbance.

The dirt road was well-worn and full of holes, ruts, and cracks. However, as they began moving across its uneven surface, they soon forgot about the road itself, for as they walked, they got their first glimpse of the decadence and depravity for which these people were soon to be judged.

Long gutters ran along the sides of the slightly elevated road. Several comatose figures lay on top of the trash, animal waste, and other unrecognizable objects. Despite being outdoors, putrid smells still wafted across the road, almost as if the gentle breeze itself were mocking them. Flies, rodents, and carrion birds could all be seen swarming around here and there, looking for a meal. The site was so revolting that Rebecca could feel the bile rising in her throat.

Noticing the horrified looks on the faces of his companions, Goliath turned to them and whispered a harsh warning. "You must not react to what you see, or we're all dead. Those who prey on fear will pick you out easily. Remember, these people are numb to this. It's routine for them. They see it every day. Act nonchalant and casual, no matter what we come across."

Taking this warning to heart and struggling to keep down the contents of her stomach, Rebecca and the others immediately concentrated on keeping their faces impassive and emotionless. It was a constant battle, for as they walked, more horrors of human immorality assailed them. The more people they passed that were leaving the city, the more they could see what Noah and his family had warned about.

Many of the travelers had features that were clearly not normal. Some had too much or too little hair; eyes that were too big, or oddly shaped; ears that looked like they belonged to some kind of animal; noses that were too long for their faces and limbs that were too long or too short in proportion to their height. In addition, there were many who walked with a limp, or suffered with other deformities due to either maltreatment or experiments that went wrong. Near the gutters, beggars called out to those on the road. Rebecca made the mistake of glancing at one of the beggars, and immediately returned her attention to the road, for the thing that called out to her was barely recognizable as a human. Rather, its mutated form looked like something out of a sick, perverted nightmare.

Even the animals bore testimony to the evil of the world. Each one Rebecca and the others passed showed signs of abuse, and many exhibited some of the same deformities and genetic tampering as their human masters.

What was even more disconcerting than the physical appearances of the people on the road was the hunted, and haunted, expressions that they wore like masks. The eyes of many of those on the road shifted constantly, as if expecting an attack from the other travelers. Several others appeared to be studying those around them carefully, as if searching for easy prey. Everyone they passed had hands that rested on the hilts of swords, axes, or other weapons, ready to defend themselves if attacked.

Judging by their stiff posture and disturbed glances, it became clear to Rebecca that her companions had observed the same thing. Goliath walked in the front with shoulders back and his hand on the hilt of Nimrod's sword, as if daring anyone to challenge him. Glancing behind her, she could see her own fear, shock, and horror reflected on the faces of Jeffrey and Jerome, whose hands also rested nervously on the hilts of their newly acquired swords. Mack, walking beside her, was pale. He gripped his sword so tightly that Rebecca feared he would injure himself.

As she studied their surroundings, Rebecca began to understand why Noah had suggested they hire bodyguards. If the road leading to the city was this dangerous, she could only imagine how bad the city itself would be. Constant vigilance would be required to live in a world of so much evil, and the weight of that vigilance could easily drive a person insane or schizophrenic. Gripping the handle of her gun beneath her robes tightly, she continually scanned those walking near them, praying desperately to God for protection as she nervously cracked the knuckles of her left hand against her thigh.

The further they traveled, the more Rebecca began to notice that not all of the travelers on the road appeared murderous. In fact, more often than not, she noticed expressions of despair and hopelessness on their faces. Their shoulders were slumped, their heads drooped, and they shuffled along weakly. Life to them was constant pain and suffering, with no hope of relief or rescue. They limped through life; their only hope was a quick death.

Rebecca recognized the expression. She had seen it before on the faces of the slaves she had encountered during her journey to the planet Ka'esch. For the first time, she began to see the Flood of Noah in a different light. To the oppressed and abused, it would serve to cut short a life that would contain nothing but pain and suffering. Grief and sadness for the whole of humankind filled her heart. Fighting back tears, she forced herself to concentrate on the task at hand. Although her encounter with the aliens on Ka'esch had been a vision, the memories of all that had happened to her were real. Drawing on those experiences, she hardened her expression and buried her feelings. As life had been on that alien planet, so it was here: *Power to the strong and intelligent, death to the weak and stupid.*

The trip to the city seemed to take forever. Finally, after an hour of walking, they drew near enough that they could begin to make out the details. The sheer enormity of the metropolis stunned them.

The twenty-foot-tall, grey walls of the city stood out in stark contrast to the vibrant green of the surrounding grasslands. From where the group stood on the road about a mile from the city, it appeared that a wide, fast-flowing river came from the west and bisected the city before exiting to the east. The portion of the city built along the southern banks of the river was divided into three clear sections by massive stone walls. Based upon what they had learned from Noah, they knew that the southwestern area belonged to the Nephilim, the humans controlled the middle section, and the area to the southeast belonged to the alfheim. According to Noah, the Blood Drinkers that had attacked them were part of this group of genetically altered humans.

The northern section of the city was built upon a plateau that rose several hundred feet up from the river and stretched out for miles. In size, color, elevation, and splendor, the northern section's majesty left no doubt as to which portion of the city housed the rulers, and which housed the servants. Magnificent buttresses, towers, and domes—each reflecting dazzling hues of color from the gemstones that were set into their surfaces—littered the landscape. A large but beautiful wall of shimmering blue split the city down the middle, and to the eyes of the visitors, it appeared that the eastern and western sides of the majestic city were locked in a never-ending contest of vanity to see which side could build the most glorious buildings and temples.

Despite the beauty of the northern section of the city, a bitter chill stole the warmth from Rebecca's body. It was not the weather itself that provided the chill, but rather it was the knowledge that the outward beauty of the shining edifices housed beings of pure evil and concealed unspeakable acts of wickedness.

Hawkers announcing their wares drew her attention back from the northern portion of the city to her immediate surroundings. As Rebecca and the others traveled the last several hundred feet toward the gate in the outer wall, groups of vendors stationed along the edges of the road called out to them, inviting them to taste and examine various foods and items of interest.

Ignoring them, Rebecca kept her focus on studying the people around her, looking for any signs of danger. The closer her group got to the gates, the thicker the crowd of people became. More and more vendors were spread out along the wall, selling to both those leaving and entering the city. Shouts rang out as vendors sought to outdo each other, snippets of conversation, and short spurts of laughter mixed with the sounds of rolling carts and animals braying, squawking, and squealing. The din was overwhelming.

Ahead, Goliath shouted something as he nodded toward a group of men standing near the wall. Or at least, they had the form of men. However, as Goliath led Rebecca and the others closer to the group, she could see that they were more than just men.

They were monsters.

For a moment, even Goliath slowed his pace as he got a better look at the mercenaries, surprise and shock registering on the holographic image that obscured his real face. Still, the shock that the giant felt paled in comparison to that which was experienced by his companions.

The soldiers stood nearly nine feet tall, with broad shoulders and rippling muscles. Each was clad in metallic armor that at one time had probably been beautifully decorated and impressive, but which was now dull, scratched, and dented. Each mercenary either held a long spear in his hands or had it resting against the wall nearby. Holstered short swords were strapped about their thick waists by heavy leather belts. The bare thighs and legs which extended down below their armored skirts and into their animal hide boots were like massive tree trunks.

The *main* sources of the visitors' shock, however, were their faces and hands. Although their basic features were human, each had unmistakable characteristics of different animals. Some had the pointed ears and rounded snouts of a cat, others had reptilian influences, including skin that looked almost scale-like. Sickly yellow spikes stuck out from the arms of two of the mercenaries, and another pair had horns protruding from their heads. In place of hands, each of their long arms ended in powerful, animal-like claws. Sharp nails that looked strong enough to slice easily through flesh protruded from the ends of each thick finger.

It was not the disturbing appearance of the mercenaries as a whole that caused Rebecca and the others to stare in shock, but rather a particular handful of the animal-like men that drew their attention. This group had course hair of various dark shades covered nearly their entire heads, except for the immediate area around their eyes, noses, and mouths. The animal-like influence of this group was clearly mammalian. In particular, two of them displayed ape-like features, while the other three had pointed ears and elongated snouts similar to a wolf.

"Oh my Lord," Jerome breathed in alarm. "They look just like… like…"

"…like Goliath and his buddy Hercules," Jeffrey finished, his own amazement reflected in his voice. "But…but how?"

Rebecca and the others stared at their giant companion in confusion, hoping for an explanation. Stopping their party while they were still several dozen feet from the beastly men, Goliath turned to face his companions, a look of impatience on his face. "I am just as confused as you are. How should I know why there's a resemblance?"

Mack suddenly inhaled sharply. When the others turned to look at him, they noticed his gaze was fixed on Goliath. "Because you know that they were made the same way you were."

"What are you talking about?" Jeffrey asked.

Still not taking his focus off of Goliath, Mack continued. "You aren't a cyborg or a Naphil. You're one of these creatures. That explains why you were so interested when Shem talked about how the Fallen Ones had perverted life with their technology."

"What are you saying?" Jerome said, glancing nervously in Goliath's direction. "Do you mean to tell me that Goliath is some kind of...of genetically altered creature from this time period?"

Goliath, who didn't seem the slightest bit bothered by Mack's accusation, was continually keeping a wary eye on those around them. Leaning over slightly to bring his eight-foot frame closer to his companions, he said, "Think what you want about me, but I really don't think this is the time or place to be having this discussion."

Trying to be indiscreet about it, Rebecca and the others looked around them to see that a few members of the crowd were beginning to take an interest in them. Wanting more answers, but understanding the delicacy of their situation, Jeffrey conceded. "Fine. But as soon as we get a chance, we need to discuss this further."

"If you're done, I suggest we get moving," the giant said. "Oh, and one more thing: these people are going to be like Nimrod. They've never heard any other languages, so we need to let Mack do *all* of the talking. Do *not* talk to each other except in the softest of whispers. Mack and I will approach the mercenaries to hire them, the rest of you wait several feet behind us. And keep your eyes open and your weapons handy." Turning to face Mack, he stared at him intently. "Whatever you think about me, put it out of your mind for now. You've got a job to do. Have you ever haggled before?"

Clearly nervous, Mack simply nodded affirmative.

"I hope it was about something more important than just a comic book or something," Goliath added with a sneer. "Show no fear. Remember, they're standing here because they *want* to be hired. The only thing you have to do is tell them where we want to go and negotiate a fair price. Offer half of the payment now, and half when we arrive. Just follow Noah's instructions and everything should go smoothly."

With that, Goliath straightened up and gestured for Mack to lead the way. With a quick glance at Rebecca and the others, Mack shot them a lopsided grin, ran his hand through his curly mass of hair, and headed off toward the mercenaries.

Following Goliath's suggestion, Jeffrey, Jerome, and Rebecca waited while Mack and Goliath approached the group. Rebecca held her breath as the two made initial contact with the men. When it appeared that all was going well, she relaxed somewhat and offered up a quick prayer of thanks.

"I hate this," Jerome whispered harshly. "Goliath obviously doesn't want us to know who he really is. If he's one of these things, then how did he get to our time, and what's he *really* up to?"

Jeffrey shook his head, his own frustration evident. "I have no idea, but I don't think he's from the past."

"What makes you think that?" Jerome said, frowning.

"Because he speaks our language, for one thing," Jeffrey replied. "And, he knows too much about our culture. For instance, just a minute ago he mentioned a comic book. Somehow I don't think someone from this time would know about that."

"But that doesn't necessarily mean anything," Rebecca countered. "We're talking about time travel. Maybe he and Hercules came to our time period and lived among us for awhile, learning our language and culture."

"And, it would explain why they have greater technology than us," Jerome added.

Seeing the wisdom in their arguments, Jeffrey swore softly in frustration. "This trip just keeps getting better all the time. I just hope lack of knowledge doesn't come back to bite us."

"It looks like they're almost done," Rebecca said.

Jeffrey and Jerome turned toward Mack to see him doling out coins to a pair of the wolf-like mercenaries. A moment later, Mack and Goliath walked toward the rest of their companions, the pair of mercenaries beside them. When they were close enough to the others, Mack made an "okay" sign with his hand. Without speaking, one of the newly acquired bodyguards moved to the front of the group with Goliath while the other one took up a position at the rear of the group.

The mercenary in front led them toward the line of people entering the city. They were forced to wait for nearly half an hour before they reached the front of the line. Remembering Noah's instructions, Mack handed Goliath several coins to be distributed to the guards at the gate. Since the bribe that Goliath offered was triple what the guards were used to receiving, they smiled at the group and let them in quickly without asking any questions.

As they passed between the thick, oaken set of gates, Mack leaned close to Rebecca. "It almost feels like we're being dishonest," he whispered. "We're giving them all of this money, but in a day it'll be worthless to them."

"Don't feel too sorry for them," Rebecca replied. "I wonder how many people they abused and cheated over the years."

Mack didn't reply, for at that moment, they left the entranceway and began walking down the wide main street of the city, their attention captured by what lay before them.

16

THE WICKEDNESS OF MANKIND

THE BUILDINGS THAT made up the city were a tapestry of architectural styles. Some blocks contained houses that were not much more than huts, while others were walled mansions that were beautiful to behold. Oddly enough, the mansions appeared almost futuristic, showing that at least some in this culture had a highly advanced knowledge of construction. In the wealthier sections of the city, wondrous marble statues of heroic figures and spectacular frescos painted in vibrant colors covered the smooth surfaces of the buildings.

However, all of the beauty and grandeur of the city was completely lost upon the visitors, for the actions and behavior of the city's many occupants demanded attention. Although Rebecca could see more of the animal-like, giant soldiers stationed at various points around the city, they seemed so accustomed to the violence surrounding them that they ignored most of it. Many of the citizens who travelled the streets were accompanied by bodyguards. Those that weren't, were either warriors themselves, or were desperate enough to risk their lives.

Even though what they had seen outside the city had sickened and disgusted the travelers, the sights that awaited them within so shocked and horrified them, that forever afterward the images became seared into their minds and haunted them in their dreams. Several times Rebecca,

Mack, Jerome, and Jeffrey felt their bodies convulse as bile threatened to expel itself from their stomachs.

As they traversed the city, it seemed to Rebecca that the sole pastime for these people must be the pursuit of new forms of wickedness. On several occasions, the two mercenary bodyguards that Mack hired had to intervene to protect their charges from the unruliness of other pedestrians.

Violence permeated the city. Despite the fact that evening was still several hours away, drunken men brawled in the streets. On occasion, one of the two brawlers would wind up dead with some sharp object protruding from a vital place of his body. At one point, Rebecca watched in horror as a man was mercilessly beating a woman on an adjoining pathway. Even young children did not escape the ruthless brutality of the adults around them.

Gangs roamed freely. From time to time, the lead bodyguard detoured Rebecca's group from the main thoroughfare to avoid a large confrontation that was occurring between rival gangs or between the gangs and the city guards. Catching glimpses of the competing groups, Rebecca's heart threatened to burst from pain as she realized that many of the gang members were barely more than children. In addition to their genetically altered appearances, the pure lack of compassion and utter viciousness that she saw reflected on their faces disturbed her greatly.

At one point, as they passed a house, they were startled as three children erupted from a doorway screaming at one another. They couldn't have been more than four years old, yet two of them grabbed the other and proceeded to attack him until blood ran freely.

Still more horrifying than the violence alone were the sexual perversions. The sounds that filled the air as people committed indecent acts with each other nearly drove Rebecca to her knees. The denizens of this city seemed to know no shame as they sought out their sick pleasures freely in doorways, alleys, and even in the streets.

If she had been riding in a vehicle, Rebecca would have closed her eyes for the remainder of the journey, but since she was walking, she was forced to settle with keeping her eyes focused on Goliath's back. Her stare was so intense that it almost seemed that she was trying to burn a hole in his back.

Although she no longer looked at her surroundings, the images that she had seen replayed over in over in her mind, torturing her with images of suffering and pain. The sounds of present suffering contrasted sharply with those of perverse pleasure, caused sickening mental pictures to flash through her mind.

More than anything else she had seen, it was the faces of the children that pounded against her psyche. Vacant stares of children whose entire existence consisted of nothing more than serving as a punching bag or plaything for vile men and women. In contrast were the hate-filled and pitiless eyes of other children, who would soon cease to be the prey and undoubtedly become the predators.

The sudden sound of laughter, cheering, and pleasant music broke through Rebecca's mental turmoil and drew her gaze. To her left, a city park was filled with elegantly-dressed people who were cheering a happy couple who stood at the end of a long aisle. Although the sight of the wedding procession amidst so much evil shocked her, that shock intensified when she noticed that the scantily clad couple was not even a man and a woman, but two men, one of which had lizard-like features.

Crushed by grief and outrage, Rebecca fought a losing battle against her emotions. Remembering Goliath's warning, she shut her eyes tightly for a moment, hoping to stem the tide of burning tears that threatened to flood her eyes. Praying fervently, Rebecca struggled for control.

The sound of rushing water mingled with the noises of a market to create a deafening cacophony. Opening her eyes slowly, Rebecca noticed that her group had now entered what could only be the center of the city. The mighty river that they had seen from a distance flowed from west to east directly in front of them. A wide-open plaza formed a semicircle with the river as its northern border and numerous shops and other buildings formed the perimeter. People streamed into the plaza from three thoroughfares: one to the west, one to the east, and the one on which she currently stood that led to the south. Across the river, the northern portion of the city rose impressively, seeming much larger and more intimidating than Rebecca imagined. Along the southern bank of the river, in the center of the plaza, stood an enormous tree, its lengthy branches stretching out to cover nearly the entire mile-wide area.

The plaza was filled with people of various shapes, sizes, and degrees of genetic modification. Tall, pale figures with pointed ears that bore an unmistakable resemblance to the vampire-like creatures that attacked her group earlier congregated near the eastern edge. Other 'humans,' who appeared to be the least genetically altered or polluted, stayed mostly to the center of the market. The western side of the plaza, off to Rebecca's left, was dominated by creatures that were yet a head or more taller than even the mercenaries that Rebecca's group had hired.

"The Nephilim!" Jerome said, speaking the name with both fear and awe, for the beings deserved both.

Standing roughly twelve feet in height, the Nephilim were truly imposing. Their bodies were broad and muscular, and, although they were hairier than the average human, they had less hair than the genetically altered animal-like mercenaries and city guards. In fact, to Rebecca's surprise, she discovered that every one of them was strikingly handsome, despite their rugged appearances. Many of the giants had thick manes of hair and beards that were intricately braided. Their skin was bronzed, making them look like great statues of gods, sculpted from polished metal. Wherever they went, crowds parted in fear and awe.

Accustomed to the sights and sounds of the city, the hired bodyguards kept the group moving. To Rebecca's dismay, they turned to the left and began heading toward the shops near the Nephilim.

A sudden shout rang through the air, drawing Rebecca's attention away from the giants. Following the sound to its source, she saw a crowd of people gathered around a makeshift stage set up not far from where she now walked. On the stage, a man called out to the crowd while gesturing toward a pitiful little girl that stood on a slowly rotating platform to his right. The girl was no more than six years old and wore nothing but a dirty tunic filled with holes and rips. Her hands and feet were bound with chains. White lines streaked down her face where tears had made paths through the dirt that caked her face.

The sight of the men leering at the child eagerly and waving money in the air was like a punch to Rebecca's stomach. Doubling over, she tried to breathe. Jeffrey's firm hands grabbed her from behind and brought her back to her feet. "We have to keep moving," he whispered in her ear. "Our bodyguards are starting to take an interest in you, as are several bystanders. Be strong, Becky. For all our sakes."

Setting her will, Rebecca nodded and concentrated on putting one foot in front of the other. The mercenary leading the group pointed to a building ahead and to the left. Thankful that their trip through the city was nearing its end, Rebecca walked on.

It was then that she heard the baby's cry. The sound seemed to carry across the wind through the competing noise of the plaza directly to her, as if calling her name. Time seemed to slow to a crawl and Rebecca lost all sense of her immediate surroundings. The yelling of the vendors, the voice of the auctioneer, and the sounds of the crowds, all faded from her mind. There, near the banks of the river, a woman carried a newborn in her arms. Two men accompanied her, both walking behind her. Fear clutched at Rebecca as she observed the coldness and cruelty in the men's eyes. The woman, by contrast, wore a blank expression, as if resigned to her course of action.

The three of them walked to the edge of the riverbank and stopped. Below them, the river foamed and frothed as it angrily crashed against the rocks. The crowds in the plaza continued on with their business, paying no attention to the trio. Yet, to Rebecca, nothing else existed *except* them.

Stepping up to the woman, one of the men reached out to take the screaming baby from her arms. Only then did the woman react. Clutching the child to her breast, she began to beg and plead with the man. Callously, the second man backhanded her while the first took the bundle from her hands. The woman collapsed to the ground, sobs wracking her body.

Dread grew in Rebecca's heart as the scene unfolded. With painful certainty, she knew what was coming. "No," she muttered softly. "Oh, God, no!" More than a hundred feet separated Rebecca from the men, and she knew there was nothing she could do. She could never reach them in time. As the man lifted the baby over the rocks, a guttural scream erupted from Rebecca's body. "NOOOOOO!"

Unable to watch the actual act unfold, she turned away from the scene and buried her head in Jeffrey's chest. Somewhere behind her, away from the tragedy by the river, a crowd suddenly erupted in cheers. Although she knew their cheers were completely unrelated to what she had just witnessed, to her overwrought mind, it seemed as if the rejoicing belonged to a host of unseen, foul beings that were relishing a victory. When the cheers died down, Rebecca could no longer hear the baby's cries.

"Shut her up!" Goliath hissed from somewhere nearby. Scanning the area, the giant noticed that Rebecca's shout, while not loud enough to carry across the entire plaza, had still drawn the attention of those standing nearby. "Everyone's staring at us!"

Mack and Jerome, who were also still in shock from what they had witnessed, simply stared at Goliath dumbly. Forcing himself to tear his eyes away from the two men still standing by the riverbank, Jeffrey wrapped his arms around Rebecca and tried to comfort her, a solitary tear sliding down his cheek.

Disturbed by the sudden attention they were receiving, Goliath began pushing the group to get them moving once more. The giant's actions had the desired effect. Stumbling to remain on their feet, Jerome and Mack realized their danger and moved as quickly as they could toward the building that their guide indicated as their destination. Then, wrapping his large arms around Rebecca, the giant picked her up and threw her over his shoulder like a sack. Shoving Jeffrey, Goliath sent him sprawling onto the ground as he let out an evil sounding laugh.

Stunned, Jeffrey adjusted his hood, which had fallen over his eyes, then looked up at Goliath in confusion. The giant merely kept laughing, and then headed off toward the building, followed by the two bodyguards who were thoroughly enjoying the 'joke.' Anger dissipating his confusion, Jeffrey leapt to his feet and charged after Goliath.

Seeing the attack, the two mercenaries tensed and gripped their weapons firmly. Waving at them to stand down, Goliath tightened his grip on Rebecca as she began to kick at him. As Jeffrey got closer, the giant took Rebecca off of his shoulder and dropped her unceremoniously to the ground.

Swearing at Goliath, Jeffrey helped Rebecca to her feet. "Just what do you think you're doing?" he spat.

"Saving our lives," Goliath shot back vehemently.

Looking around, Jeffrey could see that although many of those who were following the actions of their group were chuckling at his predicament, most had lost interest and had turned their attention back to their own business. Realizing that Goliath had pretended to steal Rebecca from him to explain her outburst, Jeffrey took a deep breath to calm his anger.

Casting a spiteful look at the giant, Jeffrey put his arm around his wife, who was still stunned by all that had happened, and led her to where Mack and Jerome waited.

"Is this Arngrim's shop?" Jeffrey asked softly as he studied the marble building that stood before them.

"Yes, according to Noah's map," Mack replied, matching the volume of Jeffrey's voice. "What just happened back there?"

Glancing over his shoulder to see Goliath and the two mercenaries approaching, Jeffrey said curtly, "Nothing. I'll explain later."

As per the initial agreement, the two wolf-like bodyguards planted their spears into the ground near the bottom of the stairs and leaned up against two thick columns to wait for their employers to finish their business.

Holding Rebecca at arm's length, Jeffrey studied her face with concern. "Are you going to be okay?"

Not trusting her voice, Rebecca wiped her eyes with the sleeve of her robe and simply nodded.

"Okay then. Mack, lead the way," Jeffrey said, looking up toward the building.

Arngrim's shop was one of many that were situated next to each other, with only a narrow, four-foot alleyway between them. Each of the marble buildings was exquisitely constructed, their magnificent facades enhanced by expertly crafted designs and carvings etched into their surfaces. Elegant and sometimes lewd statues of human-like figures stood amongst the columns that held up the roofs of the porches. Brilliant flowers placed in clay pots added color to the grays and whites of the marble, while long green vines snaked their way up the sides of the buildings and columns from small gardens placed in various locations.

Unlike the other shops, the one that belonged to Noah's friend didn't have guards standing out front, or the thick, metal bars on its windows. Also, instead of statues of humans, two hideous gargoyles stared down at Jeffrey and the others. The obsidian eyes of the stone beasts seemed to watch the strangers every move and their toothy maws hung open wide as if waiting to devour anyone who came too close.

Shivering involuntarily under the statues' unnerving gaze, Mack mounted the stairs and headed up toward the ornately carved double doors that guarded the entrance to Arngrim's shop, the others following closely behind him. "Those things remind me of the creepy demon-dogs from Ghostbusters," he said, trying to keep his nerves under control as they reached the top of the steps. As he continued speaking, his eye never strayed from the statues. "I keep expecting to hear the thud of the Stay Puft Marshmallow Man from *Ghostbusters* as he comes down the street...that stupid grin on his face..."

His voice trailed off as he approached the gargoyles. To his horror and dismay, he noticed that large, dark, red splotches stained the ground beneath his feet. Swallowing nervously, he passed between the stone sculptures and walked up to the entrance. Through the darkened windows set in the wooden doors, Mack could see signs of movement from within. Taking a deep breath, he placed his hand on the door handle, opened it, and stepped inside.

17

ARNGRIM'S SHOP AND JEROME'S SECRET

THE MOMENT THE door swung open, the intoxicating fragrance of sweet incense assaulted Mack's senses. After he had taken no more than two steps into the room, he felt his muscles begin to relax as the pleasant smell infiltrated his body. The tendrils of incense that floated lazily about the room, combined with the filtered sunlight from the darkened windows gave the shop a relaxing and disarming atmosphere.

The spacious, eighty-foot by eighty-foot-square room was filled with row upon row of wooden shelves, each filled with all manner of objects from everyday items such as parchment and ink, containers filled with an assortment of liquids, and small statues to metal tools, knives, and weapons. A handful of other shoppers, accompanied by their slaves, moved in and about the merchandise, while two fierce-looking Nephilim stood against opposite walls, watching everyone intently. As the newcomers stepped inside and closed the door behind them, one of the giants eyed the group suspiciously, his gaze sweeping over them with interest.

Along the back wall of the shop, Mack could see a long counter covered with a plush cloth, its deep red fibers adding to the overall relaxing ambience. Standing behind the counter was an eight-foot-tall, thin man dressed in fine robes of purple and silver. Long, silvery hair spilled down the sides of his pale face and rested upon his shoulders, the tips of his pointy ears sticking out from beneath the shimmering locks like stones beneath a river. His eyes, which were too big for his head, were black in color and reminded Mack uncomfortably of a black hole that could suck a person's soul out of his body just by looking at them.

Behind him, Mack heard Jerome whisper, "It looks like one of those Blood Drinkers! Be careful, Mack." Agreeing with Jerome's assessment of the man, he nodded and kept his gaze fixed straight ahead.

As Mack and his companions approached the desk, the man finished his business with another customer, then turned his dark eyes toward them. The shrewdness of the man's scrutinizing gaze gave Mack the feeling that he could read his thoughts. A cold sweat broke out on Mack's brow as he realized with certainty that, whether due to the incense or some power that the man held, it would be impossible to lie to him. When the man spoke, his melodious tenor voice rose and lowered soothingly. "Welcome, honored guests. Can I interest you in one of our fine new blades? All have the ability to send a current of electricity down the blade, shocking your enemy. One slice cuts twice as deeply as a normal blow and makes your foe writhe in pain for several seconds."

Mack shook his head, both to decline the offer and to try to rid his brain of the fogginess brought on by the incense. "We...are you...are you Arngrim?" he managed at last.

The man raised one eyebrow and his smile dipped momentarily. "Alas, no. My name is Vidarr. Is there something I can help you with?"

Mack glanced back at his friends and received a reassuring nod from Rebecca, who smiled back at him, then pulled her hood lower, covering most of her face. Goliath, though appearing relaxed and focused on examining a large metal tool of some kind, was actually keeping a close eye on the Nephilim, while Jeffrey and Jerome were standing close by, their eyes scanning the room for signs of danger.

Turning back around, Mack addressed Vidarr once more. "No...no thank you. Would you be able to tell me where we might find him? It is of utmost importance."

Although the man smiled, his black eyes and pale complexion made the expression appear anything but friendly. "I'm sure it is. However, Lord Arngrim is not to be disturbed. Perhaps if you would like to leave a message for him, I will see to it that he gets it. You can expect a reply within a week or so."

It took a moment for Vidarr's words to penetrate Mack's muddy thoughts. "No," he said slowly, his forehead wrinkled in concentration. "No, that won't work. A week is…a week is too long. The Flood comes tomorrow…"

Vidarr frowned at Mack's last statement. "The Flood?" he said, his voice low and menacing. "Surely you can't mean the Flood predicted by that fool, Noah."

Realizing his mistake, Mack tried to salvage the situation. "No, no, of course not. I…I…my house might get flooded, and…and I need Arngrim to help me."

Vidarr nodded slightly and the two Nephilim approached. Turning to face them, Goliath drew his sword. The enormous beings simply laughed. Their twelve-foot height made Goliath look small and insignificant, and there was no doubt in Mack's mind that he wouldn't stand a chance if it came to blows.

"Wait!" Mack called out. "There's…there's no need for violence! We were just leaving."

A sudden flash of light flew past Mack's ear and struck Goliath in the back. Immediately, the holographic image surrounding the giant flickered once, but remained in place. Fortunately, the dim light and smoke in the room must have prevented Vidarr or the Nephilim from noticing the brief change in the giant's appearance. Goliath's body began to convulse wildly, and a second later, he crashed to the ground.

Mack whirled around too quickly and nearly lost his balance, his body still under the influence of the strange incense. When he recovered himself, he saw that Vidarr was staring at him, a wicked-looking device resembling a kind of wand in his hand. Looking out at the rest of his customers, who were staring in interest at the confrontation, he called out, "The shop's closed. Come back in thirty minutes."

One of the Nephilim herded the patrons out the door, then shut and locked it behind them. With the store now empty, Vidarr focused on Rebecca and the others, who were still rooted to the floor.

"Now, let's start over," he said without smiling. "Remove your hoods."

Mack did as he was instructed and wordlessly indicated that the others were to do the same. Vidarr stared at them curiously for what seemed like an eternity. "Who are you? You do not appear to have any enhancements, yet you are not of Noah's family. Where do you come from? And do not try to lie, for I will know if you do."

Fear began to grip Mack's heart. Seeing her friend's growing terror, Rebecca reached over and placed a reassuring hand on his arm. "God is with us," she whispered.

Wiping sweat from his brow with the sleeve of his robe, Mack closed his eyes and fought to gather his courage. Regaining a semblance of calm, he opened them once again as he responded to Vidarr's questions, careful to keep his voice from shaking. "Forgive us. But we *are* from Noah's family. However, we are not from around here. We came to seek Arngrim's help. That is all."

"And who is that?" Vidarr said, pointing toward Goliath. "His sword looks like one of our designs. How did he get it? We do not sell our technology to just anyone."

Mack stuttered, praying that he would be able to talk their way out of this. "Our...our r-r-relative, Noah, is friends with Lord Arngrim. I-I-I'm sure you're aware that he helped Noah construct the Ark."

The man nodded slightly and gestured for Mack to continue.

"We...hired this one to be our bodyguard," Mack said, pointing toward Goliath. "We don't know who made the sword, but he got it from one of Noah's relatives."

Goliath began to stir, causing the Nephilim to tense slightly, their eyes looking eagerly at the 'giant' as if hoping for a fight. Vidarr studied Mack, while Rebecca, Jeffrey, and Jerome stood silently next to him, wishing they could understand what was being said.

Making up his mind, Vidarr addressed the Nephilim. "Take the sword and bring it to me." The Nephilim did as requested, laying the sword that Goliath had taken from Nimrod on the counter. Running a hand down the blade lovingly, as if caressing a lover, Vidarr examined the craftsmanship of the blade. "Yes…although it is not as fine as one of our own, it will bring a good price."

Turning his attention back to Mack, he stared coldly at him. "Lord Arngrim is finishing a special project that requires his full attention, which is why he left the running of the shop to me. He is in Valhalla, and I am not certain when he will return. I will pass on word to Lord Arngrim that you were trying to contact him. If he wishes to see you, he will look for you at Noah's residence. Now, the Jotun," he said, indicating the two Nephilim, "will *escort you* out of the shop. I will consider the sword payment for the delivery of your message."

The words seemed to strike Mack like a physical blow. "No. We… we can't wait! We have to see Arngrim NOW!"

Vidarr's large black eyes grew even wider in anger. "You will not dictate to me what to do! You will leave now, or you will become test subjects for my new technology. If it were not for the fact that Lord Arngrim was a friend of your relative, you would already be screaming for death in my workshop. Now get out of here!"

Stunned, Mack turned and stumbled toward the door. Not understanding what had transpired, but not liking the results of the conversation, Jeffrey, Jerome, and Rebecca all followed quickly after him, fear gripping them tightly. A Naphil picked up Goliath, who was just regaining consciousness and shoved him toward the door. Once outside, the Naphil threw Goliath toward the steps. Still groggy from the attack, he fell and rolled down the steps into the street. Laughing uproariously, the two Nephilim headed back inside and shut the door.

Mack and the others ran down the steps, constantly glancing over their shoulders as if expecting to be attacked at any moment. Reaching the street, they stood near Goliath and stared back at the shop, their hearts beating rapidly in their chests. Slowly, Goliath crawled toward the stone column near the steps and propped himself up against it. After several moments of doing nothing more than breathe, Jeffrey finally looked at Mack questioningly. "What...what happened in there?"

His nerves having calmed sufficiently, Mack motioned for the others to move off the street and into the four-foot alley between Arngrim's shop and the neighboring building. Goliath, still weak, moved over to sit against the cold marble wall of the building, his eyes closed as he listened. Mack quickly told the others what Vidarr had said, keeping his voice low so as not to be overheard by those passing by on the street. When he finished, Jerome stared at Jeffrey, fear reflected in his eyes. "What are we going to do now? Arngrim was our only hope! We're at a dead end. I...I can't die here! I need to get back to my family!"

For once, Jeffrey had no words of consolation. They had tried, and failed. Now, it seemed there was nothing left to do but wait for the end.

"Oh, shut up!" Goliath said, opening his eyes and staring coldly at Jerome. "I'm so sick of your whining."

A sudden rage welled up in Jerome, causing him to turn on Goliath. "You're telling *me* to shut up? We wouldn't even *be* in this predicament if you and your ape-man buddy hadn't tried to kill us in the first place!"

Goliath, almost fully recovered from his encounter with Vidarr stood to his feet, his huge frame towering over Jerome. "Oh, so the coward has found his backbone, has he?" he said, taunting the smaller man. His own frustration at their situation, as well as the humiliation just visited upon him by Vidarr and the Nephilim served to fuel his own rage. "*My* fault, huh? That's right, I'm the big bad guy, and you're just the innocent victim, right? Well guess what, you're no different than me. Hercules and I did what we did for the money, just the same as you. In fact, if it hadn't been for *you*, we wouldn't be in this situation either!"

The blood drained out of Jerome's face, leaving his dark skin ashen and sickly. Realizing he had pushed too far, he simply stared at Goliath without replying, a pleading look on his face. Jeffrey, Rebecca, and Mack all looked at Jerome, a feeling of dread settling into their hearts. The five of them stood in silence for several seconds, the tension in the alley palpable.

"What's he talking about, Jerome?" Jeffrey asked, fearing the answer.

Jerome blinked, as if coming out of a trance. Glancing at Jeffrey, he stammered, "I…I don't know."

"Since we're all probably going to die tomorrow, I think it's time we're honest with each other, don't you?" Goliath said, his voice mocking. "You go first. Why don't you tell all of your friends about your little side job."

Jerome stared at Goliath, a mixture of anger, fear, and guilt carved into his face. "How…how do you know?"

"You first," the giant reiterated, a cruel smile twisting his lip.

Jerome stared at the ground for several seconds without speaking. Hot tears fell onto the stone pavement beneath his feet as he began his explanation, his voice low, causing the others to strain just to hear him. "When Joy got into that car accident on her prom night, Tarshwa and I… we…we were so scared that she would die. But, she made it. She lived…

"But once she recovered, the…the medical bills started pouring in. We used up what little savings we had, including the kids' college funds. After awhile, we were forced to sell some of our things just to keep our heads above water. And then…" he paused, his throat constricting. "I figured out a way to get us out of the debt."

He looked up at each of them, his eyes full of remorse. As his gaze settled onto Jeffrey, he continued. "I…I'm so sorry, Jeffrey. *I'm* the one that sold the technical specs for the gravity control device."

Jeffrey, Rebecca, and Mack sat motionless, their minds paralyzed by shock. Jeffrey, his face revealing his conflicting emotions, reached out and placed a hand on Jerome's shoulder. "Why…why didn't you tell us? You should have asked us for help. We could have…"

"I didn't think it would be that big of a deal," Jerome said. "Who cares if some Arabs got hold of the blueprints to a gravity control device? It's not like it's a weapon."

"But you sold it to *terrorists*!" Jeffrey shot back, his anger rising. "Imagine what they could do with that technology!"

The statement hung in the air until Goliath's slow clapping suddenly broke the stillness. "Bravo. Nicely done. You worked on their sympathy to deflect their anger."

Jeffrey spun to face the giant, a disgusted look on his face. "So, how do you fit into all of this? How did you know about Jerome selling the plans?"

Goliath smiled crookedly. "Did you really think the terrorists would be content with the technical specs of a gravity control device when they knew that an even *greater* piece of technology had been discovered? No. They wanted the technical journals for the pyramid as well. But they knew it would be extremely difficult to accomplish. So, they hired the best mercenaries they could find."

"You and Hercules, I suppose," Jeffrey said in sudden understanding. "But that doesn't explain your advanced technology or why you resemble those bodyguards."

Goliath's head snapped around as Jeffrey finished the sentence. "The bodyguards!" he said in concern. "Where are they? They were supposed to wait for us."

Two large forms suddenly blocked the narrow alleyway, their shadows falling upon the group. Turning as one, Rebecca and the others barely had time to brace themselves before the animal-like men attacked. One of the former bodyguards dove directly into Goliath, knocking him off his feet. The second sprang upon Jeffrey and Jerome. With a few well-placed blows from his fists, the attacker sent the two men sprawling onto the ground, blood flowing from their split lips and lacerated faces.

Springing into action, Rebecca fumbled with her robes in an attempt to reach her gun. With Jeffrey and Jerome down, one of the wolf-like warriors turned his attention on Mack and Rebecca. Mack, hoping to avoid a blow, dropped to the ground and covered his head. Ignoring him, the mercenary swung at Rebecca. Reacting swiftly, she ducked the attack, her Marine training kicking in. Rolling to her left, she regained her feet and finally pulled her weapon free.

But she was too late.

Sensing that the thing in her hand was some kind of weapon, her attacker kicked out at her, sending the pistol flying as it discharged, missing its target. Weaponless, Rebecca tried to kick her opponent, but he used his size and strength to quickly overpower her.

Pinning her to the ground, he stared at her hungrily, his expression striking fear into her heart. She could tell that he wanted more than just her money. Memories of the horrors she had witnessed on the streets during their journey through the city flashed through her mind, causing her to cry out in panic. Seeing his victim's fear only served to inflame her attacker's excitement.

Glancing around, Rebecca searched frantically for someone to help her. What she saw caused despair to overwhelm her. Goliath appeared unconscious, as did Jeffrey and Jerome. The other mercenary stood over Mack as he pulled the pouches containing the coins from beneath his robes and handed them to him. No one would come to her rescue. "Oh God!" she cried out, closing her eyes to ward off the sight of the grotesque animal-like man above her. "Father, save us!"

The sound of something large whistled through the air, followed by a bone-shattering thud. The weight on top of her disappeared, causing her to open her eyes in surprise. The body of her attacker lay several feet away from her, its arms and legs splayed out in all directions. Glancing back toward Mack, she watched in awe as an enormous hammer with a rectangular head made out of metal slammed full force into the chest of the second mercenary, sending his body flying several feet down the alley. Before the hammer hit the ground, it suddenly reversed direction and began flying back toward the street. Watching in dumbfounded amazement, she saw a thin line of bluish light pulling the handle of the weapon back toward the outstretched hand of its master, like the recoiling of a whip.

Rebecca sucked in her breath at the sight of the figure, dread and terror seizing her heart in a vice-like grip. For standing at the edge of the alleyway was an enormous being that exuded power and strength. Although he was in the form of a man, Rebecca knew with frightening certainty that this thing was not a man at all. Her rescuer was one of the sons of God, a false god…a demon.

18

ASGARD

REBECCA STARED UP at the being, her heart beating rapidly. He stood at least a foot higher than anyone they had seen thus far, including the twelve-foot-tall Nephilim. His barrel-shaped chest was covered with a brown leather tunic replete with golden symbols and runes that hung past his waist and was cinched with a wide yellow belt. Matching wraps of yellow cloth were wound tightly around his massive legs, starting at his knees and ending at the tops of his ankle-high leather shoes, keeping his tan pants held tightly against his skin. Gauntlets of the same dark leather were strapped tightly to his otherwise bare forearms. He wore no helmet on his head, but had his thick, rust-colored hair pulled back tightly into a braid that was draped over his left shoulder. His beard was gathered into two short braids that hung down from his chin like fangs. Brushing aside the flowing, dark blue cloak that was draped over his left shoulder, the man slipped the handle of his mighty hammer through his belt.

Although Rebecca knew that this man, this *thing*, was pure evil, she was nevertheless caught off guard by his handsome appearance. His face had a rugged beauty to it that captivated her, and his majesty and power were enticing. The eyes that stared down at her were like deep pools of darkness that could see straight into her soul and read her innermost thoughts.

A voice suddenly spoke from somewhere near the false god. Blinking, Rebecca felt the spell that had bound her loosen its hold. Looking toward the source of the voice, she saw a much smaller figure standing next to the false god, its pale face and clothing was all too familiar.

"A Blood Drinker," Rebecca heard Mack mutter from somewhere behind her. Glancing in his direction, she saw that his skin was deathly white and he was shaking noticeably. Catching her gaze, Mack stared back at her, his voice quivering. "It said, 'That is them, Mighty Thor.' That's the Norse god of thunder! And the vampire thing is…is dressed like…like one of those we fought off outside the Ark. We must have missed one. If it followed us all the way here then…then it knows where the pyramid is located!"

Battling with her own fear, Rebecca didn't reply. A command from Thor brought her attention back to him. The false god seemed to be studying her, and, based upon his expression and narrowed eyes, he did not like what he saw. A Naphil suddenly squeezed into the alley and before Rebecca could react, she felt his massive arms scoop her up and carry her out of the alley. Other Nephilim entered the cramped space between the buildings, each one returning with another of her friends. The giants dropped Rebecca, Mack, Jeffrey, and Jerome onto the ground in front of Thor and, after yanking off their robes, they proceeded to remove any and all items they found from their captive's pockets, including Rebecca's gun, their commlinks, Noah's money pouches, and the swords they had acquired from the Blood Drinkers. Once the Nephilim had finished collecting the items, they shook Jeffrey and Jerome roughly until they awoke. As the two men came to their senses, they shrunk back from their captors in shock. Mack and Rebecca reached out to their friends and the four of them sat huddled close together on the ground, surrounded on all sides by Thor and his entourage.

"What…what's going on?" Jeffrey said, his face marked with fear and confusion.

Rebecca barely had time to explain the situation before the demon-god barked a command. The six Nephilim soldiers forced the group to their feet and began herding them toward the river. The captives walked along in silence, their fear preventing their minds from formulating words. Around them, crowds of people stared in curiosity and amusement, hoping that perhaps their god would hurl the prisoners into the mighty river. The same thought occupied the minds of Rebecca and her companions as well, causing them to tremble visibly. Rough hands pushed and half carried the group to keep them moving, the captors growing more and more agitated with the prisoners' lack of cooperation.

Although Thor led the group to the riverbank, it was not the rocky location where the baby had been so callously discarded. Instead, he led them to a pair of magnificent golden gates that were set into a twenty-foot-high marble wall on the northern side of gigantic "World Tree" that towered over them in the center of the courtyard. The wall extended away from the gates only a short distance before ending at the steep banks of the river. The gates appeared to be guarding nothing more than a short, cobblestone walkway that ended at the river's edge. Standing at attention were two Nephilim, one on each side of the gate. The giants each held a wicked-looking sword in front of them, the points resting against the ground.

As Thor and his entourage drew within ten feet of the gate, one of the two sentinels pressed several buttons that were set into a panel on the marble wall. A moment later, the gates began to swing open of their own accord.

Before the terrified captives could begin to guess as to why they were being led to this gate, they drew back in surprise as a multi-colored beam of energy leapt forth from the end of the cobblestoned walkway. The ten-foot-wide beam shimmered as the light of the evening sun struck it.

Without fear, Thor strode toward the rainbow-colored light bridge and began crossing it, followed by the Blood Drinker. As the Nephilim pushed the prisoners toward the bridge, the gates began to close behind them.

"The Bifrost Bridge," Jeffrey whispered, having finally found his voice now that the immediate threat of death had receded. "They're taking us to

Asgard." Stepping onto the bridge, Jeffrey could see that it rose at a gentle angle across the river and ended at a pair of identical gates on the edge of the city of the Aesir.

"What is the Bifrost Bridge?" Rebecca asked quietly as she glanced at their captors to see if they were going to punish their victims for conversing. The giants, however, didn't seem to care.

"In Norse mythology, it's a burning rainbow bridge between Midgard and Asgard," Jeffrey replied. "And if the rest of the legends are true, then the bridge will end at Heiminbjorg, the residence of the god Heimdall. He guards it from the Jotnar, which, we now know, are the Nephilim."

The conversation ceased for the next several minutes as Asgard's majesty and beauty overwhelmed the captives with each step they took toward it. The steep cliffs that led from the river up to the walls of the city made it appear as if the ground itself was lifting the city of the gods into the air in worship. Rebecca and the others could now see that the bluish glow that they had seen from afar was some kind of energy field that ran down the center of the city, dividing it into the separate domains of the Aesir and Vanir. Another gate was set into the wall on the Vanir side of the city.

Risking a glance behind them, Jeffrey scanned as much of the plaza as he could see. Unfortunately, the trunk of the massive tree blocked most of his view. "Did anyone see what happened to Goliath?" he asked, keeping his voice low.

Rebecca and Mack both shook their heads, the latter fighting hard to keep his gaze fixed upon their destination and not on the ever-widening gap between them and the raging river below. "I didn't see any of the Nephilim pull him out of the alley. Perhaps they didn't think he was one of us because of his height," Rebecca said, trying to keep her own nerves in check.

"Well, if he's still alive, perhaps he can get back to the pyramid and tell the others what happened," Jeffrey said.

"A lot of good that will do," Jerome said, near panic coloring his voice. "There's no way they're going to be able to rescue us while we're surrounded by beings that make the Nephilim look just like wimps."

"No kidding," Mack said finally. "Now I know how Frodo and Sam felt. I feel as tiny as a hobbit next to these guys."

Taking his hand in her own and squeezing it gently, Rebecca tried to give him a reassuring smile, but the gesture merely served to communicate her own uncertainty. "Pray, Mack. We are never alone. There is always hope."

Nodding, he returned his gaze to the gates before them as he joined Rebecca in silent prayer.

Once they had reached the top of the bridge, the gates of Asgard swung open. Standing just inside the gate was another of the false gods. Instead of the leather armor that Thor wore, gold-trimmed, silver armor protected this being's enormous body. A shining helmet studded with a pair of horns sat atop his head and covered much of his blonde hair. One of his hands lay on a large animal's horn that hung from a strap around his torso, while the other held a fifteen-foot-long spear that rested on the stones beneath his feet.

"Heimdall," Jeffrey whispered to the others while Thor and the gate-keeper exchanged brief words. A moment later, Thor looked back at the Nephilim and indicated for them to follow. As the captives passed between the gates, Rebecca saw that Heimdall was staring at her and Mack with disgust, the hand holding the spear twitching in irritation. Shrinking under the perusal, Rebecca nervously began cracking her knuckles against her thigh.

The splendor of the rose-colored walls of the gatehouse was completely lost on Rebecca. For although the tapestries, statues, and architecture around them was more beautiful than any place she had ever seen, the pervasive sense of evil that surrounded her leeched away any positive feelings she might have otherwise enjoyed.

Human slaves scurried quickly out of the way as the god of thunder passed. Rebecca felt an intense sadness as she guessed at the many ways in which these poor people had been abused and mistreated by their 'gods.' Yet, despite her feelings of compassion, she also knew that these people had rejected their true God, and were living with the consequences of that choice.

Two genetically-altered human slaves opened a pair of massive, eighteen-foot doors as Thor approached. Without even glancing at the humans, the false god led his captives and their guards into a room that contained several circular, metallic vehicles, each roughly ten feet in diameter. On the opposite wall was a large open doorway that led out into the streets of the city. The sides of the circular vehicles were four feet high and thin handrails rose up several feet above that, wrapping around the entire perimeter of the craft. Although a few of the vehicles had plush chairs mounted to their floors, Thor strode over to one that was devoid of furnishings.

Rebecca and the others stood transfixed by the sight of the machines. "They look just like Nimrod's floating UFO thing!" Mack whispered, giving voice to the thought that had entered each of their minds.

"Nimrod must have figured out how to recreate some of the pre-Flood technology," Rebecca stated, thinking of the sword that Nimrod had wielded.

"But how?" Jerome wondered. "Noah said that the 'gods' were very stingy with their technology, not to mention the fact that he didn't use any of this technology on the Ark."

Thor climbed up into one of the flying machines and commanded the prisoners to do the same, ending any further conversation. Once they were aboard, Thor pointed to the Blood Drinker and three of the Nephilim, who proceeded to climb onto the machine.

As the second soldier began stepping onto the platform, however, the third one gave out a surprised cry and fell into him. The second Naphil backhanded his clumsy companion, who staggered backward, his face reflecting both confusion and anger. Frustrated at the delay, Thor replaced the soldier that tripped with one of the others, who promptly climbed aboard the craft. Dismissed, the other three Nephilim turned and headed back toward the gate, the one still nursing his wounded pride and split lip. Taking the controls of the craft, Thor brought the vehicle to life and piloted the ship through the open doors, leaving the gatehouse behind.

After the brutality of Midgard, Rebecca was surprised to find that Asgard appeared deceptively peaceful. For the most part, the city seemed quiet and serene, but its beauty and calm gave her the disquieting feeling that they were viewing a tomb; beautiful on the surface, but filled with death and rotting flesh. The streets were filled with mostly human slaves and an occasional Naphil guard. Only a relatively few other flying discs travelled the sky.

Closing her eyes to the sights, Rebecca tried to pray. However, although she struggled desperately to focus her thoughts, her mind couldn't seem to put together a cohesive sentence, almost as if something was interfering with her prayers.

Opening her eyes, Rebecca saw their destination looming before them, the wind stinging as it whipped against her face. A magnificent structure rose up from the center of the city, unlike anything she had ever seen before. The outer walls of the building were in the shape of a hexagon. Breathtaking buttresses and walkways ran from the tops of the outer walls toward the central portion of the building, which had a pyramid-like shape. Atop the pinnacle of the pyramid was a large hall that rose fifty feet into the air and was topped with a domed ceiling that seemed to pulsate and swirl with its own inner light. Rows of thirty-foot-high windows lined the outer walls of the hall, adding to its grandeur.

"Valhalla!" Jeffrey exclaimed in awe.

Rebecca turned to look at her husband. Her sudden movement caught his eye, and he returned her gaze. The world seemed to fade away as they stared into each other's eyes. Uncertainty, regret, fear, pain, love, despair—all were reflected in her husband's face. What would become of them? What would happen to Jeffrey? The memory of the vision she had experienced on the Ark came flooding back to her. In her mind's eye she once again saw Jeffrey screaming in agony. They were entering a stronghold of evil. Demonic false gods inhabited this place, and her husband was still lost. As far as she knew, if he were to die now, in this place, his soul would be cast into hell forever because of his own willful rebellion. Tears began to well up within her eyes. Shutting them tightly, she felt them slide down her cheeks. A solitary prayer formed in her mind, finally breaking through the interference. *Save him, Lord. Save my friends.*

The craft descended, causing Rebecca to look up to see that they were passing over the outer sections of the building. Thor expertly guided the vehicle between the archways and buttresses, flying so close to the structures that his passengers ducked reflexively as the flying machine dipped and turned. At last, the pilot brought the craft to rest on a balcony that jutted out from the pyramid-shaped central building two-thirds of the way up the sloped side. One of the Naphil opened the door of the vehicle, stepped onto the platform, and ordered Rebecca and the others to disembark.

Taking up the lead once more, Thor strode down the hallway that led from the balcony into the interior of the building. The high, fifty-foot ceilings were held up by thick, white columns and lit by glowing cylinders mounted on the tops of the columns. Lavish frescoes covered the blood red walls, depicting scenes of mighty battles, heroes killing vicious beasts, and gods seducing human women. The marble floors were streaked throughout with swirls of white and tan coloring. Stopping before a door, Thor pressed a button mounted on the wall. Immediately, the door slid into the wall, revealing a small, square room fifteen feet across.

Ushering the others inside, Thor entered last and pressed another button on the inside wall. The door slid closed, sealing them inside. A moment later, the familiar hum of a gravity control device rose up through the floor. Rebecca felt the unmistakable sensation of moving upward and suddenly realized that they had entered an elevator. After several seconds of travel, the elevator slowed to a stop and the door opened.

Rebecca and her companions followed Thor out of the elevator and were immediately struck by the vista that surrounded them. They stood at the end of a rectangular hall two hundred feet in length that was oriented from east to west. On either side of the hall, thirty-foot tall windows allowed them to see for miles to the north and south.

Short flights of steps led up three separate tiers, each a quarter of the length of the room. Thick, plush, red carpet with golden edging covered most of the fifty-foot width of the room and extended the full length. At the far eastern end of the hall, a set of enormous wooden double doors were set into the wall. Standing guard on each side of the doors, as well as standing along the walls of each of the three tiers, were women of such otherworldly beauty that the captives gasped audibly.

The women stood an average of ten feet tall. Graceful plumes of swan feathers adorned their shimmering helmets, leather boots, and silky, red capes. Their silver armor was perfectly fashioned to highlight their curves, yet left their muscular arms bare except for slender ringlets of silver and gold that encircled their smooth skin. Rivers of golden hair cascaded out from under their helmets to flow down their exquisitely-formed features and came to rest upon their shoulders. Slender, yet deadly spears were gripped comfortably in their hands, leaving no doubt that the women could wield them expertly.

Rebecca didn't need her husband or Jerome to tell her that these were the Valkyries, the beautiful women who, according to legend, ferried the souls of warriors from the battlefield to Valhalla. Although she knew these women were not fallen angels like Thor, she guessed that they were the female equivalent of the Nephilim.

Turning away from the goddess-like women, Rebecca gazed out the southern windows to stare at the city of Asgard below. Beyond that, across the river, she could see the three distinct sections of the lower city: Jotunheim, Midgard, and Alfheim. And there, off to the southeast, resting on a hilltop, was the Ark.

A harsh order from Thor snapped Rebecca and the other captives out of their awestruck perusal of the hall and the magnificent view. Leading them across the carpeting, the group climbed the steps and crossed each of the tiers until they stood before the double doors. Bowing slightly to their god, the Valkyries grabbed the large metal handles and opened the doors.

Another even longer hall stretched out before them. The room's only furnishing was a solitary throne that rested high up on a dais. Although the room was occupied by nearly a dozen beings of enormous girth and height, their might and strength were all dwarfed by the sheer, unbridled power of the one that sat on the throne, awash in the blinding rays of the sun that streamed in through the windows behind him.

Here was Odin, ruler of Asgard, lord of Valhalla, and mightiest of all the Norse gods.

19

ODIN

THE PERVASIVE SENSE of evil that emanated from the room so over-powered Rebecca and Mack that they were forced to their knees, their breathing labored. Everything within Rebecca's soul screamed at her to flee from this room, but she knew that she was trapped. *Jesus, help!* she called out mentally. Suddenly, verses from the Bible that she had memorized burned through her mind, pushing back against the darkness surrounding her. Reaching out a shaking hand, she caught Mack's arm. Nearly mad with terror, he stared back at her dumbly. " 'Be strong and courageous. Do not be afraid or terrified because of them, for the LORD your God goes with you; He will never leave you nor forsake you.'[1] 'Greater is He that is within you, than he that is in the world.' "[2]

Light returned to her friend's eyes. Nodding slightly, he grasped her arm tightly and together, they stood to their feet. Only then did they realize that Jeffrey and Jerome were both lying on the polished floor, their bodies curled into fetal positions. Even the Nephilim guards and the Blood Drinker were on the floor, prostrated before their god.

Looking around at the other demon-gods that filled the chamber, Rebecca realized that they appeared agitated. Their handsome features were twisted in disgust as they assessed the two humans who failed to bow before their gods. Rebecca could feel the unadulterated loathing that radiated from them. In particular, several Nephilim dressed in priestly robes seemed ready to attack the strangers and rip them limb from limb.

"Bring them to me," Odin commanded from his throne, his voice laced with a dangerous edge.

Thor pushed Rebecca and Mack forward, then grabbed Jeffrey and Jerome in each hand and unceremoniously dropped them at the foot of the dais. "Who are these humans?" Odin asked. "Where did they come from?"

As Thor motioned for the Blood Drinker to step forward, Mack and Rebecca looked up at the false god. The design of the chamber was such that the sunlight was reflected through the windows behind the throne, making it seem as if it was Odin himself that produced the light. Staring through the blazing brightness, Rebecca and Mack could see that the ruler of this realm was powerfully built and physically impressive. Armor made from the scales of some giant reptilian creature covered his torso and hung down over his thighs like a skirt. Long pieces of matching armor were strapped to his bare legs, and his feet were shod with thick leather sandals. The luxurious red robe that covered his arms and wrapped around his body was made of a material that sparkled in the light, making it seem to come to life as he moved. A regal helm studded with gems rested atop his head, his long white hair reaching to just past his shoulders. His lengthy white beard rested atop his massive chest and reached nearly to his jewel-encrusted belt.

Jeffrey and Jerome, still huddled on the floor near the door, began to rouse. They tried to stand, but soon gave up, their fear paralyzing them.

Keeping his voice low so that only Rebecca could hear, Mack began translating as the Blood Drinker spoke.

"Almighty Odin, King of the gods, I and my brothers went to the false prophet's home and burned it as the Lord Loki had commanded us," it said, glancing nervously at one of the demon-gods that stood near the base of the throne, his body shrouded in a dark cloak.

"Loki, what new mischief is this?" Odin demanded.

A wicked cackle erupted from the being as he looked up at the king.

"That crazy old man and his obnoxious boat has been a blight on our city for too long. I thought it time to put an end to him and silence his talk about this one, 'true' God. So, I hired the Blood Drinkers to do it. They have proven themselves useful on several occasions."

"But not this time, it would appear," Odin said. "For unless my eyes deceive me, the boat still sits on the hill. It seems that your pets were beaten by a tiny group of humans—and pure-bloods, by the look of them."

Loki cast a baleful glance at the vampire-like creature. "Yes, explain yourself. How did these wretches defeat your entire gang?"

The genetically altered human glanced nervously between the two false gods before coming to rest on Loki. "All went as planned at first. The houses and animal enclosures burned swiftly. The liquid quickly destroyed the lock on the gate, allowing us inside the wall. But…but, as we were moving the materials into place with the devices you gave us, we were attacked from behind by these four and an altered human. When we turned to fight them off, Noah and his sons came out from the boat. We were trapped between them."

"And only you escaped?" Loki said with a sneer as he edged closer to the creature.

Quaking in fear, the blood drinker spoke rapidly, hoping his explanation would spare him from his master's wrath. "When the battle turned against us, I hid, knowing that any information I could bring back to you about our strange attackers would be worth more than my death. So, I waited all night out in the cold for them to come out of Noah's boat. I followed them, even though the sun burned my eyes and flesh."

Growing weary of the creature's tale, Odin waved his hand impatiently. "And what did you discover about them that is so important you felt compelled to disturb me?"

"After they left Noah's accursed boat, they travelled through the forest and across the plains into Alfheim," the vampire-like creature said. "There, they entered a pyramid about the size of a human house."

"A pyramid?" Odin echoed, his interest suddenly piqued. "But there are no pyramids in Alfheim."

"I know, my lord," the creature continued. "But there is now. They left the pyramid, entered the city, and went to Arngrim's Shop." The king of the false gods frowned, but said nothing. The creature continued. "While they were inside, I went to find the mighty Thor so that we might bring them before you for questioning. For you see, my lord, not only are they strangers, but they speak gibberish, as if they were mad. Only the one with the curly black hair seems capable of normal speech. Look! Even now he is speaking his strange words…"

The sudden interest in his translation efforts caused Mack to stop short, leaving the rest of the Blood Drinker's sentence unfinished. Sensing the eyes of everyone in the room resting on him, Mack nearly fainted in fear. Beside him, Rebecca squeezed his arm tightly, the pain returning his focus.

"Who are you?" Odin demanded. The rest of those assembled in the room waited in hushed anticipation.

It took Mack several seconds to find his voice. When he did, it came out broken and trembling. "W…we…we are…family members of Noah."

"You have heard what this one has said about you. Explain yourself," Odin said.

Building on the story he had concocted for Vidarr, Mack began. "We came from far away to visit with our relative. We traveled here in the pyramid, much like the flying circles you use in your city. We were having trouble with our vessel, and Noah said that Arngrim might help us fix it."

Odin's eyes narrowed skeptically. "What god gave you access to the technology for a flying structure?"

Mack swallowed nervously. "We…were sent on an errand by…by our lord Aslan," he blurted out.

Smatterings of conversation broke out around the room. Raising his hand, Odin silenced them. "I know all of the gods from the other realms, but I have never heard of this Aslan. What was the errand?"

Beads of sweat dripped down Mack's neck as he felt his story beginning to unravel. "To...to seek out Arngrim. As I mentioned, we needed him to help fix the vessel."

Based on Odin's dark expression, Mack knew he wasn't buying it. "And why do your friends speak so strangely? Are they mad?"

Mack looked down at his friends, hoping for inspiration. "They... they have...speech impediments, mighty Odin," he lied, hoping the false god would believe him. "It is from a genetic enhancement experiment that went wrong. After living with them for many years, I have learned to understand them though."

Considering his statement, Odin leaned back on his throne. "So they can hear, but not speak properly." Mack tensed, suddenly realizing the flaw in his lie. "Do not speak unless I give you permission and do not look at your friends."

Odin turned his gaze to Rebecca and said, "Raise your left hand."

Knowing that she was being addressed, she looked desperately to Mack for translation. When he didn't return her gaze or speak, she knew that something had gone wrong.

The corner of Odin's lip curled, his eyes boring into Mack. "You are a foolish man to lie to me. I will have the truth from you, and then you will beg for death." Leaning forward, Odin turned his gaze toward Thor. "Take them to the dungeon. I will deal with them tomorrow. I have more important matters to attend to."

Mack felt his insides knot up with fear. *Tomorrow? The Flood begins tomorrow!* he thought in despair. *Locked inside a prison, we have no hope of escape. And it's all my fault. If only I had been able to come up with a better story, then perhaps...*

"I knew you would be interested in them, my lord," the vampire-like creature said with a bow, drawing Mack out of his reverie.

Looking at the Blood Drinker in disgust, Odin waved him away in dismissal. "Loki, give him a few coins for his services."

"Yes, my king," Loki said as Thor and the three Nephilim grabbed the prisoners and pushed them toward the exit.

"Now, Dellingr, what is this nonsense you are spreading about a star falling from the sky?" Odin said, turning his attention toward one of the other false gods standing near the throne. Their conversation faded into the background of Mack's mind as he and the others were ushered through the double doors.

"Mack, wh…what happened?" Jeffrey said hoarsely, finally coming to his senses now that they were out of Odin's throne room and the doors were closed behind them.

Not having the courage to look them in the eyes, Mack simply stared straight ahead as he replied. "We're to be locked in the dungeon. Odin will come to question us tomorrow."

Next to him, Mack heard Jerome suck in his breath in fear. "Tomorrow?" he echoed loudly as he and the others were led through the double doors. "We can't just let them lock us up! The Flood is coming! We'll all drown!"

The words were barely out of his mouth when the floor beneath their feet began to shake and tremble, knocking everyone off their feet, including Thor and the Nephilim. For several terrifying seconds, no one moved. Once the tremor had passed, Thor rose to his feet, followed by the three Nephilim, who looked at each other with uncertainty.

"Did you feel that?" Jerome gasped. "It's already starting!"

At his outburst, Thor turned around to face Jerome, his expression hard and threatening. Jeffrey, seeing the danger, put both hands on Jerome's shoulders and spoke in a harsh whisper, hoping to talk some sense into his friend. "Get a hold of yourself! We're weaponless and surrounded by a god and three Nephilim, not to mention the Valkyries."

Jeffrey's words fell on deaf ears as Jerome's panic consumed him. "NO! We've gotta get out of here now!" Breaking free from Jeffrey's grasp, Jerome pushed him aside and turned to run, his friends stunned by his sudden movements. The guards, however, alerted by his shouting, were prepared for anything. Before Jerome had even taken two steps, the guard closest to him backhanded him with one of his massive fists, sending him sliding several feet across the smooth floor.

"JEROME!" Rebecca shouted as she prepared to run toward the unmoving body of her friend. Stepping in front of her, Jeffrey prevented her from moving.

"Becky, stop!" he commanded, trying to calm her. "They'll just do the same to you."

Taking her eyes off Jerome, she looked at her husband, and then glanced around at Thor and the Nephilim who were ready should any of the other captives try anything. Still distraught, but seeing the wisdom in Jeffrey's words, Rebecca slowly relaxed as tears came to her eyes.

Satisfied that the rest of the captives were restrained, Thor commanded one of the Nephilim to pick up Jerome. Striding over to his crumpled form, the giant reached down, grabbed him, and slung him none-to-gently over his shoulder like a sack of grain. Opening the elevator door, Thor ushered the group inside.

As they descended, Rebecca stared at the Nephilim carrying Jerome, searching for any sign of life from her friend. However, from where she stood, it was impossible to tell. Lowering her head, she prayed fervently. Next to her, Jeffrey and Mack both stared at the wall, each lost in his own thoughts.

The trip to the dungeon cell was nothing more than a blur in Rebecca's mind. She vaguely recalled leaving the elevator, and being led through a guardroom and down several darkened corridors that smelled of death and decay. When she and her friends were shoved into the cell, she stared at her surroundings numbly.

She had seen these walls before. They were the same dark stone walls she had seen in her vision aboard the Ark. Except, in the vision, it had been Lisa and Awken that were huddled in the dark corner of the cell. Which could only mean one thing:

Akwen, Lisa, and Dr. Eisenberg were in danger. Thor and the Nephilim were going to find the pyramid!

20

NOAH'S DIARY

DR. YAAKOV EISENBERG opened his eyes as the tremor passed through the pyramid. Across the room, an empty, ceramic bowl fell off the small table and crashed to the hard, stone floor, sending broken shards scattering everywhere. The moment the shaking ceased, the door to his room flung open rapidly as Lisa entered, a look of stark terror on her face.

"Doc! Doc, are you okay?"

"Yes, Lisa. I'm fine," he calmly replied, despite his suddenly racing heart.

"What was that?" she asked, her face pale. "Has it started already? I didn't think the Flood was coming until tomorrow!"

"It is the birthing pains," he answered, both for her sake and his own.

Relaxing somewhat, Lisa began picking up the broken pieces of the bowl. As she did so, Dr. Eisenberg saw her hands shaking nervously. Once she had finished, she threw the pieces away and began heading toward the door, her face lined with anxiety. "I'm glad you're okay, Doc. Try to rest again, and call me if you need anything."

"I will," he said as she departed.

Closing his eyes, he tried to relax. Try as he might though, he could not shake the unsettling feeling that rested heavily upon his

191

heart. Somehow he knew that it was more than just the aftereffects of the earthquake. Something had happened to Rebecca and the others. Pushing himself up, he grabbed a pillow and put it between himself and the wall so that he was in a comfortable sitting position. He was surprised to discover that, despite his moving around, the pain from his sword wound had lessened dramatically. Thankful that the pain would not be a distraction, he bowed his head and began to pour out his concern for his friends' safety toward heaven. Immersed in prayer, he lost all track of time.

Finally, after nearly an hour, he felt the urgency inside him shift toward the rolled parchment sitting on the shelf not far from where he sat. Climbing carefully out of bed, he crossed the room, wincing slightly as the dull throb in his side reminded him of its presence. Ignoring the pain, he picked up the thick scroll and shuffled back over to his bed. Once he had returned to his previous sitting position, he paused, and then examined the scroll.

He caressed the parchment reverently as if it were a sacred object. Studying it, he took note of every area where the individual pages had been glued together before being rolled. Although he felt a twinge of guilt at the fact that Jeffrey and Jerome had stolen the scroll from Noah during their escape from the Ice Age, it was overshadowed by an even stronger impression that he was *meant* to read it. Perhaps by reading Noah's diary, he would find some useful bit of information that could help him and his friends escape the coming Cataclysm, or give him insight into this world prior to the Flood. Taking the edge carefully in his left hand, he unrolled it far enough to reveal the first page. The time that he and Mack had spent pouring over the technical journals for the gravity control device and the pyramid made him familiar enough with the language to read it, even though he couldn't speak it.

His heart began to pound as he looked down at the words. No other human had read these words for nearly four thousand years. With his hands shaking slightly, he gazed down at the flowing handwriting and began to read…

YEAR 1556, SECOND MONTH, SEVENTEENTH DAY

The account of Noah, son of Lamech, son of Adam.

Yahweh, the creator of the heavens and the earth, spoke to me today. In all of my five centuries of life, I have waited for this day, praying that it would happen. Yet the message I received from Him has left me…unsettled and disturbed. I pray that by putting my thoughts down on parchment, I will be able to better sort through my feelings. Also, these words will be a permanent memorial to my family and me about what the Mighty One—glorious are His ways—accomplished through His servant.

Since my earliest childhood memories, I remember struggling with how a loving God could allow such evil in the world. Now, I have a partial answer to that question: although He gives His children free will to choose obedience or rebellion, those that choose rebellion will not be allowed to go unpunished forever. A day of reckoning must come, for Elohim is also a just God.

And the day of that judgment has now been proclaimed. Those that do not turn from their wickedness and choose the path of salvation that He has provided will perish in the coming Cataclysm…

Dr. Eisenberg paused in his reading, his thoughts turning to his friends. Even if they managed to somehow escape from the Flood, another Cataclysm awaited them. Death would eventually claim them, and if they did not accept the path of salvation that God had provided… *Oh Lord, help these young people realize the truth before it is too late. You spared my life for a reason. Use me in any way possible to reach them,* he prayed.

Turning back to the scroll on his lap, he skimmed passed several paragraphs that paralleled the account found in the Torah. Skipping over several other entries, he finally spotted one that caught his attention.

YEAR 1592, FOURTH MONTH, TWENTY-FOURTH DAY

I was attacked again today. Fortunately, my cousin was there to pull me away from the mob before they were able to kill me. Ra and his pantheon of false gods have convinced everyone in the region that I *am the cause of their crop failures. How will they turn from their wicked ways, oh Lord, when they are convinced that what is evil is good and what is good is evil? Their hearts are so hardened.*

Elohim, I know you told me that you would save me, my sons, and our wives, but the Ark is going to be so big, even with all of the animals, plants, food, bedding, and all the rest, surely there is enough room for many other families. Will no one accept the message of salvation that you have proclaimed? I feel so alone, Lord. Is it even worth it for me to preach? Perhaps the people in the realm of Zeus will repent...

Rolling the scroll further, Dr. Eisenberg glanced at several more entries, some dealing with Noah's struggle to continue preaching in the face of increasing persecution, others describing the challenges he faced while designing the Ark, and still others detailing the setbacks and problems he encountered while actually constructing it. Passing over several pages about the menagerie of animals, a small entry suddenly caught his attention.

YEAR 1656, SECOND MONTH, TENTH DAY

Grandfather Methuselah died today, just seven days before the Cataclysm is to begin. As much as I had hoped and prayed that he would join us on the Ark so that we would have his wisdom and knowledge, I am also thankful that he will not have to witness the destruction. Having been among those who learned the history of the creation of the world firsthand from Adam, it would probably have been too much for him to bear.

I regret that we will not be able to bury him with his fathers, as there is no time to journey to the Garden. Although I wish I could see it one more time, the sight of the cherubim and their flaming swords that guard the entrance to the Garden still fill me with awe and dread, even after all of these years.

As Dr. Eisenberg began reading the next entry, his eyes grew wide in shock and his heart began beating faster in astonishment.

YEAR 1656, SECOND MONTH, FIFTEENTH DAY

We are now only two days away from the beginning of the Cataclysm. Eema and I, as well as the rest of my family, have been fighting against our own fear and uncertainty. But I praise the Almighty for His mercy. His loving kindness never fails. For just as we were beginning to despair and lose heart, He sent us encouragement in the form of a group of strangers.

A gang of Blood Drinkers burned down my home, the menagerie, the mill, and all of the other buildings. Then, they somehow destroyed the lock on the gate and would have succeeded in burning down the Ark, had the strangers not arrived at that exact moment. Once the threat was removed and the lock replaced, I invited the visitors inside.

Although their story is a fascinating one, I have chosen not to relate it here, as I fear their tale could cause unforeseen damage to future readers. But I praise God for sending them to us today, as I was finally able to witness a person repent of his sins and accept Elohim as the one, True God! It has given me hope for the future. Perhaps mankind can be redeemed. Thank you, Lord, for this much-needed encouragement. I only regret that after they leave tomorrow morning, I will probably never see the strangers again.

After pausing to thank God once again for Mack's conversion, Dr. Eisenberg continued reading.

YEAR 1656, SECOND MONTH, SEVENTEENTH DAY

Today is the day. As I write this, I sit in the garden aboard the Ark and the morning sun is streaming through the window above. The air is so beautiful and crisp that the idea of what lies ahead seems so absurd. However, in the distance I can see massive clouds such as I have never seen before beginning to form. How long will it be before I see the sun again? When will the waters begin to fall?

An unnatural calm has settled over the animals. They know it will start soon. The earth has begun to tremble. The first time it happened, Eema nearly fainted with fright. Each time, the tremors are bigger and last longer. One has already struck this morning. I wonder how many more will pass before the Righteous Judge releases His full wrath.

No matter how I try, I cannot keep my hands from shaking. My stomach is tight, and I know it is worse for Eema and the other women. They have already begun grieving. Even as I write, tears are welling in my own eyes. My soul is so heavy—the burden is crushing me. Oh Mighty One, if only there were some other way…

All of the rest of the hatches are closed, and now I must close this last one in preparation, for I don't know when it will begin. Elohim, remember us…

YEAR 1656, SECOND MONTH, SEVENTEENTH DAY

I cannot sleep, nor, I fear, can anyone else in my family. Even now, I can barely see through the tears filling my eyes, and I cannot stop the trembling in my hands. And I make a vow before my Lord this day that I will teach my children, my grandchildren, and all of their offspring for as long as I draw breath about the consequences of sin. For as long as I shall live, I will never be able to blot out the memory of what happened today.

We knew that something was amiss when the animals suddenly began to stir. The bleating of sheep, the cawing and squawking of the birds, the lowing of the cattle, the roars of the cats, behemoths and dragons. All began to wail in terror.

Eema remained inside to comfort my terrified daughters-in-law while my sons and I rushed to the door of the Ark. What we saw there chilled our souls. A great mountain engulfed in fire fell out of the sky! Although we could not see where it landed, the accompanying tremor knocked us from our feet.

The impact must have set off a chain reaction within the earth, for the ground heaved and buckled. Great fissures opened up in the ground. Far off in the distance, we saw the giant plumes of smoke billowing up from the tops of mountains to mingle with the massive storm clouds above. Flashes of electricity sparked around the peaks while liquid fire began to run down the side, burning everything in its path as it slowly made its way towards Asgard.

Still on our hands and knees, we watched in horror as great walls of the city collapsed inward, crushing thousands of people. Within a matter of a few minutes, wildfires raged all throughout the city. The woods to the south burned rapidly. The destruction appeared so great, that even my sons and I began to fear for our lives. May He forgive our lack of faith.

Then, our fear changed to compassion and pity as we watched the people begin to empty out of the city. They ran up the hill, many laden down with whatever possessions they could carry. Even facing certain death they clung selfishly to that which was useless. Riots broke out in the streets as wicked men died while they squabbled over trinkets and baubles.

Before long, the bottom of the hill on which the Ark rested was swarming with people, all desperate to reach the safety of the Ark. The cries for mercy from the multitudes rose up from below, carrying even over the continued rumble in the earth. Overwhelming grief filled my soul. Standing to my feet, I tore at my robe, a cry of anguish escaping my lips. I beseeched the Creator for mercy and begged him to temper His wrath.

Looking back toward the people climbing the hill, I called encouragement to them from the doorway of the Ark. So intent was I on rescuing as many as possible, that I never once considered what would have happened had they all reached us with the door open. In their panic, they would have crowded the Ark and we all would have perished.

But the Almighty God, in His wisdom, did not leave it up to me.

Shem's cry drew my attention to the Eastern horizon. A wall of white and blue was rapidly growing, filling the edge of the sky for as far as we could see. For several minutes, we simply watched in confusion as it grew, wondering what new terror was about to befall the inhabitants of our world. But it wasn't until the first droplets of water splashed across my face that I knew with horrifying certainty what it was.

Only later did I truly comprehend what had happened. The blazing mountain that fell from the sky must have landed in the ocean. Like a rock dropped in a pond, enormous ripples of water spread out from the mountain in all directions. What we saw coming toward us was a wall of water!

I urged those climbing the hill to throw down their useless items and climb quicker. But there was no way that they could have heard me. The wall of water had already begun crossing over the land, ripping up trees by their roots and sweeping away everything in its path. The wall was not high enough to reach the top of the hill where the Ark rested, but I knew that everyone caught on the slope would perish instantly.

The mighty wave crashed down, shaking the earth with its fury. Millions of people and animals perished in that first wave. Most of Jotunheim, Midgard, and Alfheim were instantly wiped away by the flowing waters. Of those climbing the hill, only the hundred or so people furthest up remained.

I will never forget the expressions of stark terror that they wore. They knew, too late, that Elohim was real and they had rejected Him. Then, as they resumed their climb to the summit, the earth shook again and a fissure opened on the side of the hill between the people and the Ark. Suddenly, from out of the darkness of the chasm, rivers of water burst forth, spraying thousands of cubits into the air. Water soon gushed from many of the other fissures until we could no longer see more than a few hundred cubits in any direction.

Suddenly, my sons and I were startled as the door of the Ark began to close. Still hoping beyond hope that the Righteous Judge would allow a few to be saved, I cried out for the Him to wait. But it continued to close. My sons pulled me back from the entrance as the door finally came to rest, sealing us inside. Falling to the floor, we held each other and wept.

It was then that the noise began. It started as a drumming on the roof of the Ark and steadily grew louder until we could barely hear one another. Staggering to our feet, we ran towards the ramp leading to the upper deck. Once there, we climbed up to the observation platform and stared out the window. The water that came out of the ground had begun falling in torrents. Closing the window, we secured it tightly and climbed down.

The world that we had known was no more.

21

THE CALM BEFORE THE STORM

LISA STALEY OPENED the door softly so as not to disturb Dr. Eisenberg. However, as she stepped into the room, she was surprised to find that her concern was unwarranted.

"Doc, you're awake," she said. However, her initial excitement suddenly changed to concern as she saw that he was sitting up in bed, an open scroll on his lap. "What are you doing? You're supposed to be resting. You're in no condition to be awake and reading."

As she stepped close to the bedside, he looked at her warmly. "I'm fine. In fact, I was even able to get up and walk across the room to get the scroll."

"Yeah, well, just don't push it," she said with mock seriousness. Pulling up a chair, she sat down beside the bed. "What are you reading? Is this one of the scrolls we borrowed from Noah?"

"Yes," he replied. "It's his diary. I had just finished reading about how Noah and his family offered sacrifices after the Flood. And before that, I was reading Noah's firsthand description of life aboard the Ark. I must say, it is very sobering reading."

"I can imagine," she said, her face serious.

"There's so much about the Flood that I have never even considered before," the doctor said. "For example, Genesis records that the floodwaters rose to be twenty feet above the mountains.[1] But what's interesting is that Noah comments in his diary about how the mountains were much bigger after the Flood. It never dawned on me that if they weren't as high *before* the Flood, then that would greatly reduce the amount of water needed to cover the mountain tops!"[2]

"But then, how did our current mountains form?" she asked.

"Probably by all of the massive upheaval caused by the Flood itself," he explained. "He describes massive earthquakes, volcanoes, and tsunamis. It is probable that they were formed by the collision of the tectonic plates.[3] Come to think of it, most people don't know this, but the layers of rock at the top of Mt. Everest are made up of fossil-bearing, water-deposited layers.[4] Scientists have even found marine fossils on the tops of every major mountain range on earth!"[5]

Surprise spread across Lisa' face. "So...so then where did all of the water go?"

"Nowhere," he said. "It's in our oceans, in the deep sea trenches. After all, three-quarters of the earth's surface is covered by water.[6] If the mountains were flattened out and the ocean basins were raised up, there would easily be enough water to cover all of the land once again."[7]

"But, if there really was a worldwide flood, how come we don't find evidence of it?" she asked honestly.

Dr. Eisenberg's face lit up with excitement. "But we do! The whole world contains evidence for it, but we are so blinded by our preconceptions that we don't see it or we interpret it wrong! I'm ashamed to say that I was the same way. Only now am I beginning to understand.

"Let me give you an example," he said, barely pausing for breath. "If the whole world had once been covered by water, what would you expect to find?"

Lisa shrugged. "I don't know."

"We would expect to millions of dead animals and plants buried in sedimentary rock layers everywhere on earth," he replied. "And that is *exactly* what we do find! They are called 'fossils.'"

"Really," she said in a playfully sarcastic tone.

"Sorry," he apologized. "Sometimes I get caught up in my teacher mode and forget who I'm talking to."

"Don't worry about it, Doc," she said with a smile. "I just had to give you a hard time."

"Anyway, as I was saying before I was so *rudely* interrupted," he teased, returning her smile, "normally, dead animals and plants decompose quickly. The only way they can become fossils is if they are buried rapidly. And within the fossil record, scientists have found fossils of fish eating each other and animals in the process of giving birth.[8] Obviously, those had to have been buried rapidly."

Not knowing what to say, Lisa remained silent. Encouraged by the fact that she was listening intently to what he was saying, Dr. Eisenberg continued.

"Even more, the fossil record contains many examples of 'fossil graveyards,' where sometimes hundreds of animals were buried in the same location,[9] and what we call polystrate fossils."

Lisa frowned, unfamiliar with the term. "What are those?"

"The horizontal layers of rock are called 'strata,' and so a polystrate fossil is one that crosses vertically through more than one layer of rock," he answered. "For instance, there are many fossilized trees in the coal regions of Kentucky that extend up through several layers of rock, including layers of coal.[10] In fact, the Flood can actually explain the origin of coal itself.[11] I can't believe I've never seen it before, but now that I understand things differently, it makes more sense to believe that those trees were buried rapidly under flood conditions rather than to believe that they were buried slowly, little by little over thousands or millions of years."

Lisa frowned. "But, I was always taught that it took long periods of time to make a fossil."

Dr. Eisenberg nodded in sympathy. "Yes. Although I knew that they could form rapidly, I used to believe that they *normally* formed slowly. And, to my shame, that is what I taught in my classes. I never told students of the instances where scientists found man-made objects, such as a hat or a wooden fence post, that had petrified,"[12] he said, his expression falling. "I didn't mention them because I wanted my students to focus on the general idea that fossils are created over long periods. I never realized how much my own preconceived ideas influenced my teaching. It *doesn't* take long periods of time, just the right conditions."

"And so now you believe that a literal worldwide flood explains the evidence better?" Lisa asked.

"To be honest, Lisa, I have much research to do," he said. "So much of geology is based on interpretation, and now that I have a different starting point, I'm realizing now just how much of what I believed was based on a foundation of evolutionary thinking. I don't have all of the answers, but I can see that my new understanding is helping me to make sense of things that were always a mystery, such as polystrate fossils."

Dr. Eisenberg paused for a second as a new thought occurred to him. "You know, when you think about it, the geologic history of the earth is not uniformitarianism, where everything has always happened at the same slow rate. Instead, it is more like the life of a soldier: long periods of boredom punctuated by short periods of terror."

Lisa sat quietly for a moment, her face reflecting the turmoil that raged within her. "But, it's just…it's just so hard to believe that one ship could contain all of the animals in the world!" she said finally. "How could just eight people take care of all of those animals?"

"I imagine we'll find the answer to those questions when we get a chance to talk to Jeffrey and the others who boarded the Ark. However, I may have at least a portion of the answer," Dr. Eisenberg said, holding up the scroll in his lap. "It says here that many of the animals were in various stages of hibernation during the voyage. So even though Noah states that they had designed the Ark to make caring for the animals possible under normal conditions, their jobs were made that much easier when the animals slept much of the time. Think about it. They would consume less food, drink less water, and produce less waste."[13]

Although the doctor didn't see it, Lisa's eyes began to pool with tears.

"I wish I had been able to be with Jeffrey and the others when they went on the Ark," he continued. "To be so close and yet not get to see it…" Laughing at himself, he waved his hand in the air in dismissal of his feelings. "You know what they say, 'if wishes were fishes we'd all have some fried!'"

Lisa couldn't help but laugh at the silliness of Dr. Eisenberg's quote. Her countenance relaxed for a moment, before turning serious once more. "It's…it's all really true, isn't it, Doc?" Lisa asked as she lowered her head, tears forming in her eyes once again.

Reaching out, he took her hand in his own. "Look at me, Lisa," he said gently. "Yes, it's all true. If your struggle is anything like mine was, your pride may not want to admit that you have been wrong for all of these years. And even more than that, you know that if the Deluge was a real event, then it points to the fact that there *is* a God, and He does judge sin."

Tears began spilling unrestrained down her cheeks at his words.

"Dearest Lisa," he said as he wiped her tears away with the thumb of his right hand, "I know you've done things that you regret. If you only knew everything about me, you might be shocked at some of the things I've done in my life. I'm definitely no saint. All of my life I lived under the condemnation of the laws of God from the Torah. I knew that I was a criminal in His eyes, and that knowledge was like a crushing weight upon me. For no matter how many good deeds I did, they would never erase my crimes."

As he continued to share his personal story with her, he relived the joy and release he had felt when he had first believed. "When Rebecca urged us to accept Jesus while we were standing outside the Tower of Babel, I don't know why, but for the first time in my life I understood what Christianity meant. It's like a legal transaction! Even though we were found guilty in God's courtroom and were given the death penalty, Jesus paid that penalty for us with His own blood! Our case has been thrown out and we are free!"

Lisa's shoulders shook as she fought against her emotions. Then, like the bursting of a dam, she began to weep uncontrollably as she buried her face in the mattress of the bed. Placing his hand on her back, Dr. Eisenberg comforted her like a father to his daughter. "Turn away from your sins and put your trust in Jesus. If you do, He will give you a clean slate."

Her eyes red and swollen, she raised her head and looked up at him. "But Doc, how could He forgive me after what I did to Becky? She was my best friend! Yet I...I..." Another bout of sobs shook her body, preventing her from finishing her sentence.

His own eyes full of tears, the doctor looked at her with a pained expression. "Although my own faith in Jesus is still new, I can tell you that from what I *do* know, I don't believe there is any sin that is so great that God would not forgive you. Look at Saul of Tarsis. He *murdered* Christians, yet God still forgave him. And I think I know Rebecca enough to tell you that even though there have been times lately when she has lashed out at you in her pain, I can guarantee you that in the big picture, she would want you to accept Jesus' forgiveness."

"But, how could I ever face her again after what I've done?" she said through her tears. "And what do I do about Jeffrey? I love him."

"You may have to give Rebecca some time, but I believe in the long run she will forgive you," he said gently. "As for Jeffrey, that is between you and God. However, I think in your heart you already know what He would want you to do."

Placing his hand under her chin, he lifted her head to look at her. "Would you like me to pray with you?" She nodded, and he smiled brightly as tears of joy spilled down his cheeks. Bowing their heads, they prayed together. When they had finished, she stood and embraced him, her guilt washed away as she was reborn as a new creation.

"Dis is not good," Akwen said in alarm as she studied the screen in front of her. Reaching over, she grabbed her commlink and flicked it on. "Lisa, Doc, we've got company."

A moment later, Lisa replied, her voice sounding oddly weak and hoarse, as if she had been crying. "What do you mean? What kind of company?"

"Dere are eight giant men heading right for us," Akwen said in concern. "And somehow I don't tink dey are part of da local welcoming committee."

"I'm on my way," she replied tersely, and the commlink went dead.

A minute later, Lisa bounded up the stairs and entered the control room. Moving over to stand next to Akwen, she studied the screen intently.

Noticing the redness of Lisa's eyes, the dark-skinned Cameroonian woman frowned. "What's wrong wit you?"

Uncomfortable under the other woman's critical stare, Lisa shook her head. "Nothing. Don't worry about it. So, what are we gonna do?"

Still frowning, Akwen decided to let the subject drop and focused instead on Lisa's question. "I don't tink dere's much we *can* do. Dey will probably jest come and inspect da pyramid. Den, once dey realize dey can't enter it, dey will probably turn around and leave."

"And hopefully not come back with a jackhammer," Lisa added, her concern clearly written on her face.

Akwen tilted her head to the side and pursed her lips in agreement. Together the two women watched as the group drew closer. "Oh my..." Lisa said in a mixture of awe and fear. "They're huge! Look at them! They must be at least eleven or twelve feet tall! Do you think those are the Nephilim that Noah was referring to?"

Akwen refrained from replying, but the tightness of her mouth and jaw betrayed her otherwise calm exterior. Suddenly, both women started as the giants sprang into action.

"They look like they are going to attack!" Lisa said in panic as the giants sprinted toward the pyramid and began to climb the outer steps toward the closed entrance at the pinnacle.

"But, dat doesn't make any sense," Akwen said in confusion. "Dey don't show any sign dat dey are surprised by da sight of the pyramid. It's almost as if dey know—"

Akwen never completed her sentence, for at that moment, the hatch in the ceiling behind them opened. Whirling around in shock, the women watched in horror as dark shapes slipped through the hole, their massive frames backlit by the sunlight that streamed in through the opening.

Lisa screamed, then dove toward the stairs, knocking over the stool that stood next to the console and sending it crashing to the floor. Akwen, eyes wide in fear, started to run in the opposite direction around the central shaft of the pyramid, but was quickly intercepted by the massive arms of one of the attackers. Despite their best efforts, the two women were quickly overpowered, their final panicked cries muffled as the giants rendered them unconscious…

A scream and accompanying crash startled Dr. Eisenberg, causing him to sit bolt upright in the bed. The rapid movement sent sharp stabs of pain through his torso, forcing him to lie back down. However, the heavy sounds of booted feet on the stairs made him fight through his soreness to sit up once more. Although he was recovering quickly from his wound, the pounding of his heart and the speed of his movements nearly doubled him over with pain. Clenching his jaw tightly to keep from crying out, he swung his legs over the edge of the bed, preparing to stand.

Suddenly, the door at the foot of his bed swung open and two enormous forms entered the room. At the sight of them, the doctor yelled in surprise, sending yet another aching jolt through his body. Approaching the bed, the giant snarled wickedly. The last thing the doctor saw was the meaty hand of the giant as it swung toward his head.

22

THE DUNGEON

THE METAL DOOR of the cell creaked open, sending a loud grating sound echoing down the tunnels of the dungeon. A moment later, Lisa and Akwen were shoved into the room toward one of the corners. The two women instinctively threw out their hands in front of them to stop their momentum against the opposite wall. Turning her head to look over her shoulder, she saw the Nephilim that had been carrying Dr. Eisenberg's limp body enter the small room, the dim light filtering in from the hallway reflecting off of his armor. The giant laid the doctor on the stone floor, then, after casting Lisa a lustful look that made her skin crawl in disgust, he turned and exited, the door slamming shut behind him.

Lisa stared at the bars on the small window of the door numbly, her mind and body completely paralyzed. Minutes passed before she was able to shake off the shock of the recent events. Movement to her right caught her attention as Akwen, exhausted from fear and mental anguish, turned to put her back against the stone wall, and then sunk lethargically to the ground. Drawing her knees up to her chest, the dark-skinned woman began to weep softly.

Coming to her senses, Lisa stepped over to where Dr. Eisenberg lay on the floor. Bending down, she checked his physical condition with concern. Relief flooded over her as she felt his strong pulse beating in his neck. Lifting his shirt, she examined the bandage that covered his wound. Seeing nothing more than a small spot of blood, she lowered his shirt and leaned back against the wall next to Akwen. Mimicking the other woman's posture, Lisa pulled her knees up toward her chest, her own eyes moist.

Oh God, she prayed, *I don't know much about how to pray, but we need Your help! If You can hear me, please do something! Help Doc to wake up, and wherever Jeffrey and the others are, protect them. Although I believe that I'd go to heaven if I die here, I want to live! But…if we don't make it out of this alive, then…please take care of my girls.*

Intense sorrow began welling up with her at the thought of her daughters, Jenny and Amanda. *I don't understand You,* she prayed in frustration. *I thought You loved Your children. If so, then why did You allow this to happen to us? Aren't You a good God? If You are, then why would You take Brad, and now me, away from my girls? Do You want them to be orphans? I believe that You exist and that You died for me, but I just don't understand.*

A soft moan escaped from Akwen's lips, causing Lisa to look over at her. Although Lisa and Akwen had never really liked each other very much, the stark expression of grief and pain that she now saw on the Cameroonian woman's face filled her with compassion. Reaching out toward her, Lisa placed her arm around Akwen's shoulder. The two of them sat leaning against each other for an indeterminate amount of time, tears streaking down their dirt-stained cheeks.

Dr. Eisenberg suddenly groaned and rolled onto his side, snapping Lisa back to reality. Taking her arm from around Akwen's shoulder, she crossed back over to the doctor and placed a hand on his arm. "Doc? Are you alright? Can you hear me?"

He groaned once more and brought his hand up to rest on his head. "Yes," he mumbled. "I hear you, but my head is pounding terribly."

"I'm sorry," Lisa apologized, "but I didn't have anything to give you for a pillow."

"I don't believe that's the cause of my migraine," he chuckled lightly.

"Perhaps it has more to do with the enormous lump on the back of my head where that big oaf hit me. What do you think?"

Lisa tried to smile at the comment, but found that her fear and sorrow were warring against her will. "Oh Doc," she began, her emotions threatening to overwhelm her once again. "What are we going to do?"

Gingerly moving into a sitting position, Dr. Eisenberg looked at her, his face reflecting a calm that helped to ease her anxiety. "First of all, where are we?"

"In the dungeon of some big pyramid-like building on the northeastern side of the city," she replied, her voice desolate.

"Then we must do the only thing we can do: pray."

"But…but, how do we know God will hear us?" she asked. "It's just…why is God allowing this to happen to us? Is it because He *can't* stop it from happening? Why doesn't He just work a miracle and get us out of here?"

"It isn't because He *can't* stop evil," Akwen said, her voice echoing hollowly off the cold, stone walls. "It's because He *won't*."

"What?" Lisa asked, a chill running down her spine at Akwen's frightening words. "What do you mean?"

Her eyes stared straight ahead, her gaze vacant. "I don't tink God really cares much about us at all. More den likely, He created us, den left us to fend for ourselves in a brutal world. He is not a God of love, but rather, a vicious, murderous fiend who kills innocent and guilty equally."

Dr. Eisenberg frowned. Even in the dim light, the pain on the woman's face was easy to read. "No, Akwen. That's not true. God saved Noah and his family because they were righteous. It is the wicked that are judged."

"And what about da children?" Akwen challenged, her eyes turning to stare at him. "Be tankful dat you were unconscious when we were brought here. You didn't have to see what dese people do to deir children. You didn't have to see how dose animal-like men took dat girl, right in da middle of da city wit others watching and…and…" Her voice became choked, preventing her from finishing her sentence.

After a moment, she recovered and continued. "Where was your God den? What did dat poor girl ever do to deserve dat kind of suffering?"

Lisa felt the words sink into her heart, poisoning her newborn faith like a cancer. Although also disturbed by her words, Dr. Eisenberg listened intently and his mind worked to figure out a way to answer her questions. "You can't lay every evil that man commits at the feet of God," he said, wondering if there was more to her animosity than just their current predicament.

"And why not?!" she shot back, her voice rising angrily. "If He's all-powerful and all-loving, den He should step in and save da innocent." As she spoke, tears began to stream down her face once again and her voice rose even higher in pitch. "I watched helplessly as God stood by and let my grandmoder waste away, each day so full of pain dat all she wanted to do was die! He could have healed her, but He chose not to. I prayed day and night for weeks. I asked God for help, but He didn't spare her, or my BABY!"

Akwen's face made a frightening transformation. Gone was the anguish and despair. In its place was pure, unadulterated rage. Looking up at the roof of the cell, she began screaming at the top of her lungs, shocking both Lisa and Dr. Eisenberg with the force of her anger.

"What had she ever done to You to deserve to suffer like dat? She was only tirteen! She hadn't even begun to live, but You let dem kill her! I hate You! Do you hear me? I hate You!" Her fury spent, she doubled over and began to sob profusely until she collapsed on the floor.

Moved by her anguish, Lisa crossed over to her and placed a comforting hand on her shoulder. However, the moment her hand brushed against Akwen's clothing, the distraught woman lashed out at Lisa vehemently. "Don't touch me. It was *your* kind dat did it to her. You American princesses, always seeking your own selfish pleasures and not caring about what happens to oders."

Lisa stepped back, suddenly afraid that Akwen might jump up off the floor and attack her. Instead, she just put her head between her knees and began rocking back and forth, her sorrow consuming her.

Dr. Eisenberg laid a gentle hand on Lisa's arm. "Let her be for now. Give her some time." Still rattled by Akwen's violent outbursts, Lisa simply nodded and moved over to sit on the other side of the small cell. For nearly ten minutes, the only sound that could be heard was the soft moaning sounds that emanated from Akwen. At last, even those faded away, replaced by a heavy stillness. Then, to her companion's surprise, Akwen spoke softly, her voice hoarse and low.

"My Ariel had begged and begged to go to da party with her friend from school. She had been working so hard on bringing up her grades, cleaning up da house for me, and taking care of her younger broder. Since school was almost over for da summer, I decided to let her go. I learned later dat shortly after she had arrived, da girls decided to switch parties. Dose bratty, older American girls pressured Ariel to go with dem until she gave in. She always tried to overcome her African heritage. She just wanted to fit in.

"When dey got to da oder party, da girls began to drink," she continued, her voice devoid of emotion. "Shortly after, I guess dey began to make fun of Ariel's hair, her accent, and her innocence. Devastated, she ran out of da party and began walking home alone." Akwen paused, her voice choked. "Da...da police...didn't find her body for almost a week. Dey were finally able to track down da men dat had...taken her."

Lost in memory, Akwen's lip curled in remembered disgust. "At da trial, da men cried and said dey were sorry, as if dat would bring back my baby. Dey claimed dey were just having a little fun and got carried away. And dose princesses...I overheard one say dat Ariel couldn't take a joke and she shouldn't have gotten so upset. Dey *dared* to blame it on my little girl."

Sliding over to sit next to her, Dr. Eisenberg bowed his head and prayed for wisdom. At last, he spoke, his voice trembling with emotion. "Akwen, I know that nothing I can say will ever take away the ache and pain of your loss. But you must not blame God for the careless and wicked actions of men and women."

Akwen looked up at him and searched his eyes. "Why not? Why didn't He rescue her?" she asked sincerely.

The doctor shook his head. "We can never know for sure. But when we don't understand something, we should always fall back on those things we *do* know to be true. God is love, and like any good father, His deepest desire is that His children love Him as much as He loves them. However, love is a tricky thing. It cannot be forced.

"When God created Adam and Eve, He gave them the choice to disobey Him," Dr. Eisenberg said softly. "If He didn't, then they would have been no better than those dolls that are programmed to say 'I love you' when squeezed. Human free will is a two-edged sword: the greater the capacity for love, the greater the capacity to cause pain. God gives us the choice, but unfortunately, many choose to reject His love, and as a result, do terrible things to themselves and others."

"Human free will still doesn't explain why God doesn't intervene more often and protect da innocent," Akwen said dryly.

"Think about it, though. If God stepped in every time someone was about to do something bad, He would be infringing upon their right to choose. In addition, where do you draw the line? Obviously, rape and murder are evil. But what about cheating, or lying, or stealing? Should He stop those actions also? Where do you draw the line? You see, in God's eyes, we are all sinners deserving of the death penalty. There are no 'innocents.'"

Akwen was silent a moment before responding. "But where is da justice? Dose men were back on da streets after serving only a fraction of deir sentence."

"I know it often seems that evil men succeed and prevail while the righteous suffer," he replied gently. "But you must also remember that this world is not all there is. Justice *will* be served, just maybe not on earth."

"But, what about my grandmoder?" Akwen asked bitterly. "You say dat evil is caused by men making bad choices, but den whose choice was it dat caused my grandmoder to suffer and waste away wit cancer?"

Dr. Eisenberg allowed silence to settle in the cell as he considered her question carefully. "Akwen, once again let me say that I in no way want to minimize your loss. I know the pain and frustration that you feel. But I urge you to consider what I say and make your peace with God before it's too late."

"I'm listening," she mumbled, even though she had turned her head to stare at the wall.

"To answer your question, I would say that there are two types of 'evil': that which happens in nature, and that which is a result of choice. And it doesn't even have to be the choices of men. As we have seen, there are evil beings out there who are trying to destroy us. Often, I believe we suffer because of the attacks of demons, even though we don't realize it. As for your family, your daughter suffered because of the evil choices of others, and your grandmother suffered because of the evil that was brought into the world by man's choice to disobey. Both man and nature must suffer until God, in His allotted time, brings the evil to its end."

He paused and studied Akwen to see how she was reacting to his words. Noting her attentive posture, he continued. "The Torah says that God called everything 'very good' when He first created the earth. There was no sin or death. There was no cancer. But, it also says that after Adam and Eve sinned, the whole world became cursed. The human race still bears the results of the curse in our bodies. That's another reason why good things and bad things happen to 'good' people and 'bad' people.

"There's also an element of free will involved in our sicknesses. How many of our physical problems could be avoided if we ate healthier foods, exercised, and slept more hours?" he asked rhetorically. "In our time, so many of the foods we eat are processed and filled with toxins that slowly destroy our bodies. We don't even know it, but we may be giving ourselves incurable diseases just by the types of food we put on our plates, and in how we store and cook them."

When Akwen looked at him, the doctor could see that although she wasn't convinced by his words, she was at least considering them. *Oh Lord, give me the words that will break through her despair,* he prayed silently.

"Let me put it another way," Dr. Eisenberg said. "I once knew a man who used to love to refurbish cars. He would spend hours and hours fix-ing them, painting them, and waxing them. He was so proud of his own car that he told all of his friends about it and invited them to come over and look at it."

Akwen gave a cynical laugh. "Doc, why are you wasting your time telling me a story? We're all going to die in a matter of hours anyway."

"That's the very reason *why* I'm telling you all of this!" he exclaimed. "If we die today, you will stand before God. I don't want anything to keep you from accepting His love before it's too late."

"I appreciate your concern, but it's going to take a lot of convincing to get me to change my mind after all I've been trough," she said.

"At least let me try to answer your objections," he pleaded. "Let me finish the story."

She nodded unenthusiastically. "Well, we've got nuhting better to do."

Praying once again that God would open her eyes, Dr. Eisenberg continued. "Before the man's friends arrived to view his beautiful car, he let his son take it for a spin. But unfortunately, the son was reckless. When he brought the car back, it was scratched, dirty, dented, and gen-erally busted up. Then, when the friends arrived, they looked at the car and said, 'What a piece of junk! You spent all of your time and money on *that* thing? What a waste!'"

Akwen studied him for a moment. "So, what are you getting at?"

"Whose fault was it that the car was damaged?" he asked.

"It was da son's fault."

The doctor smiled. "Don't you see? It's the same with us and God. We often blame Him for the poor condition of the world and for all of the evil, but He didn't make it this way! He made it perfect, and we messed it up. It's because of man's sin that there are tornados, hurricanes, and—"

A sudden shudder ran through the stone cell, causing small streams of dust to rain down upon them and forcing Dr. Eisenberg to stop mid-sentence. The three prisoners froze, fearing that the entire structure above them would come crashing down. After nearly a full minute of silence, they let out their breaths and relaxed.

"…and earthquakes," Lisa finished, her voice tinged with apprehension. "They're getting stronger, aren't they?"

"Yes, they are," Dr. Eisenberg said in resignation.

"What does it all matter anymore?" Akwen said dully. "We're going to die soon and, since God won't help us, my children will be left witout a moder, and my husband witout a wife."

"I wouldn't give up hope just yet. God has a way of coming through when we least expect it. I sometimes think He likes a good story as much as the rest of us," he said wryly. Growing more serious, he continued. "But even if He doesn't choose to rescue us, it doesn't mean He doesn't love us, or our families. Often, it is only through suffering that our true character can shine."

Akwen's eye's narrowed. "What do you mean?"

"I don't remember the exact wording, but there is a verse in the New Testament that says that God works out things for good for those who love Him.[1] The Scriptures are replete with stories of men and women who suffered, yet God brought good out of a bad situation. God cares more about our character than our comfort."

Pausing, he glanced over at Lisa and saw that she was also being impacted by his words. "Take the story of Joseph, for example. He was sold into slavery by his own brothers, yet God used that horrible evil to eventually save millions of people, including the very brothers that committed the evil act.

"Look at our own situation," Dr. Eisenberg said, holding out his arms in an encompassing gesture. "Many bad things have happened to us on this journey. But if it hadn't been for those things, I may have never understood the truth about Jesus. Because we're facing death, we are forced to come to grips with our own mortality and realize that we can't do things on our own. We must never doubt in the darkness that God has revealed to us in the light."

Placing a comforting hand on Akwen's shoulder, he continued. "A famous Christian writer named C. S. Lewis once said, 'God whispers to us in our pleasures, speaks to us in our conscience, but shouts in our pains: It is His megaphone to rouse a deaf world.' So maybe, just maybe, one of the reasons that God sent us on this trip was to force us to realize that the Bible is true and that Jesus really *is* the Messiah. Isn't our eternal salvation more important than our physical comfort?"

Akwen looked over at him, tears filling her eyes once more. "But den, what good came out of da loss of my daughter and grandmoder?"

Dr. Eisenberg shook his head sadly. "I don't know. I wish I could give you some simple answer, but frankly, there are some things we may never know this side of heaven. However, that doesn't mean that there *isn't* a good answer. I am convinced God loves you and has your best interests in mind. He also sees the big picture; He knows the future. He wants you to love Him and trust Him, even when you don't understand. You may not know why God allows suffering in your life now, but perhaps in five or ten years, you will look back and see God's hand."

"If I should live dat long," she stated sarcastically.

"Hopefully you will," he said, attempting a reassuring smile.

"I don't buy into everting you've said, but you have given me a lot to tink about," she said after a few moments.

"Akwen, I have one more final point," he said, leaning closer to her. "Joseph was able to forgive his brothers, and it brought healing to his whole family. I'm afraid that if you do not forgive the men who killed your daughter, the bitterness will destroy you. It will *consume* you. Jesus died on the cross for the sins of the world, including you *and* those men. Pray that He will help you forgive."

The woman snorted derisively. "Dat would be impossible."

"With God, it *is* possible," he said, then moved slowly over to where Lisa sat, leaving Akwen to her tumultuous thoughts.

Several hours passed uneventfully. Lisa, Akwen, and Dr. Eisenberg slept fitfully on the cold stone floor, awakening intermittently whenever another tremor would roll through the building.

Sudden footfalls echoing down the corridor outside their cell roused them. A Naphil soldier appeared at the door to their cell, unlocked it, opened it, and motioned for them to follow him. Surprised, the three prisoners climbed to their feet and did as commanded, wondering at what new fate awaited them. Two other guards fell in behind the prisoners as they walked down the corridor.

After traveling down several more hallways and through two more locked doors, the group entered a medium-sized room that appeared to be some sort of guard room. The prisoners felt their hearts leap with excitement as they looked upon the other occupants of the room.

"Doc! Thank God you're okay!" Rebecca called out as Dr. Eisenberg, Lisa, and Akwen entered the room. Although she wanted to run to embrace him, the Naphil standing behind her put a restraining hand upon her shoulder. Next to her, Jeffrey, Jerome, and Mack stood silently, surrounded by three more of the twelve-foot Nephilim soldiers.

"We're all fine," Dr. Eisenberg said as he, Lisa, and Akwen were herded into the center of the room where the others waited. Before the friends even had a chance to welcome each other, the Nephilim began leading the prisoners out of the guardroom and up a flight of stairs.

The guards led them down several deserted hallways; the dim artificial lights mounted on the walls created an eerie atmosphere full of shadows and darkened alcoves. Glancing out a window, Dr. Eisenberg could see that the first rays of sunlight were beginning to make their ways over the horizon. *This is it. This is the day the Flood will be unleashed,* he thought in concern. *Lord, even if I don't make it, please save these young people. Help them to get back to their families.*

A nudge from Jeffrey broke into his prayers. "Doc," he whispered, "something's wrong here. Did you notice the way the guards are looking around anxiously? It's almost as if they're trying to keep us from being seen. And there's something familiar about these hallways."

The Naphil guard behind Jeffrey smacked him in the back of the head. Taking the hint, Jeffrey said nothing more. After nearly ten minutes of walking in silence through the darkened hallways, they finally reached their destination. Two double doors opened into a large cube-shaped room over one hundred feet in each direction. To the prisoners' utter shock and amazement, the majority of the room was taken up by a large, two-story pyramid.

"It's the Pyramid of the Ancients!" Mack said, dumbfounded. "But…but how?"

Before anyone could even venture a guess, the door of the pyramid opened. At the sight of the figure that walked through the entrance and down the steps toward them, each of the travelers felt a terrifying sense of recognition pierce through them.

Sucking in a panicked breath, Mack stuttered, "D…dear God, help us! Is…is that who I think it is?"

Jeffrey swallowed hard, trying to hold back his own fear. "I'm afraid so. It's the alien corpse from the workshop…the designer of the pyramid!"

23

MYSTERIES REVEALED

THE PRISONERS WATCHED as the figure strode toward them confidently. As the being drew closer, Jeffrey felt his stomach clench into knots. There was no mistaking it now. He recognized the large brows, deep-set eyes, sharp teeth and ape-like appearance, for it had haunted Jeffrey for many nights after he had first discovered the body in the dusty chamber. And now, here it was, moving and breathing like a creature risen from the dead.

Stopping to stand in front of them, the ape-like man crossed his arms against his chest. As he did so, Jeffrey noticed that he wore the exact same robe that they had seen on the dead body, the deep purple and silver colors shimmering in the light of the large room. The man's coarse, brown hair was combed straight back and covered the sides of his face and neck, but left the pinkish skin of the cheeks, mouth, and eyes untouched. Staring up at the seven-foot-tall being, Jeffrey could tell from the look in his eyes that this was no brute. The dark brown orbs resonated with a shrewd intelligence, as well as a disturbing malevolence.

The doors behind them suddenly opened again and two other figures entered the room. The sight of the twelve-foot-tall beast-like men sent another shiver of recognition through Jeffrey's brain. The creature on the left had the same contorted, wolf-like features and wore the same finely-crafted leather armor as the other alien that he, Jerome, and the rest of the team had discovered along with the pyramid. The other figure had two, five-inch curved horns sprouting out of his head and a snout similar to a bull. The creature's overall features reminded Jeffrey of some kind of mutated Minotaur.

As the two newcomers entered the room, the ape-like man called out an order to the Nephilim guards and waved his hand at them in dismissal. Turning on their heels, the seven soldiers exited the room, leaving the prisoners alone to face the robed man and his two henchmen.

The man with the ape-like features studied each of them in turn, a wicked smile splitting his grotesque features. After a few moments, he spoke, his voice coarse and grating. When Mack didn't translate immediately, Jeffrey nudged him. "What did he say?"

With his face pale from fright, Mack stuttered, and then fell quickly into his role as translator. "He…he said, 'Welcome, travelers.'"

The figure frowned at the sound of the strange words. He spoke again, focusing his attention on Mack. "Why do you use such odd speech with your companions?"

"My…my friends developed a different set of words to use," he said nervously, remembering his failed encounter with Odin. "It has been so long since they have used the original words, they have forgotten them."

The man stared down at Mack ruefully, and then began to laugh, the harsh sound reminding the visitors of nails scraping against a chalkboard. "You do not have to lie to me, little man," he said, amused. "For I know where you came from, or should I say, 'when' you came from!"

When Mack finished translating his pronouncement to the others, a new wave of shock and confusion flowed through them. "How do you…who…who are you?" Mack stuttered.

Clearly relishing the surprise on the prisoners' faces, he bowed slightly to them as he introduced himself. "I am Arngrim. And I would like to offer you my sincere thanks for completing my pyramid and bringing it back here to me."

"What?" Jerome said breathlessly once he and the others had gotten the translation from Mack, who had nearly fainted at the ape-man's statement. "*His* pyramid?"

Drawing immense pleasure from their confusion, Arngrim let out another laugh. "Although I must admit, you are much shorter and weaker than I had thought you would be. But that will just make it that much easier…" he said, more to himself than to the others.

"We don't…we don't understand," Jeffrey said. "Noah told us that you were his friend and that you might be able to help us fix the pyramid. How did you get it here?"

"So, I have my *cousin* to thank for sending you to my shop," he said. "I will have to make sure I express my appreciation to him for doing me that great service. I was quite distressed that you had not arrived where I expected you to."

"Your…*cousin?*" Jeffrey repeated in astonishment.

"Yes," he said. "His grandfather and my grandmother were brother and sister. Only *his* foolish grandfather continued to hold to his outdated religious notions and failed to embrace the wonders that genetic enhancements could provide. My grandmother, and my parents, had no such convictions, for which I am eternally grateful."

Jeffrey stared ahead blankly, his forehead becoming lined with confusion and disillusionment at the man's revelation. Next to him, Jerome gave voice to the words that were repeating themselves over and over in Jeffrey's mind like a broken record. "He's not an alien at all, but a genetically altered human!"

With crushing certainty, Jeffrey realized that he had been wrong all along. The bodies they had found in the hidden chamber had not been aliens. The pyramid was not some space ship that had brought those creatures from another galaxy. The last bastion of his belief in evolution had been destroyed. Rebecca was right. He could deny the evidence no longer. God *did* exist, and His judgment was about to be poured out upon the planet.

At that moment, Jeffrey knew with certainty that when he died, he would have to face *Him* and give an accounting for everything he had ever done. The thought was like a physical blow, knocking the wind out of him.

Misinterpreting Jeffrey's inner turmoil, Arngrim continued. "It appears that the thought of genetic modification unsettles you. Yes, it was one of the greatest gifts that the gods handed down to us. They showed a select few of their 'disciples' how to do it, and we have been busy playing around with the knowledge ever since. Although they wouldn't allow us *mortals* to experiment with *their* bodies, we got to watch as they altered the structures of their own offspring," he said, pointing to the two animal-like giants that stood guard behind the captives.

"This new breed of Nephilim are magnificent, aren't they?" he continued, his face beaming with a sickening pride. "They are not just a mixture of gods and humans. They also contain the best elements from the animal kingdom. Some they made more beautiful, and some they made more...useful."

Glancing back at the two monsters, with their twisted faces, yellowed teeth and blood-shot eyes, Jeffrey felt the bile rise in his throat.

"You said...you said that we didn't arrive where you expected," Rebecca said, her voice trembling with fear. "How did you know we were coming?"

"Have you not guessed yet?" he replied once Mack had translated Rebecca's question. "Obviously not. Well, then, let me enlighten you by starting at the beginning."

As he began to speak, he walked in circles around the captives, his eyes studying their expressions. It was almost as if he knew his words were bound to produce shocked reactions in his captives and he didn't want to miss a single one of them. "Noah and I are nearly the same age. I can't say that we *grew up* together, for his family shunned mine because of our superiority," he said with a sneer. "But over the years, we developed a...a working relationship.

"My brilliant mind eventually attracted the attention of Loki, who brought me under his tutelage," he continued. "I became one of the few men who were taught the secrets of the gods! Under their supervision, I was allowed to tamper with the very building blocks of nature itself! I became like a god! With my knowledge, I altered regular, imperfect humans and helped to create entire races and strange creatures."

Jeffrey shivered at the words, remembering the Blood Drinkers and the monstrous human soldiers they had hired.

"After several hundred years of study, Loki gave me permission to share some of the more primitive technological devices with the masses. So, I opened up my shop in the city. I believe that it brought Loki no end of enjoyment to watch how the foolish humans used the technology to destroy each other. In particular, he received great delight in watching them use the swords that discharged energy. He savored the times when he could witness their bodies squirm and convulse as the current shot through them."

Disgusted, Rebecca let out a soft groan, which only served to bring a smile of pleasure to her captor's face. "But I digress. One day, Noah came to me to ask for help with his little Ark project. He, of course, had no knowledge of the fact that I had been given access to some of the gods' secrets. In his simple-minded innocence, he still believed that I was just a genius inventor. Intrigued by his own highly developed intelligence, I decided to help him build his vessel."

Arngrim paused in his narrative, his expression hardening. "I worked with him for over half a century, forced to constantly listen to his ravings about God's judgment. At first I simply laughed at him and dismissed his preaching, content to use the money I earned from him to finance my own endeavors. But as time went on, I realized that Noah was no fool. He truly believed that what he said was true. His careful, detailed construction of the Ark was proof enough of his sincerity.

"And then, one day, I came to the shocking conclusion that he was right," he stated with simple finality.

"What?" Dr. Eisenberg said in surprise. "You...you *believe* that the Flood is coming?"

"Yes," Arngrim replied coldly. "I had been talking to one of the astrologers who had been studying with the gods and he told me of a great falling star that he had observed in the heavens that was heading directly for the earth. When he told me approximately when it would strike the planet, and that it would fall in the ocean, I realized that it coincided directly with Noah's prediction. Furthermore, I have overheard the gods on several occasions cursing Yahweh, the Creator, so I knew He was real as well."

"Dear God," Rebecca said in sudden understanding. "You created the pyramid to escape the Cataclysm! The pyramid is your version of the Ark! You plan to travel into the future to a time *after* the Flood!"

Arngrim smiled wickedly as his prisoners reeled back in shock from the revelation.

Mack stopped translating momentarily as he turned to face the others in shock. "That's why the pyramid was designed with a kitchen, bathroom, and bedrooms. And that's why the beds were so big!"

"The beds!" Dr. Eisenberg exclaimed in horror. "He's going to take women with him to breed with! In time, his children would easily overpower Noah and his family! He'll conquer the whole world, subjecting Noah's descendents to slavery!"

"And wit his technology, he will be unstoppable!" Akwen added.

"I see you are beginning to understand the depth of your folly. Perhaps you aren't as stupid as you look," Arngrim said, grinning perversely as he continued with his explanation. "I realized that if I was to survive, I would have to begin work right away on my own project. Besides, by this time Noah had learned of my involvement in other unsavory business ventures. Naturally he disapproved, and we had a…a disagreement."

"Yeah, I bet," Jerome added sarcastically under his breath.

"Fortunately, during the time that I had worked with my masters, I learned where they kept their most hidden secrets," Arngrim said boastfully. "It was there that I learned how to break through the very boundaries of time and space. In their arrogance, the gods have discounted Noah's warnings. They foolishly believe that with their combined power they can prevent Yahweh's judgment. I'm not willing to take that chance. If they succeed, then I will just arrive and continue to serve them. But, if they are wrong, then *I* will become the master!"

"That means that the 'gods' don't know that he has created this pyramid!" Dr. Eisenberg said softly, a tiny sliver of hope working its way into his heart.

"That's why we were put in a different cell than you!" Rebecca added. "We were captured by Odin, who seemed to know nothing about the pyramid, but you were captured by Arngrim's men!"

"Which is how dey were able to open da outer doors of da pyramid," Akwen stated. "Dey must have had some special access code given to dem by Arngrim. But how did dey get da pyramid here?"

"Mack, ask him that question," Jeffrey said, the small hope beginning to take root. "Perhaps if we can keep him talking, Odin's men will come looking for us. If we can't escape ourselves, we have to at least stall long enough until the Flood occurs."

Swallowing his fear, Mack translated the question.

Arngrim answered confidently, thoroughly enjoying the moment. "Simple: they flew it here."

Akwen stared in shock. "How is dat possible? Da pyramid wouldn't power up! Da controls were locked!"

Crossing over to stand in front of her, Arngrim leaned down to look intently at her. "And who do you think locked the controls? *I* am the one that set the pyramid to return here to me and *I* am the one who set it to lockdown once it arrived."

"But why?" Jeffrey said in confusion after Mack had finished translating Arngrim's statement. "I don't understand. What do we have to do with all of this?"

The man's ape-like features darkened. "That is the regrettable part of my story. You see, everything was going according to plan until I started working on the core. The design turned out to be trickier than I had expected. I failed several times to create a core that would be strong enough to withstand the strain of time travel.

"Finally, when I had solved the problems, I realized too late that I had used up all of the materials I needed on the failed cores," he sneered. "A new shipment was set to arrive weeks ago, and I would have had enough time to complete the project. However, as fate would have it, the shipment was attacked by a contingent of Tiamat's soldiers."

As he related the incident, the prisoners could see his anger beginning to rise. "The fools had no idea what they had done to me! When I discovered that the shipment was gone, I realized that there wouldn't be enough time to wait on another shipment. I was left with only one option.

"I took all of my blueprints and notes and put them in my workshop with the nearly complete pyramid," he said, his face becoming confident once again. "I decided to seal up the workshop, knowing that someday in the future, someone would break the seal, find my notes, and, with their curiosity burning, they would complete the project. But, the moment they turned it on, it would follow the programming I placed into it and return back here to me."

"So dat was why we couldn't control it," Akwen breathed in frustration.

Although Mack did not translate her statement, Arngrim's comment made it seem as if he guessed at what she had said. "I give you credit, though. You gained more control over my Ark than I would have thought possible. I had programmed it to land here in this room. When it didn't arrive, I nearly went insane with anger. Then, when Vidarr brought me word that a group of strange, pure-blooded visitors had come looking for me, I realized the truth."

A sudden thought struck Jeffrey with the force of a lightning bolt. Turning to Jerome, he gazed at him intently. "Did you hear what he said earlier? He sealed up the chamber with the technical journals and pyramid. But he wasn't in there himself!"

Jerome's eyes widened. "Yet we found his dead body as well as the body of one of his Nephilim guards!"

"Which means," Jeffrey continued, trying hard to contain his excitement so that Arngrim wouldn't suspect anything. "Something else happened to force him to lock himself in there."

"But what?" Jerome countered. "And how do we know that we haven't somehow changed things by being here?"

"I don't know, but we have to keep stalling," Jeffrey said.

"Why did you put the book with the information on how to build a gravity control device in the antechamber?" Dr. Eisenberg asked curiously, causing Jeffrey and Jerome to cease their private conversation. "And how did you keep it from being destroyed by the Flood, yet accessible to people in the future?"

"Simple. I didn't want just *anyone* to stumble upon my Ark," Arngrim stated after receiving the translation from Mack. "They may have unwittingly destroyed it in their ignorance. No, I needed to make sure that whoever found it would be advanced enough in technology to be able to finish it. So, I created a test. If they were intelligent enough to follow my instructions to build a gravity control device, then they should be able to complete the pyramid also. To ensure the survival of my blueprints, I sealed the antechamber with an anti-gravity field that was set on a time delay. Several years after the Flood was over, the field would disappear, allowing the antechamber to be uncovered."

"There's still something I don't get," Jerome said. "How is it that Nimrod also had the technology to create a core for the Tower of Babel that was identical to the one designed for the pyramid?"

When Mack had finished translating the question, one of Arngrim's eyebrows rose questioningly. "So, you say that one of Noah's descendents created a core that fit my pyramid. Very interesting. It would seem that my young cousin actually followed my instructions. That is good. That is very good indeed."

Disconcerted by anything that their captor might consider to be "very good," Jeffrey frowned. "What instructions did Noah follow?"

"Not Noah," Arngrim said with a smirk, "but his son, Ham. Out of all of Noah's three sons, he was the one that showed the most promise. Whenever we got into a debate, Ham seemed the most sympathetic to my views. Several years ago, he came to visit me without his father's permission. At that time, I tried to convince him to take some scrolls on his father's Ark that represented the knowledge and history of the gods so that future generations would know what our world was like before the Cataclysm."

An image of the library in the Tower of Babel flashed before Jeffrey's eyes. "That's where all of the legends of the pre-Flood false gods came from!" he said, stunned.

"Yes," Rebecca said, her eyes wide. "Ham must have hidden the scrolls aboard the Ark. After the Flood, he must have used the information in the scrolls to teach his children about the false gods. Once the people dispersed after God confused their languages, the truths of the pre-Flood world became embellished and turned into legends and myths."

"But, that still doesn't explain how Nimrod was able to build an exact replica of the core," Dr. Eisenberg said.

Arngrim folded his hairy claw-like hands into the folds of his robe. "When I learned that I would not be able to complete the pyramid in time, I sent a messenger to Ham immediately with a package. I knew that if I wanted someone to be able to have the technology to complete the pyramid, I would have a greater chance of succeeding if the world already had the knowledge in their hands."

"The package you gave Ham was the technical blueprints for gravity control and the pyramid!" Jeffrey said.

Even as Arngrim nodded in acknowledgment of Jeffrey's comment, Lisa had already begun speaking. "So that's why the technology that Nimrod had is nearly identical to the technology before the Flood! The gravity control devices, the core, the flying platforms—Ham had the specs to create all of it!"

"And after the dispersal at Babel, no one could read the blueprints anymore," Rebecca added. "Which is why the technology was lost, except for a few of the devices that survived, such as the ones the Mayans had—"

Rebecca was cut off in mid-sentence by a mighty earthquake that knocked everyone to the floor, including the Nephilim guards. When the trembling ceased, Arngrim quickly jumped to his feet, the confidence that graced his expression moments ago having evaporated.

"It seems that this world's time is nearly up," Arngrim announced as the guards and their prisoners regained their balance. "Fortunately for me, while you languished in the dungeon, I spent the entire night preparing for my journey. And so, I thank you once again for finishing *my* Ark and bringing it to me. It is time for me to depart. My lovely concubines are already on board, and I don't want to keep them waiting any longer. The New World awaits its master!"

Even before Mack had a chance to finish his translation and realize what was happening, Arngrim spun around and headed back toward the pyramid.

"Wait!" Jeffrey called out, causing the Nephilim guards to quickly take up positions on each side of the prisoners, the lengthy spears in their hands turned sideways to prevent the prisoners from moving either forward or backward.

"Oh, God!" Lisa called out in fear. "He's going to take the pyramid and leave us here to die!"

Jeffrey felt his own mouth go dry as he realized that there was no escape now. Once the pyramid disappeared, they would be doomed. "We have to stop him! There's only two guards. If we all attack at once, they won't be able to catch—"

The shaft of the thick spear butted into the side of Jeffrey's head, sending him crashing to the floor dazed. Staring down at the puny humans less than half their size, the wolf-like Nephilim soldiers began to salivate, as if hoping for a fight.

Lisa knelt down next to Jeffrey attempting to staunch the flow of blood that was trickling down his face from the small cut he had received from the spear. Dazed, he and his companions looked on in despair as Arngrim, master and creator of the Pyramid of the Ancients, stepped through its entrance and shut the door behind him.

24

ARNGRIM'S FURY

REBECCA FELT A hollowness settle in the pit of her stomach as the door of the pyramid closed. Beside her, she heard Lisa begin to weep softly. Then, to Rebecca's surprise, she heard her begin to pray. "Oh Lord, please take care of my girls. Jesus, protect them."

Turning to face her one-time best friend, who was still kneeling next to Jeffrey, she stared at her, conflicting emotions of compassion and hate rushing through her. Sensing Rebecca's perusal, Lisa looked up at her, an expression of utter regret and sorrow on her face. For several long moments, the two women stared at each other in silence. Rebecca could almost feel the silent plea for forgiveness that was expressed in Lisa's eyes. Yet, Rebecca's mind rebelled against what she knew was right, bringing back images of Lisa's betrayal to use as a shield to ward off any feelings of compassion for her friend.

Jeffrey sat up slowly, drawing Lisa's attention. She helped him to his feet, and then surprisingly stepped away from him to stand next to Mack. Rebecca's gaze lingered for a moment, then scanned the faces of each of her other friends, their faces mirroring her own feelings of defeat and grief. The two Nephilim guards, although keeping an eye on the prisoners, were nevertheless watching the pyramid with intense interest.

The sensation of someone's hand slipping into Rebecca's own broke through her swirling emotions. Glancing to her right, she saw Dr. Eisenberg smiling sadly at her; the resignation she saw reflected in his expression caused another pang of sorrow to sweep through her.

"We have little time left, Rebecca," he said. "Will you go into eternity harboring unforgiveness in your heart?"

Turning away from his convicting gaze, Rebecca stared at the pyramid. A blue glow began to appear under it as the engines revved up. Tears burned her eyes as she considered his words. "You're right, Doc. It's just…it's just so hard to let go of my hate."

"Ask God to give you the strength," he said softly.

Casting him a grateful smile, Rebecca took a deep breath and stepped over to where Lisa stood staring at the pyramid which had begun to rise off the floor. As she touched Lisa's arm, she turned toward her. Then, without a word, Lisa fell into Rebecca's arms and began to weep profoundly, her words of regret spilling out like a flood. "Becky, I'm so sorry. I'm so sorry…" Moved by her friend's brokenness, Rebecca embraced her, tears running freely down her own cheeks.

Lost in the emotion of the moment, Rebecca was startled when Mack spoke next to her, the confusion in his voice jolting her back to their current predicament.

"What's he waiting for?" Mack asked.

Breaking her embrace with Lisa, Rebecca looked over at the pyramid and noted with interest that it was still there, hovering several feet off the floor.

"Maybe he's just toying with us," Jeffrey stated, his right hand still pressing against the small wound on his head.

Suddenly, to the surprise of everyone in the room, the engines began to slow down and the pyramid came to rest on the floor once again.

"What the…?" Mack said, his brows furrowing in confusion.

Before anyone could even begin to venture a guess as to the cause of the turnaround, the door of the pyramid opened once again and Arngrim strode out, his face reflecting his fury.

At his approach, Rebecca and the others instinctively shrank back. However, the bull-like guard behind them used his spear to keep them from retreating further.

Reaching out with one of his hairy, claw-like hands, Arngrim grabbed the front of Mack's robe threateningly. "What did you do to it?!"

Nearly collapsing in terror, Mack stuttered a reply. "I…I…don't…. don't know. What…what's wrong with it?"

Arngrim narrowed his eyes. "As if you don't know. Tell me how to fix it. NOW!"

"Pl…please. I honestly don't know what's wrong with it," Mack pleaded. "Perhaps if…if you told me—"

Anger raging through him, Arngrim threw Mack to the floor of the chamber. "I don't have time for these games. The ship will not travel through time!"

Cowering on the floor, Mack stared up at him. "We didn't do anything to it! We were never able to control it much."

The ape-like man's face suddenly relaxed. With a supreme effort, he reigned in his rage. "I will make a deal with you. If you tell me how to fix it, I will take you and your friends with me. You can serve me as slaves, but at least you will be alive."

Mack trembled, his voice strained. "We can't help you fix the pyramid. WE DON'T KNOW HOW!"

Leaning over Mack, Arngrim's eyes widened as he lost the tenuous control of his anger. "You *will* tell me what I want to know, or you *and* your friends will suffer!"

Without Mack's translation, Rebecca and the others were forced to merely watch in fear, wondering what was happening. Straightening up, Arngrim suddenly froze as if listening. Outside, in the corridor, the faint sounds of booted feet could be heard in the distance. After a moment, he turned back to Mack and spoke again, then barked out a command to the two guards. Immediately, they picked Mack up from off the floor and began herding the prisoners toward the exit. The bull-like guard opened the door, looked both directions down the hallway, and then began leading the group quickly through the halls, Arngrim following close behind.

"Mack, what's going on?" Jeffrey whispered as they were ushered down a stairwell.

On the verge of tears, Mack began to explain. "The pyramid won't work! He thinks *we* did something to it, and he doesn't believe me when I tell him we didn't!"

"So where's he taking us?" Jeffrey asked as he glanced behind them at the agitated form of their captor.

"He wants to…force us to talk," Mack said, looking like he was going to be sick. "Jeffrey, help me! It's going to be just like it was with Nimrod at the Tower!"

Before Jeffrey could respond, he heard Jerome suck in a breath sharply. Whipping his head around, he began to search for the cause of Jerome's reaction. "What? What's wrong?"

Pale and shaken, Jerome looked at Jeffrey, his eyes wide. "Don't you recognize this place? Don't you realize where we are?"

As Jeffrey looked closer at their surroundings, the blood drained out of his face. "Oh no."

"What? What is it now?" Rebecca asked, deep lines of concern carving themselves into her features as she studied the horror-stricken faces of her friends.

"Dis is da floor above da chamber containing da pyramid!" Akwen stated.

Now that it was brought to her attention, Rebecca could see the columns with their intricately carved designs and lettering. Although she had only seen the actual dig site a couple of times, she understood that her companions knew it well from the years they had spent studying it. If they were above the chamber, that could only mean that Arngrim was taking them to one place.

His workshop.

The Nephilim guard brought the group to a halt at what appeared to be a dead end passage. Arngrim made his way to the front of the group, looked around to make sure no one was in the vicinity, then depressed a hidden section of a nearby column. Suddenly, a portion of the wall moved backward revealing a staircase hidden beneath the floor, a blue glow preventing anyone from entering. Moving his hand to a column on the opposite side of the stairs, the ape-like human pressed another hidden button and the blue field disappeared.

Arngrim led the way down the large stairway, the Nephilim guards following behind with the prisoners. As they descended, Rebecca remembered the sense of disquiet and foreboding that she had felt when she had entered the ruins for the first time and viewed it with new understanding. This place *reeked* of demonic power and activity. Jeffrey and the others hadn't just made a simple archaeological discovery, they had uncovered a stronghold of evil.

When they had all arrived in the antechamber, they could see that another blue field surrounded the wall opposite the stairs. Stepping over to the wall on the left side of the small room, Arngrim inserted a special key-like object into an unremarkable hole. A second later, a tiny, square panel opened up next to it, revealing three buttons. Pressing the one on the left, they heard the wall covering the top of the steps slide back into place, sealing them in. Arngrim then pressed the center button, and they watched as the blue field surrounding the door to the workshop disappeared. Opening the door, he stepped through it. Hearts beating rapidly, the prisoners followed as the Nephilim guards shoved them from behind.

A poignant sense of déjà vu struck Rebecca as she entered the chamber. However, based on the expressions on her friend's faces, she knew it was even stronger with them, for while Rebecca had arrived years after the chamber had been discovered, her husband had been the first person to set foot in the room for thousands of years.

The dimly-lit room was in nearly the same condition as it had been that day years ago when Jeffrey, Jerome, Mack, and Akwen had entered. The main difference being that instead of broken glass, pottery, and other items lying all over the floor, they were organized in an orderly fashion on the shelves and tables that lined the room. In addition to that, the only other things missing were lots of dust, and two dead bodies.

One of the two "missing corpses" stopped and turned to face the captives once they had all entered the room. "Bind their hands and stand them against the wall so they can watch," Arngrim commanded. Grabbing a length of rope that hung from a hook on the wall, the two guards immediately set about fulfilling their master's command. As they did so, Mack began to plead once again.

"Please! Mighty Arngrim, we...we honestly don't know why the pyramid won't work! Why won't you believe me?"

"Because you are just like Noah: stubborn," he responded coldly. "The only thing you understand is pain."

As he made this last statement, he took from a shelf a pair of items that reminded Mack of the gravity control devices that they had used to carry the core out of the Tower of Babel. Only when combined with Arngrim's words, the seemingly innocent objects suddenly took on a sinister air.

"Go back upstairs and wait outside the hidden entrance. Make sure we are not disturbed," Arngrim said to the bull-like soldier, who promptly turned and left the room. Returning his attention to his now bound prisoners, he smiled wickedly. "Down here, no one will hear you scream. And as you know, I have no time to be patient. You will tell me what I want to know, or I will torture you, then begin killing you one at a time."

Mack began to sob, memories of the Tower of Babel and Nimrod flashing through his subconscious once again. "I already told you," he gasped, "we didn't do anything to the pyramid. We started it up and it brought us here!"

"But you obviously were able to gain some control!" he spat back at Mack. "How? What did you change?"

Mack glanced over at Akwen, then turned back to face Arngrim.

"We…we have a robot that hooked into the computer. Maybe it did something."

Arngrim's brows creased skeptically. "Are you referring to that circular machine with eyes that sits in the control room?"

"Yes!" Mack said hopefully. "Maybe if you start it up—"

"My guards already disposed of the machine," Arngrim said coldly. "You told the machine what to do. You *must* know what it did."

"NO!" Mack shouted back. "The only thing we told Elmer to do was try to get control of the movements of the ship! He didn't do anything to keep it from traveling through time. We never had any problems… Wait!" he shouted suddenly. "The core that's in the pyramid now is the new one we got from Nimrod in the Tower of Babel! Maybe there's something wrong with it! We installed it *after* we got here!"

Arngrim shook his head. "Nice try. But if that was so, then why does the pyramid have power at all? The only thing that doesn't work is the actual time dispersment field. You are hiding something, and I am going to find out what it is."

Moving over to stand in front of the others, he stared at Lisa, Akwen, and Rebecca intently. "Perhaps watching these puny female friends of yours scream in pain as I remove their appendages one by one will loosen your tongue. So, I think I will skip your own torture and jump immediately to applying pain to a third party. What do you think?"

"Please…Oh God, please NO!" Mack cried.

Grabbing Rebecca's arm, he shoved her toward the far wall, the gravity control devices held aloft in his hands.

"NO!" Jeffrey suddenly screamed, guessing as to the evil man's intentions. Rushing forward, he ducked the swinging spear from the wolf-like Naphil guard and lunged at Arngrim. Sensing the attack, Arngrim turned just as Jeffrey plowed into him. As they crashed to the floor, Arngrim twisted his body like a cat so that he landed on top of Jeffrey, knocking the wind out of him.

Rebecca screamed and tried to club Arngrim with her bound wrists, but he deflected her blow and struck her, sending her tumbling to the floor, stunned.

"So, you want to volunteer to be first?" Arngrim snarled at Jeffrey, who continued to writhe on the floor in pain. "Fine. We'll start with you then. I don't have time to do this the right way, so we'll just have to improvise." Picking Rebecca up from the floor, he tossed her back toward the others, then reached down, grabbed the gravity control devices, which he had dropped in the attack, and mounted both of them into brackets on the wall. Activating the devices, he adjusted the setting of the blue energy beam so that it was nothing more than a thin line. Shutting them off again, he grabbed Jeffrey violently and placed his bound wrists in between the two devices. Turning them on once again, he watched in satisfaction as the blue beam passed between Jeffrey's wrists and head.

Hanging off the floor by his wrists, Jeffrey began to kick out at his captor in defiance, but it only served to enrage Arngrim further. A sickening thud reverberated in the chamber as Arngrim's massive clawed fist backhanded Jeffrey across the face, rendering him temporarily unconscious. Across the room, Lisa screamed out in protest, while Rebecca stared ahead numbly, suddenly realizing that this was what she had seen in the vision while aboard the Ark.

Grabbing a heavy table that rested against the wall, Arngrim moved it into position in front of Jeffrey. Within moments, Arngrim had used more of the rope to tie each of Jeffrey's feet to the legs of the table, effectively suspending him in midair at a forty-five-degree angle.

Reaching into a hidden area of his robe, Arngrim produced a foot-long dagger that seemed to shimmer in the dim light of the room. "Do you know what this does?" Arngrim asked, holding the dagger up before Mack's eyes. "...besides the obvious, of course. This dagger produces an electrical current on the blade that causes the body to convulse. Would you like to see a demonstration, or will you tell me how to fix the pyramid?"

Lisa and Rebecca wept openly now, the sound torturing Mack as he stared up at the man with tear-streaked eyes. "Oh God! Please help us!"

Not understanding Mack's words, which had been spoken in English, Arngrim assumed that Mack was ignoring him. Walking over to Jeffrey, he touched the tip of the blade into his prisoner's back just far enough to break the skin, then squeezed the hilt, causing the energy current to pass through Jeffrey's body. Screaming in pain, Jeffrey twisted and contorted, trying to move away from the dagger.

"Time is running out!" Arngrim yelled, his agitation building. "Tell me!"

"I DON'T KNOW!" Mack screamed as he collapsed onto the stone floor, sobbing. "How can I tell you something I don't know?"

"You *do* know!" Arngrim yelled back, grabbing Mack's face in his claw. "I'm done wasting time. Tell me what I want to know now, or I'll finish with this one, and move on to another of your friends!" To emphasize his point, he let go of Mack, crossed back over to stand by Jeffrey, and then shocked him again with the dagger.

Filled with grief, Mack looked over at Jeffrey, whose bloody face was beginning to swell from the blow Arngrim had delivered. "I'm so sorry, Jeffrey."

Staring back at him, Jeffrey nodded painfully. "Don't worry, Mack. You did your best."

Enraged by the pitiful exchange, Arngrim grabbed Jeffrey and spun him around so that he faced downward toward the floor, crossing the ropes that bound his feet. "This is your last chance! TELL ME NOW!"

Bowing his head, Mack prayed quietly. "God, have mercy on us."

Letting out a howl of fury, Arngrim brought his arm up above Jeffrey's back. Time seemed to slow to a crawl as the man summoned all of the strength of his genetically enhanced muscles and brought his arm down on his victim's back. The sickening sound of breaking bone was drowned out only by the excruciating scream of pain that emanated from Jeffrey's lips.

25

THE BEGINNING OF THE END

"JEFFREY!" REBECCA SCREAMED in anguish as his broken body went limp. Sinking to her knees, she leaned forward and began rocking back and forth. Placing her bound hands on the back of her neck so that her arms covered her head, she fought to block out the world, her mind replaying the last few terrible moments over and over. *Oh God, where are You!* she prayed, her soul in agony.

Another earthquake suddenly passed through the floor beneath their feet, causing everyone to cry out in surprise. When it was over, Arngrim stood, his fear beginning to grip him. Fighting against it, he let out a roar that served to inflame his anger, effectively extinguishing his momentary weakness. Taking up his dagger, he slashed the ropes tying Jeffrey's ankles to the table legs, causing his body to swing forward and crash into the stone wall where it hung limply.

Turning around, Arngrim strode over to Mack and lifted him to his feet while the wolf-like Naphil guard continued to stand watch over the other bound prisoners. "You truly are stubborn! You pretend to care for your friends, yet you would rather watch them suffer instead of giving me the information I seek! You are all going to die in the Flood if you remain silent. Wouldn't it be better to just tell me? If you do, I promise I will take all of you with me."

Outraged at what the ape-like man had done to Jeffrey, Mack stood firm and glared back at him. "Then it looks like we'll all die together! I know the condition of my soul, and I'm ready to meet my Maker. How about you?"

Arngrim brought his hand back to strike Mack, but then restrained himself. "But...you *don't* have to die. I will...I will make you a *king* instead of a slave. I will give you your own country to reign over. You will have riches, women, *power!*"

Seeing the other's growing desperation, Mack laughed in derision despite his inward distress. "You know what, I actually *do* know how to fix it," he lied, "but I would rather die than allow you to pervert the human race! So you can just go to Hades, along with the rest of the vile people of this world!"

Infuriated, Arngrim struck Mack with his fist and threw him to the floor. Drawing his dagger, he lifted it, preparing to thrust it deep into the stunned man's heart. Still reeling from the blow, Mack bowed his head, expecting to feel the bite of the blade at any moment.

"Halt!" came a command from the doorway. Jerking his head toward the voice in surprise, Arngrim slowly lowered the dagger and backed away from Mack.

"My...my lord Odin!" he stammered at the sight of the thirteen-foot giant that stood in the entryway. "How...how may I be of service, O Great One?"

Striding over to stand beside the ape-like man, Odin surveyed the room. Utterly confused by the sudden appearance of the false god, Rebecca and the others stared up at him in shock while Mack remained unmoving on the floor, hoping to escape the notice of the massive being. "You can begin by telling me what's going on here," Odin commanded, a frown creasing his face.

"I...I...these puny humans sabotaged one of my...special projects that I was working on," he muttered.

"Don't waste your time trying to hide the truth," Odin said force-fully. "Did you actually think I wouldn't find out about your little secret workshop? These creatures are somehow connected to that pyramid. Are you really so foolish as to think that you could sneak it into my fortress without my knowledge? Now, before I lose my temper, tell me: what does it do?"

Like a thief caught stealing a precious gemstone, Arngrim's foul heart began to beat rapidly in fear. "My lord, it was…it was going to be a surprise for you! I was going to show it to you when it was finished."

Grabbing the much smaller man by his robes, Odin lifted Arngrim over six feet off the ground and brought him up to eye level. "I don't have time to waste with your foolishness! Do you think me ignorant? I know that the falling star is almost here and I know what it portends. I've seen your pyramid, and I know that it can somehow save you from the coming destruction. Tell me, does it work? If it does, then I may forgive the fact that you stole the information from your gods!"

"For…forgive me, merciful lord Odin. I wanted to make sure I could get it working before I informed you of its existence." Arngrim begged. "I…I did make the pyramid with the capability to traverse time, but although the energy core is functional, the time dispersant is not working! These…humans…did something to it."

Throwing him unceremoniously to the floor, Odin stared at the prisoners menacingly. "Perhaps you were too kind in your methods, Arngrim. *I* will make them talk!"

All at once, an earthquake that seemed to shake the very foundations of the earth sent everyone, including the false god to the floor. Unsecured items on the shelves and tables crashed to the floor, sending shards of broken glass and pottery scattering around the room. Although the worst of the shaking had subsided, the ground continued to tremble beneath them, making it difficult to stand. Then, before anyone could fully recover, a blinding light lit up the room from where Odin had stood the moment prior. As the light dimmed, the prisoners saw the outline of what appeared to be a man clad in gleaming silver armor begin to take shape, a five-foot broadsword with a jewel-encrusted hilt hanging at his side. His strength and size matched that of the false god that still remained on the floor at his feet. Brownish-gold hair flowed to his shoulders, and as he turned to look at Rebecca, she gasped as she stared into his luminous eyes.

Their color was a deep violet.

"SIKARIS!" she sobbed in recognition, her soul leaping within her. Although it had been four years since she had last seen the angel that had been her companion and teacher during her time on the planet of Ka'esch, she could never forget the fathomless depths of his eyes.

Sikaris cast her a warm smile, then his expression hardened as he reached down and wrapped his muscular arms around Odin's neck, yanking him to his feet. Dragging the demonic god toward the entrance, Sikaris called out to Rebecca, his voice calm yet firm. "It has begun. Rebecca, you must get to the—"

His words were cut short as Odin came to his senses and jabbed his elbow into Sikaris' side, forcing him to release his hold on the false god. Taking advantage of his opponent's momentary distraction, Odin spun around, lowered his head and rammed into the angel's torso. His legs pumping, Odin lifted Sikaris off the floor and drove him through the door and up the stairs.

"Sikaris!" Rebecca yelled in concern as he disappeared from sight. She started toward the door but the massive body of the Naphil guard blocked her path. The wolf-like giant raised his spear at Rebecca and the others menacingly, when his body suddenly jolted as if a heavy weight had landed on his back. Unsure if their eyes were playing tricks on them, Rebecca and the others watched in confusion as light seemed to bend oddly around the giant's head. For a brief instant, shock and surprise registered on the creature's face. Then, his head twisted grotesquely to the side, the sound of cracking bones causing the onlookers to start at the sickening sight. Neck broken, the body of the Naphil slumped to the floor.

Having watched the strange events of the last minute, Arngrim rose to his feet and began running toward the door, unadulterated fear written on his face. However, as he was about to pass the fallen body of the guard, light began to shift in the same peculiar fashion as before. Suddenly, Arngrim flew backward as if struck by something heavy. As his body hit the floor, his head cracked against the ground with a dull thud and he ceased moving.

Bewildered, Rebecca and the others remained rooted to the shaking floor. Holding his right hand up to staunch the blood from the cut Arngrim's blow had dealt him, Mack climbed to his feet. "What the…? What just happened?"

Suddenly, another form began to materialize in the center of the room. Taken aback, the group watched in astonishment as an eight-foot-tall man dressed from head to foot in reflective silver armor appeared. Four wicked-looking horns protruded from the top of the helmet just above a V-shaped visor.

The helmeted head turned toward the former captives as a deep, gravelly voice spoke. "What are you waiting for? Let's get moving!"

"Goliath?" Dr. Eisenberg suddenly said in awe. "Where…where did you come from?"

"No time!" he said harshly as he sliced through their bonds with a small knife. "That warrior that materialized out of the light told Rebecca to get going. But, where to?"

Shrugging off her shock at the quick turn of events, Rebecca ran over toward the wall where Jeffrey still hung. Reaching his side, she began to stroke his hair as she examined him. At her touch, his eyes fluttered open weakly. "Becky…" he murmured. "I…I can't feel my legs…"

She blinked rapidly, fighting back a new wave of tears. "Shhh. Don't talk. We're gonna get you out of here." Turning toward the others, she called out to them. "We've gotta get Jeffrey down. Jerome, grab that other set of gravity control devices. If we can adjust the settings of the ones holding him, maybe we can make a kind of gurney like when we carried the core out of the Tower of Babel. Goliath, help me get him down. I can't reach the devices on the wall."

Scowling beneath his helmet at the delay, Goliath reached up and deactivated the devices while Rebecca and the others supported Jeffrey's body. He groaned in pain as they moved him over and laid him down on the table to which his ankles had previously been tied. Withdrawing a small syringe from a compartment on his belt, Goliath stuck it into Jeffrey's arm.

"What are you doing?!" Rebecca cried in fear as Jeffrey's head rolled to the side and ceased moving.

"I sedated him," he replied coldly. "I took it from the med kit aboard the pyramid after our encounter with Nimrod. We have no time for any further questions, let's get going."

"But where?" Lisa said as she glanced nervously at the entrance to the workshop as if expecting Odin to return at any moment. "Should we go to the pyramid?"

Akwen shook her head. "It doesn't work! What good will dat do us?"

"No," Rebecca replied. "To the Ark! It's our only hope!"

"But then we'll be trapped in this time period for the rest of our lives!" Jerome cried.

"Maybe not," Dr. Eisenberg said. "We now know where this chamber is buried. After the Flood, we could dig it up and perhaps build a new core. Remember, the original broken pyramid that we found in the future lies just behind that wall," he finished, pointing toward the false wall that sat opposite the entrance.

"The journals are on the pyramid upstairs," Mack said, his body still shaking from the recent emotional exertion. "How will we know how to build a new core?"

"We don't need those," Dr. Eisenberg said rapidly. "Ham has a copy of the blueprints on the Ark with him. It would take years, but we could eventually return to our time!

"It seems we have no other choice," Rebecca said. "But the Flood has begun. How do we get to the Ark?"

"While I had my cloaking device activated, I scouted out this area," Goliath reported. "There's a room not far from here that has a couple of those floating platforms. We could fly one of those."

"Great! Then let's get these devices calibrated so we can lift Jeffrey and get out of here," Rebecca said, a small glimmer of hope beginning to rise within her.

Within moments, they had the makeshift gurney set. Jerome and Mack each grabbed a set of the devices and steadied themselves as Lisa, Rebecca, and the doctor transferred Jeffrey's limp body over to it. Once they were ready, Goliath reached down and picked up the spear from the dead Naphil, then led the others toward the exit. He and Akwen led the way up the stairs but stopped suddenly as Dr. Eisenberg called out to them from below.

"Wait! There's one more thing we have to do," he said. Standing in the antechamber, he shut the door leading to the workshop, and then moved over to the hidden side panel.

"We don't have time for dat!" Akwen cried out.

"We *have* to make time for it!" Dr. Eisenberg replied. Copying Arngrim's previous motions, he activated the anti-gravity field, sealing the room. "If we don't, the chamber won't survive the Flood and we'll be stuck without a time machine!"

Seeing his point, Akwen remained silent, yet agitated by worry.

"Well, I'll be a monkey's uncle!" Mack said, his eyes wide in sudden realization. "It's just like in Terminator. It was the guy that went back in time that was the *cause* of what they found in the future! The reason we found that corpse with a broken neck in the future was because of *Goliath*!"

"Can we contemplate the ramifications of time travel later?" Lisa said as Dr. Eisenberg finished closing the hidden panel. Shaking his head in wonder, Mack followed Jerome as they carefully climbed the stairs with their precious cargo, followed immediately by Lisa, Rebecca, and the doctor.

When the group reached the top step, they congregated in the wide hallway and looked around nervously as if expecting a team of Nephilim to set upon them at any second. Beneath their feet, the building began to shake once more as another tremor struck, causing them to grab the walls for support. Once it had passed, Rebecca ran over to a nearby broken window, her face radiating deep concern. "Where is Sikaris?"

"Who?" Jerome asked.

"The angel that saved us," Rebecca replied as she continued to stare out the window, searching the courtyard below for any signs of him.

"Who knows?" Goliath said tersely as he looked back at Dr. Eisenberg, who had just finished activating the protective field over the antechamber. As the doctor pressed the button to conceal the stairs with the movable wall, Goliath began heading off down the corridor, the massive spear in his hand held ready to strike.

Chaos reigned around every turn. Soldiers fought one another as if they had suddenly been stricken insane, screams rose from behind closed doors, and several times Rebecca and the others were forced to step over bodies that lay on the floor in pools of blood, one of which they recognized as the bull-like Naphil that had been working with Arngrim. However, through it all, the escapees went unchallenged during their short trek to the room containing the floating platforms.

Opening the door to the room, Goliath's face screwed up in anger behind his helmet. A lone Naphil soldier stood upon the only platform left in the room. A set of double doors leading out of the building stood open at the end of the fifty-foot room. Turning at the sound of Goliath's entrance, the soldier snarled at him, and then returned his focus on operating the controls of the machine. Letting out a feral cry, Goliath reflexively hurled the spear in his hand at the giant, catching him in the shoulder and preventing him from pressing the controls and moving the platform. The force of the impact sent the soldier flipping over the edge toward the floor, where it lay, unmoving, upon impact. Running up to the giant, Goliath swiftly made sure it wouldn't wake up to threaten them again as the others entered the room behind him.

"Hurry!" Goliath called to them as another shockwave shook the building.

Not needing any prompting, his companions were already moving swiftly to climb aboard, while setting Jeffrey carefully into the back of the machine. As Dr. Eisenberg stepped onto the surface, he collapsed onto the floor, holding his wounded side in pain, and leaned against the four-foot wall of the vehicle.

"Do you know how to drive this thing?" Mack asked Goliath in concern.

"What do you think?" he shot back in annoyance. "Akwen, can you figure it out?"

"I'll try," she said, quickly moving up to stand at the controls. "I watched da giants dat captured us pilot one of dese when dey brought us here. It looks simple enough." Grabbing what she had observed to be the throttle, she moved it forward slightly, causing the platform to glide forward smoothly. After a few moments of experimentation during which the group thought the room was going to come down around their ears from the continuous earthquakes, she moved the circular vehicle out of the room and into the open.

What the group saw as they exited the building took their breath away. Dark, rolling clouds hung in the sky above them blotting out the sun. Blades of flashing lightning lit up the sky with angry slashes. To their left, an explosion sounded, causing them to whirl around in fright. Even though it was several miles from the edge of the city of Asgard, the explosive sound of the top of a small mountain breaking off and sliding downward toward the plains below was deafening. Thick, molten lava spewed from the open face of the mountain like a grievous wound, oozing down the southern mountainside toward the city. The glowing magma rolled over the landscape, burning up everything in its path.

Turning the platform, Akwen headed away from the volcano. Ahead of them to the south, massive crevices had opened in the earth, swallowing entire city blocks. The streets that remained were filled with people, some running in flight, others fighting with one another, and still others looting and pillaging. Fires raged everywhere throughout the city, the mighty gusts of wind fanning the flames into an inferno and spreading it rapidly across the city. In the distance, just on the outskirts of the city, geysers of superheated water shot upward thousands of feet into the air. Those unfortunate enough to be anywhere in the nearby vicinity of the water was scalded as it fell back to the earth in torrents.

Buffeted by the wind, Akwen fought hard for control as the platform dipped and tilted precariously. Goliath pointed toward the distant image of the Ark on the hill as he shouted to be heard over the roar of the gusts. "There it is! But you need to take us lower! We'll get smashed to pieces by this wind!"

Nodding, Akwen complied, dropping them at a steep angle toward the city below. As they neared the river, rain began to pour down, pelting them and forcing them to cover their faces for protection. Reflexively, Akwen let go of the control stick and threw her hand up in front of her to protect her skin from the bite of the water, causing the platform to shift abruptly. Pushing her aside, Goliath, who was protected by his armor and helmet, grabbed the controls, quickly leveling out the wobbling platform.

Ignoring the sting from the driving rain, Dr. Eisenberg suddenly climbed to his feet, his face white with fear. "NOOO! We must turn back!" he shouted in panic.

Startled, everyone turned to face him. "Why? What's wrong?" Goliath called out.

"Because, I read Noah's diary!" he stated. "I know the order of events for the Flood! We're too late! Look!" he shouted, as he pointed toward the east.

Gazing in the direction indicated by the doctor, the companions stared in horror as a wall of water filled the horizon, heading toward them at a terrifying speed.

26

ESCAPING THE CATACLYSM

SIKARIS GRUNTED HEAVILY as Odin slammed his shoulder into his torso. Pushed by the momentum of the attack, Sikaris flew backward out of the workshop. His legs shoving mightily against the ground, Odin leapt up the steps three at a time, carrying his opponent with him. Reaching the top, he crossed the width of the hallway and crashed hard into the opposite wall, his body bearing down on Sikaris. Before the angel could recover from the blow, Odin struck him twice with his massive fists. Stunned, Sikaris fell to the floor.

Snarling down at him, Odin moved his face to within inches of Sikaris' own, his noxious breath causing him to gag. "How does it feel to have a physical body, my old friend? It holds many advantages for our kind, but pain is certainly not one of them." As if to accentuate his point, he grabbed the angel's hair and hit the back of his head against the floor, causing Sikaris to yell in pain.

Forcing himself to fight against the throbbing in his head, Sikaris kicked out at the false god. His foot connected with Odin's abdomen and sent him stumbling down the hall where he landed on his back next to a large window. Climbing to his feet, Sikaris glared at his foe as he began walking steadily toward him. "We are no longer of the same 'kind,' my 'old friend.' You made your choice of whom to serve. Now you will face judgment for that choice!"

Odin twisted and leapt to his feet as Sikaris charged. The two giant combatants grappled with one another for several seconds, neither gaining the upper hand. Muscles straining, they fought desperately, each attempting to throw the other off balance.

As they struggled, the demon-god's appearance began to change. His once tan skin darkened until it became nearly as black as night. The long white hair and beard shriveled and became little more than twisted threads. His skin began to crack as horns and spikes began to push their way to the surface, like thorns breaking through parched ground. The pupils of his eyes blackened and the whites turned a blood red color while his fingernails elongated into yellowish claws.

"It's...too bad...your human worshipers...didn't get to see...how repulsive...your *true* appearance is," Sikaris grunted as they wrestled. Odin merely snarled in reply, his cracked lips rolling back to reveal a mouthful of razor-sharp teeth. Suddenly seeing an opportunity, Sikaris threw his weight sideways. Caught off guard, Odin fell with him and they crashed through the window.

As they plummeted toward the courtyard below, the demon-god twisted his bulk so that Sikaris would take the brunt of the impact. The stone pavement buckled as the two beings crashed into it. Recovering quickly, Odin grabbed Sikaris and flipped him over onto his armor-plated stomach. Using his knees and hands, the demon pinned his foe to the ground. Enjoying his advantage, he grabbed Sikaris' by the hair and pulled his head back, a look of perverse ecstasy on his cruel face. "So, your Master must have some special purpose for those particular sludge bags if He sent you to protect them. You wanted them to get to somewhere. The Ark, perhaps? Somehow I doubt it. That would probably interfere with *His* plan to restart the human population. No. It must be something else."

Suddenly, the muscles in his left eye began to twitch as the answer came to him. "Could it be that the pyramid actually *does* work? Yes, that's it, isn't it? That fool Arngrim either lied to me, or was himself deceived. How else could you expect to save them?"

Pushing Sikaris' face back into the stone of the courtyard, Odin rose to his feet. Looking upward at the blackened clouds above them, he let out a roar of triumph. As he did so, he tore at the armor made of reptilian scales until it hung in tatters, revealing his broad, muscular chest. A moment later, two black, leathery wings protruded from his back.

"If I am going to be sent to the Abyss, then I will at least do everything in my power to confound the plans of the Enemy!" he screamed down at Sikaris. "If *I* can't use the pyramid, I will certainly make sure those sludge bags won't either!"

Finally coming to his senses, Sikaris spun around as Odin's wings gave a powerful heave, propelling him into the sky. As Sikaris jumped to his feet, a pair of blazing white wings materialized on the angel's back. *Almighty Warrior, grant me Your strength and speed!* he prayed, then leapt into the sky after his enemy.

Lightning raged across the heavens and the wind howled in his ears as Sikaris closed the gap between him and the demon. Glancing behind, Odin's eyes narrowed angrily at the doggedness of his pursuer. Swerving up and around the archways and buttresses of the outer courtyards of Valhalla, Odin reached down with his right hand and withdrew his sword from the sheath that hung at his side. Free of its bonds, flames burst forth over the entire six-foot blade, adding its own blazing light to the sporadic flashes of lightning.

Stopping abruptly in mid air, Odin swung the weapon at his attacker. Narrowly dodging the strike, Sikaris swooped downward, then reversed direction and came up behind his opponent. As Odin spun around to face him, Sikaris drew his own sword. Holding the gleaming silver blade aloft, the angel of light dove at the angel of darkness. Sparks flew as the sword blades clashed, showering the warriors with pinpricks of light.

With their wings beating heavily to fight against the raging wind, the combatants traded blows back and forth, their muscles straining with each thrust and parry.

"You cannot win!" Sikaris yelled above the roar of the tempest. "You lost the day you joined Lucifer! The Lord of creation reigns and *His* will be done!"

Enraged, the demon feigned an attack with his sword, but instead kicked out at Sikaris, causing him to fall momentarily toward the ground. Taking advantage of the slight reprieve, Odin flew toward the entrance of the hangar that contained the pyramid.

Using his downward momentum, Sikaris turned his fall into a dive. Picking up speed, he suddenly swerved toward Odin, making up the distance rapidly. Just as the demon was about to enter the hangar, Sikaris crashed into him from below. The force of the blow stunned the two beings, sending them tumbling into the angular walls of the building. With their limbs entwined, the two warriors began sliding down the wall toward the courtyards below. Odin released the grip on his sword and instead began to tear at Sikaris. Dropping his own sword, he fought to keep the wicked claws at bay as the pair continued their descent.

Lightning flashed once again, briefly illuminating several flying buttresses and walkways as they flew by. Finally breaking through Sikaris' defenses, Odin grabbed his neck in one hand and began to squeeze his nails into the tanned flesh. Grasping at the claw with his own hand, Sikaris fought to pry the fingers away. Suddenly, both of the giant beings felt the breath leave their bodies as they crashed into one of the lower walkways several stories above the ground. The impact broke the marble walkway free, causing it to collapse. Stunned, Sikaris and Odin lost their grip on each other. Seeing the ground rushing up toward him, the angelic warrior spread his wings and managed to slow his fall just enough to keep from smashing full force into the ground.

Sensing something coming rapidly toward him, Sikaris turned to see a large section of the marble walkway falling down on top of him. Calling upon every ounce of strength in his legs and wings, the warrior propelled himself to the side, narrowly escaping the massive structure as it crashed to the ground.

In all of the confusion, Sikaris momentarily lost sight of his foe. Muscles protesting at the strain caused by the battle, he rose to his feet, searching the area for any signs of Odin. A glint of silver metal to his left caught his attention. Running over to his sword, he bent to pick it up. Yet, as he reached out to grasp the hilt, an enormous weight bore down on him, knocking him to the ground.

"It really is a shame that you didn't join our side," Odin said as he used his full weight to keep Sikaris down on his back. "You are quite a skillful warrior."

"Look at yourself, Odin," Sikaris yelled in reply. "You use your God-given talents and abilities to pervert and destroy men, who are made in the very image of God!"

Freeing one of his hands, the demon grabbed Sikaris' silvery blade. Pointing the tip at his enemy's throat, he screamed in rage. "*WE* were His only children until *they* came along. *WE* had power, but yet He chose to place them *above us!* And to make matters worse, He commands us to *protect* them! *They* are the ones who deserve death, and my true brothers and I have given it to them! Today we strike at the heart of our Maker. Even in defeat, we win. For in order to undo what we have done to His precious humans, He is forced to wipe them out and start over!"

Sikaris shook his head sadly. "No, you haven't won. Noah and his family still live, and through them, the Promise still lives. One day the seed of woman will strike the head of the serpent! You have LOST!"

Screaming in unbridled rage, Odin tensed his muscles, preparing to decapitate his enemy. Suddenly, an earthquake shook the ground, causing a fissure to open in the earth several feet to the left of the combatants and causing Odin to lose his balance. Reacting quickly, Sikaris kicked him toward the fissure. The demon dropped the sword and rolled to the edge, his claws raking the ground to keep from falling into the gaping hole. Leaping back to his feet, he laughed raucously. However, a deeper rumble from inside the cavernous opening within the earth caused the laughter to die on the demon's lips. Turning to stare into the chasm,

Odin's eyes grew wide with horror. With his opponent momentarily distracted, Sikaris dove forward and kicked, sending the fallen angel over the edge.

Letting out a shriek of panic, Odin spread his wings to arrest his descent. Pumping them hard, he fought to rise out of the newly formed crevasse. However, as he neared the lip, the fountains of the great deep burst forth from inside the earth, the superheated jets of water pulverizing the physical body of the once mighty Odin, lord of Asgard.

The moment Goliath saw the approaching tsunami, he jerked the controls hard, turning the platform around.

"Can't we just fly *over* the water?" Jerome asked fearfully. "That way, once the wave has passed, we could continue on to the Ark."

Dr. Eisenberg shook his head sadly. "You felt the winds earlier. We'd be knocked out of the sky!"

"Did the diary say how high the waters of the tsunami reached?" Goliath asked the doctor, his eyes darting to his right, gauging how much time they had before the wall of water hit them.

"It said that they reached almost to the Ark," Dr. Eisenberg replied.

"Good. Then only the bottom section of Valhalla will be hit," Goliath said. "Once the wave passes, we can try for the Ark again."

"But the door will already be closed!" Dr. Eisenberg said.

"Then we may have to land on the roof and climb through the window!" Goliath shot back, his voice strained as he looked at the rapid approach of the tsunami.

"Can't this thing go any faster?" Mack asked as panic filled him. "We're not gonna make it!"

Gritting his teeth, Goliath tightened his hands on the controls. He knew Mack was right. Every flash of lightning showed that the water was now less than a mile away, and although the platform was climbing upward toward Valhalla, the machine was too slow. They were going to be swept away.

Suddenly, the platform shot forward with a burst of speed, causing all of the passengers on board to grip the railings and walls tightly for support. Surprised, Goliath nearly let go of the controls. "What the...? I'm no longer controlling it!"

Peering through the curtain of rain that struck her face, Rebecca left Jeffrey's side and looked over the edge of the platform, her pulse quickening. "It's Sikaris! He's pushing us!"

Jerome, Mack, and Dr. Eisenberg, who were all in the back of the circular vehicle, followed her gaze, their eyes widening in shock. "Thank you, Lord!" the doctor breathed in relief. "You have not forsaken us!"

Turning their attention back to the wave, Rebecca and her companions watched in fascinated horror as it passed beneath them by little more than a dozen feet. Sobered by the complete destruction caused by the wave, they stood in silence for several moments.

However, once the threat of the tsunami had dissipated, Goliath grabbed the controls again, attempting to regain command of the platform and turn it around to head back toward the Ark. When the machine didn't respond, he turned his helmeted head toward Rebecca questioningly. "That angel friend of yours is not relinquishing control of the platform. He's taking us back to Valhalla. But why?"

The companions exchanged confused glances as Sikaris guided them through the open doors of the hangar that housed the time machine. Setting the machine down, Sikaris, who now appeared only half as tall as before, stood to face them, his expression calm, but intense. "You must hurry! This structure will not last much longer!" he said. Even as he finished speaking the words, a tremor shook the building, causing pieces of the ceiling to fall to the floor around them.

"But, where are we to go?" Dr. Eisenberg asked as he climbed out of the circular platform, his wounded side throbbing. "The pyramid doesn't work!"

Sikaris smiled reassuringly. "Yes, it does! I don't have time to explain now. Just trust me."

The travelers exchanged shocked glances, and then sprang into immediate action. Akwen and Goliath headed directly for the entrance to the pyramid while Mack and Jerome lifted Jeffrey carefully out of the platform, Lisa following close behind.

Stepping over to where Sikaris stood, Rebecca smiled weakly up at him. "I never thought I'd see you again. Thank you for saving us."

"Thank our Father," he replied. "Now, I must go. There is still much work to be done."

Turning away from her, he walked back toward the open doors. "Wait!" Rebecca called after him. As he turned to face her, she rushed toward him and wrapped him in a warm embrace. At first, the angel was startled by the contact. However, after a moment, he folded his strong arms around her.

Breaking the embrace, Rebecca stepped back. "Will I ever see you again?" she asked.

"Most assuredly," Sikaris replied. "But for now, I have another mission to complete."

"Where are you going?" she asked in concern.

Reaching out with his right hand, he touched her forehead gently. "Father, open her eyes," he prayed.

Suddenly, Rebecca gasped in shock. Looking through the open doorway, she saw that the sky was filled with angelic beings battling against a horde of demonic foes. Yet, far in the distance, she saw a beacon of light on a hill. The more she studied it, however, the more it became clear that the light did not emanate from one source, but was actually the combined brilliance of many smaller lights formed in an oval shape. In the center of the blinding radiance was a large, rectangular wooden vessel.

"Oh…" Rebecca breathed in sudden understanding, a tear sliding down her cheek. "Those lights are angels, aren't they?" she asked. "They're guarding the Ark!"

"BECKY!" Mack yelled from the door of the pyramid. "Akwen's bringing up the engines! We've gotta go!"

"Yes, dear one," Sikaris replied. "And I must join them, as you must join your friends. I will see you again soon. Rest assured, the battle belongs to the Lord! His purposes will be fulfilled." With that, Sikaris turned and leapt out into the rain, his body taking flight over the rising waters.

Rebecca turned, and then sprinted toward the entrance of the pyramid. Debris rained around her as the building shook. Leaping up the stairs, Rebecca dove into the time machine. Immediately, the door closed behind her and the whine of the engines increased. As she and Mack made their way up the stairs and into the control room, the pyramid and everything in it, began to fade.

"It's working!" Akwen shouted in triumph. "Da pyramid is phasing!"

The now transparent machine began to rise up and out of the building. Silence descended heavily upon the travelers as they stared at the destruction around them. Valhalla began to crumble as the initial tsunami wave receded, causing the enormous undercurrent to scour the land. Lava had reached Asgard's northern border and began eating away at the once beautiful city. Jeweled towers fell into the magma and burned brilliantly while magnificent marble walls melted like wax.

Water continued to shoot forth from beneath the crust of the earth and torrents of rain fell from the blackened sky, causing the water level to rise quickly. The once mighty river that had separated the northern and southern sides of the city now merged with the floodwaters. The entire city was completely submerged, as was much of the terrain for miles. Only remnants of the northern portion of the city of the Aesir and Vanir still stood atop the plateau. However, the travelers knew that before long, even that would disappear.

God's judgment had been swift and sure. The wickedness of mankind and their demonic deceivers had been obliterated.

As the pyramid ascended higher and higher into the sky, the last thing that Rebecca saw was a lonely ship sitting atop a grassy hill. Inside its walls was the hope of mankind: the last remnant of animals and humans who would survive to repopulate the earth.

———

Arngrim slowly opened his eyes and realized that he lay on the floor of his workshop. His head throbbed and he could feel a giant lump forming on the back of his head. Outside the chamber, he could hear strange rumbling and swishing sounds. The lights around him flickered several times, threatening to go out completely. Moving carefully over to his worktable, he pulled out a hand-held lamp-like object. Shaking it so that it began to glow, he held it aloft and scanned the room.

As his eyes came to rest upon the dead Naphil soldier lying in the middle of the floor, memory of the recent events came rushing back to him. Immediately his heart began beating rapidly, like some wild animal was trapped within his chest and fought to get out. *The Cataclysm!* his mind screamed in panic. *Has it...Am I...trapped?!* Rushing over to the door as fast as his aching body would carry him, he tried to open it. He pulled and pulled on the handle, crying out wildly in terror and panic. "NOOOO!" he screamed in anguish as he collapsed on the floor, sobbing.

After several minutes, his rational mind began to regain control of his body. Climbing to his feet, he spoke out loud to himself in an effort to calm his nerves and think clearly. "Those pathetic humans must have sealed the chamber. That means I have only a few hours of air left. My only hope is to...to try to get this pyramid to work. It *has* to work!"

As he began to cross back to his worktable, he tripped over the dead body of the wolf-like, Naphil soldier. Swearing, he kicked the thing in the side. The lights flickered again, and he knew that before long, he would be left with nothing more than his portable lamp for light. Staring down at the dead creature, Arngrim felt as if its sightless eyes were mocking him. Not wanting to be left in the dark with the dead thing, Arngrim grabbed the edges of the soldier's armor and dragged the body toward the storage room along the eastern wall. Opening the door, he pulled it inside and dropped it. His task complete, Arngrim hurried out of the room and closed the door behind him.

Crossing back over to his worktable, he heard the crunching sound of broken pottery and glass on the floor. Remembering the violent shaking caused by the earthquakes, he realized that many of his tools, containers of oil, grease, and other items had fallen off their shelves and were now scattered around the room, most completely unusable.

Sitting down at the table, he began pouring over his technical journals, searching desperately for any possible way to alter the design of the pyramid. Eventually, the lights went out permanently, leaving him in complete silence and darkness except for the glowing lamp. Desperate, he lost all awareness of time as he scoured through his own designs, seeking some small hope.

Before long, Arngrim's eyelids began to droop and he felt an acute sense of weariness sweep over him. Putting the hood of his robe over his head to keep out the chill, he leaned over his worktable and placed his head against it. *Maybe I'll just rest for a moment,* he thought sleepily. *Just for a moment...*

Several days later, the glow of the portable light began to dim, then slowly went out, plunging the chamber into complete darkness, where it would remain undisturbed for thousands of years...

27

GOLIATH'S STORY

AS THE PYRAMID entered orbit around the earth and began traveling through time, Rebecca felt every ounce of strength drain swiftly out of her body. Feeling weak, she sank down onto the floor of the control room.

We made it! she thought as she rested her hands against her head.

Although she felt like crying, her body had long since used up its store of tears. Instead, she sat unmoving, her mind and body numb from the recent trauma and stress. *Thank you, Father, for getting us through this,* she prayed. *Now if only Jeffrey...* Her eyes flew open in sudden remembrance. Standing quickly, she stepped passed Mack, Jerome, and Dr. Eisenberg, who were all sitting on the floor, each lost in his own thoughts.

Catching the movement out of the corner of her eye, Akwen turned her head and watched Rebecca leave. As the Cameroonian began turning back around, she suddenly spotted a metallic object sitting against the wall. "Elmer!" she cried. Leaving her post at the controls, she ran over to inspect the robot. Seeing no sign of damage, she spoke a quick command. "Elmer, power on."

Without hesitation, the droid's gravity control devices began to whir as Elmer's head rose up out of its body. "Greetings, Dr. Nancho. How may I be of service?" it asked in its high tenor voice.

Akwen laughed as her eyes filled with tears of joy. "Elmer, you're alright."

"That is an odd statement, Dr. Nancho," the machine replied. "Why wouldn't I be alright?"

Smiling at the droid's response, she explained. "Because da pyramid was taken over by an evil man while you were powered off. He told us dat you had been destroyed."

"He was clearly mistaken," Elmer said calmly. "All of my systems are fully functional."

"Arngrim probably wanted to study him later," Dr. Eisenberg said. "He lied to us."

"Well, I'm very glad you're still functional!" Akwen said, then made her way back to the controls. "Now, I would appreciate it if you would plug into da ship and help me out."

"It would be my pleasure to assist you," Elmer replied as the droid hovered over to the computer terminal that Akwen and her crew had installed in the pyramid when it had first been discovered.

As Akwen arrived in front of the console, she noticed Goliath studying the controls and dials, a frown on his face. "So *when* are we heading to now?" he asked Akwen. The stool that she had once used had been replaced by Arngrim with a throne-like chair that was much too large for her, forcing her to stand. It was, however, a perfect fit for Goliath, who now sat comfortably in it, his helmet resting on the floor next to him.

"I don't know," she said. From the tone of her voice, Goliath could tell that she was not pleased by her own answer.

"What do you mean?" the giant replied in a low voice that bespoke of his agitation. "Didn't you set the machine to take us back to our own time?"

Turning to face him directly, Akwen frowned. "I was in such a hurry to just get us out of dere, I didn't want to take da risk of trying to go *forward* in time. We have never been able to do it before, and if it didn't work, we wouldn't have had time to try again. So, I just dialed da counter back and launched."

"How much farther back did you dial it?" Dr. Eisenberg said in sudden concern as he stood.

Akwen swallowed uncomfortably. "Seventeen hundred years or so."

"Why so far?" Goliath asked.

"I don't know," she replied in annoyance. "I just spun da counter. Only after I started da launch sequence did I realize how far it went back."

"Can't you change it?" he said, leaning forward in the chair.

"I don't tink so, but we can try," Akwen said. "Elmer, can we change our destination?"

The droid communicated with the computer, then replied. "I am sorry to inform you that we cannot."

Akwen nodded. "We have to wait until we land. But it shouldn't be a problem. In da past, our jumps only went a maximum of a tousand years or so. If dat is da case now, we should stop about…3350 B.C."

"Do you remember what date it read before we launched?" Dr. Eisenberg asked as he crossed over to look at the controls.

Akwen nodded. "It was at minus 2732, I believe."

Dr. Eisenberg raised one of his eyebrows in mild surprise. "Something just dawned on me," he said looking over at Mack, who still sat on the floor near Jerome. "Do you remember what number was on the time dial when we found the pyramid?"

Mack looked pensive for a moment, and then replied. "Yeah, I think so. Wasn't it…1650 or something like that?"

Dr. Eisenberg nodded. "Close. It was 1655. Think about it. The dial stopped keeping time when it was sealed up in the chamber by Arngrim. So, the year 1655 must have been the year the Flood occurred when you count from the beginning of creation. That means…" He paused midthought as he did the calculations in his brain. "If we go back a thousand years, we will be at the year 655."

"At least we don't have to worry about food," Jerome stated. "From the looks of it, Arngrim stocked the pyramid with enough supplies to last us for several months."

"That's all well and good," Goliath said, "but does anyone have any idea how we're going to fix this blasted ship so that we can get back home to our own time?"

"I don't know, but I tink we have a better chance now dat Arngrim removed da virus dat was controlling da pyramid before," Akwen replied.

"That sounds encouraging," Dr. Eisenberg said hopefully. "But going back to my original concern, if we continue on until the time you set on the dial, then we'll travel all the way back to the dawn of time!"

Jerome's head snapped up at the statement. "Is that even possible?"

"It's a moot point," Goliath said, turning his head to look at the three men. "The pyramid will likely stop after a thousand years anyway. Besides, you're assuming that the dawn of time was only six thousand years or so from *our* time. But, according to the big bang, this universe is billions of years old."

"You still don't believe, do you?" Mack asked.

"I know what we saw back there, and I believe it was real," Goliath answered. "But as for the origin of the universe, no one knows what really happened. I'm not going to spend my life worrying about it. I've got enough problems."

"But what you believe about where life came from directly relates to what you think is going to happen to you when you die," Dr. Eisenberg said. "What could be more important than that?"

"Stop trying to convert me, old man," Goliath spat back. "Let me live my life, and you live yours."

Saddened, the doctor remained silent as Goliath simply reclined in his chair and relaxed.

"By the way," Mack continued, "What happened to you when Thor attacked us near Arngrim's shop? You sure saved our bacon!"

Still staring ahead at the control console, Goliath responded. "When I came to my senses after being struck by that Naphil and saw Thor standing there, I quickly activated the cloaking device on my armor. Fortunately, Thor and his lackeys didn't have enough time to count our group and the alley was narrow, allowing only one soldier in at a time. This made it much easier for me to hide.

"I followed them as they took you across the rainbow bridge," he continued. "I will admit that it was quite tricky. Since the cloaking device only bends light, it causes some visual distortion as I move. This meant I had to move slowly and wait for the right opportunities, otherwise I would have been seen by Thor, his soldiers, or any of the other guards along the way."

He paused, then finally turned to face Mack and the others, his wolf-like features frowning slightly. "The most difficult part was at the guard-house. I thought for sure that the god that stood at the gate had seen me. Fortunately, by the time he turned in my direction, I had moved into a shadowed corner and remained still, making me effectively invisible. Then, when I realized that you were all boarding that circular platform, I knew I would lose you if I didn't do something. So, I shoved one of the guards from behind as he was climbing onto the vehicle."

"That guard stumbling was a diversion?" Mack asked with an amazed grin.

Goliath nodded slowly, his own expression lightening at the memory. "While the two soldiers argued and Thor reprimanded them, I climbed up the opposite side of the machine and hunched down on the floor in front of you, next to the handrail."

Mack looked shocked. "You were there for the whole trip to Valhalla?"

The giant's grin widened.

"You're slicker than a Jedi master using a mind trick!" Mack stated.

"But, if you were with us all the time, why didn't you break us out of that dungeon earlier?" Jerome asked.

"There wasn't enough room in the lift for me to sneak in without being noticed," Goliath explained, "so, I didn't know where you had gone. By the time I figured out that you had gone up to the top floor, you were being taken down to the dungeon. It took me most of the night to prepare a plan to get you out, but by the time I was ready to put it into action, those guards came and took you to Arngrim. I followed, but knew there would be no way to overpower all of those guards by myself. So, I waited."

Akwen turned to face him at his last statement, her face dark with accusation. "Why didn't you step in to help us *before* dat monster broke Jeffrey's back? You took him and his guard out easily enough afterwards. Why did you wait so long?"

Bristling at her tone, Goliath stared back at her, his anger beginning to flare. "When Arngrim took you down into his workshop, I was stuck several floors up. It took me a few minutes to figure out where he had taken you. As I searched the area, I discovered the room with the flying platforms. When I finally found that bull-like guard standing at the end of the wide hall, I recognized where I was. But before I could do anything, Odin arrived. Fortunately, after he dismissed the guard, he opened the hidden entrance for me. However, knowing that I could never take him out by myself, I waited again, hoping for the right opportunity."

"Which Rebecca's angel friend conveniently provided," Jerome said. "Well, I for one am very glad you arrived when you did. I sure thought we were goners."

Still frowning, Akwen narrowed her eyes. "And just what would you have done if dat angel hadn't shown up? How long were you going to wait?"

Goliath returned her glare. "Look, I helped you out, didn't I? What more do you want? I wasn't going to risk my neck needlessly if I knew I couldn't rescue you. You should be thankful. If it weren't for me, you'd all be dead. "

Akwen backed off, even though her face was still hard. "I *am* grateful. But I also know dat da only reason you even saved us is because you knew dat witout us, Noah wouldn't take you on da Ark and you couldn't pilot dis pyramid alone…"

Her voice trailed off as a disturbing thought entered her mind. "Wait a second. You said you were stuck a couple of floors up when Arngrim took us to his workshop, but he never took us in a lift. We went down da stairs. You should have had no problem following us. You weren't 'stuck,' were you? You were *on da pyramid*!"

Jerome, Mack, and Dr. Eisenberg glanced back and forth between Akwen and Goliath in shock. Leaning back in his throne-like chair, Goliath smiled sardonically as he returned Akwen's stare. "Don't take it personally," he replied. "I didn't see any way that I could rescue you at the time, so I figured there was no sense in me dying also. I made my way to the entrance of the pyramid while Arngrim talked to you. When he turned to go inside, I was already on board. I figured that I would hitch a ride and watch how he controlled the ship. Once we had arrived after the Flood, I would kill him, and possibly his two women if they posed a threat, then take the pyramid. Depending on how well things went, I had even considered coming back to get you."

"Yeah, right," Jerome muttered under his breath.

"Speaking of Arngrim's concubines, what happened to them?" Mack asked.

"They probably just left the pyramid when the Flood began," Dr. Eisenberg surmised.

Her anger still roiling, Akwen refused to be sidetracked. "So, when Arngrim couldn't get da time machine to work, dat's when you knew you had to go to plan B and rescue us! It's so nice to know dat we're such a strong priority for you."

Goliath shrugged. "What did you expect? After all, ours is a relationship of convenience and survival. I *am* a mercenary, after all."

"That reminds me," Mack said. "Doc, guess what? It turns out that our giant friend here isn't a cyborg *or* a Naphil. He's actually a genetically altered human!"

The doctor and Akwen both stared at Goliath in surprise. "But, how is that possible?" Dr. Eisenberg asked. "As far as I'm aware, genetic manipulation of human DNA has not progressed that far in our time."

"It just goes to show that there is a *lot* that the average person isn't aware of, at least as far as science goes," Goliath said snidely. "But I can assure you, Herc and I are not alone. The knowledge of how to mix human and animal DNA is progressing rapidly."

Dr. Eisenberg's expression fell. "Meaning that, soon, our own society may begin to reflect the pre-Flood one, except the Cataclysm that we will face will be the *final* judgment of mankind."

"Anyway," Mack said after an awkward silence, "we found out quite a bit more about our giant friend here."

Knowing the direction the conversation was about to take, Jerome stood. "I think I'll skip this part of the discussion, if you don't mind. I'm gonna go take a much needed nap."

As Jerome descended the stairs, Mack continued. "So, Mr. Goliath, correct me if I get any part of your story wrong. You and your buddy Herc were mercenaries that were hired by a terrorist group in Iraq. They had already bought the technical specs for the gravity control device from Jerome —who needed the money to pay for his daughter's medical bills—" he explained to Dr. Eisenberg and Akwen, whose eyes grew wide with surprise, "but the terrorists wanted to get their hands on the technical journals of the pyramid. Am I right so far?"

Goliath remained silent and seemingly uninterested in Mack's summary of events. Taking the giant's silence as approval, Mack continued.

"Once Hercules died and things turned against you, you lied to us and told us that you were a cyborg that would blow up if we 'killed' you. When we arrived in the Ice Age, Noah called you a Naphil because you resembled some of the genetically altered Nephilim."

"Congratulations," Goliath said dispassionately. "You figured out my secrets."

"Not all of them," Mack said. "How is it that you got a hold of such cool technology? I mean, those holographic grenades you used when you originally attacked the base were amazing."

The giant remained silent for a moment, contemplating whether or not to answer his question. "Let's just say that the people who 'created' me have friends in high places as well as access to all of the latest gadgets."

"And they just let you use that stuff to do mercenary jobs for *terrorists*?" Mack asked incredulously.

"Herc and I had a bit of a…falling out with our original employers," Goliath stated. Standing, he began crossing over toward the stairs. "I've had enough of your questions. Now, if you don't mind, it's been a long couple of days. I'm going to get a little well-deserved sleep." With that, he headed down the stairs and disappeared.

"Gee, he sure is a barrel of laughs," Mack said sarcastically.

"Despite his past and his selfish motives, he did still save our lives. And for that, we do owe him our gratitude. It just goes to show that God can even use selfish mercenaries to accomplish His goals," Dr. Eisenberg said. Using the wall for support, he grunted in slight pain as he climbed to his feet. "Goliath does have a good point, though. It *has* been a couple of long days. I think I will retire also."

"Yeah, me too," Mack said as he rose. "Y'know, Doc, there's one more thing that still bothers me though."

"And that is?"

"When we sealed Arngrim in the chamber, he and the soldier were both dead on the floor. But that's not how we found them in the future. Did we alter history?"

Dr. Eisenberg raised his eyebrows. "We may never know. But consider this: Arngrim may not have been dead, just unconscious. He may have lived a little while longer before his air ran out."

Mack harrumphed. "I hadn't thought of that. Man, time travel messes with your head."

A few moments later, the two men had left the room. Sitting in the oversized chair, Akwen closed her eyes and breathed a heavy sigh of relief. Within a minute, her exhaustion overwhelmed her and she nodded off to sleep, Elmer whirring quietly next to her, his sensors monitoring the pyramid as it continued to travel further and further back in time.

28

CONFESSIONS

AS REBECCA ENTERED the room, she saw Lisa glance up at her from where she sat beside the bed. With eyes red and puffy from crying, Lisa stood and walked toward Rebecca. Lowering her head and averting her eyes, she stepped quickly passed her and left the room, leaving Rebecca alone with her husband who laid unmoving on the bed.

Closing the door, Rebecca crossed over to stand next to the bed that had once been occupied by Dr. Eisenberg. As she drew near, Jeffrey turned his head to look at her, his own eyes moist with tears and his expression grim.

"Hi," Rebecca said simply, forcing herself to smile despite the ache that she felt in her heart. At the sight of her husband's broken body, she fought against the tears that seemed to demand release.

"Hi," Jeffrey replied softly. "I'm…I'm glad to see you. I…we…we need to talk."

Uncertainty plagued her, causing her heart to pound. *What does he want to talk about? What's going to happen to us, Lord? So much has changed. Where do we go from here?*

Not knowing what to say, Rebecca sat in the chair that Lisa had recently vacated. "How are you?"

Jeffrey turned his head to stare at the wall of the room as he spoke, his voice pained. "I'm alive. But, it looks like I'll never walk again. My legs are completely paralyzed."

"Oh God, Jeffrey," Rebecca said as the tears came. "I'm so sorry."

"Yes. God," he repeated, almost inaudibly. Turning back to look at her, he smiled weakly. "Rebecca, I believe now that God exists."

Rebecca took his hand in both of hers, her expression radiant. Seeing her excitement, his expression fell. "I know what you're thinking, but before you say anything, let me finish. I believe God exists, but I can't serve Him."

Rebecca felt a dull ache in the pit of her stomach. "I...I don't understand. Why do you say that?"

"Because..." he began. As he continued, he stared ahead at the door of the room, his face blank and expressionless. "Because I've done terrible things."

Breathing a sigh of relief, Rebecca leaned closer. "But Jeffrey, we all have. That's what is so wonderful about what Jesus did. 'While we were yet sinners, Christ died for us.'"[1]

Jeffrey pulled his hand away from hers as he shook his head. "No. You wouldn't say that if you knew what I'd done."

An intense feeling of sorrow mixed with dread settled in her spirit. Afraid of the answer, she nevertheless asked the question that she knew she needed to ask. "What have you done?" she asked softly.

A profound stillness filled the room as Jeffrey struggled with his own inner turmoil. When he finally spoke, it was like the voice of a man sentenced to death. "I've done many terrible things in my life. I've stolen things, cheated on tests, and lied to people to further my own ambitions, just to name a few. But, more than all of that, I did things that I know God would never forgive me for."

Rebecca wanted to tell him how Jesus could forgive any sin, no matter how bad, but she bit her lip, knowing that now was not the right time. Without even looking at her, Jeffrey continued, his voice dull and even.

"I've never told this to anyone. Not to Jerome, my parents, or even you. Back in February of 2016, when I was working on my bachelor's degree at Northern Illinois University, I was dating this woman named Jaime. It was late on a Friday night and I was heading into Chicago to meet up with some friends to party. Jaime called me on my cell phone and was upset that I was leaving town. We started to fight. I yelled at her and told her she was being overly dramatic, which only made her more frustrated. In anger, she blurted out the real reason she was upset."

Rebecca felt her insides go cold at the direction the story had taken. She gripped the bedframe tightly; her heart seemed to have stopped beating in her chest.

Lost in his own memories, Jeffrey took no notice of Rebecca's tension. "She…she was pregnant with my child."

Oh God! she sobbed inwardly as the full implications of what he was telling her sank in. For years, she and Jeffrey had tried to have children, but she was unable to conceive. Now, the truth hit her like a slap in the face, confirming her worst fears. If Jeffrey had a child, then that meant that her barrenness was *her* fault. *She* was the one who couldn't have a baby. *GOD!* she cried out inwardly in anguish. *Why have you done this to me? Why have you made it so that I cannot experience the joy of motherhood?*

Glancing over at her, he realized his words had cut her as deeply as any weapon. Wanting to comfort *her* this time, he reached out and grasped her hand. "Bec—Rebecca, I'm sorry. Do you see now why I've never told you? I knew you wanted to have a child, but…maybe we just shouldn't talk about this anymore."

Brushing away her tears, Rebecca shook her head emphatically. "No. It's okay. I'll be alright. Please, Jeffrey, no matter how painful it is, I want to know everything."

Still unsure, Jeffrey studied her for several seconds before letting go of her hand and continuing. "When she told me the news, I was…I was driving on a bridge that straddled the expressway. It was probably nine o'clock at night, and it had been snowing lightly all day. By that time, the snow had become heavier, but I was determined to go to Chicago.

"The entrance ramp to the expressway was on the other side of the bridge. This particular ramp connected to a county round, and with the weather being so bad, there was almost no one out that night. When Jaime told me the news I...I became so scared and angry that I wasn't paying attention to what I was doing."

Swallowing against the lump in his throat, Jeffrey continued as tears began spilling down the sides of his face. "There was a slight hill at the end of the bridge. I was so upset that I...I turned onto the ramp without waiting to see if anyone was coming over the hill first. As I turned, I heard this horn blaring at me. I dropped my phone and swerved onto the ramp, my car sliding into the guardrail. But...but the other vehicle wasn't so lucky."

The muscles in Jeffrey's face and lips quivered as he began to weep softly. "It was a bus! The driver tried to keep from hitting me and lost control. It...broke through the guardrail and...and fell onto the expressway. I watched in shock, not wanting to believe that it was happening. All I knew was that I had to get away from there. I took off and didn't look back, paranoid that someone had seen me. Somehow, I made it to a hotel and spent the night there. But, I didn't sleep. All I could see was that bus going over the rail."

Overcome by emotion, Jeffrey stopped momentarily. When he had regained enough control to speak, he continued. "I found out later that the bus had been full of kids coming back from some winter church retreat. Ninetee—" his voice cracked and he closed his eyes trying to fight back the wave of guilt. "Nineteen of those kids died that day because of me. *Me*, Rebecca. *I* killed them! Nineteen families lost their children *because of me*! And twelve others were seriously injured. One little ten year old girl was...paralyzed."

Jeffrey looked down at his shattered body and sighed. "No one ever knew that I was the one to cause the accident, and I was too afraid to turn myself in. Well, justice has now been served. Not a day has gone by that I haven't been tortured in my soul because of what I did. And now,

I will live out the rest of my days being tortured in my body as well. It's only fair."

Compassion filling her, Rebecca reached up to stroke his hair, but he pulled his head away from her. "Please don't touch me. There's...there's more. After the accident, I was so scared, and I began to drink heavily for several weeks. During that time, Jaime came to talk to me. We began to fight again about...about the pregnancy. We were both worried that it would ruin our chances at finishing our degrees. But, more than that, I...I felt that I should not be allowed to bring a child into the world after what I did to other people's children so...so I told Jaime she had to terminate the pregnancy.

"She...listened to me and went through with it," Jeffrey said. The blood drained out of his face, leaving his skin cold and clammy. "But it destroyed her. She began drinking and doing drugs. Before long, she dropped out of school altogether and went back home. I never found out what happened to her after that."

Numb with shock and pain, Rebecca sat unmoving, her expression unreadable. Since she was unable to have children herself, she had always been particularly sensitive about the issue of abortion. Finding out that her own husband had encouraged another woman to kill his own child sickened her and made her want to scream at him in rage. Praying to God for help, she tightened her grip on the bed until her knuckles began to ache.

"So you see, Rebecca, I didn't *want* to believe in God," Jeffrey said softly. "I bought into the doctrine of evolution, not so much because I believed it, but because the alternative was too unbearable to think about. For if there was a God, then I would certainly not be worthy of His love. I deserve to go to hell."

She knew she should say something to him, but her emotions were too raw to be trusted. Seeing the pain in her eyes, Jeffrey felt the weight of his guilt increase.

"Then, when you became a Christian, I knew that our marriage wouldn't last," he stated. "I couldn't stand to be around you because you were a constant reminder that someday I'd have to account for what I'd done. And so…so I turned away from you. Oh God, I betrayed the woman I loved!"

Sobs wracked his body. Covering his head with his arms, Jeffrey moaned loudly. "I destroyed Jaime's life, I destroyed the life of my unborn child, I destroyed the lives of those children on the bus, I destroyed Lisa's life, and I've destroyed your life! I deserve to die! I deserve to be judged!"

Moved to compassion, Rebecca bowed her head and wept as she prayed. Long minutes passed with neither one speaking. Jeffrey's remorse eventually evaporated, leaving him drained and exhausted. Placing her hand on his arm, Rebecca spoke, her voice quivering. "Jeffrey, I'm…I'm glad you told me. I wish I could simply tell you that none of this matters to me, but that wouldn't be the truth. I need some time to process this. However, I will tell you that I know that God has always known what you did, and He is willing to forgive you.

"That's the main thing that sets Christianity apart from all other religions," Rebecca continued. "They teach that mankind has to *earn* salvation. But, Christianity teaches that 'all have sinned and fallen short of the glory of God.'[2] 'There is no one righteous, not even one.'[3] God's forgiveness is a *gift*, Jeffrey. We can't earn it. While Jesus hung on the cross, He forgave the very people who mocked Him, beat Him, and put the nails in His hands. If He could forgive *them*, surely He can forgive you."

Although Jeffrey remained silent, Rebecca could tell that he was listening.

"I've heard it said that our own 'goodness' is like having a jumping contest to see who can get closest to the moon!" she said. "No matter who jumps the highest, every one of us is still nowhere *close* to reaching it. God is a holy God. In His eyes, all sin is equal. There are no 'bad sins' and 'not-so-bad sins.' God will forgive you, Jeffrey. You just need to ask Him."

"I wish I could believe that," he said hoarsely.

Standing, she looked at him one last time. "Don't just take my word on it. I encourage you to read it for yourself. I'll leave you the small New Testament I carry around in my jacket pocket," she said as she laid the small book on the bed. "I recommend starting with the book of John. I'll send Mack or someone to stay with you. I'll be praying…for you, for me, and…for us." Moving away from the bed, she opened the door and left the room, leaving him alone.

Feeling a heaviness in his heart, Jeffrey sensed the weight of his guilt beginning to crush him once again. Then, remembering Rebecca's suggestion, he reached down, picked up the New Testament, and began to read.

29

THE DAWN OF TIME

THE PYRAMID SHOOK violently, causing Akwen to fall out of the throne-like chair and jolt her awake. Immediately, all traces of sleep were brushed aside as she leapt to her feet and began studying the controls. Before she had even figured out what was happening, the walls and everything within the ship, including her own body, began to turn transparent.

"Elmer, power on!" Akwen called out to the droid, who had gone into 'sleep mode' shortly after she had dozed off.

"How may I—" he began.

"Plug into da computer!" she cried out impatiently. "Find out what's happening!"

"What's going on?" Jerome asked as he reached the top of the nearly invisible steps with Mack, Dr. Eisenberg, Goliath, Rebecca, and Lisa hot on his heels.

"How should I know?" Akwen replied as she frantically looked at the controls in front of her. Suddenly, her eyes grew wide in shock and her rapid movements ceased.

"What's wrong? What did you find?" Goliath said as he and the others came to stand behind her.

"Da…da time dial," she said, her voice full of apprehension. "It's at minus 4385!"

"Then what I feared has come to pass!" Dr. Eisenberg said. "We've gone back to the beginning of time!"

"But, I thought you said the pyramid would probably stop and recharge after a thousand years or so!" Mack said, looking at Akwen accusingly. "Why didn't you wake us up and tell us that we had overshot the mark?"

Akwen spun and shot him a glance that was filled with such intensity that Mack took a step backwards. "Like da rest of you, I fell asleep because I was exhausted from spending a night in a dungeon and trying to survive! So *excuse me!*" she spat, drawing out the last two words for emphasis.

"We're not blaming you for anything, Akwen," Dr. Eisenberg said gently. "You deserved to rest as well."

"This is the first time we've made a jump with the core we took from the Tower of Babel," Lisa pointed out. "It must be stronger and able to hold more of a charge."

"Oh great!" Jerome commented as he stared through the now translucent walls toward the pristine earth below them. "So what does it all mean?"

The engines, which had shut off immediately as the machine jolted out of time, suddenly began to rev back up, this time in reverse. "I think we're about to find out!" Goliath stated as the pyramid started to descend toward the planet.

"I have full control of where we land," Akwen stated as she grabbed the controls. "Does anyone have any preferences?"

"Yeah right!" Jerome said sarcastically. "We're at the dawn of time! There's nothing down there yet but wide-open country!"

"Actually," Dr. Eisenberg interjected in order to prevent another outburst from the pilot, "we *cannot* be at the very beginning of time."

"Why do you say that?" Lisa asked.

"Simple: The sun has already been created; there is dry land; and, we can see greenery, meaning that plants have already been created," he replied. "If we had arrived at the *very* dawn of time, then we either wouldn't see anything at all or the earth would be completely covered with water and there would be no sun."

"At least, according to a literal reading of Genesis," Jerome added.

"Based upon the original Hebrew, a literal reading makes the most sense," Dr. Eisenberg stated. "Those who say otherwise are inconsistent in how they interpret ancient documents. There is nothing in the original language of the text to indicate that it should be taken as anything *but* a historical narrative. And, as we have seen firsthand, the *literal* interpretation of the Flood was the correct interpretation."

"So if we aren't at the beginning of time itself, then when *did* we arrive?" Rebecca asked.

"We won't know until we get down there," the doctor said. "But, based on the time dial, my guess is that we have arrived very shortly *after* the original creation week."

"Dis is all very interesting, but it still doesn't answer my question," Akwen said. "Where should we land?"

"If we have indeed arrived after creation was finished," Dr. Eisenberg said, "then we should be able to locate the Garden of Eden!"

"What?" Lisa questioned. "But, how do we know where that is?"

"The Torah says that God planted the Garden in the east and that a river flows out of it before branching into four great rivers!" Dr. Eisenberg said excitedly.

"But there's still an awful lot of land to cover," Jerome said.

"We've got the time, and Akwen can control the ship," the doctor added. "So, we stay at a relatively high altitude and fly above the east coast and look for rivers or anything *not* wide-open country."

"Why?" Goliath asked bluntly. "Why waste time trying to find this Garden? Why not just land, change the dial to the future and go home?"

"Because, we're not even sure we *can* go home to the future," Dr. Eisenberg replied. "The machine didn't work when Arngrim tried to use it and *we've* never been able to travel forward in time. Besides, don't you have even the slightest bit of curiosity to find out what the Garden looked like?"

When none of the others answered his question or disputed his logic, Akwen nodded in affirmative. "It's settled den." Grabbing the controls, she focused her attention on the giant orb beneath them.

As the pyramid descended through the pristine atmosphere of the beautiful planet, Akwen guided the ship to the southeastern tip of the large supercontinent. She kept the pyramid high in the atmosphere so that the travelers would have a clear view of the surrounding landscape. Only a handful of light, fluffy clouds drifted around them, allowing them to see for miles in every direction. No one spoke as Akwen guided their craft northward along the coast in search of the four large rivers.

"I don't see any big rivers yet," Jerome said, his voice tinged with awe, "but check out the Quetzalcoatlus! And over there, near that small lake is a herd of Pachycephalosauruses and..."

"...and elephants," Dr. Eisenberg finished for him. "Or maybe mammoths. They look like a mixture of both."

"Well, if we do get stuck in this time period, at least we'll have plenty of stuff to explore," Mack stated.

"What are you talking about?" Lisa said nervously. "I don't want to get 'stuck' anywhere. I want to get home."

Mack looked apologetic. "I was only saying that there are worse places to get stuck. Such as *days before the Flood*."

"Can we please just focus on finding dis Garden, if it even exists," Akwen stated. "Dere's no sense worrying about getting 'stuck' anywhere until we find out if da pyramid is even broken."

After nearly twenty minutes more of searching, Mack suddenly called out. "Look! There it is! The four rivers and a...a wall!"

The others stared in the direction that Mack indicated with his extended finger until they began to see it as well. "There *is* a wall!" Rebecca said in surprise. "It must be nearly forty feet high and seems to stretch on for miles! I never realized the Garden would be so big! But...but I don't remember the Bible saying anything about a stone wall covered in thorny vines!"

Dr. Eisenberg frowned. As he spoke, Akwen piloted the ship lower and closer to the outer wall. "It doesn't. But perhaps—"

Before the doctor could continue his thought, a stream of fire flashed across the sky between the pyramid and the wall. It took the travelers a moment to realize that the source of the fire was a gigantic sword that was being swung back and forth by an enormous, blazing figure that hovered before them. "HOLD ON!" Akwen called out as she pulled hard on the controls to turn the ship.

Although she knew it should have been impossible, Rebecca felt the heat of the sword penetrate the walls of the pyramid. As Akwen turned the vessel away from the Garden, Rebecca felt the heat decrease gradually and the sudden terror that had been squeezing her heart began to relent. Turning to look behind them, she could see through the transparent walls that the being was not pursuing.

Swearing in exasperation, Goliath turned to face Dr. Eisenberg. "What…what just happened? What was that thing?"

Clearly shaken, the doctor swallowed hard before replying. "It must be one of the Cherubim that God placed to guard the Garden after Adam and Eve sinned."

"A what?" Goliath asked.

"A Cherub," the doctor repeated. "It's a type of angel."

"But if it's already guarding the entrance to the Garden of Eden, then that means we must have arrived some time after the Fall," Rebecca said.

The doctor nodded in affirmative, his face downcast as he stared at the tops of the trees that stood inside the wall. "It appears that this bird's-eye view will be all we'll ever see of the Garden of Eden."

"So what do we do now?" Akwen asked.

Dr. Eisenberg thought for a moment. "I think we should continue circling around the Garden. Perhaps we can find Adam and Eve."

Although the idea of trying to locate a literal Adam and Eve still seemed absurd to Akwen, she nevertheless decided to follow the doctor's suggestion. Several minutes passed as she piloted the pyramid east along the southern wall of the Garden, making sure to keep the ship a healthy distance from the stone structure. Rounding the southeastern corner, Akwen and her companions gazed northward along the eastern wall. Several miles away, they could see a wide river flowing out from an opening in the wall. Before the river had traveled more than three miles, it began to branch off to become four separate rivers that each flowed in different directions.

However, it was more than the river that had captured the attention of the visitors. The being of blazing light that had nearly attacked them now hovered over the river where it flowed out between the walls. The flaming sword grasped in its hands flashed backward and forward threateningly. Fear of the power that exuded from the angelic being washed over the travelers once again. Turning the pyramid away from the entrance to the Garden, Akwen flew low over the terrain near the river.

Rebecca's sudden cry startled everyone in the room. "Over there! Look!" To everyone's amazement, they saw the figure of a man dressed in the skin of a lamb standing on a rocky outcropping that overlooked the raging river below. As Akwen guided them closer to him, the intense expression of sorrow and regret caused Rebecca to ache with sympathy. However, at the same time, apprehension filled her spirit as she realized what it was the man was about to do.

"Oh no…" Rebecca breathed softly. "We have to hurry!"

"Why, what's wrong?" Dr. Eisenberg asked in concern.

"I think he is contemplating suicide!" she said. "He's going to jump into the river!"

30

ADAM

"WHAT?" JEROME SAID in shock. "But, Adam *can't* commit suicide. If he does, then…then all human life would cease to exist!"

"Exactly!" Rebecca said. "I somehow don't think God would allow him to do that, but then again, there's a lot I don't understand."

"Akwen, can you set us down on the ridge behind him?" Rebecca asked the pilot.

The Cameroonian woman didn't reply, but simply nodded her head and directed the pyramid toward the spot that Rebecca had indicated. Within moments, the ship came to rest on a grassy knoll about fifty feet from the outcropping on which Adam stood.

"I don't think it would be wise for all of us to go together," Dr. Eisenberg said. "Adam has never seen any other humans except Eve, and it may frighten him. Especially you, Goliath. You should remain behind."

"What do *I* care if my presence frightens him?" the giant sneered.

"You might care if you scare him and he falls onto those rocks in the river," Jerome said. "Because if that happens, you, and the rest of us, will cease to exist!"

Before Goliath could respond, Dr. Eisenberg interjected. "Our presence here may have consequences that we cannot yet fathom. It would be best if we limit our exposure to Adam. With that in mind, I think only Mack should go speak with him."

"You've never been concerned about messing with time before," Goliath commented. "Why the sudden concern?"

"It has *always* been a concern of mine," the doctor responded. "However, most of the time we were just fighting for our own survival."

"Not to mention how do we know that God hasn't sent us here specifically to *save* Adam?" Mack added. "Didn't we save the Ark from being burned?"

"Good point," Dr. Eisenberg said. "So, unless there are any further objections, I think Mack should leave immediately."

Within less than a minute, Mack left the pyramid and was jogging out across the grass toward Adam, his heart pounding heavily within him at the thought of who it was he was about to meet. As he drew closer, he slowed to a walk so as not to frighten the man who still faced the river and seemed oblivious to Mack's approach.

Suddenly, Adam threw his head back and let out an anguished cry, startling Mack and filling him with a profound sense of loss. Dropping to the ground, Adam threw his arms over his head and pulled his legs under him.

Mack watched in silence for several seconds, not wanting to intrude on the man's grief. Finally, as if sensing his presence, Adam slowly looked up from where he was curled on the ground. His piercingly blue eyes grew wide as his gaze fixed upon the stranger. Adam quickly leapt to his feet, surprised by the man's sudden appearance.

Despite his shock and trepidation, Mack could tell that Adam was strikingly handsome. He was the very essence of manhood. His body was muscular and toned, and his skin was a beautiful, reddish-brown shade, standing out in sharp contrast to the white of the lamb-skin clothing that covered his torso and waist. A full head of shoulder length, sandy-brown hair flowed around him, blown by a gentle breeze.

The two men simply stared at each other for nearly a minute. Finally,

Mack came to his senses and muttered a greeting. "Oh, um…hi! I'm… my name is Mack."

Adam's eyes narrowed in confusion. "You are not a Cherub."

Mack shook his head and smiled. "You're definitely right about that. I'm a man, like you."

"But, how can that be?" Adam asked. Suddenly, his countenance fell and his eyes drifted toward the ground beneath his feet. "I see. Because I have failed, the Mighty Creator has made another man to replace me." Adam turned back to face the river once more, causing Mack's heart to leap into his throat.

"NO! Wait!" Mack cried. "That's not it at all. I am…God has not replaced you! I am here to tell you that…that you must live! You are the father of all of mankind."

Adam turned back to face Mack, his mask of confusion once more in place. "But, who are you?"

Mack gestured to him to come closer. "I would feel more comfortable if we could talk over here, *away* from the edge."

Adam did as Mack asked, although he seemed confused by the other's request. When he drew within ten feet of his strange visitor, Adam stopped and waited for him to explain further.

Clearing his throat, Mack continued. "This is going to be hard for you to believe, but I am actually one of your…your descendents! I have traveled here from the future in that machine over there," he finished, pointing to the pyramid that rested behind him.

"You are one of my descendents?" Adam repeated. "But, how can that be?"

Mack's mind reeled as he considered just how little Adam must know about anything. He had no concept of culture, or languages, or technology, or probably even the most basic of things like rope, fire, or tools. If the time dial was right, then Adam was less than a year old, even though he appeared to be in his early twenties.

"This machine behind me allows me to travel through time," Mack said. "Many years from now, you and your wife will have numerous children, and those children will have children, so that in hundreds of years from today, there will be many people on the earth."

Adam nodded. "Yes, the Creator told us to be fruitful and multiply."

"Exactly!" Mack said excitedly. "You may not understand this completely, but *I* am one of your children's children's children. This machine behind me has allowed me to travel through time to meet you."

Perplexed, Adam stepped closer to his visitor. Stopping to stand in front of him, he reached out and touched Mack's face, hair, and clothing. Unnerved by the man's perusal, Mack stood frozen in place, staring up at the six-and-a-half-foot-tall man that was *the* patriarch of all mankind.

Finally, Adam took a step back and dropped his arms to his sides. "Why have you come?"

"It's a very long story," Mack said with a grin. "We came seeking help. And when we saw you standing over the river, we wanted to stop you from killing yourself."

"'Killing myself'?" he repeated in shock. "Why would I do that?"

Mack frowned. "When we saw you on the edge by the river, we thought…we thought you were going to jump in."

Adam's expression took on a hint of fear. "I could not do that. I *have* thought much more about death recently. But I could never leave Eve alone." Disturbed by the very idea of taking his own life, Adam changed the subject. "You said 'we' a moment ago. Why?"

"I've come with friends," Mack answered. "They are still in the pyramid."

"I would like to meet them, but I must first find my wife," Adam said.

"Where is she?" Mack asked, suddenly worried. It didn't dawn on him until now that she was missing.

"If you are truly my descendent, then you must know my terrible shame," he said, his head dropping low and his voice reflecting his deep regret and sorrow.

Mack nodded solemnly. "Yes. How long ago were you ejected from the Garden?"

Without looking up, Adam answered. "Today. Not long ago. When we were cast out, Eve and I were so filled with our own shame and regret that we could not bear to be near one another. She went off by herself to the other side of the river."

Raising his head, he stared at his visitor with such intensity in his eyes that Mack took an involuntary step backward. "Can you truly fathom the depth of our shame? We disobeyed our very Creator: the one who gave us life, and who created all things! We *deserve* death. And death will come soon.

"If you truly are my descendent, then you have probably never seen the inside of the Garden, have you?" When Mack shook his head, Adam continued. "Do you believe that this world is beautiful?"

"Yes! Compared to the time during which I live, this world is spectacular," Mack answered.

Adam's depression only deepened. "You only say that because you never saw what the world was like before. When I look around, I see that even now, things have begun to change. I even saw a pair of animals fighting one another. Can you understand? My sin has affected *everything*! Everywhere I look, I am constantly reminded of my failing."

Mack walked up to Adam and put his hand on the man's shoulder. "But there is hope! God has not abandoned you or Eve. You do not know this, but in the future, one of *your descendents* will give birth to the Savior, who will rescue the world from sin. He will open the door to eternal life."

"The Promise…" Adam muttered.

"What?" Mack said, confused.

"Just before the Creator banished us from the Garden, He made a promise that there would be enmity between the offspring of the serpent and Eve's offspring," Adam said. "He said to the serpent that 'he will crush your head and you will strike his heel.'[1] Could this be of what you speak?"

"It could be," Mack answered honestly. "I'm not the expert on those things, but it sounds about right. I think Rebecca might have said something about that."

"Rebecca?" Adam asked. "Is that your wife?"

Mack blushed. "No. She's just a good friend. Let's go find Eve, and then I'll introduce you to the rest of my friends."

"I must go to her alone," Adam said. "She and I must talk first. Then, I will bring her back here to meet you and your companions."

Mack agreed, and to his great surprise, Adam stepped forward and embraced him. "Thank you, my son, for reminding me of the Creator's Promise."

Not knowing what else to do, Mack simply smiled dumbly. "You're welcome."

With a renewed sense of purpose, Adam went off in search of his wife, leaving Mack alone on the hillside. For several moments, he just stood in silence, reviewing the conversation with Adam in his mind. Finally, he turned and made his way slowly back to the pyramid. Shaking his head in wonder, he smiled broadly, his spirit soaring.

31

ANSWERS

NOT MORE THAN an hour after Mack had returned to the pyramid to tell the others what had happened, Adam and his wife arrived at the entrance to the strange structure. Having watched them approach through the exterior cameras, Mack met them at the main door and escorted them inside.

He was immediately stunned by Eve's beauty. Her brownish-red hair flowed luxuriously over her shoulders and seemed to glisten, even in the interior lights of the pyramid. Her skin was tan and flawless. Still, despite her outward, perfect beauty, it was her eyes that captured Mack, for their dark brown depths contained both intelligence and sorrow. One look at her caused him to momentarily forget his surroundings and his companions.

Once Mack had recovered from the intoxicating effect of Eve's beauty, he introduced Adam and Eve to the rest of his companions—including Goliath, who used his armor to once more disguise himself as a normal, albeit tall, human. Mack then took Adam and Eve on a tour of the pyramid. Under other circumstances, he could tell that Adam would have found the entire structure fascinating. However, still weighed down by their overwhelming grief and guilt at being cast from Eden, both he and Eve found it difficult to stay focused on the intricacies of the structure.

Sensing their uneasiness and apprehension about the strange machine and its occupants, Mack decided to cut the tour short.

Intercepting Mack and his guests as they finished viewing the inside of the structure, Rebecca invited the man and his wife to eat with her and her companions while they waited for the pyramid's core to recharge. They accepted, but due to their feelings of discomfort at being indoors, Rebecca and the others took the food outside, where the group sat on the plush grass. Using the gravity control devices, Jerome and Goliath brought Jeffrey out so that he could join the group.

As they ate, the conversation was initially dominated by Mack answering any questions that Adam had. The travelers found that nearly everything that they took for granted was new and fascinating to the man and woman. Despite the seriousness of the day's events, Adam was thankful for the distraction, while Eve seemed to withdraw into herself as she leaned against him, half-listening. As Mack described various concepts and ideas, Adam became increasingly intrigued, especially when Mack talked about different languages and cultures, as well as the differences in skin color and body shape that was exhibited by the travelers.

As the meal was drawing to an end, Rebecca and Dr. Eisenberg began to ask questions of their guests while Akwen, Lisa, Jerome, Jeffrey, and Goliath merely listened in interest.

"I never imagined that Adam would be so *hot!*" Lisa whispered to Jerome who sat next to her in the grass.

Jerome threw her a wry look. "No kidding! I can't take my eyes off of Eve either! She is *drop-dead gorgeous!* I suppose I never really gave it any thought. After all, I never believed that they were real people to begin with. But I guess that if you accept that they were real, which I can't deny now, then it would make sense that they'd be beautiful. I mean, God made them perfect, and since traits for beauty are inherited, they must already have all of that information in their genetic material. I imagine it'd be several generations *at least* before ugliness starts to even creep into the population."

"But I don't get something," Lisa asked, "if Adam and Eve are the only two people alive, then who do their kids marry?"

Jerome snickered. "I've always wondered that myself. That was one of the questions that made me wonder about the accuracy of the Bible. How do you think Doc would answer that one?"

"There's one way to find out," Lisa replied.

While Mack continued to converse with Adam and Eve in their language, Jerome reiterated Lisa's question to Doc. "The Bible talks about Adam's son Cain going off and marrying his wife. But where did he find her? Are there other people around?"

Dr. Eisenberg smiled. "That is a common question that people have asked over the years. First of all, the Bible *doesn't* say that Cain 'went off and married his wife.' It says that he left, then his wife conceived."

"What's the difference?" Jerome asked.

"The difference is that his wife *left with him*," the doctor clarified. "Cain didn't meet her *after* he left his family.[1] Also, when you study the Torah, it says that Adam called his wife Eve because she 'would become the mother of all living.'[2] It says that our first parents *also* had other sons and daughters."

"Aw man, you're not suggesting what I *think* you're suggesting, are you?" Mack asked, disgust written all over his face.

The doctor nodded. "I am. Cain must have married his sister, or possibly his niece."

Seeing Mack's reaction, Adam asked him what was being discussed. While Mack tried to come up with some way to explain their conversation, Lisa responded to Dr. Eisenberg's statement.

"But how can that be?" she asked. "If he married his sister, then wouldn't their children have been born with birth defects?"

"No, they wouldn't," the doctor replied. "What causes birth defects?"

Lisa thought for a moment before responding. "Mutations in the genes of the parents, isn't it?"

"That's right. The closer a man and woman are in relation, the more similar their genes are," Dr. Eisenberg explained. "So, in our time, if a brother and sister marry, their children are likely to have some deformity because they will inherit the same mistakes from both mother and father. However, if a man marries a woman who is *not* closely related, they will have *different* mistakes in their genes. Since the child will receive one set of genes from each parent, and since good genes tend to override or mask bad genes, serious deformities are avoided."

"Exactly," Jerome replied. "Which means that if Cain married his sister, then they would have all kinds of deformities."

The professor raised a finger to halt Jerome's assumption. "Not exactly. You are making a critical error in logic. You are doing what too many scientists do when considering questions from the *past*. You are assuming that everything that we see in *our* time applies to *this* time."

"But why shouldn't we?" Jerome replied. "Science is science. The laws of genetics don't change."

"I'm not saying that the laws of genetics must change. What I *am* saying is that we have to take what we see in our times and extrapolate backward in time using logic," he clarified. "Think about this for a moment: Is the genetic load of mutations in the human race as a whole increasing or decreasing with each generation?" he asked.

"Increasing," Jerome answered. "Every generation has more mutations in their genes than the previous one."

"Precisely," Dr. Eisenberg said. "Which means, if you go back in time, the genetic load would be less and less until you reach a time when there *were* no genetic mistakes," he paused, glancing at Adam and Eve. "It's kind of like making a copy of a copy of a copy. The further you get away from the source, the more fuzzy the image."

Rebecca sat up straighter in sudden understanding. "So, Adam's descendents could have children without deformities because their genetic information was pure."

"Okay, I'll give you that, but doesn't the Bible forbid marrying your close relative?" Jerome asked. "How could it do so and yet imply that it was okay for Adam's family? Is it sinful or not?"

"Again, you must understand the timing and reason that God gave the laws," the doctor explained. "First, the law against marrying your sister and other relatives was given by Moses, which was well over two thousand years after creation. With our modern understanding of genetics, we can now understand why God gave that law at that particular time. He knew that the genetic load was at a point where it would start to cause their children to have deformities. This is a perfect example of how, when the Israelites followed God's laws, even if they didn't understand them, they were healthier than those nations around them."

"Actually, doesn't the Bible record that Abraham married his half-sister?" Rebecca asked, joining the conversation.

"Yes, it does," Dr. Eisenberg confirmed. "And he was the father of the Jewish nation. So, Jerome, to answer your question, it was *not* sinful to marry your sister *before* the Mosaic law, but afterward it became so in order to protect the people from physical deformities."

"Uh…can we change the subject?" Mack asked. "Our guests are starting to really wonder about the details of what we're talking about, and I can't keep dodging the point forever."

As the conversation returned its focus back to Adam and Eve, Rebecca found her gaze turning to Jeffrey, who sat silent and morose several feet away from her. Although she wondered what he thought of meeting and talking to the real Adam and Eve, she knew that now would not be the time to ask. She closed her eyes momentarily and began praying for her husband and friends.

She knew that Dr. Eisenberg and Mack had come to accept Jesus as their savior, and Doc had told her that Lisa had as well. Yet, despite all they had seen and experienced, Akwen, Jerome, and (to a degree) Jeffrey still seemed too stubborn to accept the truth. However, she could also tell that each of them, including Akwen, had changed. She prayed that God would continue to work on their hearts and minds until they finally accepted His love.

Opening her eyes, Rebecca continued to pray as she half-heartedly listened to the conversation. Suddenly, a strange prickling sensation traveled down her spine, causing her to look around expectantly. Something, or someone, was coming closer. Although she couldn't see anything just yet, her spirit knew that a supernatural presence was drawing near.

"What is it, Rebecca?" Dr. Eisenberg asked in concern as she stood to her feet and began looking around.

She was about to reply when she saw a figure begin to materialize ten feet in front of her. Just as she felt a twinge of fear begin to flow through her veins, she recognized the being. Relief flooded over her, yet his presence was so powerful that she still found it difficult to stand.

"Sikaris!" she exclaimed breathlessly as she looked up at him. She noticed that he was no longer wearing the gleaming armor, but instead was dressed in a simple white robe. "I'm so glad to see you again," she said as she stared into the angel's violet eyes expectantly.

"Dear Rebecca, I told you that we would surely meet again," he said, his voice firm and comforting. "Rise. All of you. Am I God that you would bow before me?"

As she stood, she turned to look at her friends. Each of them, including Goliath, was lying facedown in the grass. Even Jeffrey had managed to roll himself over despite his paralyzed legs in order to turn away from the angelic being. Although her friends had seen him once before, his power and might had been partially masked by their own fear and the presence of Odin and the other false gods. Now, however, they felt the full weight of his majesty. Next to her friends, Rebecca could see that although Adam and Eve were still seated on the grass, Eve had her face buried in her husband's chest, while he had his turned away from Sikaris in shame.

Walking over to Adam and his wife, Sikaris crouched down and spoke to them softly. To her surprise, Rebecca found that she understood him, despite the fact that he was speaking in the Language of Eden. "Fear not. Although you have disobeyed the Lord, and have received your punishment, I have come to tell you that you are not forgotten. You will not commune with the Creator the way you once did, but know that He will always hear you and respond to your needs when you cry out to Him. He will never leave you, nor forsake you, but you will still have to deal with the consequences of the sin that you have brought into the world."

Standing, Sikaris spoke louder, addressing all of them. "You have brought encouragement to the firstborn among men. But now it is time for Adam and his wife to leave you. They must begin their new life and you must return to your home."

Adam rose to his feet. Crying softly, Eve joined him. Together they bid farewell to Rebecca and the others and thanked them. As they turned to leave, Sikaris stood before the couple and touched each of them on their foreheads. Without looking back, they turned and walked away from the visitors.

Turning his attention to Rebecca and the others, Sikaris spoke. "I have altered their minds so that they will not remember you. Their memories of this encounter will be nothing more than strange dreams to them. But they will *always* keep with them the feelings of encouragement that you brought. For you have reminded them of the Promise, which is to be their primary purpose for living."

"Is that…is that what happened to *everyone* we have met on this journey?" Rebecca asked. "Have you altered their memories as well? Will Noah and his family remember us?"

"Yes and no," the angel replied as he walked over to where Jeffrey lay on the ground. Lifting him, Sikaris set him back on the cushions that Rebecca and the others had set out for him. His face white as a ghost, Jeffrey watched silently as the angelic being smiled at him, then stood and walked over to stand near Rebecca once more as he continued speaking. "I have not altered the memories of anyone else you have encountered. Do you not remember that when you first met Noah he remarked that you looked familiar? It is because he remembered meeting you before the Flood."

"Then why did you change the memories of Adam and Eve?" Rebecca asked.

"Because they are still too young and innocent to fully comprehend all that you have showed them," Sikaris replied. "Remember, they are not yet a year old, even though they appear to be much older."

Dr. Eisenberg, having finally recovered his voice, spoke tremulously. "Oh servant of the Most High God, forgive my ignorance, but how do you know about our previous meeting with Noah? Were you there with us?"

Sikaris nodded. "God sent me to watch over you. I have been with you from the very beginning. At the Lord's command, I was with you when Goliath and Hercules attacked you. I was with you when you were captured by the Mayans. The Creator sent me to meet you on the streets of Corinth and direct you toward the vendor who could help you. It was *I* who took control of the pyramid to direct you to where Noah and his family lived during the Ice Age. The Lord guided me to protect you at the Tower of Babel, and aid you during the time before the Flood."

Rebecca and the others stared at him with expressions of shock and awe. "You...you were the one that guided the pyramid to Noah's cave?" Mack asked. "And all along we thought it was a virus in the computer systems."

"Indeed, Arngrim *did* program the pyramid to return to him," Sikaris explained. "I only intervened to pilot the ship when you arrived during the Ice Age."

A look of hurt and betrayal spread over Rebecca's face as she glanced at Jeffrey, "But, Sikaris, if you were with us all along, then why did you wait so long to help us before the Flood?"

Sikaris' expression filled with compassion. "I am sorry, Rebecca. But there are some things that I do not have the power to prevent. When you arrived before the Flood, you entered a time where the power of the enemy was at its greatest. I was very limited in what I could accomplish. I was forced to watch and wait for the time when God's judgment was poured out: for I knew that only then would the enemy be distracted enough for me to act openly. That is why I did not intervene until the very beginning of the Flood."

Placing his hand on her shoulder, Sikaris looked deeply into Rebecca's eyes which were filled with tears. "I am a created being, like you. I do not understand all that the Almighty Lord of Hosts does or allows. But rest assured that He always has a purpose. Nothing happens without His knowledge or permission. What man means for evil, God uses to accomplish His will, even though we do not always understand how," he said, looking directly at Akwen, who quickly turned away.

"Uh…Sik…your majesty," Mack fumbled for the right words, "can you…can you travel through time?"

"No, I cannot," the angel replied, frowning slightly at being called "your majesty." "Even though we have a much better understanding of space and time, the Mighty God has limited us so that, like you, we cannot travel through time. This was, in fact, one reason for the Flood. Odin and Arngrim had discovered the key to time travel, and the Lord could not allow them to use that knowledge, for in their hands, they could have used it to accomplish many acts of evil."

"But, if you can't travel through time yourself, then…then how were you able to follow us?" Mack asked.

"I traveled the same way you did," he replied. "I was with you in the pyramid."

Mack's jaw dropped. "Y…you mean that you were riding along with us the whole time?"

Sikaris nodded. "My kind has the ability to remain unseen by human eyes if we choose."

"If that is the case," began Rebecca, "then how did you get here now? When we saw you last, you were heading *away* from the pyramid to go protect the Ark."

"The Mighty King made an exception for me this one time," Sikaris said. "He allowed me to stay behind and assist my brothers in the defense of the Ark. Once that was completed, He opened time and space to bring me here. But unless I return with you on the pyramid, I will be left in this place in time unless the Almighty were to intervene again for His purpose."

"Return?" Jerome said at last. "Does…does that mean that the pyramid works?"

"Yes," Sikaris confirmed simply.

Each of the travelers let out a sigh of relief. For the first time since their journey began, they knew that they would be able to return home. Tears of joy began to spring forth in their eyes as they turned to one another and laughed.

After several moments, Rebecca turned her attention back to Sikaris. "How come the pyramid will work now when it never worked before? Did you fix it?"

Sikaris shook his head. "No. It has always worked."

Rebecca and the others exchanged confused looks. "What do you mean?" Rebecca asked at length.

"The only thing that prevented you from traveling back to your own time initially was Arngrim's pre-programming. Once he had the pyramid in his possession, he removed that restriction."

"Den why couldn't he travel forward into time?" Akwen asked. "Did you stop him?"

"Yes," Sikaris stated. "As I mentioned previously, Arngrim could not be allowed to use the machine."

"So, if the machine is working properly, then why did we suddenly jolt out of time when we arrived here?" Rebecca asked.

Sikaris regarded her with a smile. "The machine was not allowed to travel further back into time because of its passengers. If you had gone back further, you would have arrived before the Fall of Adam and Eve. But that was a time before sin. Your presence was not allowed, for you are descendents of Adam after the Fall, and so you carry sin within you. As such, you were therefore prevented from going any further into time by God's holiness."

Rebecca and the others were silent for several seconds as they processed all that they had learned. At last, Goliath spoke, saying the one thing that had been on their minds from the moment the pyramid had first launched. "Then there is nothing preventing us from going home. I say we pack up our things and get moving. No more side trips. Once the core is charged, I say we see how far it will take us."

The others nodded their agreement. Despite their excitement, Rebecca felt a sense of pain and despair. *What will happen when we get there,* she wondered. *What will happen to Jeffrey? What about Lisa? How can we just return to "life as usual" after all we've been through?*

As they sat quietly on the grass, Sikaris walked over to stand beside Mack and Dr. Eisenberg. "You have both done well. Plant the seeds of your faith deeply so that the evil one will not be able to snatch it away from you. Mack, you have a family now. Let your Eternal Father teach you. Know that you are His son, and that nothing can separate you from His love."

Stepping over to Jerome, he looked down at him. Unable to meet the angel's gaze, Jerome stared at the ground. "Jerome, you have allowed sinful man to poison your understanding of the truth. You have rejected the Savior because of the actions and false teachings of men. Read the Word of God to find the truth. Then, teach it to your family, for the Word will bring life to all who read it."

Tears fell from Jerome's eyes as Sikaris moved to stand before Goliath, who rose to his feet. Despite his obvious fear, the giant fought to maintain his composure in the face of the angelic being. As the others watched, Sikaris' expression became stern. Goliath's knees began to shake until, unable to stand further beneath the gaze of the angel, the giant collapsed to the ground.

"Goliath, wicked men have filled your life with pain," Sikaris said. "Because of this, you have used your pride and hatred as a shield. As long as you do so, you will never experience true love or joy. Do not seek revenge on those who have wronged you. They will receive their punishment in due time. Instead, you must release your hatred. Only then will you be truly free." Goliath didn't respond, but simply huddled on the ground.

Moving away from him, Sikaris went to stand in front of Akwen, who immediately began to weep. "Akwen, you have also used pain as a weapon against others and against your Maker. You must trust Him to bring justice to those who hurt your daughter. But you must also

remember that, in the eyes of a holy God, the sin that those men committed was no greater than your own sins. You have let bitterness rule
your life and rob you of joy. Forgive those who have wronged you, even
as Christ has forgiven you." Akwen continued to weep as Sikaris continued on to Lisa.

Kneeling on the grass, Lisa had her head bowed and was praying
silently as the angel approached. "Lisa, daughter of the King, know that
your sins are forgiven by both your Savior and by the one whom you
have wronged. However, the consequences of your sin still remain. Trust
has been broken, and strong bonds of friendship have now been sev-
ered. Yet, you must persevere in your new faith. Seek out others who are
mature in the Lord and let them guide you. And you must teach your
daughters the truth before it is too late. They are already being enticed
by the world. Pray for them, and seek out answers to the questions they
have about God." Lisa nodded and glanced up at Sikaris, who smiled
warmly down at her and placed his hand on her head.

Turning, Sikaris strode over to where Jeffrey lay several feet away.
As he approached, Jeffrey put his arms over his head as if trying to hide
from the angelic being. "Jeffrey Evans, you also have broken a sacred
bond and deeply wounded the one you vowed to love. Many hard years
of rebuilding the trust you once shared lie ahead. But they will be made
all the harder if you continue to reject the Savior's free gift of salvation.
He knows your sins, and He is willing to forgive you. Only by receiving
His forgiveness will you be able to be at peace."

Taking a small step backward, Sikaris directed his next comment at
both Lisa and Jeffrey. "Both of you by now have realized that what happened to Rebecca on 2021PK was more than just a dream. It was a vision
given to her by the Lord of all Creation. As I was with you on this journey,
it was I that was with her on *that* journey. Look at me," he said gently.

Compelled by his command, Jeffrey, Lisa, and the others looked
up at him and gasped in shock. Where the handsome angel once stood
was a bizarre, six-foot-tall, cat-like creature with black, bat-like folds of
skin that stretched between his muscular wrists and his powerful ankles.

Golden-brown hair stuck out from the creature's scale-like skin. The only indication that any of the onlookers had that this was the same angelic being that spoke to them moments before was the deep, violet eyes that stared down at them reprovingly.

"This was the form that I took when Rebecca first met me," Sikaris said. "You would do well to trust her word in the future. When you return home, listen to her and learn about God's magnificent creation. But remember, that as with all that you learn, you must *always* check it with scripture. For man is fallible, but the Word is infallible."

Having finished his admonitions, Sikaris turned toward Rebecca as his form reverted back to his angelic appearance. "Dearest Rebecca, you have done well. You heeded my warning and built your faith on the Rock that cannot be shaken. Great will be your reward."

Taking a deep breath, she asked the question that had been on her heart since the moment Sikaris had arrived. "Can you…can you heal Jeffrey?"

Sikaris cupped her face in his hands. "Dearest Rebecca, I am sorry. I have not been given the authority or the power to heal either his body or his soul. That is something that only God Himself could do."

Lowering her head, Rebecca began to cry softly, her hope evaporating. Then, as she considered what Sikaris had said, her thoughts began to race and her heart beat wildly. Staring up at him, she could see that he had already guessed what she was thinking. "Would He allow it?" she asked. "Would it change anything?"

Sikaris looked down at her and smiled. "I believe that in His eternal wisdom, He has already made provision for you to do what is in your heart."

Hugging Sikaris briefly, Rebecca released him and looked around at the others, her hope renewed. "Gather everything together! We've got to be ready to move out as soon as the ship is powered up."

"What is it?" Dr. Eisenberg asked. "What's wrong now?"

"Nothing's wrong. It's just that we *do* have one more stop to make before we go home," she said as she looked over at her husband, her heart swelling with excitement.

32

FORGIVEN

PIECES OF CLAY and straw rained down from the roof onto those gathered in the house below, causing them to look up in surprise and shock. The crowd of bearded men filling the moderately-sized, brick dwelling began to whisper among themselves, causing the teacher to pause in his exhortation. As more and more of the ceiling began to fall, it became clear that someone was tearing up the roof. The clay and straw soon caused those directly under the widening hole to become angry and protest loudly. However, since the house was filled from wall to wall, the men began to push and shove against those around them, trying to get out from beneath the falling debris.

Three of the religious leaders, dressed in their fine robes, became indignant that the intruders would be so calloused as to not only interrupt the meeting, but would be so rude as to drop roofing materials down on them. The owner of the home began to complain loudly about the damage being done to his roof as the rest of those gathered in the room spoke to one another with voices filled with anticipation.

Yet, through all of the commotion, the master remained silent, observing everything that was transpiring with interest.

Finally, when the hole was wide enough, the onlookers below watched in amazement as a man lying on a mat was lowered through the opening. On the flat roof, four figures could be seen holding ropes that were attached to the mat, gently lowering it down. Men jostled each other, some trying to get out of the way, and others hoping for a better view of the event.

Outside the house, a woman wearing a robe with the hood pulled up fought desperately to reach the door of the house. However, the crowd was so tightly packed that she could not get through as everyone was pressing in to see and hear the teacher. With her entry into the house barred, she made her way to a window, where she felt her heart leap with excitement at the scene that was unfolding within. Climbing up on the window ledge, she was able to see over the heads of the crowd inside and let out a gasp as she caught a glimpse of the teacher standing near the far wall. Grabbing the edge of the window for support, she swayed as tears blurred her vision. Although he looked stronger than she had expected, he was not as handsome as he had been portrayed. However, she knew beyond a shadow of a doubt that he was the one she sought.

She was gazing upon her Lord and Savior, Jesus of Nazareth.

Inside the building, Jesus looked up at the four men on the roof, a smile spreading across his face. Although the evening sunlight made it difficult to see their features clearly, it became quickly apparent to him that three of the four men had a deep love for their paralyzed friend. Even more than their love, they contained a faith far greater than most that he had encountered in his ministry. Even the fourth man, who was by far the tallest of the group, seemed confident that this teacher from Nazareth would heal his companion.

As the mat settled onto the floor right in front of the Master, a hush fell over the crowd as they stared expectantly at him, wondering what he would do. Crouching down, Jesus looked at the man, his face radiating compassion.

Jeffrey felt his heart constrict and the blood leave his face as Jesus looked at him. Jeffrey turned his head away as the guilt and shame of his past burst forth into his consciousness. Why had he allowed the others to bring him here? Here he was, lying before *Jesus the Christ!* Although he had always denied that Jesus was the Son of God, one look into his eyes and he knew the truth. The realization caused him to nearly faint with shock. Jesus *is* God, and His holiness and justice could not allow sin to go unpunished.

Jeffrey knew the Ten Commandments, and he felt as if the very stone tablets upon which they had been written were crushing his body. *You shall not murder.* In his mind's eye, he saw the saw the bus crash through the railing and fall onto the road below. He also saw the hollowness in Jaime's eyes following the abortion. *You shall not commit adultery.* He remembered the look of betrayal that had crossed Rebecca's face as she learned the truth about his affair with Lisa. *You shall not misuse the name of the Lord your God. You shall not steal. You shall not lie. You shall not covet. You shall have no other gods before me!* Images flashed through his mind of times when he had broken each of them. He was guilty, and he knew that hell would be his final destination when he died. The weight of his guilt caused his breathing to become labored and, for a moment, Jeffrey thought that his heart might rupture. *Oh God, please forgive me! I know I don't deserve it, but please...please forgive me!*

Then, as he was about to succumb to his pain, Jeffrey heard a gentle voice speaking to him as if from a great distance. For several seconds, his mind couldn't comprehend the words. Suddenly, their meaning hit him, bringing with them a rush of intense emotion.

"Take heart, son; your sins are forgiven."

As the words permeated through Jeffrey's soul, he felt the weight that was suffocating him lift. For the first time in his life, he felt free! The chains that had bound him for so many years had suddenly dropped away. Despite all that he had done, the God of the universe had forgiven him. Jeffrey suddenly realized that although he had come for physical healing, that was not what he had needed most. He needed healing in his *soul*, and God, in His wisdom, had given Jeffrey what he needed, not what he wanted. He knew in that moment, that even if he was never able to walk again, he would worship God and serve Him until death.

Tears of gratitude and relief rushed forth as Jeffrey's body heaved with sobs. Feeling Jesus' hand on his shoulder, Jeffrey turned and grasped it as if he was a drowning man in the ocean and it was his only lifeline.

He remained in that position for what seemed like hours, losing all sense of time. Gradually, he began to realize that the crowd in the room was murmuring. Although they were speaking in Hebrew and Aramaic, Jeffrey was familiar enough with those languages to understand them.

"Why does this fellow talk like that?" one whispered.

"He's blaspheming! Who can forgive sins but God alone?" another asked quietly.

Suddenly, Jeffrey understood. They didn't believe that Jesus was God! From their perspective, he was claiming a privilege that only God commanded. Only an extremely foolish or arrogant man would presume to forgive someone who committed wrongs against someone else! However, what the crowd failed to see was that Jeffrey's sins *had* been committed against Jesus, for He was the Lawgiver. He *was* God.

Looking at the crowd, Jeffrey could see that many of the prominent members, especially the teachers of the law, were scowling at Jesus. Although Jeffrey didn't know if Jesus had heard their mutterings, the teacher nevertheless stood and faced them, his countenance darkening as he returned their glares.

"Why are you thinking these things?" he challenged. "Which is easier: to say to the paralytic, 'Your sins are forgiven,' or to say, 'Get up, take your mat and walk'? But that you may know that the Son of Man has authority on earth to forgive sins…"

Jeffrey swallowed the lump in his throat. The entire room around him seemed to disappear as he looked into Jesus' eyes. Jeffrey felt as if he were a spectator, watching the scene unfold. Then, he heard Jesus speak the words that sent his heart racing.

"Get up, pick up your mat, and go home."

Before the words had even left Jesus' mouth, a rush of heat flashed down Jeffrey's spine. However, instead of burning pain, it was a soothing warmth that infused strength into his body. Before he even tried to move, Jeffrey knew what had happened. More tears came, but this time, they were tears of unadulterated joy!

Laughing and crying simultaneously, Jeffrey sat up and began bending his knees. Gasps of wonder and shock spread through those gathered in the room and those who had been looking through the windows and the open door. As Jeffrey rose to his feet, he could hear many offering praise to God. Yet most of the crowd's reaction was lost on Jeffrey, for his senses were focused solely on the man standing before him.

A plethora of emotions hit Jeffrey simultaneously. He wanted to cry, laugh, jump, bow in reverence, and grovel in humility. Not knowing what to do, he simply stood facing Jesus. Then, catching him completely off guard, Jesus laughed and embraced him tightly. The sound of the teacher's laughter was infectious, and as Jesus released him, Jeffrey let out a huge guffaw. He couldn't remember a time in his life when he had felt this happy, carefree, and full of life.

Finally, after sharing a full, joyous laugh together, Jesus placed his hands on Jeffrey's shoulders and looked him in the eye, a smile on his face. "Now, take your mat, and *go home!*"

Jeffrey's eyes grew wide in wonder. Somehow, the way Jesus said the last two words, Jeffrey knew that *he* knew where his home really was. Nodding, Jeffrey reached down, and grabbed the makeshift stretcher that Jerome and the others had made for him. Looking up through the hole in the ceiling, Jeffrey saw the joyous faces of his friends staring down at him. Raising his fist in the air, he let out a triumphant cry. "Hallelujah! Hallelujah!"

Three of the four men were beside themselves with joy, praising and glorifying God as they turned to find their way down the steps from the roof, while the fourth man followed behind them, a look of wonder on his face.

Turning to face Jesus one last time, Jeffrey stared into his dark brown eyes, his emotions threatening to burst open once again. "Thank you. Thank you, Jesus," he said, his voice choked and trembling.

From somewhere behind him, Jeffrey heard a tearful, familiar voice calling out his name from near the door of the house. Recognizing the voice, his heart skipped a beat as heat flooded through him. Bowing quickly to Jesus, Jeffrey turned and made his way across the room as people did their best in the cramped space to make a path for him.

As he reached the doorway, he saw Rebecca forcing her way through the crowd toward him, the hood having fallen back from her head. His heart ached at the sight of her. Reaching out, he grabbed her and pulled her into his arms. Burying his face into her neck, he stood motionless for several moments, simply breathing in the scent of her. He felt her hot tears soaking into the robe he was wearing.

"I'm so sorry," he said as he held her tightly. "I've been so foolish. I…I love you, Rebecca. I loved you before, but now…now I *know* you. I share your beliefs, and I understand what's important to you. I see everything so differently. Please, will you…will you teach me all that you've learned?"

Pulling away, she looked up at him, her face wet with tears. Then, as if hearing someone call to her, she glanced over Jeffrey's shoulder to see Jesus staring at her. Rebecca felt his gaze pierce her heart as a warm smile spread across his face and he nodded once.

Fresh tears raced down her cheeks as she turned her attention back to her husband. Her head cocked to the side and she swallowed hard in an attempt to control her raging emotions. "I will," she said softly, her voice quivering. She knew that it would take some time to rebuild the trust that had been lost, but she felt a calm sense of reassurance settle over her. Their marriage would survive.

Muscles in Jeffrey's face twitched as he fought to retain control of his own turbulent feelings. He had been given a second chance in life: first from God, and now from his wife. He vowed he would not squander those gifts. "C'mon, Rebecca. Let's go home."

Taking his hand in her own, she gave him a lopsided grin. "Please, call me Becky!"

33

HOME

"**ACCORDING TO DA** time dial, we should be arriving in da next couple of minutes," Akwen reported to the others as she studied the controls in front of her.

Everyone had gathered in the control room, eager to see evidence that they had indeed arrived back at their own time. Looking around the room, Rebecca studied each of her friends in turn, her mind thinking back on the events that had led them to this point. They had been attacked by two genetically altered humans, captured by Mayans, robbed by thieves in Corinth, met so-called 'Neanderthals' living during the Ice Age, entered the Tower of Babel, attacked by living dinosaurs, met Noah and demonic false gods, witnessed the beginning of the Flood, met the first humans, spoken with an angel, and witnessed a miracle at the hands of Jesus Himself. None of them would ever be the same again. She wondered what would happen to them now that they were home. Some friendships would undoubtedly grow stronger now that they shared a common faith, yet other friendships, she feared, had been irreparably damaged.

Jeffrey spoke, breaking into her thoughts and bringing her back to the present. "Well, everyone, I think it would be wise for us to decide where we'll land before we arrive." Glancing over at Goliath, Jeffrey studied him intently. "We still have some unfinished business to discuss."

"Yes, we do," the giant responded, his tone inflectionless as he returned Jeffrey's stare. He sat in the throne-like chair calmly, his helmet resting on the floor next to him.

For a moment, Jeffrey wondered if Goliath enjoyed removing his helmet and revealing his real features. He guessed that it was an intimidation tactic, and, looking at the faces of the rest of his friends, he figured it still worked, despite the fact that they had been working so closely with the giant for the last several days. Of course, Goliath's true appearance had been hidden from them most of the journey by his armor's holographic capabilities.

Taking a deep breath, Jeffrey's expression softened. "Goliath, although our relationship didn't start on the best of terms—"

"That's the understatement of the millennia," Mack mumbled.

"—our shared experiences have drawn us together," Jeffrey finished, ignoring Mack's comment. "I think I speak for us all when I say that we want to thank you for everything that you've done for us. Although I'm not so naïve as to think that you did it all out of the goodness of your heart, I'm also smart enough to realize that we probably never would've made it without you. I don't know where you stand on things after all you've seen, but I know that it was no accident that you attacked us when you did. God had it planned from the beginning."

The giant remained silent, his expression unreadable as Jeffrey continued speaking.

"I don't know if you'd ever be willing to trust us enough to accept us as friends, but I will never forget what you've done for me personally," he said, his voice cracking slightly. "You didn't have to help Mack, Jerome, and Dr. Eisenberg when they carried me to Jesus, yet you chose to do so. For that, and for saving our lives on more than one occasion, I'm forever in your debt. If you ever need anything, know that you would be welcome in my home."

Unaccustomed to expressions of gratitude, the giant simply inclined his head in acknowledgement.

"That is, of course, if you still promise to give us the detonator to the explosives you placed inside our bodies," Rebecca added, her expression a mixture of uneasy humor and serious consideration.

Her comment finally cracked the giant's somber mask, causing a grin to spread over his features. "You don't have to worry about any explosives, Rebecca. Hercules and I never planted anything inside you."

Although Rebecca was relieved to hear him say the words, a part of her still had a nagging doubt. As Goliath studied the reaction of Rebecca and the others, he laughed out loud. "Well, Jeffrey, judging by the somewhat skeptical looks on some of your faces, it appears that we still have a ways to go to work on our trust."

"Forgive me, Goliath," Rebecca grinned. "Old feelings sometimes die hard. I believe you."

"With that out of the way, we still need to decide where to land," Jeffrey said.

"Doesn't that kind of depend on what's going to happen to the pyramid once we arrive?" Dr. Eisenberg asked. "Do we plan on turning it over to any government officials, are we going to hide it, or do we want to destroy it?"

"Destroy it?" Jerome repeated in surprise. "I know this thing's dangerous in the wrong hands, but think of what we could learn about the past! I say we hide it somewhere, and then we can use it without anyone else knowing."

"That will not be possible," a deep voice said suddenly from behind them. Startled, the group turned to see Sikaris standing near the stairs, once more dressed in his plain, white robes.

At the sight of the angel, everyone in the room grew somber and silent. Although this was the third time they had seen him, they still felt overwhelmed by his presence. Rebecca was the first to recover her voice. "What do you mean? Why wouldn't that be possible?"

"You have all seen the potential that the pyramid has for producing evil," Sikaris replied, his voice taken on a dark edge. "It must not remain in the hands of finite humans. Therefore, once I have taken you home, I will pilot the craft into the sun, where it will be destroyed."

As her companions pondered the angel's pronouncement, Rebecca felt both a strange sense of loss and relief flow through her. Jerome's suggestion about traveling back into the past to study history firsthand had filled her with excitement, yet knowing the catastrophic consequences that could result if the machine accidentally fell into the wrong hands caused her stomach to knot. Despite the fact that her scientific curiosity would never be satisfied, the idea that the machine would be destroyed made her sigh in relief.

"Where…where will you drop us off?" Jeffrey asked.

"Wherever you wish," Sikaris replied.

"Do we have to choose one location for all of us, or can we each decide where we want to go?" Dr. Eisenberg asked.

Sikaris smiled. "You may each choose your own destination. However, we are limited by the fact that we must not draw attention to the pyramid. The location must be somewhat distant from any main population centers."

Jeffrey looked around at the others questioningly. "Where do we want to go? Part of me thinks we should go back to Iraq and try to explain what happened."

After all they had been through, facing a host of government types who were undoubtedly going to drill each of them for probably days and even weeks was the last thing Rebecca wanted to do. There would be time for that later. Glancing at the others, she could tell that their thoughts were running parallel to her own.

"Not yet," Mack said. "I don't know about the rest of you, but I don't feel like facing the 'inquisition' just yet. I think I'd like to take a little vacation in the good ol' U.S. of A. I've got some friends in Atlanta I haven't seen in awhile. "

"I, for one, just want to be by my family," Jerome said.

"Me, too," Lisa said softly. "I miss my girls." As she spoke, she caught Jeffrey looking at her. A sudden, intense ache of what might have been constricted her breathing, causing her to quickly avert her gaze.

Fighting to control his own emotions, Jeffrey cleared his throat and forced himself to focus on the discussion at hand. "Doc, what about you?"

"I would also like to see my family," he replied. "I'd like to visit Nathan and the grandchildren in Oregon."

As Jeffrey turned his gaze to Akwen, he noticed that some of the normal tension in her features had disappeared. "My family is in Cameroon. I will go dere."

"I just want to go home," Rebecca said as she placed her hand lightly on Jeffrey's arm. Looking down at her, he nodded, and then turned his attention to Goliath.

"What about you?" he asked the giant. "With the exception of Akwen, it looks like the rest of us will be going to the United States. Where do you want to go?"

Goliath's face took on an odd, pensive look. "I've been thinking a lot about it, and frankly, I'd like to go to some remote spot in the mountains. I don't want to return to Iraq. There's nothing for me there. Somewhere secluded in the Rockies would do fine."

Jeffrey's eyebrows rose in surprise at his reply. Mack, however, started snickering. When the others turned to look at him, he said, "I've got a feeling there's going to be some new 'Bigfoot' sightings up there this year!"

The entire group, including the stoic giant, laughed lightheartedly at the comment as the engines stopped. A moment later, the walls of the pyramid became translucent. Beneath them, the Earth spun slowly while man-made satellites floated in orbit around the planet. Far in the distance, the space station *Independence* appeared silent and still, oblivious to the presence of the new arrival.

Taking her husband's hand in her own, Rebecca's eyes brimmed with tears. "We've made it! We're finally home!"

"Yes," Jeffrey replied, his voice full of emotion. "Home."

Epilogue

JOURNAL ENTRY #8

IT'S BEEN SIX years since my last journal entry. I had forgotten all about it until this morning, when I found it tucked away in a neglected drawer. Listening to the previous seven entries dealing with my trip to Ka'esch, I felt it would be fitting to offer one last entry.

Two years have passed since the day I arrived at the dig site in Iraq... Has it truly only been two years? Who would have thought that so much could change in such a short time! God, You are awesome!

When we returned from our trip back in time, Jeffrey, Mack, Doc, Jerome, Akwen, Lisa, and I did eventually have to go through debriefing with the government. We had all agreed not to tell them everything that happened, since they would likely not believe us. So, we only told them about our trip to Corinth, but we left out everything else, especially Goliath's presence. However, we did tell them about meeting Sikaris, otherwise we would've had no explanation as to the disappearance of the pyramid. As expected, they didn't believe us. Fortunately, though, when Sikaris piloted the pyramid into the sun, he kept it visible so that NASA was able to track it from the Independence. *Knowing NASA and the government officials, they're probably having fierce debates as to who Sikaris really was. They'll probably never accept the truth. Most will likely think he was an alien. Whatever the case, they finally released us and let us return home.*

I regret that, despite the fact that we got the pyramid working properly, we were unable to return to the Ice Age to give back Noah's diary. It seems that when Arngrim was preparing the pyramid for his own journey, he left it behind. It's possible he didn't even know what it was. Then again, as Mack had pointed out to me, it may have been God's will for us to take the diary from Noah. After all, we may have inadvertently altered history if we had returned it. Perhaps God didn't want His Word to contain a full, detailed account, but rather just a summary containing the main details. I guess that will be just one more question I'll have to ask Him when we meet face-to-face in eternity.

Our trip through time changed each of our lives drastically. Yet, despite all the difficulties we encountered and the physical and…emotional pain we've suffered, I believe that we are better off. It just goes to show how God can use even bad situations to bring about good.

Mack wrote everything down and published our story as "science-fiction." He now travels around the country speaking about the proofs for a literal understanding of Noah's Ark and a global flood. He's also engaged to a wonderful woman and is doing very well for himself.

Jerome has given up field work and become a full-time professor at Northern Illinois University. The last I heard, he had paid off his daughter's doctor bills and had even begun attending a local church with his family. He seems much more at peace, and has even become a generous giver. I think it's likely that he's trying to assuage his guilt for selling the gravity control plans. Lord, continue to work in his life.

Doc decided to retire and is living in Oregon near his son and his family. Every Christmas he sends us wonderful paintings, as well as pictures of his grandkids. He's such a typical, proud grandfather! Since Christmas is only a couple of weeks away, I expect to get a new package from him any day now.

I haven't heard much from any of the others. I know Akwen returned to Cameroon to be with her family, and she is involved with a robotics business there. Although the government took Elmer back, I heard that Akwen had built another droid of her own based on Elmer's specs. Doc told me about his discussion with her in the dungeon of Valhalla, and I often wonder if she had ever accepted Christ. I continue to pray for her every day. Bring her the peace she seeks, Lord.

Although I haven't talked to Lisa since we returned, I found out through some mutual friends that she's doing well, despite the fact that she has her hands full raising two teenage daughters!

No one knows anything about what happened to Goliath. It was always so difficult to figure out what he was thinking or what he was feeling, I have no idea if what happened to us had any impact on him. Then again, being a genetically altered human who's DNA is part animal, I'm not even sure if salvation is possible for him. Only God knows. Maybe he'll surprise us and turn up someday.

As for Jeffrey and I, it has been a long road. I wish I could say that everything returned to normal once we got back, but life isn't like that. In the past couple of years, we seem to take two steps forward and one step back. Actually, I shouldn't say that. It has been more like three or four *steps forward and one step back. The changes I've seen in him have been profound. Sure, he still makes mistakes, as we all do, but he's trying, and with God's help, all things* are *possible.*

It took me some time to begin to trust him again, but now that God is the center of our marriage, we're discovering an intimacy that goes deeper than anything we've ever experienced. So even despite our occasional setbacks, I believe that our relationship is stronger now than before…before our jump through time.

When I first had the idea to go to Jesus to ask for Jeffrey's healing, I had simply hoped that he would be one of the multitudes that Jesus had healed during His ministry. When we arrived and saw how crowded the room was, I remembered the story of the man being let down through the roof. I only hoped to copy *that story. Never in my wildest dreams had I imagined that Jeffrey would be* the *paralytic in the biblical account!*

Furthermore, in the back of my mind, I held the hope that perhaps Jesus would heal my…my womb as well. But when He looked at me, I knew that God had something else in store for Jeffrey and I. Something greater.

When we returned home, Jeffrey expressed to me his desire to adopt! He told me that watching those children on the streets of the city in Midgard made him realize how hopeless the lives of orphans could be unless someone intervened. Also, he didn't want women to feel the need to abort their children because they didn't want them to grow up unloved. And so, not only have we adopted one beautiful little girl that we've named Joy, but as of next Monday, Jeffrey and I will be opening an orphanage! Although I can't have children of my own flesh and blood, God has given me many *children to watch over and nurture.*

God truly is a miracle-working God. Each day, I watch as He draws Jeffrey closer and closer to Him. Not long after we returned from the trip, we started attending church together. Before, I couldn't even get Jeffrey to set foot in the place unless there was a wedding or a funeral. What's more, he has even begun taking classes to learn more about God. He especially loves the apologetics classes, as I knew he would. We read books together and enjoy discussing what we're learning. We had always shared similar hobbies and activities, but our new passion for God's Word and for sharing the Gospel has brought us closer than ever before.

Our travels in the pyramid taught me many things. I realize now that although we escaped the Cataclysm of Noah's day, there is a greater Cataclysm to come: when this world perishes and God makes a new heaven and a new earth. I am grateful to God that, through faith in Jesus, I, and now Jeffrey also, will escape that *Cataclysm as well.*

Because of the pyramid, the accounts in the Bible, especially in Genesis, have become so personal and meaningful to me now. When I hear people compromise Genesis or doubt the truth of the Scriptures, I can't help but get frustrated and angry. Yet, I have to remind myself that I did the same before we went on our journey. Jeffrey and I continue to study and teach others what we learned about the true *history of the earth. We teach about the Ice Age, the Ark, the Flood, what happened to the dinosaurs, the formation of geologic structures, and so much more.*

There are so many proofs out there for the truth of God's Word. If only people would take the time to seek, they would find the answers. But then again, the truth is staring them in the face every day. God's creation pro-

claims His glory, and it can be seen in the lives of His followers. Once people accept that God's Word is true, then, and only then, are they able to truly make sense of the world. More than all that I have witnessed and learned, I now understand that the greatest proof that God exists is His Word.

To God be the glory!

AFTERWORD

I CAN IMAGINE that many who read *Escaping the Cataclysm* will ask, "Do you *really* believe this stuff? Demon-gods, genetically-altered humans, time travel, gravity control devices, dinosaurs living with humans and going on the Ark, and a literal Noah's Flood? This stuff can't be real."

Well, let me reiterate what I wrote in the foreword of this book: what I have presented is merely one idea of how things could have happened, and although some of my ideas and conclusions sound a little far-fetched, they are based on research (see the footnotes). So, when you begin to consider the ideas logically, they make more sense than one might initially think. I would like to offer you, the reader, a little insight into why I included these particular ideas into my plot.

Before I go any further, let me make it clear that I do *not* believe that time travel is possible or will ever *be* possible, at least not on *this* earth. That part of the story is *purely* fictional.

First, when one begins with a biblical worldview of human origins, one begins to realize that God likely created Adam and Eve to be highly intelligent. In Gen 2:19–20, it states that Adam named all the animals and birds. Contrary to evolutionary thinking, there is no reason to believe that our earliest ancestors (Adam and Eve) were dumb brutes. After all, they were created by God as full-grown adults with speech capabilities and a communicable language. The instant they were created, they were able to speak with God, each other, and the serpent.

With that assumption, let us now consider how much a person can learn in a lifetime. Even with just an average lifespan of eighty years or so, a person can earn multiple degrees, learn dozens of languages, and master numerous trade skills. Now multiply that by ten! If one takes Genesis literally (which we really have no reason *not* to take it literally), then people before the Flood lived to be over nine hundred years old! Granted, at least the first several generations were probably forced to expend nearly all of their energy just surviving. Still, one would think that after several hundred years from creation, after cities were established, learning would increase greatly.

If you are somewhat of a skeptic about the intelligence of ancient man or are simply interested in more information about this fascinating subject, I would highly recommend the book *The Puzzle of Ancient Man* by Donald Chittick. Although his book deals with post-Flood populations, I believe that we can get a hint of what the pre-Flood world's technology looked like by studying the technology of the cultures that appeared shortly *after* the Flood.

Next, let us consider the controversial question: who were the Nephilim? It is beyond the scope of these notes to answer this question in detail. Many books and articles have been written on the subject. I will, however, try to give a brief summary of the various beliefs. If you are interested in more information, I would recommend visiting the Answers in Genesis website (www.answersingenesis.com) or www.gotquestions.org.

Below is the main passage in question from Genesis 6:1–5 (NIV):

> When human beings began to increase in number on the earth and daughters were born to them, the sons of God saw that the daughters of humans were beautiful, and they married any of them they chose. Then the LORD said, "My Spirit will not contend with humans forever, for they are mortal; their days will be a hundred and twenty years."

The Nephilim were on the earth in those days—and also afterward—when the sons of God went to the daughters of humans and had children by them. They were the heroes of old, men of renown. The LORD saw how great the wickedness of the human race had become on the earth, and that every inclination of the thoughts of the human heart was only evil all the time.

In order to determine who the Nephilim were, one needs to determine the identity
of the "sons of God." This is precisely where the difficulty lies. The three most prevalent views are as follows:

1. They were fallen angels (demons) that bred with human women and had children, who were called the Nephilim.
2. They were men who were *possessed* by fallen angels and bred with women.
3. They were the godly line of men from Adam to Seth who fell away from God and had children with women who served false gods.

The article on the Answers in Genesis website discusses each of these views at length. Based on my research, the idea that the sons of God were fallen angels appeared to be the most commonly held belief and had the most potential for storytelling!

Before I leave this particular topic, let me end with a quote from the AiG website that puts this in perspective: "It is not crucial to biblical authority, since each side in this debate, for the most part, is using the Bible as authoritative to make their case."[1]

So, if one accepts that the "sons of God" were demons, then a couple of questions come to mind. What kind of interaction would they have had with humans? What kind of knowledge and technology did they have? We might find a hint to the answer to the first question in Genesis 6:1–5 passage quoted previously. In reference to the Nephilim, it says, "Those were the mighty men of old, men of renown."

In my research, I came across a book that connected this passage with ancient legends and myths of gods and their children. The stories of Perseus and Hercules spring to mind. Certainly in those stories, they became "men of renown." Other cultures also have stories of demi-gods (half-human, half-god) that accomplished amazing feats. Could there possibly be a connection between the demi-gods of mythology and the Nephilim?

To further strengthen the connection, it is interesting to note that many of these same cultures have stories of giants. Norse mythology calls them the Jotun, the Hindus call them the Daityas, the Greeks had the *gigantes* (from which we get our modern word *giant*), just to name a few. Is it coincidence that so many ancient cultures had so many similarities in their myths, or were they based in part on reality?

In his book *Flood Legends*, Charles Martin makes this statement, "Since the late 1800s, mythologists have come to see myth as not *wholly* fictional, but instead as *embellishments* of truth. In other words, a 'complex' myth may, in fact, have a perfectly 'reasonable' footing in 'reality.'"[2] It is this idea that helped spark my vision of the pre-Flood world.

Add to all of this the idea that if demons really did set themselves up as gods, they might use some of their advanced knowledge of genetics to begin toying with humans. It stands to reason that they would know at *least* as much as modern humans do about the manipulation of genes. If this idea were true, it might also explain some of the other strange things presented in some of the ancient myths such as medusa, elves, mermaids, unicorns, etc. Perhaps the demons knew how to successfully mix the DNA of different creatures. After all, some of our modern *Dr. Frankensteins* are currently working on this possibility. (Just do a quick internet search on the topic and you may be surprised by what you find.)

Let me reiterate once again that this particular line of reasoning is *purely* speculation. However, when one takes all of this into consideration, it begins to paint the very interesting picture of the pre-Flood world that I have presented in *Escaping the Cataclysm*.

FLOOD LEGENDS

When I set out to write novels dealing with real scientific issues, I invariably end up with topics I wanted to discuss, but just couldn't find a way to include it into the plot of the novel without bogging down the story. One such topic is the existence of flood legends.

Although many people are not aware of it, there are legends about a worldwide flood in nearly every culture of the world. In the book *Dinosaurs by Design*, Dr. Duane Gish says that there are over two hundred and seventy such stories. To view a chart listing several of these legends with their corresponding biblical similarities, visit www.AnswersInGenesis.org and search for the article entitled, "Flood Legends" by A.J. Monty White, Ph.D. Below is a summary of just a couple of these accounts.

In the Chinese flood legend, the only people to escape the flood were Fuhi, his wife, three sons, and three daughters, the same number of people in the Genesis account of Noah. In the Hawaiian story, Nu'u and his family built a great canoe and filled it with animals. After the flood, only he and his family were the only humans to survive.

Despite the fact that these legends have numerous *differences*, they also contain many *similarities*. Many critics point to the differences as proof that the accounts were describing different events. However, although this makes sense of the discrepancies, it does *not* explain the similarities. How could so many stories from all over the world share key similarities unless they had a similar source?

A sampling of similarities within the various stories includes:

- Man in transgression
- Divine destruction
- Favored family
- Destruction by water
- Humans and animals saved
- Universal destruction

There are several more similarities in addition to these.

So, if the legends *did* have a similar source, then why the differences? The answer lies in the account of the Tower of Babel in Genesis 11. After God confused the language at Babel, the human race scattered all over the earth with those with whom they could communicate. As the Flood account was retold over the years, some of the details became altered and changed.

For more on this topic, I highly recommend the book, *Flood Legends: Global Clues of a Common Event* by Charles Martin.

I hope you have enjoyed reading my novels as much as I enjoyed writing them. If you have been intrigued by some of the scientific research I have presented, I *highly* encourage you to do your own research. There is only a limited amount of real information I can present in a novel. Hopefully it was enough to whet your appetite for more. To this end, I have included a list of suggested websites, books, and DVDs that deal with the topics presented in *Escaping the Cataclysm*, as well as numerous other fascinating topics on biblical authority and the creation/evolution debate.

My earnest prayer is that this information would be a stepping stone that would either strengthen your faith in Christ if you already believe, or help lead you toward the conclusion that the Bible *is* true and it *can* be trusted. Then, I pray that you would make the greatest and most important decision of your life by accepting Jesus as your Savior!

Keith A. Robinson
November, 2010

SUGGESTED MATERIALS

WEBSITES

www.answersingenesis.org—The official website of Answers in Genesis, one of the largest Creation ministries in the world.

www.icr.org—The official website of the Institute for Creation Research.

www.discovery.org—The official website of the Discovery Institute, the "think tank" for the Intelligent Design movement.

www.creationscience.com—This website contains the complete, FREE online edition of *In the Beginning: Compelling Evidence for Creation and the Flood* (7th Edition) by Dr. Walt Brown.

www.evolution-facts.org—This website contains the complete, FREE online edition of *Evolution Cruncher* by Vance Ferrell. This paperback is based on a 1,326-page, three-volume Evolution Disproved series.

www.christiananswers.net/creation—This website has lots of great material, including the entire video *A Question of Origins* available to view for FREE online.

http://www.leestrobel.com/—Lee Strobel was a former atheist and has now written several books investigating the Christian faith, including *The Case for the Creator.*

BOOKS AND MAGAZINES

Noah's Ark: A Feasibility Study by John Woodmoorewrape
Noah's Ark: Thinking Outside the Box by Tim Lovett
The Young Earth: The Real History of the Earth—Past, Present, and Future by John Morris
The Puzzle of Ancient Man: Evidence for Advanced Technology in Past Civilizations by Donald E. Chittick, Ph.D
The New Answers Book 1, 2, & 3—Ken Ham, General Editor
Answers Magazine: Building a Biblical Worldview—especially Vol. 3 No. 2, April–June 2008 and Vol. 3 No.4, Oct–Dec. 2008

DVDS AND VIDEOS

Incredible Creatures that Defy Evolution, Vol. 1, 2, & 3 with Dr. Jobe Martin—Exploration Films

Unlocking the Mystery of Life—Illustra Media

Icons of Evolution—Illustra Media

The Privileged Planet—Illustra Media

A Question of Origins—Eternal Productions (This entire video can be viewed online for FREE at www.christiananswers.net/creation.)

For a list of other products, visit the Answers in Genesis website at www.answersingenesis.org

NOTES

CHAPTER 3

1. Snelling, Andrew, Ph.D. "A Catastrophic Breakup: A Scientific Look at Catastrophic Plate Tectonics." *Answers Magazine*, April–June 2007, Vol. 2 No. 2: 44–48.

CHAPTER 6

1. Luke 13:24,25
2. Woodmorappe, John. *Noah's Ark: A Feasibility Study.* Santee, California: Institute for Creation Research, 2003, p. 59–63.

CHAPTER 7

1. Lovett, Tim. *Noah's Ark: Thinking Outside the Box.* Green Forest, AR: Master Books, 2008, p. 25.
2. Woodmorappe, John. *Noah's Ark: A Feasibility Study.* Santee, California: Institute for Creation Research, 2003, p. 75.
3. Ibid p. 25.
4. Ibid p. 21.
5. Ibid p. 76.
6. Ham, Ken, ed. *The New Answers Book 3.* Green Forest, AR: Master Books, 2009, p. 52.
7. Woodmorappe, John. *Noah's Ark: A Feasibility Study.* Santee, California: Institute for Creation Research, 2003, p. 20.
8. Ibid p. 25.
9. Ibid p. 27.
10. Ibid p. 153–154.

CHAPTER 8

1. Ham, Ken, ed. *The New Answers Book.* Green Forest, AR: Master Books, 2006, p. 145–146.
2. Ibid p. 144.
3. Woodmorappe, John. *Noah's Ark: A Feasibility Study.* Santee, California: Institute for Creation Research, 2003, p. 26–27.
4. Ibid p. 34–35.
5. Ibid p. 84.
6. Genesis 9:2
7. Ibid p. 97–98.
8. Lovett, Tim. *Noah's Ark: Thinking Outside the Box.* Green Forest, AR: Master Books, 2008, p. 32–33.
9. Ibid p. 42–45.
10. Ibid p. 37.
11. Ibid p. 37.
12. Ibid p. 38.

CHAPTER 9

1. Woodmorappe, John. *Noah's Ark: A Feasibility Study.* Santee, California: Institute for Creation Research, 2003, p. 64.
2. Ham, Ken, ed. *The New Answers Book 3.* Green Forest, AR: Master Books, 2009, p. 42–43.
3. Ibid p. 39–48.
4. Woodmorappe, John. *Noah's Ark: A Feasibility Study.* Santee, California: Institute for Creation Research, 2003, p. 3–13.
5. Ibid p. 13.
6. Deuteronomy 14:6
7. Woodmorappe, John. *Noah's Ark: A Feasibility Study.* Santee, California: Institute for Creation Research, 2003, p. 8–10.
8. Genesis 9:3

CHAPTER 14

1. "Air Bubbles, Amber, and Dinosaurs" U.S. Geological Survey, June 01, 2009. http://minerals.cr.usgs.gov/gips/na/amber.html (accessed December 16, 2010).

CHAPTER 19

1. Deuteronomy 31:6
2. 1 John 4:4

CHAPTER 21

1. Genesis 7:20
2. Ham, Ken, ed. *The New Answers Book*. Green Forest, AR: Master Books, 2006, p. 137.
3. Ibid p. 137.
4. Ibid p. 137.
5. Walt Brown, Ph.D. *In the Beginning: Compelling Evidence for Creation and the Flood*. Phoenix, AZ: Center for Scientific Creation, 2001, p. 41.
6. Ham, Ken, ed. *The New Answers Book*. Green Forest, AR: Master Books, 2006, p. 135.
7. Walt Brown, Ph.D. *In the Beginning: Compelling Evidence for Creation and the Flood*. Phoenix, AZ: Center for Scientific Creation, 2001, p. 40.
8. Ham, Ken, ed. *The New Answers Book 3*. Green Forest, AR: Master Books, 2009, p. 93–94.
9. Snelling, Andrew A. "The World's a Graveyard." *Answers Magazine*, April–June 2008: 76–79.
10. Ham, Ken, ed. *The New Answers Book 3*. Green Forest, AR: Master Books, 2009, p. 95–96.
11. Morris, John. *The Young Earth: The Real History of the Earth—Past, Present, and Future*. Revised and expanded edition. Green Forest, AR: Master Books, 2007, p. 106.
12. John D. Morris, "Are Human Artifacts Ever Petrified?" Institute for Creation Research, http://www.icr.org/article/are-human-artifacts-ever-petrified/ (accessed December 16, 2010).

13. Woodmorappe, John. *Noah's Ark: A Feasibility Study.* Santee, California: Institute for Creation Research, 2003, p. 127–135.

CHAPTER 22

1. Romans 8:28

CHAPTER 28

1. Romans 5:8
2. Romans 3:23
3. Romans 3:10

CHAPTER 30

1. Genesis 3:15

CHAPTER 31

1. Genesis 4:15,16
2. Genesis 3:20

AFTERWORD

1. Hodge, Bodie. "Who Were the Nephilim?" *Answers in Genesis.* July 9, 2009. http://www.answersingenesis.org/articles/aid/v2/n1/who-were-the-nephilim (accessed December 13, 2010).
2. Martin, Charles. *Flood Legends: Global Clues of a Common Event.* Green Forest, AR: Master Books, 2009.

ABOUT KEITH A. ROBINSON

Author of *Logic's End, Pyramid of the Ancients,*
and *Escaping the Cataclysm*

Keith Robinson has dedicated his life to teaching others about the evidence for creation and against evolution. The Origin of Life debate has been his passion and his calling since he first began researching the topic in 1998. Since the release of *Logic's End,* his first novel, he has been a featured speaker at Christian music festivals and churches, as well as appearing as a guest on numerous radio shows. In addition, he is also the Extensions Director of the Creation Science Society of Milwaukee.

The publication of *Escaping the Cataclysm* marks the completion of his first trilogy. Mr. Robinson is currently working on study guides to accompany each of the books in the Origin's Trilogy, and plans to write other action/adventure novels dealing with apologetics issues.

When not writing or speaking, Mr. Robinson is a full-time public school orchestra director at Indian Trail High School & Academy, he serves as the Principal Violist of the Full Score Chamber Orchestra in Zion, Illinois, and he is a professional freelance violist and violinist in the Southeastern Wisconsin/Northeastern Illinois area. He currently resides in Kenosha, Wisconsin, with his two sons, Alejandro and Sebastián, and his one-hundred-pound, old-English sheepdog named Osa.